UNRAVELING ELEVEN

JERRI CHISHOLM

Entangled Publishing, LLC
10940 S Parker Road
Suite 327
Parker, CO 80134
rights@entangledpublishing.com

Entangled Teen is an imprint of Entangled Publishing, LLC.

Visit our website at www.entangledpublishing.com.

Edited by Stacy Abrams
Cover Design by LJ Anderson, Mayhem Cover Creations
Cover images by
Swillklitch/ GettyImages and
Hzpriezz/shutterstock
Font Design by Covers by Juan
Interior design by Toni Kerr

TP ISBN 978-1-64937-098-3
Ebook ISBN 978-1-64937-112-6

Manufactured in the United States of America

First Edition November 2021

10 9 8 7 6 5 4 3 2 1

entangled teen
an imprint of Entangled Publishing LLC

UNRAVELING ELEVEN

To j.a.p.

At Entangled, we want our readers to be well-informed. If you would like to know if this book contains any elements that might be of concern for you, please check the back of the book for details.

CHAPTER ONE

"Eve. Don't move."

The voice is low and hoarse in my ear.

A moment ago, my fingertips grazed the back of his neck as we kissed. My other hand curved over his large shoulder and pressed firmly into muscle. It was the first time we had stopped walking since escaping Compound Eleven, the first time we had even acknowledged each other, because for the past hour we have been too preoccupied and too overwhelmed.

Too mesmerized.

I think it's the feeling of earth beneath our boots that's to blame. That and the twinkling night sky overhead. We are used to concrete below and concrete above. But more than anything, it is the staggering realization that the heat won't kill us after all.

It won't even hurt us, despite all we've learned, all we've been taught. Everyone back in Eleven thinks it's a sauna up here, a killing field—practically upon impact. Yet an hour ago, we discovered that nothing could be further from the truth.

In time, as our shock wore off, our pace slowed, and we held each other—we kissed, celebration thundering like laughter in our ears. Then Wren went still.

Now his tendons stiffen. They lock him in place. He murmurs to me again, "Don't move."

The stars overhead offer enough light to see that he stares at something over my shoulder. His gaze is steady and his mouth is tight. I think it's the closest thing to alarm that his face can register.

Around his neck, my hands curl into fists, ready for violence—always ready for violence. My stomach binds. For a fleeting moment, I feel like I'm belowground again. I start to laugh the thought away, but then I hear it: the rustling of leaves, a gentle yet poignant indicator that we are not alone. An image flashes in my mind of guards decked in protective suits, dragging us back by our ankles, guns trained on our temples—

No. It's impossible they know of our escape.

Except nothing is impossible.

We thought it was impossible to survive aboveground, then we stepped outside. And so, against Wren's words, I turn.

I turn and see something I have never seen before.

Something completely unexpected, completely foreign to those who dwell in tunnels below the earth's crust. "An animal?" I mutter, and as I do, the large beast's ears twitch. Like it knows it's being talked about. My arms drop to my sides; otherwise I am still. Back straight.

It stands in a clearing twenty feet away, and if it weren't for its beady eyes that catch in the moonlight, it wouldn't be noticeable at all. It would fade into darkness. I stare at it, partly with fear that is inborn, but also with awe.

If only the beast weren't so vaguely yet distinctly threatening...

Maybe I'm imagining it. Maybe my muscles *could* defeat it—I grew up in the Combat League, after all. I've been fighting those larger and seemingly stronger than me since I was nine years old. Or maybe it *is* a gentle beast.

But I know that can't be true, and Wren knows it, too. Silently his hand wraps around mine. He pulls me backward: one step, two. The beast watches us retreat, then its heavy skull lifts ever so slightly. It takes two steps forward.

Now I can see its paws, and they are the size of Compound Eleven's dinner plates. Curved knives line each one.

"Should we run?" comes a strained voice that I barely recognize as my own.

Wren shakes his head. "I don't think so." Once more, he tugs at my hand. So once more, we retreat like we're walking barefoot on glass, and this time the beast is still. This time it doesn't follow.

Suddenly I am hopeful.

Off in the distance comes a sharp cry—one of the birds that calls this strange world home. The beast's ears flick.

Another two steps back we go.

This is good; this is very good. Soon we will slip out of sight, nothing but a distant memory. And more importantly, we will be nothing but a distant memory to the guards of Compound Eleven, too. They will not drag us underground after all. Nothing will.

And then the heel of my boot hits something hard along the ground. A root, maybe, or the lip of a rock. I catch myself before I tumble.

Still, it was jarring. Still, my pulse quickens.

It must have been jarring for the beast, too, because now something has changed.

Now its head is lower than a second ago and its ears are flat. Now a sound reverberates from its stomach, bubbly and guttural at the same time. Now my heart pounds twice as loudly as before.

"We need to—" Wren begins urgently, but there's no chance to finish.

The beast charges.

Immediately our muscles spring into action, propelling us away, hurtling us into a sprint for our lives. Twigs snap underfoot as we shoot farther into darkness, up a small hill, then down a steep slope littered with narrow trees. We are fast, our bodies built for speed.

But Wren's legs are longer than mine; he is faster. Under the glow of the moon, I see his head shift in my direction, and I see his gait slow.

As his hand reaches for mine, I scream at him to keep going—

Maybe he listens. I doubt it, but maybe. I wouldn't know, because something strikes my back with enough force to break my neck. A fraction of a millisecond passes since impact, then I'm facedown. My fingernails wedge with dirt. My forehead opens on a jagged rock.

On your feet, Eve.

Before, I was fearful, an advantage to the beast. No longer, because now the lemon juice has spilled. Now I'm primed, and I'm ready. A fighter.

But then it pulls itself onto its hind legs, and it's taller than even I am. Half a second later, a paw lined with blades slashes at me, and I swing backward in time to hear it slice the air, my innards barely spared. A heartbeat later, I punch it square in the nose.

I'm used to the feeling of a human nose squashing under my fist. I'm used to the sound it makes and the stinging of my knuckles. I'm used to the look of shock and panic shooting through my opponent's eyes. But this is different. There is no dull crack of bone, and there is no shock, panic, or pain. All that happens is that the blackened lips of the beast pull away in obvious anger, and as they do, they reveal a terrible sight. Yellow daggers, some of them as long as my ring finger.

This is not an opponent I can defeat.

There is no sense in punching or kicking. There is no sense in rooting around my boot for my blade. This creature is already equipped with blades. And speed. And strength.

Just as when I stare down the barrel of a gun, I'm completely powerless.

The gun.

Instead of groping around my waistband for my own weapon, I launch myself at the beast and throw my arms around its neck, tuck my head against coarse fur. This is the safest spot until Wren can shoot it. Otherwise it will gore me with its claws, gut me with its teeth—all before I can pull the trigger.

I hold on with every ounce of strength and scream at Wren to shoot. I hold on, but barely.

It resists my grip as fiercely as I fight for it. It jerks and shakes, and through it all, I wait for Wren. He must be near. He must.

He must have the gun cocked.

He must.

I can't hold on for much longer. And as the thought passes through my head, its paw is beneath me, my grasp is wrenched free, I am thrown onto my back so that the inky night sky is spread out before me.

The sound of fast, heavy footsteps, then my vision is clouded by blackness.

CHAPTER TWO

Blackness. I was born into it, and I will die in it, too.

At least I was able to taste freedom first. That was my goal; it was always my goal. And it is better to be dead and free than caged and alive.

I must not forget that, as I take my last breaths.

That's when I finally hear the blast of a gun.

The beast collapses on me, its weight as devastating as the daggers lining its mouth, and I scream. Or I would if I could force air to my lungs. Claws tear through my clothes. Pain clouds my vision.

Then it lifts.

Oxygen. And the ability to move, even if gingerly. Blood rushes to my extremities and dribbles from rips in my skin. When my eyes clear of tears, I notice that the beast has lost interest in me. Its sights are set on Wren and Wren alone, and the realization makes me smile.

The blast of another bullet, then another. Another. They echo through the trees like poetry. Belowground they explode, like a punch to the face. Normally I hate the sound, but right now the shots wash over me in waves. Then the earth tremors.

I don't know how many bullets it took to defeat the deadly creature, but I hear the clatter of discarded metal on rock and know we are down a gun.

Then Wren is above me, concern rippling over his handsome features. Quickly it passes. Now a scowl contorts them—those wide-set eyes, his kind mouth, that straight nose. "Are you *laughing*?" he shouts. "I thought you were dead!"

Now I laugh harder.

He sighs. His hand turns my head, and his fingers trace the wound over my eye.

"A rock," I explain as I catch my breath.

"Mm. I think you'll live. What about the rest of you?"

Hands slip down my body, and I wince as his fingers find the tears in my clothing that have given way to tears in my skin. "They're not deep," he says eventually. "You're lucky."

I wrap my arms around his neck. "Next time, shoot quicker."

"I defend my timing completely," he says as he presses his forehead to mine, angling it away from my cut. "I wanted to see what that thing was made of." He glances at the fallen beast through the darkness. Then he glances at me, and I see humor dancing in his eyes. "I wanted to see what *you* were made of, too."

I laugh softly. "And?"

He frowns, then presses his lips together as if he's deep in thought. "Tough as nails, Eve," he finally concludes.

I grin; I can't help it. Because we are free. We can kiss, and shout, and run. We can search for my little brother, Jack, who was cruelly expelled from Compound Eleven at the tender age of three. We can do whatever we like—forever.

There's no more need to fear Daniel or Landry. There is no need to cower at the sight of the guards, not that I ever gave them the satisfaction—that particular form of torture is finished. Same with the low-hanging ceilings and the recycled air. The injustice at being born on the second floor where I'm treated like garbage, where my job options are so severely circumscribed. No longer am I a citizen of a ruthless regime, one that massacres its own people at will.

Now I am free. Forever free. Forever *free*. Because the scorched earth is scorched no longer. We can survive up here.

Wren and I—and the thought sends a shiver down my spine. How did an unlucky person like me get so lucky?

No matter that my body is bruised from the beast—I pull him as close as possible so no air can separate us. I feel so light; even with his weight on top of me, it's like I could float to the night sky. I feel so secure; I could let my muscles go soft. I feel so happy; I can't believe that even for a second I was ready to die.

For a long time, we just lay there, breathing in unison, digesting it all. Then Wren says in a husky voice that tickles my cheek, "We should get some sleep."

I lift my head to better look at him. "Here?"

"Or maybe we could find a bed nearby," he says, pinching me. "Of course *here*."

I laugh, and as we make ourselves comfortable, I realize what a new experience this will be. Not just sleeping on the ground instead of a hard, dusty mattress. Not just sleeping aboveground instead of below. But sleeping with a boy next to me, as well.

I decide to be brave and tuck myself into the curve of his body where it's warmest, and I find that it's not scary at all. It feels safe here next to Wren—it feels like home.

In time, our breaths grow longer. As my eyes become heavy, I know not only will I go to sleep with a smile on my face, but for the first time ever, I'll wake with one, too.

. . .

Sometime later, the call of the birds lifts me from my slumber, and I find myself grinning ear to ear—just as I predicted. It's because lightness fills my retinas, and I didn't even have to switch on a lamp. It's because I'm not just waking up to sunshine; I'm waking up to *freedom*.

It's everything I ever wanted. No, that's not true. It's *more* than I ever wanted, because I have Wren here by my side. And now we have nothing but time on our hands—nothing but time to explore this strange new world and search for Jack. Because even though the beast we encountered in the night, the one that lies in a crumpled heap nearby, was dangerous and clearly deadly, there's too much beauty up here. It's paradise. And it's impossible to believe that Jack perished in paradise.

Dying underground, on the other hand, is easy. Compound Eleven is hell—death is just a small sidestep away, a trip to the left, a tumble to the right. Yet Jack was released into this oasis, and I know he thrived.

Just like Wren and I are going to.

Gingerly, I move Wren's arm from around me, then sit upright. I wipe sleep from my eyes and gaze around—left and right, up and down, in every direction. The problem with my certainty that my brother is still alive, I think, is the vastness of the space up here. It's completely foreign to someone like me. It's unfathomable, hard to wrap my brain around. And it means he could have gone in any direction, could have traveled endlessly—still, to this day.

But maybe not. Maybe he stayed nearby, living among the surrounding trees, because it's the closest thing to home that he knew. My chest expands with excitement at the thought.

Then I draw away from Wren, careful not to wake him. The morning air feels dewy and fresh, and aside from the endless call of birds, it's silent. So silent, I can hear my boots as they echo dully along the forest floor, toward the fallen beast. I drop to my knees next to it, then run my fingers over its coarse fur.

Now that I'm not fighting for my life, I can appreciate the texture of the coat and the thickness, too. I study its claws, note how beautiful the arc of its skull is. I even begin to mourn the fact that this sprawling creature died under our hand. Because the last thing I want to do up here is destroy.

But as I finally settle myself onto a large rock nearby, I realize that I don't want to be destroyed, either. So maybe life up here is a balancing act. Maybe in the old world, things skidded off center. Maybe humans, left unchecked, destroy, destroy, destroy.

I can't let that happen.

Wren's voice pierces the silence. "Enjoying yourself?" He is awake now, watching me.

I let my legs dangle over the edge of the rock. "Just a little," I say, and my tone is playful.

For a while, he says nothing—he simply contemplates me with his brow furrowed, like he's deep in thought. "It's good to see you so happy," he finally says. Then, before I can respond, he adds in a lighter tone, "I take it you don't object to the constant chatter those things make?" He gestures to the treetops. As if on cue, a black bird caws into the morning.

"Things? I believe they're called *birds*, Wren."

"Ah," he says theatrically. "Aren't you knowledgeable."

I bow my head.

"They're loud." And he stifles a yawn. "A few more hours of sleep would've been nice. And maybe a proper mattress."

"Of course you'd want a fancy mattress," I scoff. *"Preme."*

He chucks a stick at me.

I kick aside the stick and throw a stone in his direction.

"Not great aim, Eve." His expression is full of feigned seriousness. "You should keep practicing—it might be the best protection we've got the next time we run into one of those things." He turns his attention to the fallen beast, no longer joking.

"I was wondering about that, too," I admit.

He walks over to me and lets his arms drape over my shoulders and down my back. "And? Did you figure out what we're going to do once we're out of bullets?"

"Run faster?" I suggest. I loop my arms around his waist and pull him close.

He bends down and kisses me on the forehead, then the nose, and finally on the lips. "We'd need a motor to outrun that thing. Do you think they can climb trees?"

I lean back and give him an incredulous look. "Why? Can *you*?"

He smiles. "Good point. Not that there was a need, but it's too bad they didn't teach us how to outwit shockingly large, strangely ferocious animals back in Eleven."

I smile, too, but then the phrase *back in Eleven* echoes through my head, and my smile falters. The problem is that I'm up here—free and happy—and my friends and family are stuck in a situation that is just the opposite. Caged and miserable.

Back in Eleven. If only there was a way to get word to them that the world has cooled. Because the twinge of guilt I feel that I get to live up here and they don't isn't one I want to endlessly carry with me. And more than that, I don't want them to be stuck underground forever.

Maybe they'll figure it out for themselves when they realize that Wren and I have vanished without a trace. Maybe the Premes in charge—like Wren's mother—will figure it out, too. Maybe all of Eleven will join us up here in the coming days.

Then Wren asks, "What's for breakfast?" and all my thoughts dissipate at once.

I blink up at him. Breakfast? It isn't something I've thought about, not even once, not since we bid goodbye to the compound. But now that he mentions it, I *am* hungry. Thirsty, too, and a small flare of panic ignites in my stomach at the realization. "Maybe we should walk around and see what we can find," I suggest, careful to hide the unease in my voice.

"Sure."

I slide off the rock and consider the ring of trees surrounding us. "Which way?"

He shrugs, then points behind me. "That's the direction we came from last night, which means the compound is that way. Do you remember seeing any food along the way?"

"I didn't notice any cafeterias," I joke. But beneath my easy tone, that flare of panic grows larger. Because Wren and I have always been served food. Food that's been grown underground, in commercial greenhouses and factories, and prepared in a kitchen by trained staff—and there's none of that up here.

So. What the hell are we going to eat?

"Let's keep heading in the same direction," I say after a while. "I'm sure we'll find something."

A minute later, we start picking our way through the close-knit trees, my gaze no longer dancing along the treetops or admiring the sun that rises slow and steady from the horizon. No, instead my eyes are trained on the ground, searching for something—*anything*—that resembles food.

CHAPTER THREE

Time passes. My brain flips from jubilation at being up here, to guilt over those back in Eleven, and finally to hunger, then back again. A nonstop cycle that becomes lopsided toward food with every hour that passes. Movement is slow through the thicket of trees, my boots are coated in dirt, and my clothes are sticky with sweat. The giant rock face that sits to the north of the Oracle is now behind us, far off in the distance, but every so often, I stop to glimpse it through the trees. Right now, it's the most familiar sight I know.

Wren is as quiet as I am, both of us focused on the task at hand—finding sustenance—but finally he breaks the silence by asking, "What's that?"

I look around, spotting nothing out of the ordinary—nothing out of our *new* ordinary, that is. "What?"

"You can't smell it?"

I walk a bit farther, and then I nod. It's a scent I can't pinpoint, and yet it's sweet and very strong. I gesture to a swell of plants that tower over Wren and me, all their branches covered in tufts of purple flowers. We edge closer, and as I run my fingers over one of the tufts, the scent becomes even stronger. Then I jerk my hand aside as a black-and-yellow insect appears, landing delicately on the petals.

"Wren," I whisper, eyeing it. Together we watch as it moves from flower to flower, pausing now and then, like it's eating or maybe collecting something. "What do you think it's doing?"

"I have no idea."

"Do you know what it's called?"

He shakes his head. Then he adds, "Do you think we can eat it?"

I gaze at him. He must be hungrier than I am. "Maybe," I say, even though it doesn't exactly look palatable. I reach my fingers forward until they wrap carefully around it and I can feel its wings beating against my palm. I start to laugh at the sensation until it's replaced by white-hot pain.

I jump, and I scream, and then Wren pulls back my fingers. Part of the insect flies away, but the rest remains embedded in my palm, surrounded by a fast-growing welt. It looks vaguely like the splinter I got when I was five, from an old can that Hunter and I were playing with. My father had to hold me down as my mother dug it out with a fork she'd swiped from the cafeteria, except she couldn't get it all, and it became infected. After weeks of sickness, I finally healed, and I was told I was lucky I didn't lose my hand. I was lucky, even, to be alive.

Right now, I carefully grip what remains of the insect, my heart thumping in my throat with a volatile mixture of fear and intrigue, then yank it free. I dig my thumb into the welt to try to numb the pain, then shout, "What *was* that thing?"

"I'm not sure," admits Wren. Then he grins. "It probably wouldn't have tasted very good, though."

I try to kick him—but I'm still doubled over, and even though I feel like crying, I find myself laughing instead. Wren watches me with an amused look on his face.

"Here," I say a few minutes later, once the throbbing begins to ease. I tear a handful of flowers from the plant and push them into his hand. "If that insect *was* actually eating them, maybe we can, too."

"That does sound logical," he says, holding them to his nose. "Except they don't smell like food. They smell like... perfume. Don't you think?"

I roll my eyes. "You think I know what *perfume* smells like, Preme? That wasn't exactly an allotment offered on the second floor."

"Your loss," he says, nudging me, then he pushes the entire handful of flowers into his mouth. Immediately he makes a face and spits them back out.

"No good?" I ask, trying to hold back my laughter.

"No good," he confirms. "I'd rather eat month-old mashed potatoes from the Mean cafeteria."

Mashed potatoes. Normally I hate those glutinous mounds of starch, which have no taste, no flavor. Right now, I realize, I'd give my ring finger for some.

A few hours later, the sun has arced high in the sky, and it's far warmer than the middle of the night, or even the morning. My clothes are soaked from sweat, and I'm more thirsty than before. Funny: I had envisioned the world up here to have large stores of water—I've seen plenty of pictures in the Preme library of land ending and water claiming its place. Yet we've been walking for hours and haven't spotted a single drop.

Wren and I no longer joke or chat—we just focus on

stomping through the overgrowth in search of sustenance. Too bad we don't know what to look for. Nothing up here resembles those mashed potatoes or shriveled peas that I was served underground. There are no tin cups waiting next to a chipped sink, either.

The flare of panic I felt this morning intensifies, filling my empty belly, and all thoughts of searching for Jack vanish as I zero in on the most pressing need standing before us.

Since I can't think of anything else, I try to remember the last time I ate. It's been a while. I was locked in my cell without food before leaving the compound, because my supposed best friend Hunter betrayed me. Before that, I was too busy mourning the Noms who lost their lives in the government-sanctioned mass murder on the ground floor—called the cleanse—to eat a thing. It's been days, I think, since I've had a proper meal.

The longer we walk, the less energy I have. Wren, too—I can tell by the slouching of his shoulders and the shortening of his stride. As the sun drops lower in the sky, our pace is no longer slow simply because of the densely packed trees. I feel like my muscles have gone soft, like pools of molasses, and navigating up and down steep slopes leaves me dizzy. My head throbs, and without the warmth of the midday sun, I find myself shivering.

Finally, after several more hours of fruitless searching, we decide to sleep next to an overturned tree, and we're both so exhausted from spending the entire day walking, so weakened from having no food or water, that we fall immediately asleep before we can say good night to each other.

• • •

The next morning when I wake, I listen to the happy chatter of the birds, feel the gentle morning sun against my cheek, even remember that I am waking in total freedom.

But I do not smile.

Wren's not in a good mood, either, and we quickly begin our search for food and water all over again.

Monotonous hours pass. Futile hours. My stomach gurgles, and hurts, and my headache returns with a vengeance. With every step, I imagine us stumbling upon water—see it sparkling under the sunlight, wide and vast like the pictures I've seen in those Preme books. With every step, I'm disappointed. At the same time, a steady stream of visuals competes for space in my brain—visuals of everything I've ever eaten back in Eleven—even simple things, like toast. I salivate at the thought.

More and more hours slide by, and that now-familiar feeling of panic grows even worse. What are we going to do? What's going to happen? Just as I start to lose all hope, I hear Wren say in a thick voice, "Eve. Over there."

I follow his gaze and spot something slinking between the trees. At first I think it's just a mirage—another trick of the eye or deceit of the brain. But when I move closer, I see that something is definitely moving, and it resembles water, except that it's brown and murky. We stumble closer, barely daring to believe it, and finally I step off the land, feel the liquid seep through my boots. I kneel down and dip my hands in, examining how it falls through my fingers, behaving exactly the way water does. "Do you think…?"

"It doesn't look like water belowground," Wren says, and I note how weak his voice sounds.

"No," I whisper. "It doesn't."

He sighs, then crouches next to me and scoops the rust-hued liquid to his lips.

"How does it taste?"

"It tastes like water," he confirms. "Just…dirty water."

It must not be that bad, because he drinks down handful after handful, and a moment later, I do the same. Because even though dirty water doesn't sound very appetizing, I've never been this thirsty in all my life, not even after a full day training with Blue Circuit—my Combat League team.

Wren is right: it doesn't taste like the water we're used to—but it's satisfying, and slowly the all-consuming panic that gripped me a few minutes ago ebbs. And maybe it's because of that—because of my sudden clearheadedness—that I spot the red berries growing along the water's edge.

I've seen food like this on occasion underground. It isn't often that Means are served fresh fruit, but once in a while we're served the leftovers that the Premes aren't interested in, and I think that's why it looks familiar. I wade through the murky water as quickly as I can, stopping when I'm right in front of it, then examine the bright red spheres.

"Have you had these before?" I ask Wren.

He stands over my shoulder and shakes his head. "They look like blueberries, aside from the color. Have you had blueberries before?"

"Not that I know of," I mutter. Then I pull a berry free and roll it between two fingers. "Is there such a thing as *red*berries?"

He tries to grin—I can see the corners of his mouth pull up, but it looks more like a grimace. "Evidently," he says.

Since we don't have anything else to eat, I shove the morsel into my mouth. Bitter, and I almost spit it out again. But it's been so long since I've had food that I swallow it down, then I pick more, fill my stomach with them, and Wren does the same, both of us ignoring how we gag with each bite.

When finally the berries are gone, we wade out of the water and sit on the forest floor, more content than before.

My head no longer pounds from thirst, my stomach no longer consumes itself from hunger, and I lay back, stretching out so that I'm spread-eagle, staring at the blue sky and the billowing clouds overhead. I feel exhausted, and I realize I've never walked so far or for so long in my life. I've never come so close to starvation, which is saying something, considering how strictly Compound Eleven rations food.

Right now, though, all is good. All is calm. I watch the leaves shimmering in the breeze and the clouds rolling by. I realize that my hand is no longer swollen and sore from whatever caused such pain yesterday, and for that I feel grateful. I feel *hopeful*.

Everything will be okay up here in paradise.

Then, just as I think about searching for Jack, Wren draws himself unsteadily to his feet. He disappears into the bushes.

At first I think he's spotted something—I almost follow him. But when I hear him vomit, I go still. All that hope and gratitude are replaced by concern, by fear, and a few minutes later, I feel it, too. Nausea. It creeps up my stomach and swirls around my brain. My skin is no longer tacky from the sun—it breaks into a cold sweat that drenches my clothes. Those shimmering leaves overhead distort sideways, then I roll onto all fours as my stomach heaves.

The vomiting is unending—again and again and again, along with the tremor in my bones and the blistering fever that leaves me curled in a ball at the foot of a tree. Somewhere off in the distance, I hear Wren groan, and I spot him, through my warped vision, clutching his stomach. I wonder if it hurts as much as mine does right now.

And as time marches on, as the symptoms refuse to vanish, as the world spins around me, I begin to wonder if we'll die here.

CHAPTER FOUR

Darkness has fallen, maybe minutes ago, maybe hours ago. All is still and silent, and I realize that at some point, the dizziness and the aches and the fever and the upset stomach must have subsided, and sleep must've kicked in. When I sit up to look for Wren, though, I find the headache has returned, and it feels like a knife straight through my skull. The world slides back and forth, like tar, and I have to lie down again.

Next my gaze scales up, down, all around, searching for Wren. Just because I survived whatever made us so ill, doesn't mean that he did, and my heart thuds uncomfortably at the thought. But when I finally summon enough energy to twist my body around, I spot him through the darkness. He lies on his side, his head resting on his arm—alive, but barely. His eyes are sunken, like hollow pits, and even under the dim light I can see how pale he is. His lips are tinged gray, they even tremor, like he walks a fine line between life and death. Probably I look the same way.

He draws in a breath, a gasp for air, then he says in a hoarse, barely audible voice, "We have to go back, Eve."

For a while I am motionless. Silent. Then the words echo through my brain. *We have to go back.* Surely he is kidding. Yes—of course he is. So I laugh at the absurdity of the statement, or at least I intend to. But my mouth is so dry, I have so little energy, that all I can do is whisper, "Good one."

"I'm serious."

I lift my head from the ground so I can better see him. "*What?*"

"We might be able to survive another day out here," he says in that hoarse voice. "And if we keep moving, we'll never be able to make it home. We need to turn back."

"Home?" I say in a strangled voice. "You call that place *home*?"

"Eve," he says in a stern voice. "We're going to *die* otherwise. We have to head back—we don't have a choice."

My stomach twists into knots. I feel unreasonably cold. "We can't go back."

"Why not?"

"Because we almost died breaking *free* of Compound Eleven. Because—because *Jack* might be up here. Because I don't want to." I shake my head, ignoring the way it aches. "I'm not going back."

"Just listen," he says, with more intensity than before. "We need to—"

"*Just listen?*" Right now emotion spikes inside my brain. I stand on shaky legs. "You *just listen*. You're suggesting we go *back* to Compound Eleven. You know, to that place that after sixteen years I finally escaped. To the place that I hated so much I was willing to *die* to leave. Remember? I was willing to say goodbye to all of it. My parents, my friends, *you*."

He exhales, then carefully he pushes himself up so he's standing, too. He grasps me around the shoulders. "Eve, I need you to think this through. I need you to use your head.

When we came up here, we came prepared to die. Right?"

I gaze at the stars that spread above us, stars that reach from one end of the sky to the other, thousands of pinpoints of light that ebb and flow like clouds do during the day. "So?"

"We didn't come here prepared to survive."

"Yeah, *Wren*, I know that. Everyone down there thinks it's a thousand degrees up here, so *obviously* we didn't think we could survive. But now we know the earth has cooled. We *can* survive. So why would we go back *now*?"

As he stares at me through the darkness, I see that even though his eyes look like pits, sunken in, hollowed out—they still manage to look thoughtful. "Because we can't," he says simply. "If we stay up here any longer, we are going to die. We have no food, no water, and not enough ammunition to survive another attack."

I go silent. Because there's pressure in my ears and the light drifting from the stars overhead just dimmed considerably. I shake my head. I try to rock the notion from its resting place. But I can't. He's right.

He's *right*.

It makes me want to erupt into a thousand fiery pieces. It makes me want to crumple into nothingness. But all I do is stand motionless, blinking back tears, thousands of them that threaten to flood this place I want, more than anything, to call home. And what does it mean for Jack? It means that even if the world *had* cooled nine years ago when he was thrown from the compound by Commander Katz, and Ted Bergess, and the guards…there's no chance he could've survived. After all, if we can't find a way to live up here, how could a young child?

Emotions, too many to count, too overwhelming to bear. How long have I clung to the hope that he somehow persisted? That he defied the odds and found a way forward? That he thrived up here in paradise? I can't believe how wrong

I was. How foolish I was. I can't believe the crushing sensation suddenly sitting on my chest.

Then I relive Jack's final moments underground, I hear his pleas, I see my mother's agony, and something inside me withers.

"Eve?" Wren asks. "Are you okay? Did you hear what I said—about us having to go back?"

I swallow deeply. "We can make do up here. We don't need to go back." I say it firmly. I repeat it under my breath, again and again and again.

The world around me grows darker, and I feel so cold, so exposed, it's like my insides are cast in ice.

"We're going to starve—"

Probably he says more. But I am sobbing too loudly to hear. I am unraveling too thoroughly to care.

He doesn't move toward me, doesn't offer words of comfort. I don't expect any. Don't want any. I just want to be left alone to cry, and I want to cry until the tears finally dry up, leaving nothing but the hardened shell of the person I have always been.

Somewhere along the line, I became far too hopeful. Maybe it was when I met Wren. Or when we shared that first kiss, in the Oracle. Maybe it stopped me from seeing straight.

But with time, my breathing slows. The tears stop and I blink up at him. "Everything you're saying makes sense, except for the part about me going back. I chose death over the compound, and that's still my choice."

His brow digs together. "I made that decision, too, remember, Eve?"

"So why are you changing your mind now?"

"Because I don't want to die! And I don't think you do, either. Not anymore. Not after seeing all this."

Partly I think he's right. After all, I wanted to find out if something more beautiful than Compound Eleven persists in the world, and now I know that it does. I wanted to feel fresh air against my skin, and touch dirt, run through open and unending spaces—and I've done that, too. But those fleeting experiences aren't enough to sustain me underground again, how could they be? So I shake my head. "I'm not going back. I'd rather die here."

"Would you? Because I don't believe you're thinking it through. When we left Eleven, we were both reeling from the cleanse, and we just wanted out. I think you also had it in your head that maybe your brother found a way to live up here, and you could, too."

I go still. "And?"

"And now you know better. I'm sorry, Eve—really. I know how much this must kill you."

"I'm not going back to Eleven, Wren," I say in a shaky voice.

For a while he just considers me. The moonlight catches his cheekbone that stands out more than it used to. It makes him look animalistic, and wild. "Then we'll both die out here," he says eventually.

I scowl. Because I can't let that happen. I can't let Wren die—not when he doesn't want to. And he won't go back to the compound without me, I can see it in the angle of his jaw. So what choice do I have?

Maybe having found this place, having experienced it... maybe it *will* be enough to sustain me. Maybe it will even make compound life more bearable knowing that Jack isn't up here, all alone...

"Don't forget I'm technically a criminal right now, locked in my cell," I remind Wren.

"They have no evidence you were planning an escape. It's your word against Hunter's. They can't verify you as a criminal based on that." Then he moves closer to me and takes my hand in his, and its warmth spreads up my arm but doesn't reach the empty pit sitting inside my chest.

"What about Daniel?" I ask hollowly. "And Landry. We have to choose jobs in a week. And they told me that once they're guards, they'll make my life a living hell. Don't think they won't. And I won't be able to fight them off anymore because, as soon as they're hired, they'll be walking around with guns and I won't." Plus there's Dennis, the black-eyed guard whose nose I broke. And Ben—someone else I must watch out for.

Under the moonlight, Wren looks at me knowingly. I squeeze my eyes shut. Because suddenly I know what he wants me to do, and it's the very thing that has always sickened me. I loathe the guards as much as I loathe Compound Eleven. And yet not only does Wren want me to return to that dreaded compound...he wants me to find a way to become a guard.

CHAPTER FIVE

The clock blinks at me. Two minutes past noon.

I stare at it, then glance at the door. The one that Wren returned the padlock to almost a week ago. The one that holds me in my cell, a prisoner. My criminal verification will take place sometime in the coming days—the one that will determine if I am guilty of my alleged crimes, but until then, there is nothing for me to do but stare at the ceiling. And the clock.

Three minutes.

They are never late.

Finally I hear the sound that makes me salivate. I drag myself from my bedsheets and grab the packet of sustenance from under the door, the only one I'm allotted each day. I go to the bathroom, where a tin mug sits. I wait for the water to run hot and as I do, I stare at the reflection in the mirror hanging over the wash basin.

The same face I have always known stares back.

For all that has happened in the preceding two weeks, I am still me. Still the same wide and even features. The ones that are sturdy, utilitarian, and decidedly not delicate. Right now my eyes are hard slits, and I deflate as I look at them. Because they are not streaked with light from the sun. They are not alive with freedom. I am more caged now than I have ever been.

And I now know that my little brother is dead, dead, dead.

Funny that I thought I would be able to do this. That I'd be able to return, and maybe accept compound life easier than before. Funny that I thought that fleeting taste of the world aboveground would be enough to sustain me down here, and that the knowledge that Jack is truly gone would somehow bring me peace.

It brings me despair. Nothing more. Nothing less. Despair that is compounded by my return to this place in the depths of hell.

I shift my gaze away from my eyes, and look at my bottom lip instead. Red, as though I bit it. Perhaps during the short bouts of fitful sleep that I manage from time to time. Then I pull back my index finger as the water turns scalding. I stick the mug under until it's full, and carry it carefully back to my desk, where I rip open the packet of sustenance and tip it in. Waiting for it to dissolve is the hardest part. Yellow and gray clumps of powder saturate slowly, taunting me with their leisurely pace.

But despite these taunts, despite the despair, at least I have a sliver of hope of a better tomorrow. It's not much—and tenuous, at best—but still it shines brightly from some remote corner of my brain, and I think it's the only thing keeping me going. The sliver of hope comes, ironically, from Wren's wish that I become a guard. He wants me to so I can protect myself, but as I've whittled away the hours stuck in my cell, I've realized there's a far better reason for finding a way onto the guardship.

It's that the guards are powerful. They have access to all kinds of places in the compound, and all kinds of resources. So maybe…maybe if I can manage to secure a position, I can find stores of food and water—maybe I can find a way to get them to the top of the earth. Guns and ammunition, too, for the deadly beasts that call that strange world up there home sweet home.

Yes. It's possible that if I can become a guard…I can find a way to survive aboveground.

Tenuous. Unlikely. Remote. But it's a shoestring of hope, and right now I think I need that more than anything.

I sigh, then glance at the door. There's a voice on the other side, but it isn't for me. Just someone yelling as they pass by.

Wren offered to come, to keep me company and to bring me proper food. He knows the passcode—it would be no problem at all for him to break into my cell. But I told him no, I asked him to stay away until my verification, explaining that I wanted to abide by Compound Eleven's rules until then. Best not to cause any trouble, I said.

But is that really why?

My fingers shake as I tilt the mug to my lips and empty its contents into my belly, the only thing keeping me from starving to death. No matter that it tastes like blood, no matter.

CHAPTER SIX

One hundred push-ups every hour. It's hard to find the energy or the will, but at least it's something to pass the time. Besides, I sleep better for it. So I roll out of bed and collapse onto the floor. Too many days without proper food has made me weak, and dizzy. The room rocks back and forth as my palms push into cold concrete, as my forearms engage.

Even through the dizziness, and the faintness, the first twenty reps are easy. They always are. It doesn't get tough until the sixties. At that point my muscles begin to scream and the desire to stop becomes overwhelming. But still it can't touch me. I have become skilled over the years at bagging up my feelings and setting them aside, just as I did when I descended the ladder back down here to hell, my features indifferent, my tears of sorrow packaged neatly on the inside.

Up and down, up and down.

Sweat seeps along my hairline and neck. I will be ready for Daniel and for Landry—I will not go soft so long as I am a member of this compound.

Up and down, up and down.

Of course I'm a member of this compound. I was born here, and I'll probably die here, too.

Up and down, up and down.

What was I thinking, believing otherwise?

Finally I pull my elbow tight to my body and roll onto my back with a groan. I blink and see a pink face looking down at me.

The face contorts with laughter. "Remember me?"

Ben. The guard I met on the fifth floor. The one who locked me in here in the first place. The one with the greedy eyes, and the thing for pretty faces. Yeah, I remember him.

"How long have you been here?"

"Long enough." He smacks his lips. "So, how many push-ups?"

"Hundred." I say it bluntly.

"Impressive. Not exactly a turn-on, though, is it? Getting out-muscled by a girl." His brows crowd together and his laughter is gone.

I want to tell him that I couldn't care less what he finds a turn-on. But I can't do that because there is a gun in his holster, one that is only inches away from his hand. My own gun is stashed in Wren's apartment on the fifth floor, a precaution in case more sweeps are performed. So—Ben has the power here, not me, and the realization makes me feel like a sock is wedged just far enough down my throat that I can't pull it out.

If I were aboveground right now, I wouldn't have to stare into his watery eyes and shrug my shoulders. I wouldn't have to inch backward on my heels so that more than two feet separate us. But I'm not aboveground, because Wren made us come back, and right now I can't really remember why.

"What'd you do anyways?" He gestures to the padlock he holds in his hand.

"I didn't do anything."

He smirks. "That's what they all say." Then his gaze touches my exposed collarbone, my bare arms. "Your verification starts any minute. Might want to get yourself dressed up a bit."

My back straightens. "It's *now*?" My criminal verification is important—if I'm found guilty of my crimes, I will be punished, and severely. "I thought there'd be some notice—"

"Thought wrong. Look, you're the only Lower Mean I've had marching orders on—usually I work the top floors, but most girls wear a blouse, maybe a skirt even." Then he grins. "Promise I won't look."

I still wear what I slept in: a black tank top with spaghetti straps and sweatpants. "I'm ready," I say, shrugging.

"Like that?"

I nod.

"You won't stand a chance. You've got Andrews as your chief adjudicator, and if you walk through the door looking like that, he'll verify you before you even sit your ass down. Not that it's any skin off my back," he adds, with a wink.

"I'm a Lower Mean. You think I own a blouse? Because I don't. Ditto the skirt." I brush by him and savor the relief I feel as I yank open my cell door. No longer am I trapped with a man and his gun.

But relief is replaced quickly by dread. Broken glass crunches uncomfortably underfoot. The neon sign across the hall turns my skin a sickly shade of green. The damp air is tainted with the smell of urine.

Focus, Eve.

My verification is important, I must think only of that. Besides, after days locked in my cell, I should be celebrating the change in scenery. No matter how slight, a whisper of freedom trumps no freedom at all.

The first door I turn to is Hunter's. Closed—too bad. I may be weak and dizzy with hunger, but the mere thought of him sends blood pumping through my arteries with renewed life. I may have to bite my tongue with Ben the guard but I don't have to with Hunter, my friend no longer. I can scream at him and curse him—both of which he deserves.

How he could turn me over to authorities after a lifetime of closeness is something that still keeps me up at night. I think it will be months, maybe years, before I can sleep easy.

I turn to Maggie's door next, but a hand lands on the small of my back and Ben pushes me in the direction of the main corridor, my thoughts interrupted, my whisper of freedom quickly silenced.

We stand before a brushed steel door on the fifth floor, along a hallway I've never been down. Around me are the same glossy surfaces I have come to associate with the Preme floor, the same white lights, too. Except it looks nothing like it did a week ago.

A week ago it sparkled. It glittered like gold. Now, after being aboveground, it looks stale, gaudy—forced and unnatural. And it isn't just up here...the entire compound looks different. It looks sadder than ever, something I didn't think was possible. It is a joke of an existence, except right now it's my reality. Probably it will always be my reality.

Ben wraps his fingers tightly around my arm.

"Do you mind?" I ask him.

He moves closer so that his stomach brushes my side. "Wouldn't want you to escape, now would we?" He squeezes me tighter.

"Escape to where? We're in a concrete box below the earth." Because unless I manage to find vast stores of food and water to take aboveground, we really are trapped in a goddamn box below the goddamn earth.

"You know, I don't remember you having so much attitude that time we met in the hallway up here. I remember thinking to myself, damn she's sweet. I'm not thinking that so much anymore."

Then he squeezes my arm as tight as he can. It burns, then it aches, but I don't let it touch my face. *I am impassive, made of steel*, I remind myself. Can't feel a thing.

The door in front of us clicks open, and a tall, unsmiling man with glasses beckons me in. The vise grip around my arm lifts and I'm pushed forward. I stumble, but I don't fall.

Inside, the walls are the same white plastic as the hall, and the bright lights are the same, too. A lone chair sits in the middle of the room, and at the far end is a table with three seats placed behind. Two of the seats are occupied, and the tall man moves around the table and sits in the third.

All three are men. Preme men. They will side with Hunter, of course they will.

"Sit," commands the man in the middle. He's wide and bald, and his thick eyebrows arch with distaste. He's more important than the other two. I can see it in the black robes he wears, and in the white tabs that hang under his chin—a uniform of superiority. "Sit," he says again.

It's difficult to do what this man commands of me, but I think of Wren and the determined look in his eye when he told me I could beat the verification, and I sit. I have to play along, just as I agreed to. I have to say my piece. I have to trust in him that this will turn out okay.

"My name is Justice Andrews. My colleagues and I will be your adjudicators today." He taps his pen as he looks me over. Then his lip curls as though he smells something foul. It's hard to tell if it's my outfit that he takes offense to or my status as a Lower Mean. Probably both.

That's okay—I'm used to being looked down upon. All second-floor Lower Means are used to scorn from the upper floors, especially from Floor Five—the Preme floor. The Premes rule the compound, and they make sure they're afforded all the luxuries the compound can offer while they do it. Luxuries the rest of us are denied. But I can't complain, because the Floor One Denominators—Noms, for short— have it far worse. No jobs mean no allotments, which mean no supplies—not even clothes, or diapers. And, since I'm one of the volunteers who passes out their lunch, I know it's scraps that they're fed, and not enough to fill a stomach.

So, let Justice Andrews be disgusted; it doesn't bother me—it *doesn't*.

"State your name," he orders.

I take a deep breath, then force my voice up an octave. I command it to be soft and yielding. "Eve Hamilton."

"State your floor."

"Two."

"State your cell number."

"12404K."

The wide man known not just as Andrews but *Justice* Andrews folds his hands and looks somewhere between content and dissatisfied. The man to his right, one with white hair and delicate features, clears his throat. He says in a crisp voice, "Ms. Hamilton, this is your criminal verification for Charge 55.4-2. Do you understand?"

Fluorescent lights buzz loudly overhead as I nod.

"A yes or no, please."

"Yes."

"Good. What say you: guilty or not guilty?"

I shift in my seat. "Not guilty."

The three men glance at one another. Justice Andrews

looks bemused while the other two are stern-faced. Then the tall one sighs. He adjusts his eyeglasses and fixes me with a stare. "Why don't you tell us about the incident that gave rise to this charge."

"I don't know which incident that was," I lie. "I don't know why I was locked in my cell. I don't even know why I'm here." Right now I'm not speaking off the cuff; I have had many long days and nights to think this through. I am practiced, and ready—my lies are polished.

The tall man checks his notes that lay in front of him. "Do you know, Ms. Hamilton, that it's against the laws of this compound to attempt to leave it for another?"

My head knocks forward with feigned confusion. "To leave? Yeah, I guess I do know that."

"We require loyalty of our citizens."

"Of course."

"Do you know a young man by the name of Hunter Thomas?"

I resist the urge to contort my face. "He's a friend of mine," I say. "How come?"

"We ask the questions, Ms. Hamilton—not you. Now, you say Mr. Thomas is a friend of yours. Is that correct?"

"For as long as I can remember. Best friends, except for the occasional fight." I give the man my best attempt at a smile.

Justice Andrews, meanwhile, seems to vibrate in his seat. He interrupts the tall man, and I can hear in his voice that he lacks the patience of the other. "Do you know where the tunnels are, Ms. Hamilton?" he demands.

"Tunnels?"

"Yes, *tunnels*. The ones that lead to neighboring compounds."

I turn my gaze to the smooth and unblemished ceiling. How different it is from Floor Two, where the ceiling is a constellation of decay. "Well," I begin slowly, "I know where one is. It runs from downstairs, from the first floor. I have a friend down there—that's how I know. I have a few friends down there actually, thanks to my volunteer work feeding the—"

"Did you ever speak to Mr. Thomas about this tunnel?"

"That's what our last fight was about, actually. It happened...I'm not sure. I think maybe the day before I noticed my door was locked."

Justice Andrews's eyes narrow. The room is so quiet, I can almost hear the crackling of his brow as he draws it tight—like sandpaper. Beside him, the white-haired man says, "Tell us about this fight."

My heart thuds harder now than before. These are important words I'm uttering. One misstep and it's all for naught. My criminal status will be verified, and I will be given a punishment. I tap my fingers against the base of the chair. I don't want to lose one of my fingers—a common punishment. I don't want to be sent to live on the first floor, either—another possibility. And, since a verified criminal would never be accepted onto the guardship, I don't want to ruin my already dismal chances of becoming one, not when so much rides on it. A series of images flash through my brain—Daniel and Landry, brandishing guns and pointing them in my direction, the deadly beast Wren and I encountered aboveground, stores of food, vats of water, swaying trees... The images taunt me. They remind me that right now, I must not slip up.

"Ms. Hamilton?"

"Um, yeah. Okay—the fight. It had to do with the job search, actually. It's stressful, you know? My friends and I were having a hard time deciding and it was causing a lot of...um—"

"Stress?" the tall man suggests. "Conflict?"

"Yeah. That one—conflict. Anyway, I told Hunter that I was interested in tunnel maintenance—"

"Did you attend the job tour for that position?"

"I missed it. But I went down there myself, maybe a day or two before we fought. I went down there and spoke with the guard—you can ask him. I told him I was interested in doing tunnel maintenance and tried to get him to open it up for me so I could look around." I pick at my finger and shrug. "Didn't work."

The white-haired man leans forward. "And your interest in this tunnel position angered Mr. Thomas for some reason?"

"He kind of lost it on me," I agree. "It's because we were supposed to get jobs in the kitchen together. You can check the records, both of us went on the kitchen tour and everything. But I just wasn't sure the kitchen was for me. He said I was betraying him." Gently I twist my hands together. "It was a silly fight, that's all. What does it have to do with my verification?"

"Your charge is 55.4-2. That's attempting to abdicate the compound. It doesn't come with a light sentence."

I stare at them, hopefully blankly. Then I whisper, "You think…you think I tried to go? What, along the tunnel downstairs? All I did was ask the guard if he could show me—I swear. Ask him. He'll tell you the same thing. I never tried to go through it, I *swear*."

"Nobody is saying you did, Ms. Hamilton," snaps Justice Andrews. He likes me the least, I am sure of it. "Mr. Thomas has alleged that you were planning on going through that tunnel the night in which you became a prisoner."

I force shock to my face. And then I deny, deny, deny. Just like Wren said.

Finally the questions stop, and in front of me the three men huddle as they deliberate my fate. They have no evidence, no proof—only a statement from my supposed best friend. A laugh of derision almost slips between my teeth, but I catch it just in time.

The two men on either side, the tall one and the one with the delicate features, they nod together. It's the wide, smirking one in the middle who's against me. Justice Andrews. I can see it from here, from my lone seat in the middle of the barren room.

The longer it takes, the more my insides begin to squeeze into themselves. My earlier bravado, if I ever had any, evaporates. The thumping inside my chest feels like it might burst bones made frail from little food. But finally, *finally* Justice Andrews clears his throat. He places his palms together, then tips his fingers to his nose. Thinking. "Ms. Hamilton. Your story seems to make perfect sense."

I sit straighter, hopeful.

"Except for one small problem, and that is that I don't believe a word of it." His eyes reduce to slivers as he glares at me. "Your demeanor here today isn't fooling me. You are a trained fighter, are you not? As brutal a monster as they come in this civilization of ours, from what I've heard. I think your rebellious attitude, one on perfect display today with your choice of outfit, did indeed spur you to plot an escape from Compound Eleven. I think you would have gone through the tunnel had you not been locked inside your cell first. I think you would have used violence to slip past the guard who protects our civilization. I think all of these things, and yet my colleagues are less sure. They are less sure.

"There is little to weigh here by way of evidence; it is simply your word against that of Mr. Thomas. Truly…*truly* it's a shame that it isn't enough to verify your status as a criminal."

I blink.

"You are hereby reinstated back into civilian life."

My heart lurches with relief. I make to stand—

He raises a hand before I do. "As I have made clear, trust you I do not. So don't think for a fraction of a second that I won't be watching you, waiting for your true colors to show, relishing the first opportunity I get to drag you back here before me." He leans backward in his chair and folds his arms. "In addition, I will be putting through orders to the Department of Security to have regular checks made to your cell. Any rights to privacy have been hereby rescinded. Do I make myself clear?"

I cringe. The last thing I need as I try to locate a supply of food and water to take aboveground are regular check-ins. And the last thing I want is even less freedom, more restraint— more *captivity*. But with no other choice, I nod. "Perfectly."

"Perfectly, Justice…"

"A-Andrews," I stammer.

He is silent, but his eyebrows lift.

"Justice Andrews," I say through gritted teeth.

"Memorize my face."

I glance at the others, but their expressions are unreadable. I look back to Andrews, then force myself to nod.

"Good. Because there is no place for a rebellion in Compound Eleven, and I will see to it that any residual rebellion in you is stamped clean out." He smiles darkly. "You are excused."

CHAPTER SEVEN

A moment later all three men push noisily back from the table. They file past me and through the door. Probably I should feel worried or even vaguely threatened by Andrews's words. Instead all I do is smile.

I am not a verified criminal, and I am no longer a prisoner. No horrible punishment awaits, and at this last thought, a balloon swells in my stomach and lifts me from my chair.

Ben waits for me in the hall. He squints one eye. "Looks like it's someone's lucky day."

"Looks that way."

"I guess my services aren't needed, then. Strictly speaking, at least."

"Not needed at all," I grumble. My boots kick quickly away.

"It's not goodbye, Eve," he hollers. I glance over my shoulder and see him grin. Something catches in his eye as he winks. "I'll be along to your cell before long. Just to check in, you know—on Justice Andrews's orders. Make sure you're being a good girl and everything."

His words make me shiver. But then I remember the

words of Justice Andrews: *As brutal a monster as they come...*

So I turn, I walk backward so that we face each other, and I return his wink. Then I'm gone, through the atrium and down the stairs to the third floor, to where the Mean cafeteria is located. It is practically empty—only a few dozen sit inside, and none of them are Daniel, or Landry, my biggest concern. After all, they have been my sworn enemies ever since I was young—cruel Floor Four Upper-Means who take joy in kicking those beneath them. They have always harbored a particular hatred for people like me. People like me who hail from below, and yet stand up to them anyway.

I sit and eat, and it doesn't matter that what I shovel into my mouth is bland and mushy—it is food, real food, not sustenance packets, not poisonous berries. Across the room, a man hands out flyers. Sully: one of the ringleaders of Lower Mean civil disobedience. The not-so-civil kind of disobedience, too. He was shot recently, I saw it happen myself, and yet here he is making the rounds through the Mean cafeteria, limping but otherwise unscathed. I hope he doesn't stop to chat with me, but I'm not a lucky person, never have been, and he tosses a flyer next to my plate. It's for a protest that is starting soon.

"You're no Upper Mean," he says to me, speaking from the side of his mouth.

I glance at him as I finish the last of the crumbs, then flash him the back of my hand. "No, I'm not."

"Not a weakling, either."

"You're two for two," I grumble.

"So why isn't your face ringing any bells? We need numbers if we want those assholes way up there to hear." He tugs at his ear, then points to the ceiling.

"I was locked in my cell until now. Is that enough of an excuse for you?"

The revelation interests him, I can see it in the way his

body bends. Immediately I regret being so forthcoming.

"Locked up for what?"

I take a long gulp of water and swipe my mouth with the back of my hand. "It doesn't matter. Look, I'll think about coming." Normally I might actually be interested in what the flyer has to say, I might even consider attending. But right now I just want to find my friends.

"What's there to think about?" he presses. "You either stand with your fellow citizens, or you stand with the Premes living the golden life. You a Preme lover?"

The words make me go still. I don't love the Premes, I don't even like them. But I do like Wren, and that fact alone is enough to put a target on my back, as far as Sully is concerned. I eye him, more carefully than before. "Have you ever met a Lower Mean that's a Preme lover? Ask a stupid question…"

My tongue amuses him—it must, because he laughs. "What's your name, anyway?"

I don't want him to know my name. I don't want him to know my face. So I push back from the table and stand, then find that I am just as tall as he is. "Don't have one," I announce largely.

"Never met a girl with no name before," he calls, but I'm already halfway to the exit.

I run a hand over my arm as I head downstairs. I have lost weight, even a bit of strength. That's fine. I will go to the Bowl today, will hit the punching bag until my muscles scream for mercy. Then I will keep punching. Right now, though, I want to find Maggie. And Emerald. It feels like it's been years since I've seen them.

And I want to find *Wren*. I know he told me that I could beat the criminal verification—that there wasn't enough evidence to verify me. But he held me for a moment too long when we parted ways. He held me and something inside his gaze wavered. He'll be eager to know the results.

Then I freeze.

Up ahead, it isn't Maggie, and it isn't Emerald or Wren. In fact, it isn't someone I need to fear. Yet it *is* my enemy. Catching sight of the back of his head makes my good mood evaporate. I see red and feel hate push against the inside of my brain.

Hunter. My best friend. My forever friend. Until I told him about my plan to leave Eleven for another compound, and he turned me in to the authorities. He's the reason I had the padlock on my cell door. He's the reason I had to undergo a verification—he's the reason why I will now have extra sets of eyes on me going forward. *Him.*

I shove people out of the way to reach him, and when I'm within striking distance, I push him so hard that he smacks against the concrete wall. He turns quickly, ready to defend himself—then he sees it's me.

Even though the lighting down here is dim, Lower Mean, I glimpse the shock and disbelief that ripple across his features. When he says my name, it's barely audible, and not because the crowds around us are loud. "E-Eve..." he stammers. "Eve, I thought—"

"Thought *what*?" I snap. "That I was locked in my cell? That I was a verified *criminal* by now?"

"But...the lemon squares. I thought..."

He stares at me like he is seeing a ghost. As if he can't quite believe I'm really here. I know why. My calling card— the mention of lemon squares to his friend in the kitchen— after the padlock was already secured to my door. Probably he thought I escaped to another compound after all...

A dark smile turns my lip. "Lemon squares? Don't know what you're talking about. *Jerk*." I shove him again, hard and quick, but this time he is ready. This time he catches himself before he strikes the wall.

I want him to shove me back, to hit me, but not once does violence stir in his eyes. His cruelty runs much deeper.

So I hiss at him, "You disgusting little *rat*." My finger jabs him in the chest as elbows from passersby knead me in the back, while memories of his betrayal flash through my brain. "You piece of—"

"Eve, *please*." Now the initial shock has gone. I am here, in front of him, and I know what he did. He *knows* that I know. "You don't understand," he starts and he wraps his arms around mine. It reminds me of that moment when I told him about my plan to leave Compound Eleven, when I was trying so desperately to secure his blessing. When I almost let myself think that *he* was the solution to my problems. That he had been hiding in plain sight all along...

"You turned me in!" I shout at him. My eyes prickle with tears, they sting with his duplicity. "You were my best friend and you *turned me in*."

"But you have to believe—"

I slap him, and it turns his cheek red. My palm stings, but I barely notice. "I don't have to believe anything," I tell him. "You turned me in. That's all I need to know—that's all I *ever* need to know. Come near me again, try to talk to me, so much as look at me...and I'll knock you out," I add. But threatening him doesn't bring me joy—and I remember that I've been working toward less violence in my life, not more.

Then, before I can register his reaction, I hear my name being called, catch sight of brown hair and an easy smile. Maggie has me wrapped in a hug before I can finish with Hunter.

Once more, my mood changes. Or it must, because I'm smiling now, and I wrap my arms around her like it's been years since our last embrace. By the time I let her go, Hunter has disappeared. She bounces on the balls of her feet and squeezes my hands. "You're *free*. That means the verification went in your favor, doesn't it?"

"How did you—?"

"What, you think I don't care what happens to my best friend? Obviously I hunted down Wren after you-know-what."

"You mean after Hunter turned me in?"

"Yep." She looks suddenly sullen. "I was going to smack him myself, but after Wren told me you decided to stay, I figured you'd rather take care of that on your own." Her smile returns. "You're *here*. I thought, that night…" Something passes over her eyes. She thought I had left for another compound. She doesn't know my true destination because she couldn't know. Nobody could. After all, it took months before I found a way aboveground, and then only because of Wren and his Preme connections.

That's not technically true: I could have killed a person to get there.

An image of Daniel's freshly slashed face burns in my brain, reminding me that I couldn't kill him even though he deserved it. The image taunts me. Makes me feel soft. Except ever since surrendering my freedom a week ago, since…Jack, I feel different. I feel hollow. Too hollow to show him or anyone else mercy.

Maybe my taste of freedom has changed me. Or maybe it's my failure up there and all its implications that has.

Maggie shakes me. "Are you awake? We should be celebrating right now! Right? Your verification went well, didn't it?"

"In the clear," I agree.

She wraps an arm around my back as we push through the crowded main corridor, toward our cells. "That's so, so great," she gushes. "You have no idea how bummed I was about, well, everything. You deciding to try out Compound Ten, first of all. Then Hunter, pulling that stunt." She sighs. "Life has been so crazy lately. And let me tell you, the past week has been off the charts."

"What do you mean?"

"Total chaos. People are pissed about the cleanse. Four guards have been killed so far, which is some sort of record. And people are pissed about that, too. They say it wasn't the guards' fault. They were just following orders from upstairs, you know? Cue more chaos."

I frown. Technically it's true. The order to shoot apart the ground floor came from the head of Health and Population Control—Ted Bergess. I am familiar with the name and with the depths of his ruthlessness. He was the one who ordered that Jack be taken, sent aboveground to wither like the discarded core of an apple, and at the mere thought I feel my insides wither, too.

Still. The guards are not blameless. They are complicit to murder. They lifted their guns, they fired their bullets. Just like Commander Katz, who would have signed off on the cleanse, who would have authorized my brother's murder...

"Have you heard the riots?" Maggie is asking. "They've been nonstop. Plus they're pulling massive numbers—triple the norm. Emerald went to a couple, can you believe it?"

"Good for her."

"I wanted to go, too, but Dad made me promise to stay in my cell. He said they're pretty dangerous."

"I bet," I say, as we turn off the main corridor. A tall girl with brown skin and thick muscles walks our way. Dimples flash, then arms wrap around my waist and lift me so far into the air, I have to shield my head from the low-hanging ceiling.

I laugh as Emerald drops me. I punch her across the shoulder, then we embrace again.

"Don't tell me they let you off!" she shouts in her deep, velvety voice. I've missed that voice. "How the hell did you pull that?"

"No evidence. It was my word against his. Plus I had a nice backstory all planned out."

"I guess you did. Does that make you a full-fledged citizen of Compound Eleven again?"

How badly I want to say no. How badly I want to renounce my citizenship, to stomp on it, to *shoot* it. Instead I say, "Yep. Reinstated back into this hellhole."

"A hellhole you chose over that shithole Ten!"

Maggie starts to laugh, but then she jumps to the edge of the hall, out of the path of two men who sprint by. Chains hang around their necks. "Protests are scheduled to start soon," she explains as I stare after them.

"And the chains?"

"They symbolize oppression."

I nod. "Fitting."

"They also make one hell of a racket," Emerald adds.

More and more pass by, some with chains, some with signs that demand equality, that threaten revolt. Shouting echoes from the main corridor. I think of the warning Maggie's father gave her and move quickly in the direction of our cells. My muscles may have softened over the past week, but I'm not fearful for myself. Only for my friend who doesn't fight.

"Well?" Emerald demands. She smacks my shoulder.

"Well, what?"

"An explanation, hello. For choosing the hellhole over the shithole and everything."

Underfoot trash crunches and crinkles, discarded pieces of aluminum jar the bones of my feet even through thick boots. Elbows clip me under the ribs. "I decided at the last minute that Compound Ten wasn't for me," I say quietly. "No big deal."

"So let me get this straight. You tell Hunter you're going to Ten. He tells the compound. Compound locks you in. Wren busts you out. Then you decide, after all that, to stay here in Eleven to be with yours truly. Right?"

"Bingo."

"Girl, that's got some bat-crap crazy in it, you know that, right?"

I laugh, even as anonymous faces push past, their breathing, chatter, and movement thunderous in my ears. It's a wonder I can even hear myself think. Off in the distance comes chanting. Screams. The clanking of metal.

There was none of that aboveground. There was nothing but peace. Well, almost nothing. I think of the beast that chased me and Wren and suppress a smile with the back of my hand. A second later my smile vanishes as I remember what came next. Dehydration. Starvation. Sickness.

Failure, simply put. And now I am back. Back in Compound Eleven.

Emerald slaps me between the shoulders, completely immune to the sounds of unrest. "Seriously, it's good to have you back. And don't worry about Hunter. I already told him that if he comes near us again I'd shove his head up his butt. Literally."

The two of them burst out laughing, and something warm floods my insides. It's more potent than the anger I felt when I saw Hunter. It is sweet and pleasant and perfectly soothing, but it also makes me uneasy.

I suppose everything does these days.

Maggie slings an arm through mine. "So," she begins slowly, "last time we talked...you and Wren were over. Is that still true?"

Sheepishly, I roll my eyes. "Not so much," I admit.

Then all three of us are laughing, arm in arm, and for a

moment in time — one fleeting moment — I don't care about yesterday, or even tomorrow. I don't care about where I am, where I'm not. In this moment I am surrounded by love, and love is all I choose, all I need.

I just wish the moment would last longer.

CHAPTER EIGHT

I wake to darkness, just as I have all my life.

It's funny—I was so close to waking forever to the rising sun. So, so close. And then everything went wrong—all of it was snatched from my grasp. I think of Wren's insistence that we come back here, and I frown. Because no matter that the world aboveground is strange and unknown—I want to be lulled awake by warmth and brightness, I really do.

Yesterday was spent mostly in front of a punching bag, and aside from Hunter, I didn't run into a single enemy. It was a good day, considering, and I was happy to see my friends again. But now I'm alone, and all I see are shadows. They creep under the door rimmed in neon. They claw their way down the back of my throat.

Fatigue isn't helping. All night I kept one eye on the door just in case Ben the guard decided to pay a visit, and my fingers curled into fists whenever my ears twitched. Right now I rub swollen eyes and groan. I touch my lip, sore to the touch, and next my neck, which feels like something is tethered around it. Like it's the compound itself, taunting me with that blissful taste of freedom.

Okay, maybe it wasn't that blissful. But since returning underground, all the bad parts from aboveground tend to melt to the periphery, and I can't believe Wren dragged me back here instead of trying harder up there. But there's no sense in harboring resentment toward him, I know that, so I set aside the thought and pull myself upright. My muscles ache, they protest, and I relish the sensation. It's a reminder of my strength and a distraction from the day before me.

It's a day I've been dreading. A day I was hoping would never come. It's a day I was actually determined to avoid.

Because today is the day my peers and I must choose a job. And I must do the unthinkable: select as my top choice that of a guard, those whom I despise most, above all others, aside from our rulers.

I must pretend that I want to be one of the cruelest, most power-drunk, most deranged psychopaths below Floor Five, the ones who attract the likes of Daniel and Landry and Zaar. The ones who commit murder simply because they want to, or because they were told to by a man sitting comfortably upstairs. To make matters worse, I am a Lower Mean—my chances of securing such a position are slim. Embarrassingly so. And if I fail, I will be without a legal gun, without clout, without any protection but my fists when my enemies come calling.

Partly it would be a relief. I hate guns, always have. And my fists have served me well over the years—there's no denying that. But if Daniel is walking the corridors with a gun, I need one, too. Besides, becoming a guard is the best shot I'll have of locating the supplies I need to survive aboveground, and I do want that.

Yes. Everything rides on today's application.

With no other choice but to face up to it, I switch on my

lamp and pull on my boots. Flashlight and knife are tucked inside, like always. I pull on a black hoodie that's old and too small, then I braid my blond hair over my shoulder. Next I knock on Maggie's door, and together we go up a floor, where we wait for Emerald. Fifteen minutes later, we squeeze onto a bench with toast in hand. The cafeteria is packed full, and the chatter of thousands claps in my ears.

I remember the sound of silence aboveground, and I long for it. I hate that I'm back here. *I hate it.*

"So much for getting our applications in first," Maggie says glumly.

"The lineup will take until dinner," predicts Emerald as she rests her head on her fist and yawns. She's usually a late riser, and it took several minutes of us pounding on her door this morning to rouse her. Bags are heavy under her eyes.

No doubt they're heavy under my own, too. I push a half piece of toast into my mouth and nudge Maggie. "What's the final decision, anyway?"

"A reporter position for the paper. But I don't want to talk about it or I'll change my mind for the thousandth time."

"Is fighting getting your number one slot?" I ask Emerald after another mouthful.

"Did they not feed you or something when you were locked in your cell?" Maggie interrupts. She lifts an eyebrow.

"Nope."

"Here. Take mine." She shoves her plate under my nose and I grab her piece with thanks.

Emerald, meanwhile, looks stern. "Blue Circuit needs me. Wins have been way down with Bruno out of the picture and you on sabbatical." She pauses theatrically. "And speaking of you... Dare I ask?"

Maggie stares at me, her glass hovering in midair. No wonder. Save for the kitchen, I didn't bother with any of the job tours. I crack my knuckles under the table. "Throw my name in for another fight," I tell them. "My sabbatical's over."

Emerald tilts forward. "Serious? You fighting as an occasional or a pro?"

"I'm not going pro."

"So what *are* you doing?" Maggie demands.

I rub a hand up and down my face and twist my braid around my finger. I stare at the ceiling, then the table. "Guard," I finally mutter.

"Huh?" Emerald leans forward so deeply that the table digs into her sternum. "What'd you say?"

"It sounded like you said guard," Maggie clarifies slowly, "but obviously that can't be true."

"Probably I won't get it or anything. I mean, obviously I won't. But that's my pick. Guard." Maybe if I act like it's no big deal, they will, too.

But one glance at Maggie tells me my efforts are in vain. "Get *out*," she shouts. "A guard—you're serious? *You?*"

"How could you not tell us that's what you were thinking?" Emerald hollers from across the table.

"I wasn't sure. I mean, not until recently."

She gazes at me, eyes unwavering. "They'd be lucky to have you."

"Thanks." I cover my smile with a piece of toast.

Maggie, meanwhile, bounces in her seat. "This is so, so good, Eve. Remember what Daniel said about not giving you a moment of peace? He won't even *think* about messing with you if you're a guard."

"That's the hope," I say darkly.

"Do you have any backup options?"

"Nope," I say crisply. Then I stand before their faces can register shock, before they can kindly suggest I put something—anything—down as my next preferred position. "Let's get this over with."

I spot Wren through the crowd at the same moment he sees me. He is dressed in black, and has clearly made a full recovery from almost starving to death aboveground. The poisoning, too. Right now he looks completely at ease among the sea of people pressing into his broad shoulders, and even though I stand in line with the others, completed application in hand and ready to submit, I push in his direction. I think I always will be compelled to drop what I'm doing and push toward him.

"Vindicated," he says in my ear when I reach his side. "I heard the good news yesterday."

"My word against his," I agree. For some reason, I don't look him in the eye.

"I thought you'd tell me yourself—"

"I had other things to do."

"Other things?" He kicks my boot lightly with his own.

Right now, that part of me that feels resentful toward Wren stirs. Quickly I push that feeling away. He was trying to help. He was trying to keep us *alive*. And yet when I jokingly say, "Are you looking for a play-by-play?" there's an edge to my voice that I can't really help.

"Still working on those conversational skills, eh, Eve?"

When I hear the warmth in his voice, I tuck my fingers into my sleeves and finally look at him. "I was hungry."

His gaze lingers on mine a second longer, then moves down my body. It is done in a methodical way, but it still makes me shiver. "You've lost weight," he notices. "I'm guessing a week locked in your cell wasn't exactly pleasant."

"You'd be guessing right."

"I offered to come. You're the one who said—"

I wave aside his words. "I know what I said." Something bubbles inside my stomach. Butterflies? Maybe. It *has* been a long time since we've seen each other. But agitation, too.

Part of the problem, I think, is that he looks no different than before we escaped Compound Eleven; his T-shirt is just as crisp, his stance just as easy. Like seeing the beautiful world aboveground didn't have any effect on him.

Maybe I'm reading too much into it. Maybe I'm just angry that I've been locked away for the past week, alone, and life has been carrying on without me out here. Or maybe I'm just a jumble of emotions, unable to decipher which way is up or which way is down.

"Is everything okay?"

"Huh? I mean, yeah. Everything's fine." I wait a while, then add to my boots, "Of course it is."

He nods, then tucks stray strands of hair behind my ear. "I know this sucks, Eve. Being back down here, applying to be a guard and everything. But at least we have food, right?"

I ignore how rigid my spine becomes at his words. Instead I push my boots closer so that the pocket of air separating us grows smaller. I want to lift my hand to his chest, want to feel his heart beating under that layer of muscle, because maybe that will make everything feel okay again. But something stops me from doing that.

"Eve?"

"I missed you," I blurt out.

He laughs gently. "Longest week of my life."

"Yeah?"

"Mmm," he mutters, and he pulls me firmly into his arms, into that masculine smell of his that makes my pulse race. I feel my muscles uncoil, and instantly I feel like I'm clinging to a rock in a current of bodies that threaten to drown me. Then I am thumped hard on my shoulder.

I almost ignore it; the hallways are full of people, after all. Why should I worry? Except I can smell a scent that is painfully familiar…

Soap, bitter and astringent. *Daniel.*

So my hands become fists, and I square myself to him. I will not cower, especially not now—not after he tried to *kill* me in the stairwell. But as I lay eyes on him, I hesitate. I even inhale. It's the deep slash that distorts his once handsome face. Never handsome to me—only to others unfazed by his cruelty.

It begins at his cheekbone, then slices across the bridge of his nose, all the way to his far eyebrow, a shiny pink line surrounded by dots—the remnants of stitching. And the start of a scar, one placed there by the blade of my knife.

"I thought you were warned," I say slowly, "to stay away from me."

He steps closer and dips his head so that he speaks directly into my ear. "You're going to pay for this, Eve. Not right now. Not with your bodyguard standing next to you, or with that blade inside your boot. But when I have a gun? And it's aimed at your head? Yeah, you'll pay." He pulls back so I can see his sneer. It makes the wounded skin, all rose-hued and shiny, buckle.

He's about to walk away, but I stop him. I grab his shirt and pull him back to me. "You'd better hope I don't have a gun of my own, then," I whisper.

He gives me one last withering look before he disappears.

"What did he want?" Wren demands.

"Same old stuff."

"That cut is your work, I'm guessing?"

I don't respond. Of course it is.

It is, and every time I blink, I see it across his face. He did evil to me, and I to him. We are square, but only for now. The second I turn my back, he'll strike again…unless I strike first. The realization makes me sigh. Because no matter how much I wish it weren't true, I'm back in Compound Eleven, at least for now. And my survival down here is not a given.

"You're bleeding," Wren says. His fingers graze my bottom lip.

I wipe at my mouth, then turn and push through the crowd. I catch up with Maggie and Emerald who are now at the front of the line, and I shove my crumpled application through the window with theirs.

"Nice timing," says Emerald, elbowing me.

I grunt in reply.

"Everything okay?" Maggie asks.

"Fine," I assure her. I stare dully through the glass partition at my application as it's stamped and filed. Nothing to do now but wait. Probably they will reject my application to become a guard. No. Not probably. *Definitely*. But not until Jeffrey Sitwell, Head of Security and father to Wren's ex, has a good laugh about it.

And then I notice something. A black-haired girl with a nose ring glaring at me. She stands a few spots back in line, her completed application folded neatly in hand. I should keep walking, I know that. I should carry on with my day. After all, my business on the fourth floor where the administrative offices are housed is now complete. But I find myself saying, "Can I help you with something?"

I can smell her attitude. I can feel it ringing in my ears.

"Maybe you can. *Bitch*." Then her lip curls in distaste, just like that of Justice Andrews, and his words suddenly snake through my head: *As brutal a monster as they come…*

"Bitch?" I repeat. Something tingles along the back of my neck.

"You cut in line. In front of Upper Means, too," and she holds up her hand to show me the number four tattooed there. "You have some—"

I don't let her finish. Instead muscles twitch, tendons engage, and I punch her in the cheek, right along the bone.

She is knocked to the floor. Her friends crouch next to her; they glance up at me with stunned expressions. I feel stunned, too. If I've been working toward less violence in my life, why did I just punch this girl who didn't really deserve it?

"Eve!" Maggie shouts from behind me.

I don't want to be scolded. Not when my brain is taking care of that all on its own. So I mutter, "Just forget it," then I straighten my hoodie and try to act cavalier. "She'll live."

"That's not really the point."

"Just *forget* it, okay?" Because I don't want to hear it and I don't want to feel even worse for what I have done—I don't want to think about it for another second. I start to walk away, but then Wren moves into my path. He stares at me, and his eyes look hard as iron. So I push to the side, away from him and the reprimand sure to come, and head toward the stairs.

There. Much better. The stairwell may be smothered in gray concrete, pipes may drip overhead, trash may collect in the corners, but at least it's empty. At least I'm alone. I have survived my first encounter with Daniel since returning underground, since slashing him across the face, and that is something. Same for submitting my application to be a guard. And now, thankfully, the rest of the day is mine.

All I really want to do is go back to bed, but the others will knock on my door and I'll feel badly for ignoring them. So maybe I'll head straight to the Blue Circuit training room instead—nobody will come looking for me there, at least not right away.

"Eve."

I stumble at the sound of Wren's voice—I miss a step and land awkwardly on my knees. When I push myself up I notice droplets of red that fan across the concrete. Blood. When I look closer I realize the blood isn't fresh. But this is where Daniel and Landry attacked me, and beat me, and tried to kill me, so I think the blood is mine.

Wren crosses his arms. His mouth is set in a straight line as he gazes at me. "Care to explain?"

"Explain what?"

"The girl."

I make an exasperated sound. Then I remind him of something. "I don't answer to you."

"Come on, Eve."

Carefully I wipe grit from the palms of my hands. I pick away specks of black that sit along the crevices. I still don't want to admit that I was wrong, so I say, "She was giving me attitude."

"One punch from someone like you can be deadly, you know that. Especially for a civilian."

"I'm a civilian, aren't I?"

He gives me a look. "You're a fighter."

The words of Justice Andrews once again echo through my head. I know Wren isn't calling me brutal, or a monster, but part of me feels like he is. And maybe he's right.

"Come on. Since when you do pull crap like that?" he continues.

I frown. "Can you save the lecture, please?"

For a moment I think he might press the point, might even make me admit that I feel badly. Then his features shift and he says instead, "I need to talk to you about something."

"Maybe later? I'm headed to the Bowl right now—I've got a match in a couple days I need to train for."

"Really?" He glances over his shoulder and up the stairs. "You think your punches need *more* work?"

"Funny," I say, "How about tonight? We can meet at the Oracle," and I stand straighter at the thought. Because it has been too long since I've seen the outside world, that is the problem. That's why my skin is tacky with sweat. That's why I squirm under Wren's watchful gaze. A trip to the Oracle will remedy all that.

But he shakes his head. "Your place. I'll be there at eight."

I roll my eyes. "I'm a big girl, Wren. I can—"

"Defend yourself against the likes of Daniel? Yeah, I get that. But what about that guard Dennis? Or Ben? You shouldn't be out after hours. Even late day, the crowds are too thin. You stand out too much." His gaze lingers on my hair, it trickles over my face. I get the sense that he is looking at me through the eyes of another and I can't begin to guess at what he sees.

I start to protest, but he wraps his hands around my shoulders and squeezes them tight. So tight my eyes widen. He says in a low voice, "You're not invincible, Eve. Accept that. It's safer if I come to you." He looks me so hard in the eye that I shiver, though I'm not altogether sure why. Maybe it's because it reminds me of when he told me we had to return to Eleven.

Sometimes, when I'm feeling particularly cruel, I forget that Wren is just as cruel as I am. I forget that he is stronger. I forget that if he thinks himself a monster—something he's told me in the past, there might be a very good reason for that, one I don't yet know.

CHAPTER NINE

I stare at my reflection in the scratched mirror that hangs over my desk. The better part of the day was spent training with Erick and Anil, my Combat League friends who fight professionally for Blue Circuit—the same team I fight for under a hobby pennant, and my muscles are now weary. My brain is, too. My teammates are disappointed that I'm not going pro, but they are excited to have me back.

The face in the mirror is pale but otherwise unblemished. Just a lip too red and a gaze too sullen. Wet hair from the shower falls limply down my back, soaking through my T-shirt. Maybe that's why I feel so cold.

Next I examine my knuckles. I hold them under the bedside lamp where the light is brightest. Probably I should visit my father soon—have my wounds cleaned properly...

The thought makes me feel like I'm filled with lead, but I know it's guilt that weighs me down. Guilt for so many things. The words I leveled his way, last time I saw him. Abandoning his dream for me to fight under a professional title. Leaving him and my mother for what I thought was forever without so much as a goodbye. I bite my lip, but then I'm distracted by knocking at my door. I glance at my watch. Eight o'clock—right on time.

When Wren enters, I notice immediately that he wears a white T-shirt instead of his usual black. Crisp as always, but white. It makes his olive skin look richer, makes his features more striking. The whites of his eyes even seem to glow, so that he looks almost unearthly. Handsome, too—and every cell in my body seems to stir in unison.

"Can I help you with something, Eve?" he asks when he notices me staring. A hint of a smile catches his lip.

Without cause, I'm at a loss for words. Maybe he can't help with anything, maybe he can help with everything. I kind of want to push him onto my bed and rip that clean white shirt from his body. I kind of want to push him to his breaking point, just to see where it is.

Just to see what he might do.

I don't know what I want or who I am. I don't know anything anymore, aside from the fact that I made it all the way to paradise, and failed. That Jack failed, too. So all I do is stand there and frown.

"Are you okay?"

"Of course."

"Of course," he repeats with an edge of sarcasm to his voice. "I don't know what I was thinking." He lowers himself onto the bed and rests one boot over the other. "How was the Bowl?"

The last time he sat there, he told me he had discovered a way to get aboveground, news I thought would forever change the course of my life. I suppose it did—I would be in Compound Ten right now but for that news. But it isn't the change I was expecting, and it isn't the change that I want. Instead...everything feels the same, when all I want is for it to be different.

Actually, that's not true. It *is* different. It is much, much worse. Because before, I had a mission: to escape Compound Eleven before jobs began. That was always my worst nightmare—serving the Premes who took my brother. Who *killed* him—I know that now, too. But here I am. And soon—when I get a job, whether it's on the guardship or, more likely, some other position the compound needs to fill—my arm will be covered in that painful memory, part of the tattooed information sleeve given to all of us on the lower floors. Perfect.

"Eve."

"Yes?"

"The Bowl."

"Oh. Right. It was fine."

"Fine," he repeats, then he leans back on his elbows and stares at me. I feel like his eyes are seeing beneath my skin to the dark recesses of my mind, and it makes me squirm.

"Yeah. I spent a few hours sparring. Trained with the guys. Same old." I start to ask him about his day, an effort to make things feel normal between us, but there comes a noise from outside my locked door and without warning, it pushes open.

Ben the guard walks leisurely inside, keys held loosely in one hand. He whistles loudly. "There's the naughty girl," he says slyly. "Just—"

He catches sight of Wren and freezes.

Wren stands. He is taller than Ben, and much stronger. They both carry guns. I'm the only one in the room with just fists to defend myself. I feel powerless, just like when I returned to the compound.

Ben's face contorts like he has swallowed something sour. "Didn't realize you had company," he says to me.

"Didn't realize you received an invitation," Wren says

coolly before I can open my mouth.

"Eve's first spot check. The first of many."

"Spot check?"

"As ordered by the great Justice Andrews. Didn't she tell you she'd be having visitors?" He sneers. "You look familiar. Aren't you from upstairs? Preme floor?"

"Yeah, I am. You can go now. She's here—your job is done."

But Ben doesn't move. "You doing her or something?" He glances me over with a scrutinizing look. "Kind of scraping the bottom of the barrel coming all the way down here, don't you think?"

My cheeks burn at his words. They make me feel small. Small and pathetic and unworthy of someone like Wren. They make me feel like he should be with someone like Addison instead.

Slowly Wren sits on the bed and runs a hand across his mouth. "If you come back," he says after a while, "you're a dead man. If you so much as look at Eve again, you're gone."

Ben's watery eyes contract. Then he twirls the keys around his finger and pockets them with a flourish. "Your call," he shouts over his shoulder, a show of nonchalance. But I catch sight of the pucker of his lip before he disappears.

He won't let me be, I know that. Nobody will. Not so long as I'm down here.

"Are you okay?" Wren asks, as soon as Ben is gone.

I shake my head. "Not really." Then I sit on the bed next to him. "Clearly I'm no safer in here than I am out there in the corridors, so let's go to the Oracle."

He wants to protest, I can see it in his eyes. But his gaze meets mine and all he does is nod.

• • •

We are almost to the fifth floor when he speaks. "Strange you didn't mention that Ben's keeping tabs on you."

"It's an annoyance, nothing more."

"Don't be rash, Eve."

"Being rash, *Wren*, would be obsessing over something I can't control."

He sighs, then glances at the side of my face. "You're going to have to take the chance on the sweeps and keep the guard's gun you lifted in your cell. Okay? I'll drop it off in the morning."

A gun for the next time Ben comes calling. Some insurance, just in case things go sideways. Yes, that could work.

"At least you'd have a gun that way," he continues. "Otherwise I'm going to make you take mine."

"Which I'd never do."

"Which you'd never do. Of course you wouldn't." He rolls his eyes as we enter the Preme atrium. "Guard guns are different than Preme guns, you know. If you're caught with it, they'll know it was lifted from one of their own."

"Meaning?"

"Meaning you might not want to stroll around the hallways with it unless strictly necessary."

"Fine, Preme. And what do I tell them if they search my cell and find it? That I was keeping it safe for them?"

He lays a hand on my shoulder. "Let's hope that doesn't happen."

"Don't tell me," hollers a voice from up ahead. "They let Houdini go?"

Bright green eyes shine with laughter as they latch onto mine. Long. He tosses his hair out of his face, then punches Wren across the chest. "Does this mean you can finally lighten up, man? Our pool team's getting crushed without you."

"Eve, you remember my friend Long?"

"How could I forget. What's Houdini?"

"You mean *who* is Houdini. And to answer your question, he's a very famed, very noble escape artist from forever ago. I did a school project on him when I was ten that never seemed to get the credit it deserved. And in case you couldn't otherwise tell, I graced you with his name in pure sarcasm."

"I told Long about your verification," Wren explains, laughing.

"Trying to abdicate Eleven, Eve? Really?"

Then, before I can reply, a scowling boy I recognize joins our group. His name is Strike, and when I met him before, he was worried that Wren was paving the way for Long to take a position in his mother's office. He has the look of a fighter and, if memory serves me, the friendliness of the same.

"Strikey!" Long shouts, clapping him on the back. Either Long isn't very good at reading people, or he's completely fearless.

Strike grimaces at the touch, but his interest extends only to Wren. He juts out his chin. "I heard about your job application."

"That's nice." Wren's voice is placid.

"That position was supposed to be mine."

"Says who?"

"I've been buttering up that entire department for months. And then you think to swoop in at the very last minute?" He steps closer and lowers his voice. "Can you guess how that makes me feel?"

Wren yawns. "I don't really care how it makes you feel, if I'm being honest."

Strike grits his teeth and steps even closer—so close that Wren can't ignore it. Before, when I saw him, he was wary of Wren. Right now his face is too flushed. He is too caught up in his own anger to feel fear or apprehension.

Why does he care so much about Wren's job in the first place? Wren wanted a computer position, and there must be dozens of computer positions available up here in Preme land.

"If you are somehow trying to intimidate me right now," says Wren quietly, "you might want to think better of it."

I don't have Wren's self-restraint, I realize, as I watch him. I am too hot-tempered. But his method proves effective, because after scowling for another few seconds, Strike disappears through the atrium.

Long ruffles Wren's hair, unfazed at how close his friend just came to getting in a fight. It makes me wonder how many fights Wren gets into up here—not a question I ever thought to ask. And yet I know Wren is a very good fighter, and so he must have plenty of experience...

"Where are my two favorite lovebirds flying off to, anyhow?" Long asks.

Wren gives him a look. "We're going for a walk, if you don't mind."

"A walk, great. I could use some exerci—"

"Alone," Wren adds, then he pushes against my back, propelling me around the sculpture of Planet Earth. He makes a face at Long over his shoulder, and against the odds, considering my day, I find myself laughing.

By the time we reach the brushed steel door housing the Oracle's emergency exit, my laughter has changed to anticipation. Anticipation of seeing the outside world, sure, but also of being alone with Wren in the very spot where we shared our first kiss. That should make everything feel normal again—shouldn't it? And yet as I step foot into the Oracle, I find I'm too transfixed by what I see to reminisce about the past or to worry about the future.

It's the electric sky, that's doing it. The most majestic shade of purple I have ever seen. Streaks of bubble-gum pink ripple through it like waves, and the white-hot sun sits off in the distance.

"A sunset," Wren observes. His voice sounds detached— not like him at all—but I'm too mesmerized by the outside world to pay it much attention. But then he moves so he stands next to me, close enough that our arms touch, and even though he stares outside like I do, I get the feeling that his mind is elsewhere.

As my fingers reach for his, he turns and walks to the darkest corner of the Oracle. Usually he moves with ease, with the kind of confidence that can come only from the Preme floor. Right now he's rigid, and that's the first inkling I have that something is wrong.

"Wren?"

He glances at me, brief and indirect, then he returns his attention to the sky. His white T-shirt glows in the muted light, and the space between us feels suddenly cavernous. "The world," he says. "Out there."

"What about it?"

"It doesn't make sense. What have you always been taught about the very end?"

I blink. Whatever I expected him to say, it isn't that. "The very end. You mean when people came down here?"

"Yes."

"That they couldn't survive out there," I say with a shrug. "The temperature was too high. Icebergs began to melt, oceans rose, cities were flooded. Complete destruction."

"It was the end of humankind. Except for those who bought a ticket underground, where the sun and the heat couldn't reach them," he finishes. "Yeah. That's what we were taught, too."

"You don't think it's true?"

"I think it's true. I've seen the pictures and the newspapers from when things became desperate. I've held the compound's originating documents. I believe the world was uninhabitable when civilization moved underground."

"And now it's changed. Miraculously."

Wren shakes his head. "Not miraculously. They said that humans were the reason it became so hot in the first place. Something to do with pollution, and their reliance on mechanics, and chemicals. But with all the humans gone, killed off or relocated into underground compounds..."

I watch the sky again, one that's now tinted black. Stars flicker to life before my eyes as I finish his thought. With all the people gone, Earth could repair itself. It could begin to cool.

And so it has.

"The thing is," he continues, "is that it doesn't make sense that we're the only ones who know. Others down there, those in charge of the compound, I mean—they *have* to know." He runs both hands through his hair, then clasps them behind his head, like he's deep in thought.

"We couldn't survive out there, Wren. Remember? You made us come back to get food and water—"

"Yeah, you and I couldn't survive, Eve. But the entire compound, with its kitchens and its water purification system— *it* could. All those underground utilities could move up here. Life could carry on aboveground, in freedom. With space. With no need for another cleanse."

I stare at him. "That would be amazing." It would be more than amazing, actually, because it would solve everything—a way to survive out there, without the guilt of leaving so many behind. "Maybe if we tell them—"

"Floor Five has a team of scientists. They monitor the world aboveground. Don't forget our water supply depends on it, and our energy. How could they monitor it and not realize that things have changed? All they'd need is a *thermometer*."

I sit on the Oracle floor and squeeze my knees to my chest. I have been so focused on my own failure out there that it never crossed my mind our rulers might already know. "But *how* could they know," I blurt out, "and not do anything about it? How could they keep that from everyone? How could they *want* to stay underground?" I shake my head. "They don't know." I'm firm in my belief; it would be too grave an injustice otherwise.

For a while, he's silent. Then I hear his boots start forward as he walks toward me. "I know it's killing you, being back here."

"It is."

"Then let's make the most of it. We're back, like it or not, so let's find out what they know. Let's find out if the Premes in charge are aware that the earth has cooled, and that we could all relocate up there tomorrow. Let's find out if they're turning the entire compound into a *prison*."

I glance up at Wren and see that his features are stern; I note the fervor in his voice; I realize how deeply he wants to uncover Eleven's secrets, if there are any. Strange. All I want to do is crawl back into bed, replay the lighter moments from outside, and forget about reality.

"Eve?"

That's not completely true. I also want to secure a spot on the guardship and look for supplies to take out there.

"What do you think?"

I startle. Then I disregard his question and say, "Do you think it would be possible to run a water pipe aboveground?"

Wren looks confused. "What?"

"Guards can access places in the compound that others can't. Maybe I could find the supplies to run water aboveground."

"Eve—"

"And maybe we could sneak food out of the kitchen from time to time," I continue, lost in a world of my own making. A world where my stay down here is temporary.

"Eve. You're thinking about yourself right now. What about all the people down there? They deserve to have a shot at freedom, too, don't they? They deserve to know that the world out there has cooled."

"So let's tell them!"

"Nobody would believe us. Ever since we were born, we were told it was deadly outside. It's ingrained. Would you believe it if someone suddenly said different? Besides"—as he speaks he drags a thumb slowly across his mouth, and I can't help but stare at it—"if it's something the rulers already know, it means it's something they're trying to hide."

"So assuming your theory is correct, if we say anything, we're walking targets," I finish.

"Dead in the water," he agrees.

"It's not going to be easy to find out," I say eventually. "If it's such a dangerous secret, it's not like you can exactly ask around."

Again he's silent. So silent that I look at him. Then he says bluntly, "I didn't apply for a computer job." Strike's anger comes back to me full-force, and I realize that even though we're a couple feet apart, it feels like we are much, much farther. "There's an opening at one of the departments," he continues. "Executive director, a senior position."

"Surely you wouldn't qualify," is all I can think to say.

He frowns. "Thanks for the vote of confidence."

"You know what I mean."

"I've already spoken with the department head. Henrik Tankard, a family friend. The position is mine."

All over my body, I feel hot. Uncomfortable. I try to give

him congratulations, but the words taste bitter in my mouth. Because it's confirmation that all these years, my life has been ruled by those with all the right connections, in all the right places. It also feels like confirmation that since returning underground, we've grown apart. "Which department?" I finally ask.

"Inter-Compound Relations."

"Inter-Compound Relations," I repeat. My voice is harsher than I intend it to be. "I thought you were going to tell me you took this job because it would be useful. You know, to find out what you need to know and everything."

"What *we* need to know."

"Right."

"That's exactly why I've taken it."

I eye him. "What good is Inter-Compound Relations?"

"First of all," he explains, "it was the most senior position available, across all departments. Even more senior than what my mother's department was offering me. Higher seniority means a higher security clearance, which means access to classified information." He pauses to knock his boot against the sole of mine. "It's also a way for me to assess and communicate with other compounds, something that may prove useful."

I should be impressed. I *am* impressed. But right now, Wren feels like a stranger, because as commendable as his objective is, along with the initiative he has shown landing himself this job, he has done it all on his own—he didn't even consult me along the way. Or maybe that's not the problem at all. Maybe the problem is that it feels like our hopes and aspirations no longer align. I want to grieve Jack, and our failure up there. I want to focus on how we can try again, and if that means becoming a loathsome guard along the way, so be it. Wren, on the other hand, doesn't seem to have any interest in returning to paradise. Instead he wants to investigate his peers, he wants to uncover the truth of what they know, and then, presumably, take action on a compound-wide scale. Commendable, yes. But burdensome, too, and lengthy, and all I want to do is go, go, go.

His objective is more just, more selfless than mine, but instead of inspiring me to be better, it makes me feel weak. Uncomfortable. It makes me have the sudden urge to be alone. Carefully, I stand. "Congratulations on the job," I say in a hollow voice.

"Are you leaving?"

I nod. "I'm tired. I'm going to bed."

"I know this isn't what you wanted, Eve," he calls, before I can go. "This isn't what I wanted, either, for the record."

I keep walking, back down to hell, unsure of whether or not I believe him.

CHAPTER TEN

The next morning, the cafeteria is once again packed tight. It hums with energy.

Interviews are today, for those positions that require them. Mine is scheduled for this afternoon. Partly I'm nervous, really nervous. Too much rides on this interview, and Wren's certainty that I'll secure a spot makes it worse. So there are nerves, yes. But the rest of me is numb. I think I've been numb since returning to Eleven.

Last night, after the Oracle, sleep was slow to find me. Frustration and sorrow made me feel weak and helpless. Then an ember of injustice flared ever so slightly inside my stomach, and I grew angry. Is Wren right? Are those in charge of our civilization knowingly holding us hostage down here? And if they are, what does that mean?

It means we have an obligation. A *burden*. Part of me wants to rise to the occasion. Part of me wants to wash my hands of it all.

Across the cafeteria, I spot Hunter. My eyes follow his every move as he searches for a seat. They aren't assigned, not formally, but everyone sits in the same spot day after day and he is no longer welcome in his. Then a girl with long eyelashes makes room for him, and I find myself scowling.

I shift my focus to the piece of toast that I push around my plate, the same thing Maggie is doing. "What time is your interview?" I ask her. I must repeat myself to be heard. Silverware clatters loudly, voices louder still. Emerald shouts to someone across the aisle, a girl with long black hair, and I rub my temple as a headache sets in.

"In an hour. Oh *God*, I'm going to blow it."

"You'll be fine," I assure her without conviction.

"But it's a *Mean* job." She pinches the bridge of her nose and groans. "*Why* did I apply for a Mean job? Why not a Lower Mean one that I could totally get?"

"Because you're awesome," says Emerald as she returns her attention to us and slaps Maggie on the back. "And awesome deserves awesome. Hey, isn't it funny that you two both applied to jobs on higher floors and I applied for a Lower Mean job even though I'm a Mean?" She makes a flipping motion with her hands.

Maggie and I are silent as we stare at her.

"Tough crowd," she mutters. Then she drums her fists on the table. "Lighten up, you guys—it'll be fine! And if you don't get your first pick, that's what the backup options are for."

"True," says Maggie slowly. "But I'd way rather write for the paper than work a factory job. Did you end up listing a backup, Eve?"

My mouth is dry. "Nope," I say, then I clear my throat. Because with no backup listed, it means that unless I somehow manage to secure an Upper Mean job as guard, I'll be slotted into whichever Lower Mean position needs to be filled. "So. Any idea what I'm supposed to wear to a guardship interview?"

"*Yes,*" Maggie gushes. "I have the perfect thing. It's a blazer that my mom traded for from an Upper Mean. It's really professional looking, and also super no-nonsense. Perfect for a guard interview, right?" She pulls back her sleeve and checks her watch. "Come on, I'll grab it for you now. I need to get ready, anyway."

Wordlessly we stand, and Emerald beckons to the girl with the black hair.

"Her name's Eunjung," Maggie explains as we walk out of the cafeteria. "A new friend of hers."

"Oh?"

"She's one of the Combat League administrators, a year up from us."

"Guess I missed a few things when I was locked in my cell." I can't keep the bitterness from my voice. "Is Kyle still out of the picture?"

"After you punched him at the party?" she asks, laughing. "He won't even look at me when we pass each other in the hall."

"Good riddance. What about Connor. Has he asked you out yet?"

"Of course he hasn't—we're *friends*. Listen, don't distract me with boy talk, okay?" She exhales loudly, then shakes out her hands. "I need to concentrate on one thing right now, and that's nailing this interview."

"Wow," I say, eyeing her. "Maggie Krauss doesn't want to discuss boys? Did I really just hear that?"

She elbows me as I pull open the door to Floor Two. Immediately I go still. Because a group of people stand on the other side, all of them peering in the direction of the sculpture that stands in the lobby, that jagged and wretched rendering of a tree. It doesn't take long to figure out why.

A body hangs from it, strung up by an artillery vest.

I glance at Maggie, then push my way through the crowd,

people chatting easily to one another. Laughter ripples here and there. Dead bodies aren't an uncommon sight in Compound Eleven, at least not down here on the second floor, so typically they aren't met with grief. Usually they aren't met with such jubilation, either. Of course, it isn't often that a guard is killed.

When I get closer, my heart thumps loudly with recognition: Dennis.

The guard with the black bead eyes. The one who shot at me, whose nose I broke. The one with the wife, the mother—

No, Eve. He doesn't deserve my sympathy, and he won't get it.

"Number five," Maggie says quietly. She stands behind my shoulder, but still I can see her shudder.

I don't blame her. It's a gruesome sight, what with his throat so obviously slashed. Blood, a deep red, pools alongside the bronze roots below. It makes the knife in my boot grow hot against my skin. It makes my insides pinch and pull in a way I don't really understand.

"We should go," I say darkly. Then I grab Maggie by the wrist and pull her through the crowd in the direction of our cells. Their delight is sickening. And yet my own stomach flutters in a peculiar way.

One fewer enemy I must watch out for.

Fifteen minutes later, I sit on my bed, alone. A black blazer is folded neatly beside me, along with a T-shirt the same color. It's the closest thing I have to dress wear.

With my outfit decided and several more hours until my interview, I smooth my hair into a low ponytail and head out my cell door. The green neon light across the hall twitches as I turn in the direction of the family cells, and gum sticks to the sole of my boot. My head pounds.

It was before the cleanse that I last saw my parents. Quickly I add up the days in my head. Two weeks, I guess, though surely that is wrong. It has been months. Years. Guilt squeezes my insides as I think of the decision I made—to leave and not say goodbye. That was something I regretted as I prepared to step into a sweltering world and die. It's something I should feel grateful for now—having the opportunity to right that wrong.

Maybe I do feel grateful; it's hard to tell anymore.

Just like always, it's my father who pulls open the door. His eyebrows inch up when he sees me, but otherwise his face is empty. No greeting, no smile, and I am reminded that when I was here last, I screamed at him. I told him that I hated him, didn't I? And that I hated fighting.

Probably he will be happy that I have signed up for another fight, then. But I don't know how he'll react to the fact that I won't be fighting under a professional title, that I have applied for a position on the guardship instead. I don't even know how to tell him.

Finally, and almost reluctantly, he stands aside so I can enter the cell that used to be my home. My mother doesn't look up from her stitchwork—I'm not sure she realizes she has a visitor at all—the same way she's been for years, ever since Jack was taken. How placid her world must be. How tranquil, to be so detached from reality. To absolve herself of any and all parental duties, and I have to resist the urge to laugh. And scream.

Then behind me, the door slams shut with a bang, and I jump.

I jump, and I turn. Before my brain can register what's

going on, my father shoves his face close to mine. He jabs a finger into the flesh just below my collarbone, except there's a plate of muscle under the skin and it doesn't hurt. I think he means for it to, though.

Next his wrath falls over me in shades, red and black and everything in between. His shouting voice claps in my ear. A criminal, he calls me. A disappointment to the family. A selfish kid who thinks of nobody but herself.

So, he heard about my verification hearing.

Before, when I was young, I would cower at his rage—I would even be sick to my stomach. But things change, people change, too, and now I just laugh. Now my voice is clear as I say, "I *am* selfish. And I *am* a criminal, even though I wasn't verified as one. Because they had me pegged right all along—I was about to leave this compound and never look back. And you know something? I wasn't even going to give you the courtesy of a *goodbye*."

No longer do I feel guilty for plotting—for *executing*—my escape. In fact, I feel like a fool for coming here in the first place.

Then he slaps me, much harder than our pre-fight ritual. This is an act of aggression. But the words of Justice Andrews snake through my head: I am a trained fighter. I am a brutal monster, as brutal as they come in a place like this.

So I strike him back, tit for tat. Not a shade less.

I blink and see my mother in front of me, wedged between my father and me, her embroidery work forgotten. Her eyes are alive with lucidity, with recognition. I expect her to scold me. Instead she whispers, "You were going to leave? To where? *How?*"

"You can't leave the compound," my father hisses from over her shoulder. He glares at me. "Any fool knows that."

"Actually, you can," I reply levelly. I stare at my mother,

and anger balloons in my brain. "Something you would've enjoyed doing, I take it? I know you hate this compound as much as I do. Maybe if you weren't so busy doing this nonsense all the time, you would've discovered what I've discovered." I march to her chair and I take up her precious embroidery work in my hands and I rip it in two. "Maybe if you had paid attention to me even once since Jack was sent aboveground, I wouldn't be so desperate for a way out in the first place!"

I throw the remaining scraps of fabric at her chest. They fall feebly to the floor.

There isn't time for her response, to hear what she has to say for herself, even though I want to. Because my father is pushing me, he is shoving me in the direction of the door. "I have half a mind to beat you senseless," he hisses as he swings it open. But my muscles engage at his words and he can't push me a step farther.

I am getting too strong.

"Watch what you say," I warn, my fury building. "You wanted a fighter? You've got one," and my muscles snap in his direction as I lunge—but only an inch. It's enough to make him flinch. Then I pull the door shut behind me with twice the force he managed.

Blood rushes in my ears. I am a fool for going. For *caring*.

They were never worthy of a goodbye, never worthy of regret. My boots move quickly, children scamper out of my way, even adults give me a wide berth. Finally I stop and take a moment to crouch along the wall, where there's more space. I breathe deeply and wait for my pulse to slow. For my anger to fade.

I shouldn't have lost my temper, I know that. But my father provoked me, and my mother's blind disregard broke me, and without sleep, and sun—I just don't have the patience.

My head rests on my knees as I pull myself into a ball and groan.

"Are you okay?"

I turn my head toward the voice and spot an old woman sitting next to me, her face carved with time. Passersby trod over her feet but she doesn't seem to notice. "I'm fine, thanks."

Her milky gaze sweeps over my bare arms. "You of working age?"

"Just about. I have an interview this afternoon."

"I went straight into the mines, no interview needed," the woman explains. "Which job are you interviewing for?"

I stare at the boots shuffling back and forth in front of me, then mutter, "Guard."

For a moment the old woman goes still. I glance at her, she glances at me, then she spits in my face. A second later I'm on my feet, more despondent than before. Although I guess I asked for it—nobody down here likes the guards. So, if I actually do get hired on, I either need to learn to deal with it, or learn to hide it.

But then along the next corridor I see a familiar face, one that makes the old woman vanish from my mind. The last time I saw that face she was chewing me out, accusing me of knowing about the government-sanctioned slaughter of her people and doing nothing to stop it...

"Jules," I say quietly.

Slowly she stops, sizes me up. For a moment I think she's going to hit me, but she must think better of it because she stuffs her hands into the pockets of her threadbare jeans. "What do you want?" she asks, and I'm struck by how hollow her voice sounds. How deep the blue lines are that ride under her eyes. Her *eyes*. They've lost their sparkle, their shine—like the cleanse has completely gutted her.

"How are you?"

"Take a wild guess, Eve."

"Probably not great," I acknowledge. "What have you been up to?"

"You know how it is. Just hanging around, waiting for the guards to come downstairs and start shooting again. Fun stuff."

I stub the toe of my boot against the concrete floor. "Anything I can do to help?"

"Not really. Unless you feel like raising a heartbroken kid who won't eat or sleep or stop screaming for his dead mother."

"Avery." His name catches in the back of my throat.

"You two were buds. Why don't you come by sometime and say hi?"

"I'd like that." I say it bluntly, as if it's true, but it's nothing more than a charade. Because seeing his face twisted with anguish would be too much for me to handle—once was enough. Even that was too much.

Before I can say anything more, I'm knocked against the back of the shoulder. A ball, thrown by one of the children who clot the hall, one of the children lucky enough to be born on the second floor. Just barely do I stifle a laugh. *Lucky* to be born on the second floor. How ridiculous. How true.

"Seen Wren lately?" Jules asks now, and there's more of an edge to her voice.

I can't defend Wren, or myself. I can, but I can't. It's too convoluted—everything is. Trying to explain it away would be saying too much, yet my silence says everything.

She shakes her head. "You're perfectly suited for each other, you know that? A pair of *savages*."

"Jules!" I call after her, but she's already gone, and I bite my lip to stop myself from screaming. A second later, I'm distracted by a rhyme, sung by a pair of children as they clap their hands. For a moment I watch them, vaguely listening...

Compound Eleven had a graveyard,
The graveyard had a bell,
The graveyard went to heaven,
Eleven went to…

Hell. That's where Compound Eleven went. Maggie and I chanted the same song when we were young, clapping our hands against each other's, just like these kids do. But that was forever ago—a lifetime, really, and right now I don't feel like reminiscing. Suddenly the kids go still, looking at me with startled eyes. Dully I realize I must be scowling, so I turn. I turn and push in the direction of my cell, dismay crushing my chest—dismay with everyone around me, but mostly dismay with myself.

CHAPTER ELEVEN

"**W**hy is it," Jeffrey Sitwell asks, "that you want to become a guard?"

Under the desk, my steel-toed boot taps against the floor. Unsteady fingers smooth my ponytail, they tug my blazer straight. The past two hours were spent celebrating; Emerald is now a professional fighter, though it was never in question, and Maggie is a writer for Compound Eleven's paper. I am happy for my friends, but now it's my turn.

I take a steadying breath and glance around the small office where I sit, one located on the fourth floor where the guardship is housed. A concrete room, no decoration or ornament whatsoever. Nothing to distract me from the two men sitting across the table.

One of them has black hair and black skin, and his name is Dirk Nkrumah. He wears the uniform of a guard, but he is no regular guard. He is the most senior guard of the compound, and I loathe him for this reason alone. Beside him is Sitwell, a man much older, a Preme, one dressed in a navy-blue suit with gold cufflinks, one with white hair and a sharply cut nose.

The one in charge of Compound Eleven's security. His skin is as white as his daughter Addison's, and I loathe him more than Nkrumah.

He leans into the desk and taps his pen against a pad of paper. "Ms. Hamilton?"

"To...s-serve," I stammer. "To serve and protect." Inwardly I bristle at my words. Not because they are generic, or cliché, or meaningless, but because of how untrue they are. I have never been protected by the guards, or served by them, either. Just the opposite. To join their ranks, probably I should tell Sitwell that I want to bully, abuse, torment, harass, and kill the civilians of Compound Eleven unlucky enough not to carry guns. Unlucky enough to be born below the fifth floor.

After all, the guardship serves Premes and nobody else, that is the crux of it, and yet the privileged Premes don't deserve their station or their status. They don't deserve the ease with which they live their lives, or their security, or the luxuries they are afforded at everyone else's expense. I hate them. In this moment I can't even think that Wren is one.

I blink, and something in the back of my brain becomes clear.

Whether the Premes know the world aboveground is inhabitable or not...they will never go, or allow others to. Life is too comfortable and safe for them down here. Why risk it all—why start fresh up there?

More and more often lately I find myself feeling nothing at all. Completely numb. But right now something bubbles in my stomach. Right now I am determined. Determined to carry on my back every last citizen of this compound born to a lower floor to the top of the storeroom—determined to find a way to bring up food and water so we can *all* survive. And with nobody left to rule and to look down upon, to kick and to kill, the Premes will turn on one another. It's inevitable.

"Something funny, Ms. Hamilton?" Sitwell asks sternly.

I force my face to straighten. "No, sir."

"You're bleeding, right here." He taps his lip.

I wipe it dry, and the disgust that distorts his face eases ever so slightly.

"I'm going to be blunt, Ms. Hamilton—it isn't often we receive an application from a…" He makes no effort to disguise the smirk that touches his face. "From a person such as yourself."

"Meaning that—"

"Meaning that our applicants come from the fourth floor, if I must put it in so many words. The guardship is an Upper Mean institution, it always has been. Mr. Nkrumah, do share with Ms. Hamilton just how many applications have come from the second floor in recent years."

"Three. Least in the thirteen years I've been around."

"And how many of those three were hired on as guards?" Sitwell continues. He speaks with a slight drawl.

Nkrumah glances at his boss. "Zero."

"My point exactly," Sitwell says crisply. "So you see, Ms. Hamilton, the chips are rather stacked against you."

I am still, except for my pulse that quickens with desperation. I need this job. So I gather my courage and my wits and I lean forward in my chair. "I'm more qualified than any of your other applicants, no matter the floor. I know I am. Who are you looking to have join your ranks? Someone brave? Strong? Someone who can fight? I've been fighting for sport since I was *nine* years old. I'll fight anyone—you'll never see me back down. You'll never see me cower."

Sitwell stirs; he pinches his brow. As though it pains him to say so, he mutters, "Yes, your physical prowess is commendable, there is that. But it takes more than—"

"I've volunteered to feed the Noms my whole life. Did you

see that in my application? Are any of your other applicants claiming something like that?"

"Again, commendable—"

"How about this, then. The job of the guards is to maintain order. At the end of the day, that's it. Keep things running smoothly. Probably you have issues most often on the lower floors. People live terribly downstairs, I can vouch for that, and so it's the most violent. The most miserable. You've lost five of your own down there in the past few weeks alone, isn't that right? I *know* those floors—inside out, like the back of my hand. Nobody can hide from me down there. You want order downstairs? Then you need someone like me enforcing it."

Silence, except for my hammering heart.

Nkrumah throws down his pen. "She's good, gotta give her that," he says slowly to Sitwell, and I notice a large gap between his two front teeth, the whites of his eyes that are tinted red. "Thing is, Ms. Hamilton, says in my notes here you recently underwent a criminal verification."

"Fully reinstated back into civilian life," I say quickly. I lift my chin higher. "I was never verified as a criminal."

"Thing is," he continues, "any involvement in the criminal verification process means an automatic rejection. Standard practice. Add to that the fact that you're Lower Mean…"

And so it's a no. I can almost hear my hopes smashing to the floor, can feel it at the bottom of my stomach. A toxic mix of disappointment and fear and embarrassment thrashes inside me as tears prickle behind my eyes.

I lean forward ever so slightly at his words. *Wren went to Sitwell?* I don't want *him* to be the reason I get this job. Truly I don't. But who am I kidding? I *need* this.

Nkrumah, meanwhile, stares at me. "Is that so," he says slowly, and something stirs in his dark eyes. It makes the back of my neck tingle.

"Normally I don't call in favors, and I don't accept bribes. Normally even someone with the surname Edelman wouldn't play a role in my decision making. But." Sitwell drums his fingers together, then fixes me with a piercing stare. "But Mr. Edelman is my daughter's boyfriend, and so I am inclined to do as he requests, at least in this instance. Your application has been hereby accepted." Wincing, he adds, "Welcome to the guardship."

Accepted.

A Lower Mean serving as a guard. A guard who has authority. A guard with weapons and access to all the compound has to offer. I can almost taste my freedom — almost. But my ears are ringing too loudly, and instead of basking in triumph, my brain hones in on one thing. *Mr. Edelman is my daughter's boyfriend.* That is what he said. *Mr. Edelman is my* daughter's *boyfriend.*

Wren is *my* boyfriend. He is not Addison's boyfriend — he isn't.

Maybe Jeffrey Sitwell, with his gold cufflinks and his pressed suit, is confused. Maybe he thinks that because they used to date, they still do. Maybe he doesn't realize that they broke up months ago — that must be it. Except Sitwell doesn't strike me as the type of man who makes mistakes.

"Ms. Hamilton? Did you hear me?"

I blink.

"You've been officially hired. What say you?"

"Th-Thanks," I stammer. "Thank you." I pinch myself, then force my gaze to my new boss — to both of them. *Be polite, Eve. Be polite until you can track down Wren.*

The rest of the meeting is a blur. Snippets of important information are passed my way. Training starts in three days. Okay. It will last for two weeks. Fine. At that time and at that time only will I be permitted to serve and protect Compound Eleven.

Sure.

A bag is shoved into my arms as I leave: my uniform, weapons, and guardship passcode inside. "Looks like you got lucky, Lower Mean," Nkrumah says quietly.

"Looks that way."

"Better bring your A game. You don't look like much of a fighter."

"Looks can be deceiving."

"I suppose they can," he says, and as he does he stares at me with something peculiar in his eyes. But I simply walk on, knowing that for now, at least, I got what I came for.

K nock, knock, knock.

Breathe, Eve.

Trying to force calm on my shoulders like it's a garment I can pull over myself doesn't exactly work. Nothing does. I knock again and suck air into my lungs. It's a mix-up, nothing more. There's no need to feel like a thousand bugs scuttle under my skin. There's no need for my hands to tremble. This is Wren.

Besides, I've been hired onto the guardship. *That* is what I should focus on. That is what matters.

But when the door finally swings open, my façade of calm shatters. I stare at him, noticing that he wears sweatpants and nothing else. A sheen covers his torso and it touches his hairline, and I almost hate him for being so handsome. For being such a distraction. I dart around him where I'm less preoccupied, into his oversized Preme apartment.

"I take it you had your interview," he says as he shuts the door.

Silently I consider the large room, the dim lighting, the couch that we've shared, the punching bag that hangs in the far corner, one he was no doubt sparring with. I wouldn't mind attacking it myself right now.

"Eve?"

"I got the job," I say. Then I glance at him. "Not on my own merit."

He crosses his arms. "Okay, you got me. I spoke with Sitwell. I told him you're like a little sister to me and I needed a favor. So?"

I gawk at him—like a *sister*. "So?" I finally repeat.

"Come on, Eve, this is good. This is the outcome you needed. You have a gun now—a legal one. Daniel and Landry and all the rest—they can't touch you."

I shrug.

He exhales, as though effort is required to keep himself calm. "Can't you just accept help from time to time?"

"I guess I should be thanking you."

"Maybe you should."

So I square myself to him. In a sour voice, I say, "Thank you. Thank you, *Wren*, for getting me the guard job. If you weren't Addison's boyfriend, I wouldn't have had a chance. So thanks. Thanks a lot."

I have the door halfway open before he shoves it closed. He stands so close his breath tickles my neck. "Eve," he says. "Wait."

So I lean against the closed door and fold my arms, I watch as he turns, then laces his fingers behind his head. The motion makes his back muscles engage; it's like watching a patchwork of gears spring into motion, gears that my fingers used to spread across—caressing, exploring… And now?

"I didn't have a choice," he finally mutters.

"So, what?" My voice sounds panicked. "That's it, we're

over? Were you even going to tell me?"

My questions make his eyes narrow. "I'm not actually *with* her, Eve—surely you know that." He looks suddenly livid. "*Surely*, after everything we've been through, that's not in question."

"So then *what*?"

"I told Sitwell I was trying to win Addison back. There was no choice. Otherwise I was just the asshole who dumped his daughter."

Win Addison back.

It's okay. They are just words. Just three little words. I swallow them down and say, "Won't he realize it's not true when he talks to her?"

"He won't, no. She thinks you and I are finished. That you broke up with me after the cleanse, and that's that."

"She doesn't think we're together," I begin slowly, "but I'm pretty sure she realizes you're not her boyfriend."

"She thinks we're in the process of getting back together."

I go stock-still.

"It doesn't change anything between us," he adds, and he cups his hand around mine like he's trying to reassure me. "It just means we have to keep it a secret until she gets bored, or fed up, and moves on."

It doesn't change anything between us? It *does*. Because I don't want to do any of that. I don't want to hide our relationship. I don't want him to pretend to be interested in Addison—I don't want him *flirting* with her.

"Don't forget that if word gets back to Sitwell about the two of us, you'll be stripped of your title," he says, as he coils his bare arm around my back. He draws me closer so that I'm pressed tight into his chest, so I'm immersed in that irresistible smell now tattooed on my brain. He kisses me along the neck, making me shiver.

I trust Wren. That is what I need to remember. But it doesn't change the fact that I don't want to be a part of it. In fact, there are a few things I haven't wanted lately. I didn't want to come back underground, for starters.

Yet I did as Wren said. I obeyed this *Preme*, just as I have obeyed Premes my entire life.

I stare into his eyes, and I start to wonder.

Maybe I wonder where my voice went, or if I ever had one at all. If being with Wren has somehow made me grow weak. Or maybe I wonder just what flashes behind his eyes when the rest of the world grows dim, when he thinks that nobody else is watching.

CHAPTER TWELVE

I blink away sleep and stare into darkness.

Today is a free day. The first of three, then training for the position of guard will begin. Already I know that Daniel will be there, Landry too—they secured positions just as I did. That should be fun—training to become a guard with my enemies. Just thinking about it makes me fill with dread.

But what did I expect?

I flick on the light as my brain races over events from the past few days. From my fight with my parents, to running into Jules. From the check-in from Ben, to seeing Dennis with his throat slashed. From learning that I need to hide things with Wren, to getting spit on by that woman, to the derision from Justice Andrews, to the violence I inflicted on the Upper Mean who called me out for cutting in line. Too much negativity. Too much darkness. From the compound, from others, from myself. What I need is fresh air. I need to feel the sun against my skin, I need space.

There's one place where I can get all that, a place where I don't need to watch over my shoulder for enemies, and it strikes me suddenly that even though I can't call that place home—not yet, anyway—I can at the very least visit.

Happily I lift myself from bed into the damp morning air and pull on my boots.

A half hour ago I was in my cell, overwhelmed by darkness. Now I step outside where all my senses are flooded with unthinkable light. Everywhere I look, the world glows, and it sparkles, and it is so deeply enchanting, so vast, that I can't believe I didn't think to sneak up here sooner.

Just like that, though, I realize something. The Oracle—and I stare at it from my spot next to the outbuilding, fear prickling along the back of my neck. Carefully I comb every inch of it for signs of movement. Because if someone spots me, the door will be forever sealed and I'll be forever trapped out here. Or down there.

I shudder at the last thought. Then, without wasting another second, I walk around the outbuilding and disappear into the trees.

It's a different route than the one I took with Wren. The trees are smaller, and more closely spaced, so that I must squeeze myself through small crevices and bend back branches to move forward. Leaves brush across my face, twigs catch in my hair. Funny—it's like I'm boxed in tight, and yet this type of encroachment to my personal space doesn't bother me in the slightest.

The longer I walk, the more I begin to think about making this place home. Maybe, once I'm a full-fledged guard, I can have someone run a water pipe to the outbuilding. Maybe I can then run it into the woods, without anyone being the wiser. As for food, the compound must have a massive store of those sustenance packets I was fed while locked in my cell. Not exactly flavorful, but at least they would keep me alive. And maybe there are other staples—perhaps in the kitchen, or the storeroom—that I can sneak out as well. Maybe I can even sneak back into Eleven as needed to replenish my supplies.

I smile at the thought, at the possibilities, and I feel calmer than I did when I woke up. All those incidents that have hounded me for the past few days—they evaporate into thin air. They seem so trivial, so meaningless, I can't believe for a second I let them affect me so deeply.

The only thing that matters is the infinite beauty of the world surrounding me. The only thing that matters is the tree that I lean against, bursting with yellow leaves. The only thing that matters is the handful of pine cones I scoop up and examine. I just wish Wren were here, by my side, exploring and discovering with me.

I let the pine cones fall between my fingers and scatter in the breeze. It feels like forever ago that I was perusing that guidebook while sitting cross-legged in the Oracle, trying to identify all the plants and wildlife on the other side of the glass. Maybe next time I come up here, I should bring that guidebook with me—

I go still.

My heart beats quicker. I used a book to help me before. So maybe a book could help me again. Maybe it could tell me which things are safe to eat. Which bodies of water are safe to drink. Maybe, if I do enough research, I could *learn* to survive up here.

If I'm right, if I can find a book on survival, if I can figure it out on my own, it means I don't have to worry about finding stores of food and water to take aboveground, I don't have to worry about sneaking back to Eleven to replenish my stock. It means I can go, go, go, whenever I want, and nothing could make my insides swell with happiness more than that.

I walk deeper between the trees, until finally I sit on a rock face that arcs down a hill. Right now I'm so full of hope, it feels like none of the horrific things I've lived through ever happened. I feel stuck in adolescent bliss.

I remember the children in the Lower Mean corridor playing the clapping game, and instead of scowling, I smile. I even find myself humming the same rhyme:

Compound Eleven had a graveyard,
The graveyard had a bell,
The graveyard went to heaven,
Eleven went to...

Hello Commander Katz,
Please give me cookies nine,
If you won't allow me,
I'll kick you in your...

Behind the stairwell door,
There was a piece of glass,
Let's throw the guards upon it,
So they cut their little...

Ask me no more questions,
And tell me no more lies,
The Premes are in the bathroom,
Zipping up their...

Flies are at the bodies,
They're buzzing at the light,

Follow the dead upstairs,
Throw them out at...

Nighttime has come early,
It's time for us to rest,
But here's the truth we've found,
Eleven ain't the best!

Well, we certainly had the last line right—Eleven isn't the best, not by any measure. Funny lyrics, yet provoking ones, although I don't think we realized at the time just how dangerous they were. Then I think about the second to last stanza—the one about flies, on bodies. On the dead, presumably, that are taken upstairs, tossed from Eleven at night.

Tossed out here.

I gaze around, this time with more unease than before. This paradise that surrounds me has seen many horrors. The destruction of the planet, the death of millions, the end of civilization. And even since the remnants of society moved underground, humankind has continued to deface it by throwing our deceased upon it, letting what used to be a scalding sun do the dirty work, just like that childhood ditty says.

For some reason, I find myself singing it all the way back to Eleven.

CHAPTER THIRTEEN

My breathing is quick and unsteady, even once I emerge onto the second floor an hour later. Outside my pace was brisk, and the journey from the outbuilding to here was anything but easy, the kitchen now jammed with people. But that isn't the reason for my thumping heart.

I think it's excitement. Excitement that the elbows pressing into my sides, the ceiling skulking overhead, the litter and glass and gum that stick to the soles of my boots— they won't be my forever. All I need to do is go to the library and start my research, and there's nothing stopping me from doing that right now.

I also need to find Wren, to tell him about my idea, to have him start doing research of his own. So, with both goals in mind, I push my way along the corridors, take the stairs two at a time. But I'm not yet at the top when I hear something unusual. The sound of angry chanting. Shouting voices. And yet here I stand outside the fourth floor. It isn't often the Upper Means rise up—why would they? But the sound couldn't be coming from any other place, and so I swing open the door.

The lobby is packed full of people. Signs are plentiful, and their message is clear. Justice for Dennis. *Dennis.* The guard with the black bead eyes, the one strung up on the Lower Mean sculpture, dead as a doornail.

They don't like it when one of their own gets killed, I think to myself, with a whisper of satisfaction. And the guards won't appreciate this demonstration, either—not one bit. It makes them look weak, ineffective.

Unrest in Compound Eleven is spreading.

I head back into the stairwell, but as soon as I step into Floor Five's glittering atrium, I notice Wren standing on the far side, and thoughts of the protest—and even thoughts of the library—vanish.

It's strange. Among the crowd of Premes surrounding him, he blends in, but he also stands out. He dresses differently, more casual than the others. He carries more muscle. He lacks their stiff upper lip and the air of arrogance. And yet he couldn't be mistaken for anything else.

So if we find a way to survive aboveground, what will he be up there? What will *I* be? My status near the bottom of the totem pole is part of my identity—it's who I am, even if I don't want it to be. How easy will it be to shed all that and start anew?

I push toward him, through the Floor Five crowd. As I round the bronze sculpture in the middle of the atrium, I notice his arms are crossed and his head tilts forward, like he's listening to someone. A second later I see that he is. He's listening to Addison.

Part of the game, I tell myself. Isn't it? Without really meaning to, I notice how crisp her white blouse is and how her hair looks so freshly brushed. Her skin so porcelain. By comparison, my black T-shirt is ripped from branches, my skin, too. Where it isn't scratched, it is red from the sun. Sweat curls the hair around my face, and my once-smooth ponytail is now windswept into knots.

I start to remind myself that it's fine, but then he laughs softly at something she says and a weight drops in my stomach. It was affectionate, that laugh. Too affectionate, and surely Wren isn't that good an actor.

A moment later I step in front of them, and it's him I am watching. Maybe I think I'll spot a tell—like guilt slashing through his features—but his eyes are even as they sweep over me, as they linger on the cuts. His brow lifts ever so slightly—he even seems to suppress a smile. "Training start early?" he asks.

"Not quite."

Then his eyes narrow. "You're covered in scratches. Where were you?"

I frown. Right now I should be the one asking questions, shouldn't I? But just as I open my mouth, something glints in his eye. A silent reminder, I think. A reminder that Addison can't know about us, that nobody up here can. A reminder that I must not upset her—a prestigious Preme.

But I don't want to bow to her. I don't want to appease her, and I don't want to be under her control. I don't even want Wren by her side, pretending to be her boyfriend.

This is harder than I thought it would be, and suddenly I wish I were still downstairs. Actually, I wish I were still outside.

"I thought *that*"—says Addison suddenly as she nods in my direction—"was over with. I thought you guys were through."

"We are," says Wren.

"So why is she here?"

"Because we're friends," he replies with a shrug. Then he punches me in the shoulder, and I catch sight of a flicker of a smile once again. "Isn't that right, Eve?"

I force myself to nod. "That's right," I say, then I punch him back, harder than I mean to. Hard enough that it stings—I know it does by the way his lips press together.

"Wren and I were in the middle of a conversation," she says to me. "Besides, I don't think Lower Means like you are allowed up here on the fifth floor. Certainly my father, the Head of Security, wouldn't approve."

Go back downstairs—back to where you belong—back to filth. That's what she means. Except she doesn't just think that I'm from filth. She thinks I *am* filth.

Right now that feeling of hopefulness that I had under the sun evaporates—it almost feels as though the entire outing was a figment of my imagination, nothing more. No joy. No bliss. Just the darkness that comes from being a Lower Mean.

Wren's eyes flash and he shakes his head, back and forth, back and forth.

I can't touch her. But I can't contain my sudden anger, either. Despite all the work I've done to change, to have less violence in my life, I feel like so much of that work was undone when we failed aboveground, when we returned here. And right now I feel myself slipping into the same old thought patterns, the same old habits. I am the hobby fighter trying to survive in a dangerous world. The girl raised among riots. Bred in brutality. I am looked down on, spit on, locked up, stripped of hope—and so when a Preme walks by with a sharp blazer and a look of contempt as he glances at me—*me*, a clear intruder on this pristine floor, with cuts across my face and arms and rips in my clothes—as he shoves his shoulder into mine as he passes just because he can, I let the old urges take over. I pivot and shove him hard from behind. He goes flying into the bronze rendering of the world.

Across the atrium, a guard starts toward me, but already my hands are raised, palms up, and I stride quickly in the direction of the stairs, my plan to search the library now ruined. "An accident," I shout, as I block out the swarm of voices swirling in my head, chastising me for being so weak, for having so little control over my emotions. "I fell right into him."

The guard accepts my lie—he must not have seen it, and I count myself lucky. Pushing a Preme is not something a Lower Mean can usually get away with.

But a hand grabs my shoulder before I can go. Bald head. Wide face—and my chest swells with a toxic mix of fear and anger. Justice Andrews. The one determined to stomp the rebellion from me, the poor man. He doesn't realize it's an impossible task. After all, if I can't reign myself in, surely nobody else can.

"I saw that," he says with a glint in his eye. "Accident my foot."

"Good," I say quickly, before he can fit a word in edgewise. "Then you saw him push me first. You saw me defend the integrity of the Lower Means. Equality and justice for all, isn't that so?" Then I wrench myself free and start down the stairs with my heart thumping in my ears.

"That was strike one, Ms. Hamilton," he calls.

I'm almost at the second floor when I find someone sitting on the step, wearing a blue and green color-block hoodie, the same hoodie he has lent me before to keep me warm. Hunter.

Seeing him makes me feel like a ball of tightly wound emotions that crisscross over one another like elastic bands. Then he turns his head and I see that one eye is black, and pretty much swollen shut, and the emotions crisscross even more. "What happened?" I ask before I can stop myself.

"Eve," he says, like he's surprised to see me. Then he shakes his head and goes back to staring at the wall.

"What happened?" I ask again. I hate him, I do—I swear I do. But still it makes my chest ache to see him hurt.

He glances at me and mumbles, "Zaar."

"Zaar?"

"He's out of the nurse's station."

"And?"

"And…he got in my face. Said he didn't get a spot on the guardship because of you—because of what you did to his knee. He's not too happy about it and wanted me to pass on the message. I guess he doesn't know we're not…"

"Friends?"

He stares at me. "I was going to say talking."

The damp air of the stairwell feels thick and tactile between us. I clear my throat. "So, then what—he punched you?"

He studies his knuckles, and I notice they're bleeding. "Only after I punched him. I don't think he'll be giving you any trouble, for whatever it's worth."

My brow knots at his words, because I don't need anyone fighting on my behalf, especially not Hunter. Definitely not Hunter. And that feeling of warmth that spreads over me? It's unwelcome. Completely unwanted. It makes my skin crawl to think that I can be touched by someone who betrayed me.

So just like that, I turn and head for the stairwell door.

"I didn't get the job," he calls before I can go. "If that makes anything better, if it makes you hate me any less, I didn't get it. It was your mention of the lemon squares in the kitchen. They think I gave you the passcode so you could steal some for me, and they can't hire someone they can't trust."

I want to laugh in his face and tell him he deserves it. The black eye, too. I want to tell him that it doesn't make anything better, because nothing ever will. I guess I'm not that cruel, though, because all I say is, "Lemon squares? Not sure what you're talking about."

"I know it was you. You match the description." His face contorts. "Him, too."

"I was locked away in my cell, Hunter, awaiting my criminal verification. Something you'd know all about."

"If you'd let me explain—"

"No."

"Eve—"

"I said *no*."

We stare at each other until he nods, defeated. "I know you weren't locked in your cell, though. And I don't think you went to the kitchen just to ruin my job prospects. Why would you kick Hugh out, tell him to come back in an hour, if that's all you wanted?"

"I don't know what you're talking about."

"He found the passcode to the lock on your door. He did, didn't he? You could've gone to Ten, just like you wanted. Yet you decided to stay...after you visited the kitchen, that is. But why the kitchen? I keep thinking about how excited you were to discover the storeroom that day..."

My entire body stiffens, then I walk out, letting the door swing shut between us. Because it's impossible that he knows my secret about the world aboveground—that it has cooled, that it is accessible through the storeroom—and it's impossible he ever could. I take a deep breath and lift my chin higher.

It doesn't matter that he's comforted me too many times to count, that he rushed to my bedside after every difficult match in the Bowl, that he snuck out soup and biscuits for me from the cafeteria whenever I was sick. No, it doesn't matter, because I am hardened and brittle now, and so I don't care that he didn't get his dream job because of me. And I don't care that he has a black eye because of me, either. I don't, I don't, I don't.

CHAPTER FOURTEEN

I rub blood from my eye and drag myself to my feet, wincing through considerable pain. Blinking through fatigue. The timer reads thirteen minutes. Thirteen minutes of full-throttle fighting. Thirteen minutes of engaged muscle, hard hits, pumping adrenaline.

Somewhere over the drum of the crowd and the stomping of boots, I hear my name announced. *Eve Hamilton. Winner.*

Before, in another life, it would make me smile. Now all I do is spit.

My opponent is slow to get to her feet, but finally ample muscles lift her from the mats. Blood streams down half her face. She is a professional fighter, a few years older than me, with black cornrows and a tattoo of red lips stamped on her neck.

The ref grabs my hand and thumps it into the air. Then Erick is beside me, and Emerald, and they guide me over the ropes and push a path for me through the pen, a pen that's thick with bodies.

"That was *awesome*, you crazy girl!" Emerald yells in

my ear. "Longest match I've ever seen." I spot her dimples through flashing lights, her wide smile, and I smile with her. Or at least I hope I do.

I can't really think straight.

But as I'm propelled in the direction of the tunnel, I remember that this might be the last time I walk this walk. Once training begins at the guardship—time will no longer be my own. And when I do get a break, I won't be spending it here. I'll be learning to survive aboveground.

Aboveground. Just thinking it makes my veins expand with joy.

Then I blink and the ceiling dissolves, and the sun is shining, the trees are swaying, and I feel a warm breeze against my swollen cheek. I should be savoring my time in the Bowl. I should be savoring the sound of victory in my ears and the feeling of thunder underfoot. But I can't think of anything except for the world up there.

I stare at the sun and sigh.

Inside Blue Circuit's training room, Anil stands from the couch to congratulate me on a tough win for our team while Emerald still cheers. They toss a towel my way and I use it to blot blood from my face. I wipe sweat from my brow. Then Erick is whispering in my ear about a visitor at the door, and I move in its direction, smiling. Probably it's Maggie, or Wren. It was a good match I put up; celebrations are in order.

But it isn't either one.

It is my father, and he's straight-faced, as usual. Immediately I glance at my hands that are coated in red. A dull sense of confusion overwhelms me.

"I'm not here to clean your knuckles," he says. His voice is stern. "You're old enough to do that on your own."

Silence.

"I noticed you didn't fight under a professional title."

My back straightens and I feel slightly more lucid than I did a few minutes ago. So, this is why he has come. "I had other priorities," I say stiffly. Victory should be my focus right now, shouldn't it? This is not a conversation I want to be having.

"Indeed. I heard from Maggie's father you're a guard now."

I brace myself. "That's right. Once training's through."

He stares at me as if I'm completely unfamiliar, as if he has never seen me before in all his years. Then he says, "Your whole life you've talked a big game about hating the guards, ever since you were small."

I stare at a smudge on the wall. Dried blood, maybe. I don't have the energy to tell him about Daniel or Landry, about how essential the position is to my survival. And I definitely can't get into the rest of it — the plan I was formulating to access stores of food and water to take aboveground, to relocate there, forever. So I simply say, "Now I get to carry a gun."

"Something else you've always hated: guns. Fighting, on the other hand, requires hard work, strength, intellect. It's a noble pursuit."

Those words delivered with such calm resolve, they make my temper spark, even through the fog. "Did you come here to give me a lecture?" My voice becomes hard and unkind — the only version of myself I know these days, at least when I'm down here. "Because if you think fighting in the Bowl is so enjoyable and so — so *noble*, why don't you give it a try? You may have fought when you were young, but times have changed. Now it's dirty, it's *brutal*. You wouldn't survive two whole minutes out there."

It wasn't a nice thing to say to my father, but that ship has long sailed. Just as I am old enough to clean my own knuckles, I'm old enough to decide when he deserves my respect and when he doesn't. And right now I shouldn't have to defend myself or my choices. Not in this instance. Fighting under a professional title was his dream for me, not my own.

Never my own.

I am about to tell him so when he surprises me.

"I came here to give you my congratulations, Eve. On securing such an unlikely position. It's completely unheard of for a Lower Mean. And I came also to tell you that your mother would like to see you."

If I'm supposed to be elated at his words, swept over with joy, I experience none of it. Instead my sizzling brain narrows in on one thing: my mother. She hates the guards as much as I do. They were the ones who plucked Jack from her arms all those years ago. She will want an explanation, I know she will. And the worst part? She deserves one.

With my father, it's different. I see that now. He trained me to be cruel enough to survive down here, and nobody can survive easier than the guards. Noble or not, in his eyes I made it.

In her eyes, I am a traitor.

Then my name is being called from inside the room, and hands wrap around my shoulders, pulling me backward. "Come on, girl—we just cracked a bottle in your honor!" Emerald hollers.

In front of me, my father grows smaller and smaller, until finally the door slams shut. And suddenly I'm grinning, maybe because I'm finally my own person, or maybe I'm just excited to have an impromptu, sweat-covered party in the tired little training room that is as close to home as I've known down here.

. . .

Muscles scream as I parcel up lentils. My head feels full of cotton balls, and the knuckles of my right hand are completely unbending. It makes for slow work, and so by the time I slide open the partition, the Noms are impatient. The first ones in line holler at me, some even cast threats. They try to antagonize. All of it washes over me completely unnoticed, words and wrath the same.

It's only when I see a small boy waiting near the back of the line that I jerk awake. *Avery.* The one who watched his beloved mother Monica die during the cleanse. I don't recognize the woman standing with him, and she doesn't recognize me. Avery, I notice, as I pass them their food, doesn't seem to recognize me, either. His eyes are glassy, he stares at the air hanging next to my bruised face.

There's a tremor in my fingers as I watch him walk away. He used to laugh, he used to call me Miss Eve. And now? Now that little boy once brimming with life is completely dead inside.

As I pass out the last of the offerings, I have to blink back tears. I shouldn't have come—I should've gone aboveground for a walk. It was a mistake, one that I won't make again.

"Surprised to see your face down here."

Blond hair. A pallid complexion. Eyes that used to sparkle but now scowl. "Jules."

She turns her packet of lentils around in her palm as she considers me. "Did you see him? Did you see Avery?"

"Yes."

"And?"

I laugh sharply in her face, and for a moment it pulls her from her rage. She looks like herself again. I make a show of wiping away my tears, then glare at her. "You seriously don't know? You think I don't give a damn? It's heartbreaking. *Obviously*, it's heartbreaking. You may be angry at me, Jules, but you still *know* me."

She is motionless, and watchful, but finally she nods. "Sorry."

"You don't have to…say that."

She chews on a mouthful of lentils. "Maggie told me the news," she says after a while.

"News?"

"You're the first Lower Mean to become a guard. Ever."

I stare at her, brassbound. It never occurred to me that she would get wind of it, or just how bad the optics would be—her good friend joining rank with the same group who slayed her people. Why didn't I come down sooner and tell her myself? I'm a bad friend, that's why. A bad person, too—Justice Andrews was right.

"I…"

"Relax, Eve."

"You mean—you're not upset?"

"Maybe I was at first. But if it's the only thing keeping you alive, well, a girl's gotta do and all that. Besides, can't imagine it's fun having Daniel, Landry, and Zaar breathing down your neck all the time. Just promise me that if the dicks upstairs give the order, you won't shoot up the rest of us."

She's trying for a joke, I think, but I don't laugh. Not even a little. Instead my gaze sweeps the room behind her. Two men exchange words and push each other, but quickly it's broken up. A group of women walk by chatting, and children play hot potato in a darkened corner with what looks like a worn-out shoe. The Premes upstairs—they've never glimpsed this. They don't know that real people live down here. They must not, to treat them like such animals. To order their *deaths* from around a boardroom table.

"I won't let that happen," I promise her. "Not ever."

She tilts the rest of the lentils into her mouth. "Good,"

she says once she's finished chewing. "So, are Daniel and the others becoming guards too?"

"Unfortunately. At least Daniel and Landry are."

"Shit."

I nod. "They say to keep your enemies close, though, right?"

"Still... Can't that boyfriend of yours do something? I thought Premes carried magic wands, for God's sake."

It's true that maybe Wren could change things for me. But my list of enemies is too long to push all on him and so self-reliance calls, just as it should. Or maybe she's asking something else. Maybe she wants to know how much my boyfriend let *her* down. How blameworthy he is, how blameworthy *both* of us are.

"There's no wand," I say firmly.

Slowly she nods, accepts it for the fact that it is. Finally. "That's a shame."

There's no need to answer. Of course it is.

That afternoon, I try my luck on the Preme floor once again. The library is full of books from the old world—it's a way for Eleven's citizens to pass one dreary day and then the next, and so surely there's a book among the thousands that specifies which plants are safe to eat, and how to find drinking water. An image flashes in my mind of taking Jules and Avery up there, of teaching them all they need to know to survive, and my mouth twists itself into a smile.

"An intruder," comes a voice. It's said with such calm, such disinterest, that I almost ignore it. But then I realize that ignoring it isn't really an option. My path is blocked, and when I finally lift my gaze, I see that it's guards doing it. When I finally find the speaker, I just about lose my footing.

Commander Katz.

The most senior man in all the compound, the very one I loathe above all others. The very man I'd actually like to *kill*—a small retribution not only for Jack's awful fate, but for the fate of all those killed during the cleanse. For all those who have endured a hellish existence on the lower floors as he enjoys his luxurious seat of authority up here on the fifth.

Right now he moves to stand in front of me, his gaze scrutinizing. Briefly I note the militaristic jacket buttoned up to his chin, the black hair swept stylishly off his face. *Be careful*, my brain screams, reminding me that even though I hate this man more than I hate any other person, I am powerless before him. Even sacrificing my own life wouldn't accomplish anything. The guards would shoot me before I could break a single one of his bones.

"Pardon?" I say in an undertone.

"You don't belong up here," he says. "You're not a Preme. You, my dear, are an intruder."

I string my hands behind my back so he can't see how much of an intruder I really am.

"What's your name? Just your first name—I don't care about the rest."

"Eve."

"Ah. Eve. And which floor do you belong on, Eve?"

"One of the Mean floors."

A thin smile spreads his mouth. "A Mean named Eve. How lovely to meet you," he says, falsely. "What is it you're doing right now?"

"I'm going to the library," I explain.

"The library is on the Preme floor."

The people surrounding us go about their business silently—listening, smirking. "Yes."

He makes a show of acting surprised. "Then why would you think you could access it?"

"The teachers used to bring us here," I say in a hoarse whisper.

He looks all around, taunting me. "Are you with a teacher now?"

I feel my face flush. "No."

"Hold up your hands."

I hesitate.

"Hold up your hands, or I'll have my guards do it." At their very mention, they step closer, mouths drawn into unfriendly lines. I feel sweat bead along my hairline.

Reluctantly I draw my hands forward, hold them up to Katz's face, and I really think about it. Think about shoving my hands forward, curling them into fists, breaking his nose and whatever else I can lay into. I could stun him, and hurt him, make him feel pain for once in his life. But I'm not ready to die, not yet.

Or maybe I am. I can feel energy vibrating inside me. Outrage and injustice, rushing against the humiliation he makes me feel. Maybe instead of dying I could incapacitate him, fight off all the guards. Maybe I could force him to the Oracle, place his hand in the scanner, open the compound to anyone curious enough to breathe fresh air, or daring enough to try to survive up there. Maybe this is the moment where everything changes. My heart starts beating harder, faster, every cell in my body building with pressure—

He bursts into laughter and turns to the atrium with his arms sweeping to the side, my window to strike swiftly closed. "A vagrant from the second floor, up here on the fifth! A vagrant insisting she's entitled to waltz into our library, that she's allowed to put those dirty fingers all over our beautiful books!"

Around the room, the tide of laughter swells, and soon the entire atrium is filled with the sound. People point at me, and if they aren't laughing, they are whispering, the guards are glowering, and my boots are shuffling backward, toward the stairs.

Finally I stumble down them; I don't stop running until I reach my cell; I don't start crying until I collapse into bed.

CHAPTER FIFTEEN

The next morning, and for the first time, I unlock the door to the guardship on the fourth floor, using the passcode I was given by Nkrumah a few days ago when I was hired. Through the door I'm surprised to find just another section of hallway. Unadorned, aside from signs, pointing the way to the guardship cafeteria, holding cells, shooting range, and—where I'm going—the training room.

I look down at my hands, just to make sure the number two is still tattooed in place. Just to make sure I'm still me. Then I stifle a laugh. A Lower Mean—here. It's hard to imagine anyone more out of place.

I head in the direction of the training room, but I don't get very far when a group of guards stalk out of a nearby room, batons hanging by their sides, uniforms on. They are all men, I notice, and all larger than I am. They don't seem to notice me, but I'm still careful to hide my hands behind my back, just in case.

They are about to start their shift, I realize, and as they push toward the door that leads to the rest of the compound, they begin a rowdy chant:

>*Don't go out tonight*
>*Unless you're primed to fight*
>*I see trouble on the way*
>
>*Secret talks I'll stop*
>*My baton on top*
>*I see trouble on the way*
>
>*You'll be black and blue*
>*My brother's ruthless too*
>*We see trouble on the way*
>
>*If you Lows unite*
>*Then you'll feel our might*
>*We'll make trouble on the way.*

Once they finish, they start it again, and I watch them over my shoulder until the last of them disappears through that door, until their endless chant becomes a far-off whisper. With a heaviness in my stomach, I slip open the door labeled training room, and gaze around a large room with rows of lockers on one side and punching bags on the other. A flag hangs from the ceiling, depicting a fist. Wire baskets overflowing with knuckle tape are drilled to the wall, and kick pads are stacked in the corner. Familiar equipment for someone like me. And yet the space is anything but familiar. This is the guardship training room on the fourth floor, after all, and I am the first Lower Mean to ever set foot in it.

I pull at the neck of the black fabric that covers me from head to toe, my official base layer. The rest of my uniform I carry by hand. I don't want to wear it. I don't want to see myself in it. It makes me sick to my stomach to think that I'm a guard.

In the middle of the room stand a group of people: the other new hires. They're all male, except for one, and mostly big. Brawny. Daniel and Landry talk quietly to each other with stern expressions—they don't see me, not yet.

Cautiously I approach the group, I even stumble over my boots, but none of them notice me, except for the girl. She turns and looks at me with eyes that are rimmed with thick eyeliner. I stare back at her with a blank expression, though I notice every detail, from her dyed red hair to her nose ring. "You one of the new hires?" she asks in a voice that is surprisingly deep.

I nod.

"My name's Maax." She sticks out a hand, and I notice a scorpion tattooed in the spot between her thumb and index finger. "We may as well buddy up now," she continues, "seeing as how we're the only members of the superior sex." She winks.

I shake her hand, relieved to have an ally. But in my periphery I watch my enemy. Both of them.

"What's your name?"

"Mine? Um…"

"You forget?"

Half my mouth twists into a smile. "It's Eve. Eve Hamilton. Nice to meet you."

"What floor are you from, Eve?" she asks with a half smile of her own. "Because I know most of the people our age on the fourth. You don't look familiar."

"That's because I'm from Two."

She raises an eyebrow. "Are you serious?"

I wait, watching. Too often I have been subjected to upper-floor scorn. Yesterday afternoon, for instance, at the hands of the leader of Eleven. Then, I was powerless, but right now I'm not, and I think my patience for ridicule has finally run out.

But she grins and something glints in her eye that looks strangely like admiration. "That's an impressive feat. Nobody gets hired from the second floor."

"Thanks," I say, but I don't mean it. I was hired because of Wren, because of the lie he told Sitwell—not because of my own merit. Then our conversation is interrupted and my thoughts are too, because Daniel turns, and his eyes find mine.

I can see his stillness. I can feel his surprise.

"What are you doing here?" he demands. He comes at me and without any warning shoves me in the neck so that I cough.

I push his hand away, then shove him right back. "Ready to start training, Daniel—same as you. Surprised to see me?"

"You're *kidding*. So Zaar was right. You did steal his spot." He looks sideways at the others. "They hired a Lower Mean loser like you over a respectable Upper Mean?"

The voices around us fade to silence.

"Do you think that talk's going to bother me? You're wasting your breath." But he isn't, we both know that.

"Seriously, though, Eve. What'd you do, sleep with someone to get a position? Wait, I know. Your bottom-feeder boyfriend Wren Edelman—"

I punch him before he can finish his sentence. He staggers back, his fingers cradle broken flesh right beneath his scar, then he attacks me with a punch of his own.

The others in our group jostle him. They push him away. My cheekbone feels like it's on fire from where he struck me.

"What's gotten into you, man?" I hear one say. He has brown skin and hair pulled into a long ponytail.

I get it—they don't know how dangerous I am. Only Daniel does. Well, and Landry, too. They know it's a fair fight he's picking.

"We're on the same team—don't forget it," booms a new voice, and out of the corner of my eye I see Nkrumah saunter through the door. His red eyes glance coolly over the purple spot on my face and the blood smudged on Daniel's. "Except for when I turn this room into a fight club, guards don't fight one another—they help one another. Got it?"

I bend down and scoop up my things, wishing the day was already over.

"Hamilton, got it?"

"Got it," I mumble.

"Good." He looks around at our group. "Cause one of our own got killed the other day, and another before that, and another before that. Five in total. By the looks of this sorry lot, one of you'll be next in line. Never hurts to have an ally on the guardship. Remember that."

Landry snorts. "Who needs allies? We've got guns."

"Yeah? Out there, they've got numbers," Nkrumah snaps. He swats Landry across the head, and I have to bite away a smile at the look on Landry's face. Nkrumah continues. "If you think a gun's all you need, you're a goner. Those five dead soldiers of ours had guns, didn't they? Happily for you, we'll be spending the next few days learning how to use what God gave you." He holds up his fists, then eyes us. "I see you haven't bothered to find your lockers. Go put your gear away, then we start."

It doesn't take long to find mine. *Hamilton* is scratched across the front, while other names above have been crossed out with a single line. I swing the door open using the toe of my boot and dump my things inside without ceremony. A few spots down, Daniel does the same.

His jaw is set, just as mine is. In my periphery I see him dab the remaining blood from his face, I see him say something under his breath to Landry. I know it's about me.

"You're more badass than you look, Two," Maax says. "Nice punch—where'd you learn to throw?"

"Hobby fighter."

"In the Combat League?" Her brow arches as she stares at me.

I nod.

"Well damn. No wonder you got hired on. Did I hear that Wren Edelman's your boyfriend? My mom used to know his—"

Before she can finish, I am shoved into the lockers, my shoulder smacking so loudly that the other hires stop and stare. Landry's white-blond hair stalks by. Daniel is right behind him, and he pulls a finger across his throat as he passes.

I will not let them get under my skin again. I *won't*.

"Don't worry," Maax says as we turn for Nkrumah. He waits at the punching bags tossing knuckle tape from hand to hand. "They're both jerks. Most of the people up here can't stand them."

I glance at her. "Really?"

"Don't look so shocked, Two." She grins. "Not all Upper Means are complete assholes."

"News to me."

She makes a face, like she's exasperated. "Didn't I just hear that you're dating a *Preme*?"

I smile. "True." Then my smile falters, because if Nkrumah hears, he will tell Sitwell, and I can't have that. Too many secrets to keep track of. Too many lies.

"Speaking of *amour* and all that good stuff, what do you think of Nkrumah? Kinda cute, right?" she asks suddenly.

"Cute? You can't be serious."

"Shut up!" Nkrumah barks at us, prompting Maax to look at me out of the corner of her eye. She slaps her hand coyly over her mouth, and I have to bite my already sore lip to stop myself from laughing.

"If you want to cut it as a guard," Nkrumah begins, "you have to know how to throw a solid punch. Today we're focusing on the cross, the jab, and the uppercut." He demonstrates each one, and I take the opportunity to look around at the others. None of them I recognize from the Bowl, and that is good. They may be larger than me, for the most part, but I am the best fighter here. I'm sure of it.

"Everyone find a bag. Cycle through each punch until you can't move your hand to your ass. Any questions?" Nkrumah blinks theatrically into the silence, then claps three times.

A minute later and I'm at a punching bag with Maax on one side and Landry on the other. I take a few strikes, but I can't get comfortable with Landry so close. *Focus, Eve.* One strike, two. I feel his touch and I punch the bag harder. I hear his cruel words curling through my brain and I punch harder still. I remember the years of taunting, the threats, the endless ridicule, and I deliver a series of blows that leave me breathless.

Now the scabs that had begun to form over my knuckles crack open. I watch closely as blood stains the hide, then, in my moment of distraction, Landry stomps on my heel. "Oops—so sorry," he says with a nasty smile.

"You might want to focus on your punches, Landry, instead of me. They're pathetic," I retort.

"You're going to get what's coming to you, Eve," he says between heavy breaths.

"I'd like to see you try," I reply. "Ask Daniel how that turned out for him. Actually, you don't have to—just take a nice long look at his face."

Now Landry squares himself to me, and I don't think his face is red simply from exertion. Same with the veins that strain in his neck. "Don't threaten me, you dirty little Lower Mean *bitch*."

Blood thumps in my ears. Adrenaline makes me bounce on the balls of my feet. He's about to attack — I can sense it —

Then we are pulled apart, and a cool metal baton pushes against my chest and against his. "Get it together, both of you," Nkrumah commands. "Right now, you play by my rules or you're off the guardship. Tomorrow, the matches begin. The two of you can be the first to fight, how's that? Sugar and spice and all things nice."

"Perfect," Landry says, his gaze not wavering from my own. "About time I taught her a proper lesson."

"Best get working on that uppercut, then," I reply smoothly. "Because I don't get out of bed for a punch like that."

"Ha, Landry," yells a boy next to us with a shaved head. "You get beat by a girl and you ain't living that one down." Then his gaze casts over me, and it's just as unfriendly.

"Go to hell, Huffy," Landry spits at him. He turns to the punching bag and lays into it with vigor. Others around us do the same. Nkrumah watches me closely and so I hit the bag with half strength, playing by his rules indeed. I won't wear myself out, though.

Too much rides on tomorrow.

Here I was, thinking the day couldn't get worse. That the hardest part of training was bickering with enemies. That the fight with Landry scheduled for tomorrow would be where my mental energy would be expended. And drained.

But I'd forgotten something, and it's the very thing that I was trying to avoid by escaping Compound Eleven in the first place. The tattoo along my arm, the information dump, so that my bosses don't need to learn anything about me, so that I can hide nothing from whatever guard or person of authority I cross paths with—it's scheduled for right now.

"It's called a data card," Nkrumah explains. "Record keepers will be arriving shortly, along with the people with the needles."

"Needles?" one boy echoes.

Nkrumah claps a hand along his forearm in reply. I see from his pushed-up sleeve that it's covered in text, but his skin tone is so dark it's barely legible. My pale skin, on the other hand, will make every last letter stand out. J-A-C-K.

"Couldn't they just hand us an actual card instead of tattooing it along our arms?" Maax whispers. "My mom said it hurts like hell."

"Actual cards can be lost," I say in a hollow voice. "We'll have this everywhere we go. Forever." Even aboveground, I remember with a sinking feeling.

Then the door to the guardship swings open and two women pushing a cart walk inside. On the top of the cart are needles and ink. On the bottom shelves are files. Each file has a fluorescent letter along the edge, and all of them are pink *Fours*. Except for one that has a neon green *Two* at the very bottom of the pile, and I can see from here that it's thicker than the rest. My family has a history, after all. A history of rule breaking.

J-A-C-K.

It was my mother who hid the pregnancy: broken rule number one. Then my father and I became rule-breakers in our own right, once Jack arrived. I stole food for him, from the cafeteria. We took pains to hide him, or at least we tried. But then I forgot to pull the door completely closed, and he was spotted, and everything changed in the most horrible way imaginable.

I feel sick at the memory, I feel sick that this memory will be etched into my skin.

The woman setting up the needles has the number three on the backsides of her hands, and the woman retrieving the files has a number four—she probably works in the administrative offices. Both of them wear sleeves that hide data cards of their own, but I know they're there. Then the door swings open again, and this time Jeffrey Sitwell steps inside, looking impatient. His hands, of course, are unblemished. Same with his arms.

Nkrumah immediately claps to get our attention. "Let's start with the oath," he calls, nodding meaningfully at Sitwell. "Get in a line and listen up. This right here is the Head of Security. Every directive we have comes from this man and his office. Clear? It doesn't matter what directive it is—if we're asked to act, then we act. Welcome to the guardship," he adds, as he gives the floor to Sitwell.

Jeffrey Sitwell straightens his sleeves. Then he says sternly, "To serve on the guardship is to serve the entire compound."

Lies, my brain screams.

"It is a privilege," he continues. "A granting of trust by those residing at the very top of this civilization. We trust you to walk along these halls in a position of authority. We trust you to bear arms. We trust that you keep peace, maintain order, that you tamp down dissidence and disloyalty." His cool gaze lingers on mine. "In exchange for granting you with this privilege, with our trust, we expect something in return. Unfettered, ardent devotion. Indiscriminate obedience. Loyal service. Get on your knees," he suddenly hisses. "Pledge it to me."

The others around me fumble into position, eager to partake in this initiation, and so I force my legs to bend, even when every muscle, tendon, and cell screams to revolt. When all of us new hires are on our knees, a slinking smile twists

Sitwell's mouth. "Say it," he commands. "Unfettered."

"*Unfettered*," the new hires call out around me.

"Ardent."

"*Ardent*," they echo.

"Devotion."

"*Devotion*."

He raises a palm. He points straight at me. "I don't hear you," he says coldly. "*Say* it. Unfettered, ardent devotion."

I feel my face pucker, but I force my mouth open and push air from my lungs. "Unfettered. Ardent. Devotion."

"Good. Now—let me hear all of you again. Indiscriminate."

"*Indiscriminate*," we repeat.

"Obedience."

"*Obedience*."

"Loyal."

"*Loyal*."

"Service."

"*Service*."

"Say it—all of it. Unfettered, ardent devotion. Indiscriminate obedience. Loyal service."

"*Unfettered, ardent devotion. Indiscriminate obedience. Loyal service.*"

"Shout it."

"*Unfettered, ardent devotion. Indiscriminate obedience. Loyal service!*"

He spreads his arms wide. "Again!"

"*Unfettered, ardent devotion. Indiscriminate obedience. Loyal service!*"

And then it's finished, and my ears ring from the silence. A thin smile curls Sitwell's mouth, he looks straight at me—the sole Lower Mean—and then he takes his leave. The other hires glance at one another, like maybe the initiation wasn't that enjoyable for them, either. Maybe Upper Means are used to garnering a bit more respect.

"What was that?" Maax whispers. "And why do I feel like I need to have a shower?"

I know exactly what she means.

"Everyone have a seat and wait for your name to be called," Nkrumah shouts. "It's data card time."

I guess the chant about obedience worked, because everyone drops from their knees to the floor. Even I do.

The boy with the long ponytail is the first to go, and as I watch him and everyone else have their data pushed into their arm, my mind goes blank. I still feel faintly sick from thinking about Jack, and from the initiation, but otherwise I can think of nothing. Not up there. Not my failure to survive when I thought I had succeeded in every meaning of the word. Not my new, unwanted life on the guardship, or my inability to reach the library—thwarted by my own bad temper, and by the commander. Emptiness, just emptiness, and I think I like it that way.

"Eve Hamilton," I hear eventually.

So I stand unsteadily, I go sit in the chair that my peers occupied. I don't cause a scene, or make a fuss. Unfettered, ardent devotion. Indiscriminate obedience. Loyal service. That's me.

The sting of the needle barely registers. I just watch out of the corner of my eye as the name Eve Hamilton is marked out along my arm. Birthdate goes next. Then my role as guard. My verification record. Finally come my parents' names...and that's when my stomach starts to flutter. More ink is loaded into the needle, then with a fresh burst of pain far worse than before, the words I've been dreading for years are inscribed into my arm.

That I had a brother. Name, *Jack Hamilton*. Born in violation of numbers, dashes, dots. A multitude of rules, all broken. Harbored against even more rules, and for three years, too. Sentenced to expulsion, the data card ends with, or so I think. But the woman returns with the needle, she makes a backslash along my skin, and adds one more word. Death.

Sentenced to expulsion/death.

I stare down at those words, at the way they're beaded with blood, enflamed and irritated, and I try to focus only on the numbness inside my bones. I try to resist sadness, anger, despair. But then I recall my mother's reaction to the same words being inscribed in her own arm, and my entire body shudders. I remember how she used her nails to slash the words apart, completely disfiguring each letter, and forever mutilating herself in the process. I guess those tapering pieces of swollen skin she left on the floor of our cell must have been nothing compared to the rest of the pain she was in.

I breathe. In. Out.

Life around me slowly resumes. The women pack up their supplies, and their files, they load up the cart and push it out the door. Nkrumah shouts orders, and the air is alive with movement. Without looking, I can tell that it's only me who reels so deeply.

Eventually a tear falls, it lands on Jack's name, soothing the burning sensation for a moment. But it's not enough.

Nothing will ever be enough.

CHAPTER SIXTEEN

Maggie hasn't stopped talking since we sat down for dinner five minutes ago. "So basically," she is saying, "I'm assigned three stories per day, which is kind of a ridiculous amount, right? Except most of the stories aren't really stories, they're more like notices, you know? Think vaccine notices, scheduled blackouts, stuff like that, okay?"

Emerald nods, a good friend, but all I do is shut my eyes. Normally Maggie's joy would make me happy. Now all it does is highlight my own misery. Besides, her love for her new job underscores how terrible mine is.

When I open my eyes again, I see that Connor has joined her. He wears a button-down shirt and a tie that's crooked. A second later, Wren sits down next to me. My heart beats faster when I realize we haven't spoken for several days, not since I found him on the Preme floor talking with Addison. I cringe when I think about what happened next—pushing that Preme.

Right now, though, I try to play it cool, but it doesn't help that he looks the way he does. Crisply dressed, well-rested, calm. Everything I am not.

"I suppose congratulations are in order," he says into my ear. Feeling his breath tickling my exposed skin makes me shiver, and I hope he doesn't notice.

Across the table, Connor makes Maggie laugh. Emerald waves Eunjung over to our table. They are in good moods—they usually are these days.

"Are you okay?" Maggie asks me. "You've been pretty quiet."

"I'm fine," I assure her, then I nudge Wren. "Congratulations, for?"

"Your fight. It was a good match. Bit long. Surprised you didn't make faster work of her."

I turn to him quickly, but he's laughing. So I roll my eyes and return my attention to my plate.

"I dropped by your cell after, by the way. No answer."

"I was celebrating, with Blue Circuit."

"Ah. And yesterday?"

"Busy."

He nods, then stares around the cafeteria. I watch him consider Sully, who makes a speech to a rowdy crowd in the far corner. Next his gaze lands on three women in the midst of a shoving match, then on a screaming baby. How different it must be from wherever the Premes dine. Yet Wren's face is level as he looks around, just as it always is. It's even mildly disinterested.

He elbows me. "How was your first day at the guardship?"

"It was okay."

"No. Really."

A small shrug. "I survived."

"Come on, Eve. I know they're out for you, Daniel and Landry. I know how bad this is."

"I'm made of steel, remember?" I say as I pull down my shirt sleeve, making sure it covers the new ink. Partly I do it so I don't have to look at it, but I also don't want Wren to see. I don't want anyone to see, because I don't want to talk about it. I want to pretend it's not there, just like I pretend day in and day out that I'm not here. In Compound Eleven.

"Yeah, I was reminded of that the other day when you shoved Derick Elmsworth in front of the Head of Justice, a guard, and about a dozen Premes. Addison's terrified of you by the way, if that helps."

I give him a look.

He grins. "Seriously. She came to your match, too." Quickly he holds up his hands as I round on him. "She insisted," he says, and once again he's laughing.

"You think this is all a joke? Because—"

"Actually, I don't," he interrupts, and his grin has vanished. "I'm trying to make light of a difficult situation. Something you might want to try."

"I don't need a Preme telling me what to do," I grumble. "And speaking of that day upstairs, it seemed like you and Addison were in the middle of a really riveting conversation. I'm sorry for interrupting that moment for you," I add, with sarcasm.

"You know the game, Eve."

"It doesn't mean I like it."

"Well, if you really want to know, we were discussing work."

I glance at him. "Why?"

His gaze meets mine, then quickly drifts away again. He rubs a hand down his face. "I know you're not going to want to hear this, but our departments work fairly closely."

"So you'll be spending a lot of time together," I finish, and I have to work very hard not to roll my eyes. I have to bite my tongue, too.

"Eve," shouts Maggie, "did you get your data card today?" and she raises her arm to reveal lettering that's outlined by swollen pink skin.

"Not yet," I lie, as she holds out her arm for Connor to examine.

"Well, I know you're tough and everything, but trust me— it hurts like you wouldn't believe."

"I bet."

Suddenly she looks more serious. More somber. She lowers her voice. "Are you, you know, ready?"

I stare at her. Because she isn't talking about the pain anymore, at least not the physical pain. I think she realizes that Jack's life and death will be imprinted on my skin, and without me even telling her. I shouldn't be so surprised. She has always been a good friend, and astute, too. Still, though, her kindness and consideration catches me off-guard. It makes my gaze cloud with tears.

But the last thing I want to do right now is cry here, in the middle of the cafeteria. So carefully, I nod, I try for a smile, then push back from the table even though my meal is barely touched. When Wren says my name I just shake my head, then wave goodbye to everyone and go to the exit. So what if I have to fight Landry tomorrow? I can beat him on an empty stomach any day of the week. I can beat him with my eyes closed.

Can't I?

A few minutes later, I turn the key to my cell door under flickering neon light. My arm, like Maggie's, throbs—but I barely notice. I feel too empty to notice anything. Then the air shifts over my shoulder.

"Eve," comes Wren's voice through the shadows. "Are you okay?"

I go still. Part of me is angry at him—annoyed that he and Addison will be working so closely. Yet the rest of me is happy he came. I even wonder if he feels the same magnetic pull toward me that I feel toward him.

"Eve?"

"I'm fine," I assure him, then hold the door open. "Just tired."

"Tired? Okay, well I won't stay long." He sits on the bed and considers me. "I just want to know what's wrong."

Everything is wrong. I'm back in Eleven. I'm training to be a guard, with my enemies breathing down my neck. Wren, on the other hand, seems perfectly content to be back underground, and spending time with his ex-girlfriend, too. I have a fight with Landry scheduled for the morning—a fight I don't have the energy for. I have Jack's *death* inscribed in my arm. I took an oath to Sitwell pledging deference and obedience to the Premes. Katz humiliated me in the atrium. He stopped me from going to the library. The list goes on.

So yes. There is plenty that's wrong.

"Eve. This is *Addison*," Wren says, and for a second I don't know what he's talking about. I can't even remember what we were discussing. "I wasn't interested in her months ago, which is why I ended things," he continues, and it all comes back to me. "And now that I'm with you? Come on."

"It's not just Addison that's the problem," I tell him, "but sure—let's discuss that."

"I'm all ears."

"Okay…well, how would you like it if I were working with an ex-boyfriend? And let's say he was still interested in me. Let's say he thought you and I were just *friends*—"

"It would drive me crazy," he admits.

It's a small admission, but it fills me with satisfaction.

"That being said," he adds, "you need to let it go. There's nothing I can do about it, not now. Anyway, she's not interested in me, she's always hanging out with Strike—"

I don't let him finish. Instead I push him off the bed.

"You're a fool, Wren, if you think she's not interested in you."

He gives me a look. "Fine. But, Eve"—his face grows serious—"I was going to die for you. Doesn't that tell you everything you need to know?"

"Actually, you decided to come back down here. Remember?"

He crouches beside me and runs a hand through my hair. "You decided that, too. And yet I've hardly seen you lately."

"I've been busy," I tell him as I gaze into his eyes.

"Yeah, you said. Anything new?"

I think about the question. The guardship is new. So is my fight tomorrow with Landry. And the data card, and my run-in with the ruler of Eleven. But I don't want to discuss those things. "I was thinking that maybe we could find a way to survive aboveground after all," I say eventually.

"You mentioned using your job as a guard to access supplies, right?"

I shake my head, then immediately correct myself by saying, "That's an option. But I was thinking it would be simpler to learn how to survive on our own, rather than depending on Eleven's resources."

"Learn? How?"

I shrug. "The same way we learn everything else—books. I'm sure there's something useful in the library, don't you think?"

"Could be," he admits, as he runs a hand over his chin. "Have you taken a look?"

"I tried. Twice."

"And?"

"And the first time I ran into you and Addison. The second time I ran into Katz."

His brow lifts. "Katz? I'm guessing running into him was even worse than running into me and Addison."

"Neither was particularly pleasant," I admit. "Do you mind taking a look in the library when you have time?"

"No problem," he says at once. "Of course, finding time won't be so easy now that work has started."

I roll onto my side so that I'm facing him. "Speaking of that, how's your big-shot job in Inter-Compound Relations?"

"Not bad, considering I have no idea what I'm doing."

His self-deprecating laugh is something I've missed, and slowly I lace my fingers between his. "Have you found anything useful? Do the Premes know what we know?"

"It's been one day!" Then he squeezes my hand. "I did learn that Compound Eleven looks like paradise compared to Compound Ten. I don't want to say that I saved you from hell, but…" Smiling, he shifts forward and kisses me lightly on the lips.

I lift myself onto my elbow as he pulls away. "Tell me more."

"It's chaos. Half its people have killed one another. They've put in multiple requests to our compound for guard back-up, all of them denied—too dangerous. It won't be long before it goes black."

"Black?"

"Extinct."

The words buzz in my head. *Half the people killed by one another. Requests for more guards. Soon extinct.* Society completely imploding upon itself.

I didn't think anything could be worse than Eleven. But I was wrong.

Suddenly his eyes harden and his features look angular and sharp in the shadows of the lamp. "The other day, when you saw me and Addison in the atrium. What were you doing before that?"

"What do you mean?"

He squints at me. "You had all those scratches, remember?" he continues. "Your skin was pink. It still is, here and here." Gently he touches my cheeks.

I burst out laughing. "That's because I snuck aboveground," I admit, then I lift my palm. "I was careful, don't worry."

"It's risky, Eve —"

"I don't need the lecture," I remind him. Then I pull myself to the very edge of the bed so that he's close enough for me to kiss. With my seemingly unending list of things that have been going wrong in my life, this feels like one thing that is very right.

I lean forward and he fills the void, his lips press against mine, and all that other stuff becomes noise, nothing more. Noise that fades away into nothingness. The only thing that matters is the two of us — together. Then, as I kiss him harder, as I twist my fingers through his hair, he sits straighter, and the way he responds to my touch makes me smile. It always has.

"It's been a long time since I've seen that," he murmurs, as his lips move to my neck.

"What?"

"You — happy."

"Maybe we should be doing this more often, then." My fingers curl under the bottom edge of his shirt.

"I definitely wouldn't object to that."

And then I go still. My smile is gone. Because I can hear something outside my door and down the hall, something that doesn't belong. A knocking, louder than a fist could make.

"What's wrong?" Wren asks. He pulls back and stares at me. Silently I get to my feet and open my cell door a crack.

Deep voices, loud and authoritative. They are at Hunter's cell. *Stand aside*, they say. *Turn out your pockets*. Guards.

But Hunter isn't a rule-breaker. He isn't a risk-taker. And so the guards must be there for another reason... *Stand aside*.

Turn out your pockets.

I shove the door closed, because suddenly I know why, and all at once there's a pounding between my ears. "Shit," I mutter. "*Shit.*"

Quickly I retrieve the gun I lifted from the guard, and my knife, gifted from my father. Two items that I'm not allowed to have. Two items that could get me in a lot of trouble.

"What's going on?" Wren demands. "What's wrong?"

"It's the guards—they're sweeping the cells," I explain in an undertone. "They hardly ever do it—it's because of Dennis." No, not just *Dennis.* After all, there were no sweeps conducted after the other guards were killed. It's because of the demonstration by the Upper Means, the one demanding justice. It put pressure on the guards to investigate, and so that's what they're doing. Funny, I don't remember Lower Mean demonstrations ever garnering such swift action.

"Dennis?"

"Remember him? The guard. He was strung up near the elevators with his throat cut." I touch the knife to my lip and try to think. *Think.*

"When was this?"

"Huh?" I am barely listening—I'm too busy searching for a hiding place for my weapons. There are none. *Of course* there are none.

"Dennis. When was he killed?"

"A few days ago."

Then something strange happens. I notice it first in Wren's body, how it stiffens. Then I notice how his mouth presses into a thin line, and how he watches me out of the corner of his eye. Like he is thinking.

Probably I should head out the door right now, sprint out of sight before the guards come calling. Instead I turn to him with my weapons hanging at my side. "*What,* Wren?"

His face is expressionless. But I think I can see it clear as day. He wonders if *I* killed Dennis—I'm almost sure of it.

Before I can level the accusation, there's a loud hammering at my door, one that can come only from a long metal baton.

I stare at the door, and I try to breathe. *Breathe.* Maybe I could convince them that I'm storing the gun for one of the other hires on the guardship. But I have no such excuse for the knife, and they will find it, they will accuse me of murdering a guard.

Then Wren is behind me and one hand lifts the knife from my fingers and the other lifts the gun. He tucks the knife into his boot and the gun into the back of his pants, out of sight. His Preme gun is removed to make room and he holds it loosely in one hand. "Answer the door."

I don't move.

"Answer the door," he says again.

"I'm not letting you take the fall," I tell him.

He rolls his eyes. "You don't need to worry yourself over me."

Outside, one of the guards is shouting. The baton pounds louder and louder against my door. I look at it, then back at Wren.

His gaze is so steady. It always is. Like he possesses something inside himself soldered in steel—something that can't easily be broken. I hope I possess it, too, but as I turn to the door and my entire body trembles, I don't think I do.

Two guards glare at me from behind face masks. All I can see are their eyes, and they look like black beads. Just like Dennis's used to look.

"What took you so long?" one snaps.

I motion behind me. "I have company." They stare over my shoulder at Wren. And then their guns are drawn and pointed at his chest.

"No!" I scream—because Wren doesn't understand. This is the *second* floor. Guards don't hesitate to shoot down here.

"Put the weapon down!" the taller one shouts.

Calmly Wren places the gun on my desk. Then he crosses his arms and steps pointedly away so that the guards can examine it.

"This is a Preme gun," the short guard observes as he turns it in his fingers. "Who'd you steal it from, huh?"

"I didn't steal it from anyone."

"Meaning—"

"Meaning I'm a Preme, obviously."

The guard rounds on Wren. He shoves his face mask to the back of his neck and presses his baton into Wren's stomach. But before he can do or say anything more, Wren lifts his unblemished hands.

The tall guard, meanwhile, knocks me across the shoulder. "Empty your pockets." I don't respond, or move—I am too scared for Wren. Then he hits me again, hard enough that I wince. I turn out my pockets.

"Boots off, too."

I do as he says. He turns my boots over, then he runs his hands along my legs and over my stomach. I barely notice. My gaze is still on Wren and the guard, who speak angrily at each other. Too much rushing in my ears to know what they say, but I know one thing: I shouldn't have let Wren do what he did. I shouldn't have let him take my weapons. They are my responsibility, my burden. Not his.

Besides, since when do I accept help?

"Time to have a look around," the tall guard says gruffly as he kicks my boots toward me.

"What are you searching for?" My voice is low and hoarse. I already know the answer.

"None of your business."

"Does it have to do with that guard who was killed a few days ago?"

"Sure does."

"I hope you catch the person," I lie.

The guard grunts, then he goes through my bedsheets, empties my desk drawers. His movements are quick and indifferent, but he pauses when he finds my guard uniform and the weapons that go along with it. He turns to me with suspicion shooting through his Upper Mean eyes.

"Nkrumah hired a Lower Mean." I say it plainly, but my eyes burst with a sudden boldness that can't be tamed. I draw up my sleeve and stick my data card under his nose. "You didn't get the memo?" I add as I yank my sleeve down again. For a while, he just stares at me, features unkind. Then with a withering look, he continues his search.

The other guard continues to question Wren. "What's a Preme doing in a Lower Mean cell?"

"Take a guess," he replies. He isn't cuffed, his boots are laced. It makes my head ache with less intensity. But still the baton is pressed to his stomach, and that's enough to make me uneasy.

"No idea."

"No? Doesn't take a genius to figure out what a guy and a girl might be doing together, alone in a room."

The guard casts a sidelong look in my direction, and I am ready for it. Braced for derision and hurt to spew from his mouth. I can see it already in his eyes: a Preme and a Lower Mean don't belong together. It's wrong, almost perverse.

I get it.

But before the words can pass his lips, the tall guard hits him on the arm. "All clear." He heads for the door without waiting for his colleague. No backward glances, no goodbyes.

The other guard, though, he does pause. "You keep

hanging out down here with Lower Means and you're going to wind up getting treated like one," he advises, and he clunks his baton against Wren's chest. "Consider it a warning."

Wren says nothing. He simply watches as the guard turns and follows in his partner's footsteps out the door.

They knock on Maggie's door next, but I don't bother to listen. Instead I shut my eyes and swear under my breath. It was close, too close. If Wren hadn't been here…

Then a series of emotions sweeps over me—a jumble of grief, outrage, relief, a sense of injustice…even a sense of longing. Tears prickle in my eyes and I feel unusually hot. Probably I should be thanking him. Instead, once the tears harden over, I say, "Better get out of here before my status rubs off on you."

"Let me guess. You didn't want my help, is that it?" His voice is every bit as unfriendly as mine.

I turn to him. "Go back to where you came from, *Preme*."

He laughs coldly. He tosses my gun and knife onto the desk and picks up his own. "With pleasure." Then he's gone, the door banging loudly behind him, his smell—the one I usually love—clouding my senses.

CHAPTER SEVENTEEN

Later that night, when I am alone and staring at the ceiling like an empty shell devoid of thought or emotion, there comes a knocking at my door.

Ben. It must be.

So far he's heeded Wren's warning—he has stayed away, he has let me be, but I guess that's over. Right now I feel reckless, so I don't bother to grab a gun before I throw open the door. I have my fists, after all—I can fight. And wasn't it my very own father who labeled it a noble pursuit?

But it isn't Ben. Not even close, and the smirk falls instantly from my face. "What do you want?" I whisper.

Hunter shakes his head. "Please, Eve," he says. "Let me come in."

He doesn't deserve it, not after he betrayed me. But then I remember all those times he *didn't* betray me. All the times he didn't let me down. All the times he actually built me up. Like when he threw me a surprise birthday party in Blue Circuit's training room. He made the decorations himself, using pieces of leftover tinfoil, cut into stars. Or the countless times he snuck me treats after a tough loss in the Bowl. Or the way he held me when the pain of losing Jack, and, in some ways—my mother, became too unbearable. Yes, sixteen years of his love and kindness force my socked feet to shuffle to the side.

He takes a seat at the foot of the bed and motions for me to join him. "Will you sit?" he asks eventually when I don't move.

"No."

He nods, like he was expecting that answer. "Did the guards sweep your cell?"

"What do you want, Hunter? Because if you came here to make small talk—"

"I didn't," he assures me. For a while, he just fidgets with an elastic band pulled from his pocket, the light from my lamp cradling his face. Then he sits straighter. "What do I want? Pretty much one thing: to go back in time—"

"Too late," I interrupt. "No such thing as time travel."

"Eve—"

"Just admit it," I say, as my voice fills with emotion. "You're a coward who doesn't like change, and you'd rather me rot under lock and key in the cell next door than see me move off to a better life somewhere else." I don't bother to tell him that Compound Ten would have been a mistake, a horrible one.

"That's not why, Eve. That's not it."

"So why don't you enlighten me!"

Instead of responding, he says, "I can't stand us not being friends. I can't. You and Maggie, even Emerald, you're my family, you're everything—"

"You betrayed me, Hunter!"

"I know I did!" he shouts, and now he is on his feet, standing directly in front of me. "I know I did. I screwed up, okay? I made a mistake—a big one, I get that. But please—*please* stop hating me for it."

My grimace gives way to a dark laugh. "A mistake? It was more than a *mistake*. Look, you got your way, okay? I'm still here, still in this piece-of-shit compound, just like you wanted!"

"Yeah, that is what I wanted! Is that such a bad thing? Is that such a crime?"

"It may as well be! God forbid you consider what I want, Hunter!"

"I did consider it!" he yells. "I did, but I also knew you haven't been yourself—"

"It wasn't your call—"

"You're right! It wasn't."

"We were best friends!"

"I know, Eve—"

"So how could you do it?"

"Because—"

"How could you do it?"

"It's just—"

"How could you do it?"

"I'm in love with you—*that's* how!"

The words startle him. I see his tall frame jerk. I see emotion cut through his eyes. Then he runs his hands slowly down his face as he contemplates the ceiling. And if *he's* startled by his words, it's nothing to how I feel.

Shock and unease and wonder claw at my brain. There's a strange humming in my ears that I can't place. Then I laugh. "Funny, Hunter," I say, even though no part of me finds it humorous. No part of me thinks it's a joke. But I need to give him an out, because even I'm not that cruel.

He doesn't take it. He just stares at me head-on. "It's the truth," he says. "For so long."

There's too much to think about right now, and now this? Hunter—in love with me. In *love* with me. All those years of friendship and closeness... All those years where we could have been even more? The shaking in my body is worse than before, but this time it isn't from anger. "Why didn't you tell me?"

He shrugs. "I didn't want to ruin what we had. I didn't know if you felt the same way. I…didn't know how."

Something rips through my chest, but try as I might, I can't put my finger on it. I really can't.

"If I had said something before…" he begins, as he sits back down on the bed. Then he stares at me expectantly.

"Before?" I ask as I sit next to him.

"You know. Before *him*. If I had told you how I felt…" He looks at me, and a shy smile flickers for an instant across his face, and I know what he's asking. If he had told me about his feelings before Wren, what would I have said? What would I have done? He wants an answer; I would, too.

"Maybe," I finally say.

"And now—"

"Don't, Hunter. Please don't." I blink; I blink ferociously, but it doesn't stop my eyes from welling, or a tear escaping. I rub it away before he can see.

Eventually he nods.

"I still don't get it," I whisper. "You love me, so you decided to turn me in?"

"I decided to do whatever I could to get you to stay. It was desperate. And pathetic. And wrong. All that stuff you said about me being a coward—I guess it's true. Because I couldn't bear to see you go, I just couldn't."

Half of me wants to wrap my arms around him and never let go. The other half wants to punch him. I don't know how to appease both sides. I don't know how to unite myself into one fully functioning, fully feeling person. I am a wreck, but maybe I'm not the only one. Maybe Hunter's brain has been pulling him in different directions for months, maybe even years. Maybe he, too, can't seem to find a way forward.

"I think you should go now," I say in a distant voice. I guess I really am my mother's daughter.

Then, for a fleeting moment in time, I think he considers doing something bold. I can almost feel his hands pressing against either side of my face, I think I can even taste his lips on mine. But all he does is capitulate to my demand, respecting my wishes. He lifts wordlessly from the bed, and I can't tell whether it leaves me feeling relieved, or disappointed, or somewhere in between.

When I'm sure he is gone, I pull my pillow onto my lap. Then I bury my face into it to muffle the hideous-sounding sob that echoes from the pit of my stomach.

Later, with sleep as elusive as my freedom, I slip on my boots. The air of the hallway is biting cold and I am reminded that it warms only when it's flooded with bodies.

All I want is to clear my head. Because right now my thoughts threaten to drown me. Every time I lay my head down on the pillow and close my eyes I see my exit to the outside world blocked off forever. I see Wren dismissing me with complete indifference. I see Hunter bleeding under my hand. Daniel and Landry are there, too, cracking their knuckles and scowling at me through the shadows.

Also I think of Maggie and Emerald, how much they enjoy their new jobs and their new friends. I think how unlikely it is they will want to leave everything to start over aboveground, if that's even a viable option. Wren, too.

Finally I think of the burden of the entire compound. Because if I do find a way to survive up there, I can't simply leave—not if everyone down here is being held hostage. Does it make me selfish that that's all I want to do? Does it make me *weak*?

I sigh. Then I focus on the feeling of my boots striking concrete, the sound of crunching glass and grit. I focus on the damp air that curves around exposed skin and the beads of light that glow orange at my feet. I focus on every sensation that doesn't radiate from inside my own toxic brain.

Around every corner I expect to see someone, someone with evil glinting in their eye. That or an attack already in progress, brutal and bloody. Or even a guard, ready to shoot. But I walk on, my boots kicking ever forward, my gait uninterrupted. I have no destination and that is good, because the longer I walk, the more my pulse slows. My brain quiets, and something resembling calm settles over me.

Before I can register what I'm doing, my fingers curl into a fist and knock sharply on a metal door. The same man from last time opens it. Hugh, and he stinks of onions.

"Remember me?" I ask.

"How could I forget."

"I wanted to let you know that everything I told you about the lemon squares was a lie. I didn't get the code to the kitchen from Hunter, but I did make it look that way."

"Why?"

"I was angry at him."

"Yeah? So why are you telling me now?"

I shrug. "Guilty conscience?"

"You don't sound too sure of yourself."

"Maybe I'm not."

"You guys are friends. You're just covering for him."

Carefully I shake my head. "We used to be friends," I clarify.

CHAPTER EIGHTEEN

As soon as I walk through the door to the fourth-floor training room, I'm body-slammed against the wall. The smell of acrid soap chokes me. So does the forearm jammed against my neck.

"I was speaking with some of my friends from the fifth floor, Eve," Daniel says through clenched teeth. "Heard from a little birdie that you and your bodyguard are toast. Can't say I'm surprised. But all the same, best if you think long and hard about your future, don't you think?"

I wrench Daniel's arm off me and gulp oxygen. His words make me bristle, but only the part about Wren and me breaking up. So, news has spread. It is starting to feel true even though it isn't. It *isn't*.

"Nobody to fight your fights now, isn't that right?" he continues. "A ballsy bitch like you ought to be a bit more careful, is all I'm saying."

"He was never my bodyguard, Daniel," I retort. "I don't remember him being around when you got that little decoration across your face, do you?"

Immediately his fist is cocked, but someone knocks him on the shoulder. One of the new hires, the guy with the ponytail. "Got a thing for her or something?" he asks loudly. "Every time I open my eyes you're up in her business."

"Screw off, French," Daniel says. "You don't know her like I do." But the interruption is enough to extinguish the fire that lit Daniel's eyes a second ago, and soon he leaves me be, turning his attention to the punching bag instead.

French sticks out a hand and introduces himself.

"Eve," I mutter, as I scan the room for Landry.

There he is. In the far corner, taping his knuckles. Those sinister gray eyes are focused. His mouth is pressed into a thin white line. I swallow and find my throat has gone dry.

Funny. This morning I woke with hunger, and I can feel a hint of it again in my stomach now. But when I arrived at the cafeteria, I realized it wasn't food that I crave...

"Yeah, I know who you are," says French. "Everyone does. Not often a Lower Mean gets hired. Look, I'm not real interested in being your friend or anything, but we're supposed to work together and all that crap, so nice to meet you." He walks away before I can reply.

"Morning," Maax grunts as she walks in, then she stifles a yawn. "Rested up for the big fight?"

I shrug. Rest was something that eventually found me, but after an eventful night, it was far too short. My brain feels sluggish, my muscles too. Not a good combination for such an important match. Together we push our belongings into our lockers, then I carefully tape my own knuckles. I give extra attention to each loop, its placement, even the tension.

"This is Sam," Maax says and she points to a boy with rounded eyes and sandy hair. He is the least brawny of our group and maybe because of that, he looks least like a guard.

"Hi." My voice is flat, my brain focused on the match ahead.

"We go way back," Maax explains. "He used to live across the hall from us."

"Yeah, your mom Fiona and I were tight," confirms the boy named Sam. He winks at her.

"Rumor is you can fight, legit," another hire says to me, this one thick-set with curly red hair. He watches my tape application with interest.

"Something like that."

"One of the perks of being Lower Mean, I guess," he continues. "Mom never let me give it a try with the Combat League. She said it was beneath me."

I peer at him from behind a strand of hair that has escaped my ponytail.

"Bern," Maax says from my side, "she's getting ready for a fight. Get lost."

"Jealous?"

"You wish," she shouts at his retreating back.

Across the room, Nkrumah claps his hands together and motions for us to gather round. "Today," he begins, "you learn how to fight. Muscle isn't everything. Better hope it's not, anyway, cause plenty of Compound Eleven is bigger than the lazy asses I see lined up here. Now, all of you will get a chance to fight today, and when you're not fighting, you're either watching, studying, or you're practicing over there." He nods in the direction of the punching bags. "By the end of the week, I expect every last one of you to be able to throw down a civilian, no matter their size." His gaze lingers on Maax, the smallest member, then on Sam.

Nkrumah motions to me and to Landry, and when we are near, he grabs our wrists. "Our first two to fight!" he proclaims, lifting our arms into the air. A few of the hires cheer, some clap. Most are stony-faced and I'd wager they're nervous for their own matches. If I hadn't grown up in the ring, I'd be nervous, too.

"Let's see what you're made of, Lower Mean," Nkrumah whispers so the others can't hear. I glance at him and see that his red eyes are eager. He thinks I'll lose; I can read it plain as day. He knows I didn't earn a spot here with the new hires and he wants to prove it.

I can't let that happen.

The others spread themselves into a wide circle with Landry and me standing in the middle. I shake out my muscles and bounce a little. I watch out of the corner of my eye as my opponent does the same.

"When I say so, you fight," Nkrumah announces. "You don't stop till I say stop. And nobody interferes unless I order them to. Clear?"

My pulse accelerates and I jump up and down with more vigor, but I'm still not warmed up. Adrenaline hasn't taken me, not without the roar of the crowd or the blinding lights of the Bowl. The will to fight doesn't burn as it should.

But then Landry's gaze meets mine, and he smirks, and I see in his cold gray eyes that he isn't scared of me after all. He knows I can fight—he has seen it on plenty of occasions. But he has also hurt me in the past. He thinks he can do it again. I can see it glowing under his skin. He thinks he can smash my head into concrete. Again. He thinks he can touch my bare stomach. Again. I hear his hurtful words hissing through my brain and, just like a switch has been flicked, I see red.

The hunger that woke me this morning returns with full force, and this time I know it isn't food that I crave or even blood. It's the opportunity to flip the script, to find my voice. The past couple of weeks, life has happened *to* me. I've been frustrated and ridiculed. Others have made my decisions.

Now it is my turn to take control.

Maybe Nkrumah says the fight is on, maybe. I can't hear anything over the rushing in my ears or the hunger roaring in my belly. But I know that Landry is suddenly lunging toward me, and I smash his nose. A cross cut, full force. It sends droplets of blood to the gray speckled floor, and the other hires inhale.

A second and a third punch find him, and when he finally lands one on me, it's barely enough to leave a bruise. "Is that all you have, Landry?" I hear a voice call, and I think by how his eyes narrow that it must be me who taunts him. I may be on his turf right now, stuck in the fourth floor guardship against my wishes, stuck in this goddamn compound against my will, but I'll make him pay for his past wrongs. I will make him suffer.

I kick him in the stomach, then in the leg. I block his punch. I land one of my own.

Then in my periphery I see Daniel, see his face red with pressure, see him dart forward to help Landry. Two against one, except Nkrumah grabs him and forces him into submission.

It's a terrible thing to be forced into submission.

Then, in my moment of distraction, Landry smashes into me and his hands wrap around my neck. He squeezes so tightly that my vision goes black, stars flash and pop through my vision, and I am on my knees.

Submission, indeed. If I don't free myself, he will kill me, and I know that Nkrumah won't call the match before that happens. So through the darkness I reach up, I find his face, I dig my thumbs into the wetness of his eyes until his grip disappears and my vision returns. My lungs swell with life.

Before my breathing can return to normal, I launch at him—no second spared. I knock him to the ground. Both fists beat the tissue of his face until it loosens, until blood covers my hands like gloves. Then he gets lucky. He clips me under the chin and I bite my tongue, jerk back from the pain. It gives him a window to force me off him and he takes it, and a moment later we are both on our feet, breathing hard.

He glares at me with hatred; his words bubble to the surface like poison. "You think I'm going to let a girl beat me? A low-level piece of *trash*?" His lips split to reveal a wide smile. "You may be one ugly bitch, but I'd rather die than let you win."

"Your choice, Landry," I growl, and as he lunges for my neck once again, I leap away, then aim a kick directly at his head.

It snaps back, and as he drops to the ground, I am on top of him—in control, finally in control. The others in the room, they scream my name. They cheer for me, I think. My knuckles may be black and blue, clotted with blood, stiff to move, but my hands find renewed life and they clench his neck like he did mine, collapsing every tendon and muscle and artery in their path.

Maybe the blood vessels in his eyes burst. Or maybe his eyes have been closed for a while now. Maybe whoever pulls so intently at my waist that they lift both me and Landry from the floor ought to give up, because nothing will remove my fingers from his neck until it collapses into nothingness and there is only air left under my strong hands.

I am in control. *I* am.

But eventually more arms find me. Eventually I'm ripped free, thrown across the room by a small army. I breathe so hard that I can't think straight. I sweat so profusely that my hair drips. I breathe, and I sweat, and I blink. I blink until the shapes around me take form, and I see they are people—the new hires that I've been forced into a room with and told to fight.

They stare at me.

It isn't with awe. Their eyes are too wide, their features too limp. They are too still, all of them.

But even their stillness can't compete with Landry's.

CHAPTER NINETEEN

Nkrumah has me by the arm. He pulls me through door after door, and I am too unfocused to know where we are, or how to find my way back. Right now, I feel like a child.

Finally he deposits me onto a chair. "Wait here," he says tersely. "You hear, Lower Mean?"

I sway a little. Then I nod.

When he disappears, I tap the heel of my boot slowly against the concrete floor. I study my knuckles, at the pattern my blood makes across the skin, seeping through fine lines like a spider's web. Landry's blood, too.

My brain tries to claw its way back to the motionless body lying on the training room floor, but I don't let it. Instead I stare at the white light overhead and will my pulse to steady. I study the concrete walls unmarked by graffiti and blink away the tears prickling my eyes.

My boot taps louder as I study each monotonous detail. Above me the light buzzes; it reminds me of the fifth floor where the fluorescent lights are constantly humming. There's a similar sound aboveground, and I cover my eyes with my hands and replay it inside my head—letting it drown out all other thoughts.

"Come with me," says a new voice, and I drop my hands in time to see Sitwell disappear through a door to my right. I stare after him and remind myself to breathe in, out. In, out.

My movements are sluggish as I enter the room, as if the fight drained me of all energy—and yet when I see that Justice Andrews sits inside, I feel more awake than before. My spine is more rigid, my skin begins to crawl. Nkrumah sits to one side of him, I notice next, and Sitwell to the other. There are no smiles or pleasantries—of course there aren't. I am about to be thrown off the guardship. I'm about to be verified as a criminal.

And then what?

I can't really think about it. I can't think about anything. Right now I am an empty shell, except for the bulletin of soundbites in my brain telling me that Landry got what he deserved. But did he? I don't know—I don't know anything anymore, so I say nothing at all. I direct my gaze decidedly to the floor as three men gaze at me.

Finally Sitwell stirs. "Mr. Nkrumah tells me there was an unfortunate incident just now in the training room."

"An understatement," Andrews says quickly. "What we have here is a murderess, plain as day."

I lift my head at his words. Everything inside of me deflates. Everything inside of me withers. "He's dead?"

"Surely you knew that, Ms. Hamilton." His eyes sparkle darkly as he surveys me.

Dead.

Shock sits beside me, but it doesn't envelop me, not yet. And deep down I think I did know. I think I knew in the training room that Landry's body was lifeless, and I have the sudden urge to throw up.

"What do you have to say for yourself, Ms. Hamilton?" Sitwell asks sharply. His eyebrows touch in the middle, disfiguring a face already twisted in revulsion.

Blood drips from my mouth, and I notice that my lip is bleeding, too. The contents of my stomach thrash more violently by the second. The light in the room grows uncomfortably bright. "I don't have anything to say," I whisper.

"Nothing?"

Get a grip, Eve. If there's any chance of saving myself from being thrown off the guardship, of becoming a verified criminal, of suffering whatever punishment they deem fit, I need to get a grip. I need to say my part—I need to give my side of the story. So I take a steadying breath and tell them, "I was ordered to fight him. That's what I did."

"It sounds like you did a bit more than merely fight the young man."

"I'm trained in hand-to-hand combat, Nkrumah knew that," I explain. My voice wavers, but I'm no longer whispering. "So maybe it wasn't a fair fight. But I was ordered to fight, and that's what I did."

"According to Mr. Nkrumah, you *strangled* him, Ms. Hamilton. Does that sound to you like a regular fight?"

"Are there marks on my neck? There must be."

"There are."

"That's because he strangled me first. I broke free, then I did the same to him."

"And he was…less lucky?"

"He would've killed me," I say. "If he was strong enough."

Andrews leans forward in his chair. "You feel no regret, do you, Ms. Hamilton." He doesn't phrase it like a question, so it sounds like he's trying to put words in my mouth.

I grit my teeth and say, "We were fighting. He wanted to play dirty, so that's what I did."

"Do you know what I think?"

"No."

"You are a mutant, Ms. Hamilton, completely unfit for civilization." He states it like it's a fact. Like he's capable of making such a determination about my character.

"Hold on," Nkrumah says. He gazes at me, slow and deliberate. "Everything she's saying is true. Landry strangled her first, saw it with my own eyes. And I ordered her to fight, I did. Ordered them not to stop till I said so."

"And did you order her to stop before she was pulled off the poor lad?"

He says nothing.

"That's a yes, then. Wrongdoing is clearly established. No matter that she was ordered to fight. When you told her to stop, it was her duty to listen."

"Except she didn't hear me."

Andrews peers at him. "Surely you aren't defending her behavior, Mr. Nkrumah."

"Not defending anything," he replies. He reclines in his seat and stretches his arms over his head. "Just trying to make sense of what happened in my training room. Not often a new hire doesn't make it through basic training."

"It's a mutant you hired, that's what happened. Do you want a mutant among the guardship?"

Nkrumah pauses, and in the silence, the sound of protest erupts beneath our boots. "Fighting for me, I do," he says eventually.

Sitwell, who had been tapping his long fingers against the table, freezes. "Are you quite serious, Mr. Nkrumah?" he asks.

"Why wouldn't I be? Do you hear that downstairs? You should see this girl fight. Maybe we should be hiring more from the Combat League."

"They are typically Lower Means, Mr. Nkrumah," he says

tactfully, then he glances at me and sighs. "We can't have guards killing one another, I know that for a fact."

"It was an accident," I say, as the sounds from below, from my floor, become louder.

"An accident," snaps Andrews. "Really?"

"Do you know very much about fighting? It's dangerous," I tell him. "There was a death a few weeks back in the Bowl— one of the professional fighters. It happens. Do you think I meant for it to? Do you think I want to walk around with that on my conscience?"

"I don't think you have a conscience to begin with, Ms. Hamilton." Then he leans forward so that his robes graze the table. He lowers his voice. "If it were up to me, you would be sentenced to death this very second. You cannot be rehabilitated into society; I see that now. Death is the only way."

My skin prickles with electricity, borne partly by fear. But there's wonder, too. To be expelled from the compound now would make things more difficult, sure. I don't yet have the know-how to survive up there. Or resources. But I do know how to sneak back inside, and Wren knows how to sneak out. It would be jarring and shocking and terrifying to be forced out of Eleven right now, but part of me hopes for it anyway.

"Mr. Nkrumah is the one who saw the incident in question," says Sitwell. "The decision as to whether there was any wrongdoing should lie with him."

"Any wrongdoing?" repeats Andrews. "A boy was killed!"

"As was a young man in the Combat League, just as Ms. Hamilton alluded to. There was no wrongdoing found in that match; it was a tragic accident and nothing more. Your own ruling, I might add."

"This girl is a killer. This is not my first encounter with her and I'm telling you, if she is not sentenced to death today, it will not be my last."

Downstairs people roar. Chains clank loudly.

"Be that as it may, I trust Mr. Nkrumah's judgment."

Andrews stares at Sitwell, as Nkrumah stares at me. Seconds give way to minutes. Finally the Head of Justice stirs. "Someone's leaning on you. Someone has you in their pocket—that's the real reason you're defending this villain. Out with it, Jeffrey."

I don't know what is said in return. The unrest downstairs is growing too loud, and my ears begin to ring. Surely Wren doesn't know what happened. Surely his alleged romance with Addison wouldn't be enough to turn Sitwell's hand *now*. Would it? I don't want to think about that. I just want to think about the world up there, and so I picture the birds skimming the treetops, I imagine the warmth of the—

"Ms. Hamilton. Ms. Hamilton!"

I blink slowly. Then I raise my chin to Sitwell. "Yes?"

"Did you have any reason to dislike the boy?"

"The boy…?"

"The boy whose death you are responsible for."

The correct answer is no.

No reason to dislike the boy whatsoever. It was an accident, there was no inciting incident, no reason or motive for wanting him dead, not in the least. But that's not the truth, and part of me wants to tell the whole story—I want anyone who will listen to know how dirty and rotten Landry really is. Was.

Self-preservation wins the battle inside my brain; I begin to cough up the answer Sitwell seeks. Except Nkrumah knows there's bad blood—he has seen us exchange words, threats, even come close to blows, and this only in the two days he's known us. He might not know the reasons for my hatred of Landry, but he knows the hatred is there.

I eye him, and he eyes me. Then ever so slightly he shakes his head side to side.

"Ms. Hamilton?" asks Sitwell.

"No." I say it quickly and clearly. "No, there was no reason for me to dislike him whatsoever."

Sitwell sighs. I stare at his cufflinks—ruby and gold ones that shine. Never would anyone beneath the fifth floor be allotted such a needless luxury. Then he says quietly to Nkrumah, "She can't be fighting the rest of the hires going forward."

Andrews stands so abruptly at the words that it sends his chair to the floor. "She killed someone—and not just anyone, I might add. Someone who resides *two floors* above her. She should be verified this instant as a criminal of our compound, not sent out there to defend it!"

"Was an accident," Nkrumah says bluntly. "Won't happen again, not on my watch."

"That's two in favor of Ms. Hamilton, Justice Andrews. I'm afraid you're outnumbered."

Andrews hammers the table with his fist, then he moves deftly in my direction. It causes his robes to billow, makes him larger, more intimidating. I brace myself, but all he does is dig his finger into my chest. "That's strike two," he says to me. His wide face is just inches from my own. "One more strike and I'll kill you myself."

Then he's gone—and the door slams loudly shut.

Sitwell stands next. But he pauses by my side, stares down at me. "You'd be well-advised to stay away from my daughter at all costs, Ms. Hamilton. Her boyfriend, too."

His words make me cringe, they make me want to laugh, and cry. But I am still too numb for them to have any effect at all.

Now it's just me and Nkrumah.

Before I can begin to process any of the events of the past hour—like Landry's death, or the verification that I so narrowly avoided—Nkrumah draws his gun. His arm rests lazily on the table, but the barrel points at me with intention. He says, "Don't think for a second I believe any of the bullshit lies coming from my mouth, or yours. An accident?" He shakes his head. "Like hell it was an accident, Lower Mean. I was screaming at you to leave that poor son-of-a-bitch alone the moment you kicked him in the face. Don't think he even came to after that one, not that it slowed you. Nah, you wouldn't stop until you knew he was down for the long one, isn't that right?"

"You didn't call the match when he was strangling me, so I wasn't exactly listening for your voice when I was attacking him. Why would I?"

He rolls his eyes.

"Look, I didn't hear you. I didn't mean to kill him."

"The others are gone, you can stop with the bullshit."

I fold my arms across my chest. "If you don't believe me, why did you help me?"

"You're a machine, completely fearless. Never seen that in my day. And for some reason, you've got Wren Edelman and even Jeffrey Sitwell in your pocket. That's two peculiar ways you wield power. See what I'm getting at?"

"Not really."

"You're exactly the kind of person I'd like to have indebted to me." Then his lips curl into a grin as wide as a Cheshire cat. "You owe me one, Lower Mean."

I don't know what kind of debt he will look to collect, but I can't argue with him, not now. So instead I sit on my hands and wait for him to finish laughing.

CHAPTER TWENTY

Later that evening I lean back until my head rests against the gritty floor of the Oracle. I stare at the sky that burns orange, at the fiery globe known as the sun as it begins its steady descent. When I returned to my cell from the guardship, there was a note shoved under my door from Wren asking me to meet him here. So here I am, waiting for him to show, undeniably nervous about the prospect of telling him about Landry.

Landry.

The other hires won't look at me. Even Maax and Sam stood away, pretended to be busy learning the mechanics of combat. I have been banished to the far corner to beat a punching bag senseless instead of human flesh.

The biggest change is Daniel. He lost his sidekick, his best friend. And under *my* hand. Today, after my impromptu verification, I watched his pallid face and his rounded shoulders, and I knew he was reeling. Deep down I didn't think he could experience such things. I didn't think grief was part of his vocabulary. Whenever he saw that I was watching, he turned away. Normally he would meet my gaze with viciousness, threaten me with his words and his fists. Our dark banter is gone, for now.

The old me would hope it was gone forever. That Daniel had learned his lesson, that he would let me be. But I am wiser now. I know it's just a matter of time before the snake eyes re-emerge. And I will have to be ready with my muscles and my weapons.

I suppose there's another reason for me to be ready with my muscles and my weapons: this morning another guard was found dead, strung up yet again on the statue downstairs. The Giving Tree is what Nkrumah called it when he told us the news. Sixteen years I have lived with it, have passed by it on a daily basis, and not once have I heard it by name.

Nkrumah is worried that guards are being systematically targeted. That a movement is underfoot. He said the sweeps turned up nothing and are being discontinued, that they are ineffective and a waste of time. So at least there's that, I suppose.

My stomach gurgles with laughter at the thought, or maybe it's with hunger. It's impossible to recognize what I feel anymore. I didn't bother with dinner tonight—eating is the last thing I feel like doing. Instead I locked myself away in my cell, where my friends couldn't reach me. They don't know about Landry; I don't want to tell them. Telling them would involve thinking about it, and if I think about it, I'll be crushed under a wave of despair so intense I doubt I'll ever be able to crawl out. So—how the hell am I going to tell Wren?

Maybe I won't.

I lift my gun from its spot on the Oracle floor and turn it over in my hands. It feels different than when I first held one with Wren. It doesn't feel as cold, or as heavy. I grip it with both hands and point it at the glass pane in front of me that's shaped like a triangle. At one time I thought a single bullet would shatter that glass into a million pieces. But it's thick; every bullet in the chamber wouldn't be enough. It would be fun to try, though.

The sound of grit crunching underfoot catches me by surprise, and I roll onto my stomach, gun leveled at my visitor.

Wren lifts an eyebrow and glances coolly at the weapon.

"Hi," I say, as I toss it to the floor and sit upright. "You left a note saying you wanted to speak with me?"

"I didn't think I'd see you otherwise."

I nod. "I've been busy."

"Yeah, I guess you have."

I am careful not to look him in the eye. "What's that supposed to mean?" I ask cautiously.

"Sitwell came to see me today."

There's a long and uncomfortable stretch of silence, and I wonder if Wren already knows what happened with Landry. "Maybe he told you I'm not to go near you or Addison anymore, then," I finally mutter, trying to steer the conversation away from myself. Away from the guardship, too.

But Wren stares at me with piercing eyes, then laughs darkly. "*That's* what you're thinking about right now?"

Once again I say nothing. I just stare past him at the shrinking ball of fire off in the distance as my brain screams: *he knows.* I should just explain my side of the story—he'll understand. It's Wren—of course he'll understand. But I can't bring myself to talk about it. Every cell in my body pulls away from the memory, desperate for it to become yesterday's news. Ancient history.

Then Wren says, "He told me what happened." His eyes are watching.

I go still. Then I say as placidly as possible, "That's nice."

"Want to talk about it?"

"About what?"

"Goddamn, Eve," he snaps, sounding frustrated—not that I blame him. "What's wrong with you? About the fact that you killed Landry. *Obviously*."

"Oh, *that*." I try to pick at my nails but they're chewed back to the wick. So I force myself to breathe deeply and screw up the courage to say, "It was a fight that went sideways, that's all. There's nothing to talk about."

His eyes narrow. "Come on. I know you. I know how much this must be eating you up inside."

I don't think he means to antagonize me with those words, but I still feel a surge of resentment. I think on some level I've been feeling resentment toward Wren ever since we returned to Eleven. And now…well. I already feel horrible enough without him heaping on the blame. So I shoot him a look, and say, "Because you're a Preme, right? So you know everything?"

"No," he says quietly. "Because I'm your boyfriend."

My heart beats faster at these words. It makes me feel vulnerable, to hear him lay our relationship status bare, to feel the surge of affection for him that courses through my veins. It makes me feel too human, when all I want right now is to feel like an emotionless machine. "He got what he deserved," I say after a while.

Wren scowls.

"You just about killed him yourself a few weeks ago," I remind him. "You would have, actually, if I hadn't stopped it. I didn't want you becoming a killer, remember?"

"And now you're one."

I flinch, but I don't think he notices. "Looks that way."

"You're lucky you aren't being punished, you realize *that* at least, don't you? Landry may have been scum, but he was still an Upper Mean."

"Lucky?" I almost snort, because even though what he says is true, the last thing I feel right now is lucky. Then I add, "Now I'm indebted to Nkrumah instead."

"What's that supposed to mean?"

"He helped me get off. Sitwell did, too. He must really want to keep you happy."

Wren sits on the Oracle floor, and I watch him out of the corner of my eye. He doesn't sit close—there's a bumper of space he leaves intentionally between us, and for a while I stare at that empty space, contemplating it sadly.

"I'm as surprised about that as you are," he mumbles. Then he shakes his head. "Eve, we barely see each other anymore. Couples typically hang out from time to time, you know."

"But I'm not allowed to see you, remember?"

"That's not—"

"Word of our breakup has already spread, just like you wanted. Daniel sure got a good kick out of it."

He leans forward. "Stop being so difficult, Eve. *Stop*."

I hold up my hands. "Okay, okay. What do *you* want to talk about?"

"Anything but that."

"Here's something interesting, then. Hunter came by my cell the other night. He told me he's in love with me. That's why he turned me in—he couldn't bear to see me go."

Wren's eyes reduce down to slits, then he laughs. "You actually think that's news to me? I can't believe you didn't clue in yourself, to be honest."

I'm silent. Rattled. Maybe because of the revelation that Wren already suspected what I did not. Or maybe I was trying to push him to anger...and it didn't work. But why would I want that? Is it because those feelings of resentment bubble closer to the surface than I realize? Or is it because I'm trying to distract myself from what happened to Landry? Trying to deflect the spotlight, trying to make someone else morally blameworthy...

"How's the new job?" I ask eventually.

"Interesting, actually."

"Yeah?" I stare at him, at the way his skin seems to glow under the setting sun. "Did you find what you're looking for?"

"What *we're* looking for," he corrects me.

"Oh. Right."

"I didn't, but I discovered something of personal interest. My father used to work there, in Inter-Compound Relations." He shrugs. "He wasn't very senior or anything, but I've come across his name a few times now on old files."

"You didn't know he worked there?"

He leans back onto his elbows, more relaxed than before. "I was only ten when he died," he explains. "And my mother refused to discuss him after that."

"Not a word?"

"Nothing."

It strikes me suddenly that Premes don't often die prematurely. Violence and suffering aren't part of their every day. I say so.

"Premes get sick, though."

"Premes get treatment, and aid. Premes get better."

He gives me a hard look. "Not all the time, Eve. He had kidney disease. One evening my mother told me the disease had taken a turn for the worse and that I needed to say goodbye. That was that."

"That was that?"

He nods, then runs a hand down his face. "I didn't even notice him going downhill in the first place."

I set about retying my laces. It distracts me from how exposed Wren's voice is. Because that emotion that I can sense—I don't like it. It makes me uncomfortable, like the bugs that crawl around the perimeter of my cell are under my skin. It makes my own emotions threaten to rush to the surface, and I don't want that. So I remind him in a more detached tone, "Well, you were only ten."

"Yeah."

"And at least you had the chance to say goodbye," I add, thinking of Jack. My mother didn't have that opportunity. He was plucked from her arms as she pleaded for his life, as she fought a futile fight. But I don't want to think of that, either.

"It wasn't like that," he says, drawing me from my thoughts. He clears his throat. "We were surrounded by people. And he wasn't himself. He kept mumbling something about bodies. Follow the bodies. I don't know what he was talking about, maybe he didn't, either. But he knew he was about to die and he was just… He was just so *scared*."

I stare at him, eyes round. "That's terrible," I finally say, because it *is* terrible, and the very least I can do right now is acknowledge it. Maybe I should do more. Maybe I should close the gap between us, place my arm around his shoulders. Offer him comfort, or even condolences, because I can tell in this instance he needs it. But my palms grow clammy at the thought, as if I'm nervous to cross that bridge. Like things have become so strangled between us lately that I can't even manage that. Finally I swallow deeply, and rest my hand on his. "I'm sorry," I whisper, without really looking at him.

"Let's talk about something else."

I nod, then return my attention to the world outside where daylight is fading. Silently I consider Wren's father, I think about his final mutterings. *Follow the bodies.* It reminds me of the rhyme that Maggie and I would clap our hands to.

Flies are at the bodies,
They're buzzing at the light,

Follow the dead upstairs,
Throw them out at night.

Then I notice that Wren watches the side of my face, and the ditty fades into nothingness. "What?"

"You wish we were still outside, don't you?"

"I do," I acknowledge, surprised by the question.

"Have you found any survival books, like you wanted?"

"No. Have you?"

He shakes his head. "Even if we do find them… You'd really want to go?"

I exhale, exasperated. "Of *course* I'd want to go."

"And finding out whether the Premes know aboveground has cooled—does that matter to you?"

I shrug, since I don't know what to say about that. It hasn't exactly been at the forefront of my mind since returning underground.

"I can't believe you," he says, sounding cross. "After all those years down there, and you're willing to turn your back on everybody? I thought you'd care about this, Eve. Don't you realize they could be holding everyone hostage down there? They could be killing them for no reason? Doesn't that bother you at all?"

"Of course it bothers me," I say sharply. Too sharply.

"No, it doesn't. You care about saving yourself, and maybe a few friends. That's it."

Suddenly we are glaring at each other. "Don't put words in my mouth."

For a while he just considers me. When he speaks again, his voice is distant. "I suppose there isn't anything I could do or say to stop you from being so angry with me."

"I'm not angry with you."

He gives me a look. "Come on. Enough with the bullshit."

"Don't put words in my mouth," I say again. "And I told you, I'm not angry. Just leave it at that."

"You've been angry with me ever since we returned to the compound."

"*Stop*."

"I can't say I completely blame you. You didn't want to come back, I get that—not that there was really a choice in the matter. Then I tell you we need to figure out if the entire compound is a prison, something I thought you'd care about—"

"Since when do you care about saving everyone?" I yank at my braid and begin twisting it between my fingers as tightly as it will go.

He peers at me from his shadowy spot on the Oracle floor. "It's funny that of the two of us, I'm the one who wants to liberate this—"

"You haven't found a shred of proof—"

"I don't need proof! I *know* Katz and the others know, so wake up! Stop focusing on your own misery and help me figure out how to *fix* this."

"Stop focusing on my—"

"Getting angry yet? How about when I told you about Addison, how you and I have to pretend like we broke up and everything. That would piss anyone off, I get that." He is yelling now. "I mean, I was just trying to help you get a spot on the guardship, but God forbid you see it that way. God forbid you see it any way except—"

"Enough, Wren," I interrupt. I am on my feet now, and pressure builds quickly inside my head—all the pressure from the past few weeks—from our failure aboveground, to the verification, to the guardship, to Landry, Landry, Landry. "I told you I wasn't mad at you. Leave it at that."

"Yeah, but you are, Eve. I can see it in your eyes every time you look at me. Which is barely ever, I might add. Just admit it. You almost had your freedom, didn't you? Then I had to ruin it. I had to make everything miserable for you. Isn't that how you've twisted it?" His brow sits low over thunderous eyes.

"I'm warning you, Wren."

"What? Are you going to fight me like you did Landry?"

"*Shut up!*" I scream, the words erupting from my stomach without warning. I wanted to push him to his breaking point, and he did it to me, instead. "Ever since we came back underground, you've called the shots. Do you realize that? The Preme says we go back, so back we go. The Preme says to become a guard, so I become a guard. The Preme says we hide our relationship, so we hide it. I've got news for you—I get that enough as a Lower Mean. I never have a say, not one say since the day I was born. The compound makes all the rules for people like me, and now you think you can, too. Isn't that right?"

"All I'm doing is trying to help—"

"*Nobody asked for your help!* The compound didn't ask for your help, and I sure as hell didn't either."

"Punch me, Eve," Wren says. He steps closer. "Punch me. It'll feel good, I promise you. Just get it off your chest so we can move on."

"That's ridiculous."

He steps close enough that his long body bumps into mine. "Scared?"

I bite my lip hard enough for blood to drip like a faucet. We scowl at each other. Finally he takes a step back and shakes his head.

"I don't even recognize you anymore. Punching that girl on the fourth floor. Pushing the Preme on the fifth. Killing Landry—accident or not—and not feeling remorse. Even your disinterest in investigating the Premes, or freeing the compound. None of it is you. Do you realize that? You used to have this innate sense of right and wrong, no matter what happened. Through thick and thin, you were good. You've lost yourself, Eve. You're not you anymore, and I want you back."

He expects a response, I know he does. But my twisted brain can't think of anything to say. It can barely process what *he* says. Partly, though, I think he might be right. I have lost myself. I haven't been good. But he's wrong about one thing: I do feel remorse. A lot of remorse, not just about Landry, but about all my bad behavior lately. And yet instead of confronting that remorse, I've been running away from it. Trying not to let it touch me. Trying not to let it consume me. And along the way, I've become someone I don't think I like.

He sighs, and suddenly he looks defeated. He looks younger and older all at once. "Do you even want this anymore?" He motions with his hand and I know he means us. And of course I want *that*, but right now there's too much pressure between my ears to respond. What happened to me? And how can I get myself back?

I peer at him, begging him without words to help me find my way.

"I'll take that as a no," he says, as he strides past me. Then, from over my shoulder, I hear him add, "We're through."

We're through. The words feel like a hot knife. *We're through.* Then, as his footsteps fade into silence, the knife twists so that I almost cry out. I sink to the floor and outside the sun has set, and I am surrounded by nothing but soul-destroying, fear-inducing darkness.

CHAPTER TWENTY-ONE

Now the darkness isn't so bad. It's a reprieve. It hides me from the world and it hides the world from me. It's the latter one that is important.

I am a mutant, a savage, a monster—truly as brutal as they come in a place like this. I shouldn't be unleashed on the world, I shouldn't be free to roam among civilization. Andrews was right all along.

Funny that I couldn't own up to that truth until now.

I lie back on my bed and shove my hands underneath me where they belong—where they will stay. Because they're stained with Landry's blood, they are bruised from punching those who didn't deserve it. They are a reminder of my cruelty.

Sleep won't come, I am sure of it—no matter that I'm exhausted, or that it's the middle of the night, or that the past few hours have been spent sobbing in the Oracle and along the blackened corridors of Compound Eleven. It won't come and that's okay.

Sleep is a comfort I am no longer worthy of.

CHAPTER TWENTY-TWO

Probably I should turn on my lamp and check the time. It's morning now, it must be.

Instead all I do is trace my index finger along my bottom lip, one clotted over in scabs. I think about the anger that enveloped me when I fought Landry and when Wren finally pushed me too far. Funny that I wanted to push him to his breaking point at one time. But he is noble and good, I see that now. Any doubts I had, came from my own warped mind. And from my own inability to face the dark person I was becoming.

I tried to cast the shadow on him, rather than look myself in the mirror.

But he's the one intent on discovering the truth about the leaders of the compound—his peers at that. He is the one intent on righting a wrong, potentially the biggest wrong imaginable.

That needs to change. *I* need to change. It's time to start thinking about everyone else, instead of myself, myself, myself.

For now, though, tears drip to my pillowcase. They choke the back of my throat. I killed Landry. I punched and pushed those who didn't deserve it. I turned on Wren. And to make matters even worse, he *broke up* with me. The words are crushing. They make me hurt in a way I didn't think was imaginable.

Then I laugh—how disgusted my father would be. Sniveling like a child, pining for a love that was never meant to be. But that's okay, it's fine. Because for a while I became what my father wanted, and it got me nowhere. It got me into this mess. I became someone I loathe, someone my loved ones loathe. Life may be cruel and unkind down here, it's true. But the only way to survive is to surround yourself with goodness, and that can't happen if you aren't good to begin with.

I wrap my arms around my stomach and groan. It hurts the most—a tight knot, filled with regret.

Every single time I stop thinking about Wren, I start thinking about Landry, about the fact that I was responsible for his death. When I tire of that, I think of the other things: what a bad daughter I have been, what a bad friend, a bad citizen, a bad girlfriend. And that brings me back to Wren. A never-ending cycle of despair.

But finally something pulls me upright, a distraction, one that comes from my cell door. Pounding, and it takes my sluggish and sleep-deprived brain a minute to realize that someone stands outside, seeking entrance.

It isn't Wren, I know that, though there's nothing in this world I want more. He won't come. Besides, he may be exceptionally strong, but he is also impossibly gentle. It isn't him. Hunter wouldn't pound so loudly, either. So maybe it's Ben. Maybe it is someone who wishes me harm. I don't care who it is, and I don't bother to take a gun with me once I drag myself from bed. So what if one of my enemies has come calling—I would deserve it through and through.

A second later, Nkrumah pushes his way inside my cell.

Light floods the room and I see that his hand hovers over his gun—he doesn't trust me. "Wakey wakey."

I use the sleeve of the sweater I slept in to wipe away the last of my tears. "What do you want?"

"I want to know why your sorry ass isn't upstairs where it's supposed to be. Don't think I'm happy at coming all the way down here, either. Six guards dead on this floor, do I need to remind you?"

"What's the difference? The others don't want me there."

He raises an eyebrow. "Since when do you care?"

"Just forget it," I say quietly. "The point is, I'm not coming."

"That's not for you to decide, Hamilton. Unless you're on your deathbed, you're expected to report for duty. Welcome to the guardship." Then he pauses and looks at me out of the corner of his eye. "What's going on with you, anyway. You been crying or something?"

"No," I say, too quickly. "Of course not. It's just… I just—I haven't been sleeping."

"Something's on your mind," he states.

"Maybe."

"Don't tell me." He blinks theatrically. "Landry? What, you suddenly grow a conscience, Lower Mean?"

"Something like that," I mutter. "Look, can I at least have ten minutes to get ready?"

"Make it five. And if you don't make it upstairs by then, there won't be a job left waiting for you."

Then he is gone and the realization that life must go on even though I'm shattered into a million unmendable pieces sinks slowly through once-thick skin.

• • •

When I inch open the training room door a few minutes later, I see that the others stand near the lockers wiping themselves of sweat. By the looks of it, they have spent the past couple of hours at the punching bags while I lay in bed weeping.

Three of the five minutes Nkrumah allotted me were spent splashing cold water on my face, an attempt to bring down the swelling around my eyes. It worked—I look fine from the outside. If only I were okay on the inside.

Deep breath, Eve.

Slowly I walk in the direction of my locker, and slowly the others notice me. One by one they turn their heads. Conversation ceases, movements stiffen. Yesterday I ignored them, I was numb, I didn't care. Maybe their reactions were the same as now, maybe, but right now they make me hurt.

Then Nkrumah is motioning to everyone. "Congratulations, Tim," he calls. "You have the honor of being today's first fighter. Bern, you too." The others move to watch the fight, and I make to follow them. Nkrumah stops me. "Suit up," he says coldly. "Grab some compound maps and take your first patrol. Third floor and fourth."

"My first patrol? I thought we had to be full members—"

"Don't care. Be thankful I'm not assigning you to the ground floor today. Understand?"

Slowly I nod.

"Don't smile out there, don't be friendly. Fear is the best method for keeping the peace."

"Okay."

"And if someone needs an ass-kicking, go nuts."

His words make me wince, because they are confirmation of what I have always known. That guards are given too much power; they can do no wrong. All I must do is put on the suit and I'm virtually invincible.

Except that's the last thing I want right now. I don't deserve to be invincible. I don't want to cause people fear. Not anymore.

But one glance at Nkrumah tells me there's no use protesting, so silently I draw on my kneepads, and elbow pads, and the heavy artillery vest. Baton and gun are positioned in their holsters, face mask is hung around the back of my neck. I grab a handful of maps, one for each floor, and am almost to the door when someone knocks me on the back of the shoulder.

"You're not staying, Two?" Maax asks.

For a second I just stare at her, surprised that she's speaking to me. "Sent out on patrol," I finally explain. "I'm not allowed to fight, anyway," I add, as I watch the others.

"Figured. So. How are you holding up?"

How am I holding up? I blink at her. "What do you mean?"

"I mean Landry croaking during your fight probably didn't make you feel warm and fuzzy inside. Even if he was a complete jackass."

A lump forms in my throat. I'm not worthy of her kindness, or her compassion.

"Sometimes shit happens," she adds, after a minute passes with me saying nothing at all.

"Lower Mean!" Nkrumah hollers from the other side of the room. Tim and Bern stand in front of him staring uneasily at each other. "Patrol, now!"

I nod at Maax, grit my teeth, then walk out the door.

CHAPTER TWENTY-THREE

At first it's foreign, walking in the skin of a guard through third floor Mean corridors I have traveled thousands of times before. It isn't the feeling of the mask hanging around my neck or the heavy artillery strapped to my chest. It isn't even the feeling of weapons at my disposal.

It's the people.

They see me coming—glance my way or catch me in their peripheral vision—and they move. Laughter is swallowed, movements grow still. Just like in the training room with the other new hires, they recognize me for what I am.

But slowly sadness consumes me and I don't really notice anymore. Right now, all I think about is how Wren is no longer mine to kiss, or to hold, or even to smell.

I take the stairs up to the fourth floor and patrol there instead. I hope that the change in scenery will be a distraction, but it doesn't work. What if he gets back together with Addison? Seeing them hand in hand, laughing, kissing…it isn't something I could handle. Not now, and probably not ever. What if it triggers the monster inside me that looms so large these days and I snap? Do something awful? Something I won't ever be able to take back?

I can never take back what happened to Landry. He was a snake, an evil piece of scum—and maybe he would've killed me if I didn't get there first, but he still didn't deserve what came to him. Nobody deserves that.

"Look who it is," comes a voice, one that makes my boots stop their endless shuffle forward.

It has been a while since I've laid eyes on Kyle, Maggie's ex, or even thought about him. Same blue button-down. Same orange hair. Same condescending sneer curling his lip. "Don't tell me they made you a guard," he continues. "Since when do they hire from the second floor?"

"Guess they made an exception."

He raises an eyebrow. "Guess so. How's your little friend doing?"

Displeasure flares in my stomach. "Little friend? Is that what you call her now that she's dumped you?"

"Not my fault I can't remember her name."

"Say it. Say her name."

"Mary. That was it, wasn't it?" He gives another snide sneer. "You lower floor girls all sound the same."

"She was always too good for you, you know."

He laughs. "You may be dressed up as a guard, but you're still a Lower Mean. Mind your manners."

"I've punched you before," I remind him. "Don't think I won't do it again."

He steps closer. "Is this the part where you pull out your gun?"

I go still. It's true that I'm armed and he isn't. I have the power right now to make him afraid, very afraid. But whenever I blink I see Landry's lifeless body lying where I left it and I shudder. I don't want to draw my gun, or my fist.

I don't want to feel powerful. I just want the weight that sits on top of my chest to lift.

"Hit me."

"Excuse me?"

"Hit me," I repeat. "I won't hit you back. I won't reach for my gun, or my baton. Come on, you know you want to."

He laughs. "I may want to knock your teeth out, Eve, but I'm not a fool. I hit you and you've got a legitimate excuse to attack. Probably to kill."

"I have a legitimate excuse to do those things anyway. I'm a guard, remember? And you may be an Upper Mean, but you're no Preme. The thing is, I don't want to attack you. All I want is to be roughed up a bit, and I know for a fact that there isn't anyone better at roughing up girls than you. Especially the ones who can't—or won't—fight."

He takes another step closer. "What's that supposed to mean?"

"Take a guess. Let me ask you, did it make you feel powerful when you hit Maggie?"

His grin widens.

"Did it make you feel like a big man?"

Nothing.

I lower my voice. "Is that the way you got off?"

Smash. A punch, square between the eyes, one that knocks me backward and stuns me into passing silence, one that will leave me with two black eyes, I'm sure. Then a gurgle of laughter escapes my lips.

It felt good. Too good.

I open my eyes to see Kyle cock his fist again. This time it gets me in the temple, stuns my brain and breaks the skin. Next he shoves me into the concrete wall, and my shoulder screams.

I keep smiling.

Another punch, then someone is yelling, and Kyle is retreating. I dab at blood. Blink. Black boots and kneepads fill my field of vision and I know it's a guard before I even lift my gaze.

Not just any guard, I soon see. This one is vaguely familiar.

"You all right?" asks the gaunt face that stares down at me. Then he frowns. "I know you... I met you downstairs, on the first floor."

"The one asking to see the tunnel," I add as my fingertips brush over the swollen tissue that now pads my face.

"Eve, right?"

"That's right."

"Thought you were interested in maintenance."

"I thought I was. Turns out I'm doing this instead."

"Not well, by the looks of it."

I lean against the wall and relish the feeling of my head throbbing. It's so intense I can't think of anything else. Just like I wanted.

"New hires should still be training, shouldn't they?"

"We are."

"In my day, we weren't allowed out for patrol until training was finished, and for good reason."

"Yeah, well, I was no longer welcome in the training room."

He leans against the wall opposite me and lifts an eyebrow. He isn't as old as my father, I notice, but he isn't young, either. I don't know why he bothers to speak with me, but I suspect that kindness has something to do with it. Because he had been kind that day I came across him downstairs. So kind it was almost unrecognizable. "Why's that?"

I make a face. "You ask a lot of questions."

My words make him smile, and if I wasn't an empty shell inside, I would smile, too. After all, last time we met, those words were his.

He kicks one boot over another. "So, tell me. What'd you do to get kicked out of training?"

"It's a long story."

"I've got time. Besides, looks like we're going to be colleagues, so no harm in getting to know each other. Name's Trevor, by the way."

"It's nice to meet you."

He nods. "So?"

"I was told to fight another hire, as part of the training. Things got out of hand." I kick at the floor. "He didn't make it."

Trevor rocks forward with surprise. Then slowly he is nodding. "You're the professional fighter from Two… I heard about the death."

"Hobby fighter," I correct him. Then I stare up the hallway because I can't look at him anymore. He is kind and I am not. He knows that now.

I expect him to walk away. The other hires hate me; it would make sense for the seasoned guards to as well. Instead he says, "Didn't look like you were putting up much of a fight just now. You should've been able to clobber a guy like that."

I don't feel like laughing, but I can't help it. "Yeah, I could clobber a guy like that with my hands tied behind my back. Maybe I didn't want to."

"Not often guards get attacked up here, on this floor. Don't mean any offense by that, either. Just stating facts."

Usually people mean offense, but I don't think he does. There's no malice in his eyes, no superiority in the way he holds his body. "Maybe I provoked him," I say.

"Like to get punched, do you?"

I run a finger over my bottom lip, feel that the scabs are getting smaller. "Sometimes pain is the best reminder that we're still human."

He stares at me for a while, then he says, "Know what the

difference is between you and the rest of the guardship, Eve?"

I shake my head.

"They'd be celebrating their first confirmed kill. Not repenting. That's the only reminder you need."

I look at him only long enough to see that he is serious.

"Don't let me find you laying down your gloves again," he adds as he pulls himself from the wall.

I lift my hand to stop him from leaving. "Do you have any?"

"Any what?"

"Confirmed kills."

"Hard to do this job for very long without," he answers.

The words surprise me, even though they shouldn't. But it's difficult to picture someone so good taking life. "How do you…?"

"What, cope?"

I nod.

Instead of responding, he says, "No amount of guilt can change the past." Just when I think maybe it *is* a response, he gives me a sad smile, then starts down the hallway, conversation complete. But he pauses just up ahead, he calls to me over his shoulder, "It *can* destroy your future, though. If you're not careful."

CHAPTER TWENTY-FOUR

I don't bother with dinner that evening. Instead I head straight for the one place where I know I can clear my head. The one place where I feel peaceful, maybe even content.

The kitchen is crammed as I slip through, and I'm sure people notice me—my cuts and bruises, being where I shouldn't be—but I don't slow down enough to notice. Probably I look too frightening for them to say anything at all.

The climb up is easy, but I'm more careful when I leave the outbuilding. Minutes pass, motionless ones, spent peering around the door in the direction of the Oracle. When I'm sure that it's empty, I edge outside. All at once I notice the way the fresh air feels against my skin, the way it pushes through my hair, and against the odds I find myself smiling.

Eventually I find movement—I must, because I am running, and this time it's in the opposite direction as before. This time I sprint up the hill toward the solar panels that power the compound beneath my boots. The wall of rock sits off in the distance, sparkling under the sun.

The solar panels seem to stretch forever. My fingers

brush over cool metal, they graze smooth glass. Then without thinking I am running again—I run at top speed until my breath grows short and my quadriceps burn. I run with my arms spread wide until I am through to the other side of the panels and the earth drops off into oblivion.

But it isn't oblivion, I soon see. It's a hill, though not a gently sloping one. This one is steep, with exposed tree roots and jagged rock. If I'm careful, I think, I might be able to scale down it, so I take a step, and another. Then something catches my eye.

It's off in the distance. It's so far away, my eyes must strain to see—they even water a bit. I guess I've never asked so much of them. I wipe them dry then shield them from the sun, but they still can't decipher what it is. Not fully.

It's unnatural—an abomination among the trees, that much I know. Straight lines, right angles. No arching beauty. No graceful movement. Instead it looks like blocks stacked together, all different shapes and sizes, except for one that is twice as tall—its top whittled to a point like a sword.

I have seen this sort of thing in the books below my feet. A city. Or at least what remains of one.

With a wild feeling in my chest, I remind myself that I should appreciate its strange and sinister beauty from here. I should enjoy the way the late-day sun warms the apples of my cheeks, then venture carefully back downstairs. Certainly I shouldn't set off for that faraway city, through the unknown, where beasts with knives for teeth lurk, where I could easily become lost—never to find my way back again.

But my body has always had an unfortunate habit of disobeying my brain, hasn't it? Besides, I have a gun nestled in the waistband of my jeans now, and the wall of rock to the north will serve as my guide. What do I have to fear?

Right away, I lose my footing. I topple down the steep

hill, and branches slice through exposed skin. Dirt wedges under my fingernails and stains my knees. When I reach the bottom, it's hard to stop the laughter that wells up from my stomach. I think to myself that I have never fallen down a hill before. I have never shouted to the birds or to the blue sky that peeks through the canopy of green. I have never kicked at leaves just to hear them rustle and so I do, I do all of it, and when I try to remember the sound my boots make against concrete, I can't.

It's the same with what happened in the training room yesterday. In this moment, that Eve doesn't exist. In fact, I'm not so sure she ever did.

I walk, and walk, but I am not completely careless. The wall of rock that lies to the north of the Oracle is the key to finding my way back again, back to sustenance, and so every few minutes I look over my shoulder and make sure I can still spot it between the leaves. On and on toward the city I go, and then without warning, the trees are behind me. A hard surface rides under the toe of my boot, one that is gray and smashed into a million pieces. Shoots of green push their way through the cracks. Beyond it, there's a horizontal box of concrete that vines clamber over, vines that disappear between thick shards of glass to the interior.

The city sits just beyond.

Buzzing fills my ears as I stare at it. The fine hairs along the back of my neck stand upright at the sight, and my pulse is unsteady. Because it is recognizable as a city, but barely.

Vines don't simply grow alongside the concrete monstrosities—they cage them, and smother them, and claim them as their own. There was a battle here, I can see that now. Nature versus humankind. The victor is obvious, and to the victor go the spoils.

There's no sense in turning back, not now, so I take a deep breath and start forward. Some of the shoots I wade through are covered with jagged leaves that slice my knuckles as I pass, but I barely notice. Maybe later I will clean them with lemon juice, but right now I tilt my head back and stare up at buildings that aim for the sky. Even strangled with vines, they look proud. Stoic. Sunlight reflects in the window panes that are still intact, something I've never seen before, and they shimmer like jewels that the Premes sometimes wear.

But even the Premes with their jewels and their privilege haven't seen something like this. It's the one thing I have that they do not.

When my neck begins to ache, I consider the horizontal box in front of me, then peer through broken shards of glass to an interior completely returned to nature. Something green and napped covers the floor, and a bird flies from one end to the other where a pile of thatch awaits.

I watch it for a few minutes, then step away, turning once more to the city. And that is when I hear something that doesn't belong. Something that feels cold against my spine. Something that doesn't match the buzzing and the snapping and the squawking that I have come to associate with life aboveground.

I think of the beast with knives in its mouth and feel a ripple of gratitude. Gratitude that I, a Lower Mean, have a gun tucked into my jeans. I reach for it and find its cool metal reassuring. Funny. Still I loathe them and the destruction they cause. Still I detest the power they bestow their owners. But right now I am the owner, and the power is mine.

One boot kicks forward, then the other, again and again

until I am past the horizontal building and closer to the pulsating remnants of the city itself. Closer to the source of the noise, too.

Two buildings stand immediately in front of me—the one to my left is a coiled metal half cylinder, like the tunnel underground that connects the Blue Circuit training room to the Bowl. The one to the right is a skeleton, its innards completely exposed to sunlight.

The sound came from the half cylinder, I'm sure of it, so I walk in its direction. Each step is careful and deliberate. My ears hum. When I am ten feet away, something black and large bursts from the top, from where the vines are thickest and I watch it fly away, laughing.

With the source of the noise uncovered, I let the gun fall loosely to my side, I walk easily around the corner of the half cylinder with my fingers gliding over its smooth metal. And then my smile falters, because there stands the true source of the noise, and it isn't a bird, and it isn't a beast.

It is a person, staring at me calmly, clear as day.

CHAPTER TWENTY-FIVE

For a moment, the thick muscles covering my stomach arc my spine. Then the barrel of my gun lifts; it points directly at the person's chest.

A young man. Not much older than myself.

He has black hair and light-colored eyes, a well-mannered face. When he speaks it's with an accent I have never heard before. "Might want to save your bullets for a proper threat, is my suggestion."

I don't move. All I do is stare at him. Because not once in all the minutes and the hours and the days that I obsessed over the outside world did I expect to find someone else up here. Sure, I hoped against hope to find Jack—but finding others? It didn't even cross my mind. Until now.

"Muji," he says, calling it over his shoulder. His hands are in his pockets and his posture is relaxed. "Muji, there's another one here."

A few seconds later, a girl with almond-shaped eyes and several piercings emerges from the metal half cylinder. "Second in a week," she says as she eyes me up and down.

"Not often they come armed."

The young man nods. "Round up the others, will you? We should make proper introductions."

Round up the others. Second in a week. The words fly through my head on repeat. Because it sounds like this girl, and this boy...it sounds like they *live* up here. Like they call this strange, magical place home. But that can't be true, because Wren and I tried that, and it didn't work. It didn't work at all.

The girl named Muji has disappeared, so I switch my attention back to the boy. He is watching me, studying me almost. The gun I have pointed at his chest doesn't seem to bother him in the slightest. I wish I was so unbothered. Instead I feel much hotter than before, so hot that sweat curls the hairs that frame my face. But it isn't the low-hanging sun doing it. Just my unsteady pulse.

"You don't have to worry," he says eventually. "We're friendly, all of us. We don't even bite." He smiles, and it's just as easy as his unusual way of speaking.

"Who are you?"

"My name's Michael," says the young man. "I'd shake your hand, but..." He nods at the gun I still refuse to lower. "Care if I ask yours?"

"Eve. My name is Eve. Eve Hamilton."

"Nice to meet you, Eve Hamilton," he says levelly.

Behind him, Muji returns with three others. She stares at my weapon. "You still have that thing out? We're not going to bite—did you tell her, Michael?"

"In so many words, I did. She's just overwhelmed, is my guess. Is that so, Eve? I take it you didn't expect to come across a real live person, is that right?"

Slowly, I nod.

"Well," says Muji, "there aren't a ton of us, but welcome

to the club all the same."

"That right there is Anne," Michael says as he points to a plain-looking girl with mousy hair and light skin. She peers at me without smiling. "If you have a question about pretty much anything, she's the one to ask. You're a walking encyclopedia, right Anne? That's AJ, standing behind her—" He points to a heavier-set young man with light brown skin indented with scars. "And that's Rex, our resident brawn." He steps aside so he can point to the last of their group. "Can practically hunt with his bare hands, isn't that so?"

Rex steps forward and smiles. He is tall with dark skin and curly hair cropped close to the scalp. "He's full of it, this guy," he says good-naturedly as he slaps Michael on the back. "But don't let him fool you—he's as quick as they come, eh, Mikey? He's the brains behind our whole operation."

"Don't mind me, asshole," Muji says as she jabs him in the ribs. She turns to me. "Rex, Michael, and I are all from Compound Twelve. Anne and AJ found us from afar. Nine, to be precise, which is about a kajillion miles north of here."

AJ laughs quietly. "The walk sure felt like it," he agrees.

My eyes comb the new faces, then I realize with a jolt that my gun has dropped—it hangs limply by my side. Still my back is rigid, still I am cautious. But these people aren't looking to do me harm, I'm almost certain of it.

"What operation?" I ask hoarsely.

Muji leans forward and tilts her head. She turns to the others. "What'd she say?"

"The operation," Michael repeats slowly. "Oh, right— what Rex said. There is no operation, Eve, not really. The only mission is to grow our numbers and stay alive—pretty simple, that. What about you—what's your story? Can't say I remember your face from Twelve."

"I'm from Eleven."

Immediately they glance at one other.

"What?"

Silence.

"Tell me," I insist.

Michael motions for the others to go. AJ and Anne walk around the far end of the building and Rex disappears inside. But Muji doesn't budge; she just crosses her arms and stares at Michael.

I stare at him, too.

"We have members who keep watch on the lids to most of the compounds within a day of here," he explains. "There's never been any action at Eleven so long as we've been around—so much so that we've mostly given up. Strange, that, seeing as how it's a more sophisticated operation than the rest."

"Sophisticated?"

He shrugs. "The glass pyramid, the whole fleet of solar panels, the outbuilding. More than the others have, I'd say. Is it not so sophisticated down below?"

For a while I just peer at him. My brain feels dull. Like it's full of the tar they use to seal cracks in the compound walls. Instead of answering him, I say, "How long have you been up here?"

"Couple of years, there about. Could be longer—it's hard to keep track of time."

I blink. "You've been living up here for a couple of *years*?"

"More or less."

"So…so it's possible to *survive*? I mean, you've found food and all that?"

"Of course."

"And you have more members than this?"

"Quite a few more. And some of them have been living up here for far longer than I have."

Now I'm silent. Because I am trying to process all he says, trying to synthesize this new information and decipher what it means for my own future. But the buzzing in my ears grows louder, and I can't really think straight.

"Are any of your members named Jack?" I finally blurt out. Then I hold my breath as I wait for his answer.

He shakes his head. "Someone expelled from your compound, I take it?"

"Years ago," I agree, as everything inside me deflates. "How'd you find one another, you and your members?"

"Through Michael's genius," interrupts Muji as she watches him, and I think it's admiration lighting her eyes. "He's got a few tricks up his sleeve. Watching the lids is one of them, probably the most effective one we've got. Sweeping the city every week is another. You may as well get out of the sun," she adds to me, motioning to the half cylinder beside us. "It may not be shooting death rays anymore, but it's still a bitch to spend the day in." Then she pauses, her brow narrowing as her gaze drops to the weapon hanging by my side. "You're going to have to turn that over if you're staying."

"Staying?" It dawns on me very slowly. I can *stay*. I don't have to return to Eleven. I can have fresh air and freedom, just like I've been longing for. *I can survive up here.* Besides, I hate the version of Eve that exists underground. Wren does, too. So, what's the point of going back?

But then I think about Maggie and Emerald. Even Hunter. And my parents. I think about Jules and Avery, and my Blue Circuit friends. I think about everyone else on the lower floors, and then I stare up at the sky; I watch the clouds stream by, unobstructed. I want to stay here more than anything, in Michael's world, but instinctively I know that I won't.

I will choose to be selfless. I will choose to prioritize the citizens of Eleven over myself. And I will do it not just to prove to Wren that I am good, but also to prove it to myself.

Besides, after the way I've behaved lately, I don't deserve a life up here in paradise—not yet. First I must return to Eleven and *earn* it.

"Eve?"

"I'm not staying," I announce.

"You're not?"

I shake my head.

"Care to elaborate?"

I don't, not really—not to strangers. So all I say is, "I have unfinished business in my compound."

Michael's forehead creases as he gazes at me. He steps closer. "You're going *back* to your compound? But how are you going to manage it?"

"The same way I managed my way out."

"You mean you weren't expelled?"

"No. Were you?"

Michael and Muji glance at each other. Muji gives a snort of laughter, but Michael is stern. "All of our members," he begins, "have been exiled from their compounds for one reason or another, including myself. To our deaths, I might add, or so we thought. As I'm sure you've clued in, the world isn't quite so deadly these days." He glances up at the sun and squints.

I glance at it, too. A breeze brushes the loose hair from my shoulders. And once again, I think of Jack. He was expelled, just like the rest of them. If these people found a way to survive, maybe Jack did, too. Maybe he *is* still alive. "None of your members are named Jack," I begin, "but are any of them kids?"

Michael grins. "How old is this kid you're after?"

Jack was three when he was sent aboveground. That was nine years ago. "He'd be about twelve."

"Could be," he says, and my entire body goes numb. "Our youngest member doesn't speak, so I don't know how old he is exactly, but I'd put him around there, maybe a little younger."

My heart stops beating. My mouth goes dry—so dry I can hardly spit out three little words. "Is he here?"

He shakes his head, and for a moment it feels like the disappointment is choking me—I can barely breathe—but then it's replaced by something powerful: hope. Because maybe that child is Jack. And even if it's not, it's proof, isn't it? Proof that Jack could still be out there, alive and well. Waiting for me.

"He's out on a hunt with some of the older members," Michael explains. "He's dead helpful, that kid." Then he gestures to the door. "Can I show you around before you go? Because if you're planning on leaving your compound for good at some point, you might want to think about joining rank. It's easier than going it on your own, or at least I imagine. Bears get pretty hungry at this time of year, and we're safer when we travel in packs. Food is easier to come by when we work together, too."

"I won't be alone," I say quickly. Then, with far more certainty than I feel, I add, "I'll be with the rest of my compound."

Michael grins. "Well, our doors are always open. Speaking of which…" And this time he turns; he walks through the doorway, inside the half-cylinder and out of sight.

Muji looks at me with her eyebrows raised, then follows in Michael's footsteps.

After a deep breath, I walk after them.

Inside, I'm still. My mouth hangs open. Because the outside world hasn't made its way in here, not in the least. Or if it did, it has been expelled again, because under my boots run wide planks instead of dirt. There are no shoots of green, no vines clawing their way in. Light floods the large space through holes cut in the metal, holes that have been sealed off with squares of thick plastic. And it's cooler here than outside, pleasantly so. The whole thing looks habitable, it *feels* habitable. Like underground, but without the low-hanging ceilings and the stained, unending concrete. Like underground, only a million times better.

Most of the space is devoted to cots, some with sheets hanging around them, some without. A series of large cupboards and worktops occupies the far end of the building, and the walls are covered with yellowed paper—charts, maps, and names scrawled across each one.

"Yeah," says Muji, after I've been motionless for several minutes, "Michael's a bit of a marvel."

"*You* did all this?" I turn to him, noticing that the sunlight from outside bathes his shoulders in light, arcing around his face like a halo.

"Not by myself, I didn't. It was a team effort. Everything is." Then he walks by me, deeper inside, gazing around at his handiwork with a hint of pride. "All our materials come from nearby buildings—the wood down here, the plastic up there. Same with our fire pit around back."

I follow after him. "And all the members sleep here?"

"Most of them," he agrees. "Not the ones on watch, obviously, but the rest do. Eventually we'll need to expand into another building, since our numbers keep climbing."

"Because people keep getting expelled from nearby compounds?"

He nods. "Back here is our drinking supply," he says next, leading me around a series of worktops to the far end of the building. He points to an assortment of plastic containers that are full of water. Then he pulls a glass from a nearby cupboard and fills it to the brim. Carefully he pushes it into my hand.

I stare at it. It looks no different than the water I receive underground. It looks nothing like the rust-hued water that Wren and I drank when we were up here.

"It's safe to drink, that," Michael assures me.

"How do you—?"

"Jugs are ones we've uncovered during our weekly roundup of the city. Properly rinsed and cleaned, fear not. Same with the mugs. The water itself is a pain, but as I'm sure you can piece together, kind of essential. First we collect rainwater, Eve, that or bring it in from a stream west of here, then boil it over a fire to kill the bad stuff. Takes ages."

I swallow a lump growing in my throat. "All that just for water?"

He smiles, and I notice how white and even his teeth are, as if he manages to care for them even up here. "Another point in favor of living in groups, not that I'm trying to sway you."

I tilt the glass to my lips and drink deeply. Immediately he refills it, and I'm grateful for his generosity. Until now, I've been too preoccupied to realize how thirsty I am.

Next he takes me to a long series of cupboards, all of them assembled from the same material as the floor. "This over here is where we keep the food." He opens one to reveal sealed pouches stacked from top to bottom. "Know what this stuff is?" He passes a sachet to me and it reminds me of the sustenance packets I received when I was locked in my cell.

"Meal replacements?" I guess.

"Bingo. Designed and made before D-Day." He smiles. "In other words, they could survive a nuclear meltdown. Plus, the city's flush with them."

Silently I return it to the cupboard.

"That's not all we eat," says Muji from over my shoulder. "That'd be sad, right? Nah, we're pretty gourmet, right Mikey?"

He nods, then turns to another cupboard. "This stuff's

all fresh," he says, revealing an assortment of baskets, many brimming with berries. None of them look like the berries that Wren and I ate. "Picked fresh every other day," Michael adds.

My stomach churns with hunger.

He must be watching me closely because he says, "Here, Eve. Have some." Then he lifts the nearest basket from the shelf and offers it to me.

When I hesitate, he insists. So I reach an arm out, one that looks thinner than I remember, and scoop up a handful.

"They aren't poisonous, I promise you," says Michael, grinning, like he can read my mind.

I shove them into my mouth and am immediately overwhelmed by the sweetness and the flavor. So much flavor. Downstairs the food is bland, without texture. What I tongue around my mouth now is completely foreign.

"Better than compound food, that."

I look at Michael and nod my agreement.

"We also send out a team of hunters every day, as I mentioned, which means meat for dinner." He rubs his hands together and grins.

"Where did you learn all this?"

"Lots of different places, in fact. Books back in my old compound, books up here, too. And trial and error, of course. It hasn't been easy, but we've more or less gotten the hang of it."

I say nothing. Maybe my own research would've taught me a few things about how to survive up here, maybe. But I don't think I ever could've learned all this.

"Overwhelming, I know," he adds. A few feet away, Muji and Rex discuss something called firewood, and I'm struck by their posture. So relaxed, so at ease. As if they don't expect violence to creep up on them.

"I pretty much had the exact same look on my face when

Muji and I stumbled up here and realized we'd be sticking around for a while," Michael continues.

"You were exiled together?"

He nods, his eyes on her back as she heads for the door with Rex by her side. "It was my fault. I've always been too curious for my own good. Muji was punished by virtue of our friendship alone. Kind of didn't have a choice but to figure things out up here—it was the least I could do."

Questions bang around my head, too many to count, and I don't know where to start. I don't know how much to say, or how little. So I pick at my thumb. I pretend not to notice the heavy silence that engulfs the metal half cylinder all of a sudden.

"What's Compound Eleven like?" he asks eventually.

"A shithole." It's an easy answer.

For some reason, he finds it amusing, and I watch him laugh—I even laugh myself. "You sure you want to head back, then? I mean, come on, Eve, look around. You're already here."

My gaze sweeps over the half cylinder's clean and cozy interior, at the blue sky that peeks through plastic, at Michael's clear eyes. For a moment, my resolve weakens. For a moment, I truly consider staying.

But I can't do that, I know I can't, even though this world up here, this civilization crafted by Michael—it changes *everything*.

"I need to go back," I say firmly. "I don't have a choice."

He peers at me through the muted sunlight. "You always have a choice." Then he squeezes my shoulder and steps out of my path. "But if you're sure."

CHAPTER TWENTY-SIX

"Have you even been eating?" Maggie asks as she stares down at me. Emerald stands in front of my desk with her arms crossed, watching me carefully. "Because we haven't seen you, like, at all. And until just now, you haven't opened your door when we've knocked, which has been about a kajillion times, by the way." She lifts my arm from the bed and lets it fall. "You look different than normal," she adds. "Kind of frail. I don't like it."

"I've been busy," I explain, only half paying attention. I'm too focused on my discovery. Too focused on Michael and the others. Too elated by my future, and the possibility that Jack may still be alive. "With work," I finally add.

She gives me a look. "Yeah, right. We're all working now. *Obviously* something's wrong. Something's been wrong ever since you were locked in your cell. And now?" She sighs. "Connor said Wren's been really weird lately, too."

Now she has my attention. "Weird? Like how?" I can hear the desperation in my voice. Can she?

"Well, he won't talk about you, for starters. And apparently he's been angrier than he's been in ages. Picking fights, barely leaving his apartment—that kind of thing. Did something happen?"

I cover my face. "He dumped me, okay?"

"*What*? Is he *crazy*? Why would he do that? I can't believe what an—"

"It's not his fault," I interrupt. "He was right to do it."

Emerald moves to the bed and lies down beside me. "Right to dump you, my ass. How do you go and figure that, girl?"

I struggle to find the words, or maybe I just don't want to say them. I finally decide on, "I…haven't been that pleasant lately."

Maggie lies down on my other side. "Punching that girl when we were submitting our applications, that sort of unpleasant?"

"I wish that's all it was." My list of bad behavior is too long to recount. Except for a pertinent one that can't really be ignored. I take a steadying breath, then I say three short words that still don't ring completely true. "I killed Landry."

Silence. Only the sound of people coming and going along the hallway outside my cell door. I stare at a wet patch of cement on the far wall as they digest the news. I even think about Trevor's words: *no amount of guilt can change the past.* I tell myself that again and again and again.

"How?" Maggie asks, eventually.

"We were ordered to fight at the guardship. It's part of training. So, we fought, things got out of hand, and…he didn't get up at the end."

"Yikes."

"Yeah."

"Did you, you know, realize?"

"During? No. Well…maybe." I claw at a hole in my jeans,

then I groan. "All I know is that I lost control. The others were screaming at me to stop and I didn't hear them. It was like…it was like I was consumed by this anger I've never felt before." I pull the hole in my jeans wider.

"Well," Emerald says slowly, "you *do* have a history with him. A pretty brutal one, actually."

"It's no excuse. You *know* it's no excuse. Besides, a few weeks ago I couldn't kill Daniel, even though I wanted to, and I have a history with him, too. Then something changed. *I* changed." I became capable of killing. Capable of *killing*.

Maggie looks at me, then says in a level voice, "Eve, I'm not going to pretend that you haven't been different since you were locked in your cell. And I'm not going to pretend that what happened with Landry is okay. But you're not a bad person. You realize that at least, right?"

"I guess." My voice is limp. It lacks assurance. How could it not?

"The thing that gets me," she continues, "is how Wren can judge you for what happened. I mean, he would've killed Landry weeks ago if you hadn't stopped him. And now he's calling you out for the same thing? Am I missing something?"

The truth is too complicated to explain. Besides, most of it stems from that taste of freedom, and the ensuing failure—it stopped me from seeing straight. And I won't tell my friends about that—not yet. I don't know how long it will take to discover the truth about Eleven, but it won't be quick, and it won't be easy. Finding out what to do with that truth, whatever it may be, will take even longer.

Besides, if the Premes know that the world has cooled, that means it's something they're trying to hide. It means that it's dangerous knowledge to have. And that means I *can't* tell my friends.

"Eve?"

"It doesn't matter," I finally grumble. "He ended things with me, we're over, that's that."

Maggie exhales. "Come *on*. You guys were crazy for each other—anyone could see it. You really think his feelings have changed? *That* quickly?"

"Evidently."

"Screw him," says Emerald. "You need to focus on getting yourself back on track, girl. Focus on *this*." She grabs my arm and shakes the muscle until I'm smiling.

"She's right," agrees Maggie. "Maybe not so much the brawn part, but definitely the rest of it."

I run a finger over my almost-smooth lip. "Yeah, well. That's easier said than done."

"If I were you, I wouldn't be beating myself up over Landry," Emerald adds. She stands and grabs the ball from my desk, tossing it into the air. "Because when I'm fighting in the Bowl I'm in the *zone*, you know? If the ref ever yelled at me to stop mid-fight, I'm not sure I'd hear him, just like you. Besides, we're trained fighters. Sometimes one blow is enough to knock someone's lights out for good."

I nod, but deep down I know that I went too far, further than I would have gone before, in the Bowl or out.

"You need to hang out with your friends more," Maggie says as she nudges me. "Seriously. You need to ease some of this pressure or you're going to burst."

I already have, I think to myself. But I don't argue, I just look at her and nod.

"By the way, it looks like you've got two black eyes forming. You know that, right?"

"Yeah, I do." I don't volunteer the fact that it was Kyle who gave them to me. Just in case she decides to ask, I change the subject. I nudge her back, playfully this time. "Has Connor asked you out yet or what?"

Instead of responding, she turns pink. Emerald grins.

I pull myself upright so I can look at her. "*Did* he?"

She shrugs. "Maybe."

"Maybe. What does *maybe* mean?"

"It means yes, okay? We had our first official date last night. But we totally don't have to see each other again if it's going to make you uncomfortable—"

I hold up a hand to silence her. "Maggie, give me a break. Just because Wren and I are over doesn't mean you and Connor have to be." Then I lie down again and sigh. "Besides, maybe now I'll still see him once in a while…"

She squeezes my arm. "I wish it wasn't like this."

I try to shrug it off, but I can't. Because I wish it wasn't like this, too. And what about when I *do* see him? How different it will be, with Connor and Maggie the ones holding hands and sharing secrets, with Wren and I barely talking…

Enough, Eve.

I turn my attention to Emerald. "What about you? Any exciting romance in the works?"

I expect her to scoff, but she's quiet. She even looks stern. Then she says, "Actually…"

"No *way*!" shouts Maggie.

"Holy *crap*," I blurt out. "Are you serious?"

"Kinda," she says, with another grin. She tosses the ball to me, and I toss it back. "I mean, what do I know, right? But yeah, there's this person, and we've become decent friends…"

"Okay…?"

"And now I'm ready to take it to the next level. I think both of us are. The problem is, we're, um… Well, neither one of us has actually been in a relationship before, so…"

"So?"

She hits Maggie in the arm. "Aren't you supposed to be

good at reading people? So how do I crank it up a notch? *Obviously*."

Maggie bursts out laughing. "I'm sorry," she says between breaths, "but come on, talk about fake problems. Flash that smile and ask the poor guy out already! Right, Eve?"

"I'm not so sure." I roll onto my stomach, and I'm grinning now. "That kind of thing could ruin a friendship, couldn't it? She needs to make sure he's on the same page *before* she makes a move. Maybe it's even safer to wait for him to do it, I don't know."

"No *way*," yells Maggie. "She already said he's ready to take things to the next level, so why bother waiting? Trust me, I waited for Connor to make the first move and it took for*ever*. She doesn't want to do that. Plus, she's obviously an ass-kicker—he wouldn't be into her unless he thought that was—"

"Hey. *Hey*. Can I talk yet?" Emerald drops the ball onto the desk, then sits on its edge. After taking a deep breath, she explains, "It's not a guy."

I stare at her. Maggie does too.

"The guy you're into...isn't a guy?"

She rolls her eyes.

"So, it's a girl," Maggie says slowly. "Even better. Eunjung?"

"Bingo."

"Oh, she's *cute*."

"No kidding. So—thoughts? Advice? Anything?"

"Wait. Why didn't you tell us sooner, Emerald?" I ask.

"What—about...that?"

"Yeah, about *that*. Did you really think we'd care who you're into? We're your friends!"

"I know. It was just...not something I was ready to talk about. Maybe it wasn't something I was sure about. But now I am."

I grin. "Well, that's awesome. I'm really happy for you."

"Me, too," adds Maggie.

She rolls her eyes again, but she can't stop the smile that spreads across her face. "Okay, guys—enough. So, do you have any advice?"

"I do," I say. "Hunter."

The others look at me.

"He has feelings for me. He told me a few days ago."

Maggie and Emerald glance at each other. "Wow," Maggie says eventually. She whistles. "I mean, I started to wonder…"

"Well, I didn't. Which brings me back to your problem," and I turn to Emerald. "Hunter waited and waited to tell me how he felt, and by the time he did, it was too late. Way too late. So, if you like this girl, let her know."

Emerald exhales. "That's good advice. Thanks."

"Okay, wait, wait, wait," begins Maggie. "Back to Hunter…"

"Yeah?"

"If he had spilled the beans sooner—"

I shrug. "Who knows what would've happened."

"But you're single now?"

"Not by choice. Besides, he *turned* me *in*." I sigh heavily. The words still have an effect on me. Maybe they always will. "Enough about that. I want to hear about Eunjung."

Maggie pokes Emerald in the leg. "She better be cool."

"She is cool. She's…awesome."

"What's she like, what's she into—come on, give us the rundown!"

Emerald hesitates, but only for a second, and I can't help but smile as I listen to her. And even though hearing her discuss her love life when my own has been so completely decimated hurts me to my core, it's worth it to see my friend so happy. Maggie, too.

So maybe, just maybe, I'm not such a bad friend after all. Maybe, just maybe, I'm not such a bad person, either.

CHAPTER TWENTY-SEVEN

"**G**et out of here, *bitch*," Daniel hisses, as he throws his things into his locker. "And don't think I'm scared of you, just because you got lucky with Landry."

His eyes have hardened over. They are no longer exposed, or raw. The shock of Landry's death has worn off, and he is himself again.

So be it. I have other things to think about. Finding the truth about Eleven, for one. That and the world waiting for all of us aboveground. A survivable world, thanks to Michael and the civilization he is crafting.

But Daniel keeps needling me, so finally I say, "You might want to watch your language. Because as far as I know, Zaar's still on crutches and with Landry out of the picture, it looks like you'll be strolling the hallways by yourself for a while. And we both know that's an awfully dangerous position to be in."

He snorts. "Think you're going to be walking the hallways with anyone? Because you aren't going to have any friends on the guardship after what you did, not here on the inside and not on the outside, either. Actually, if I were you I'd go crawl into a corner and *die* already."

I shut my locker as calmly as I can. "I have plenty of friends, thanks. And don't forget the pair of you tried to *kill* me, two against one. When Landry and I fought, it was a fair fight, it was a fight to the death, and I happened to win."

Others stand around us listening, but I don't care. Let them hear how terrible Daniel is. Let them realize that even though I wasn't justified in taking Landry's life, I was justified in fighting him with my all.

"Hamilton," says Nkrumah from behind me, "get going on patrol."

I glance over my shoulder in time to see that he casts a long look Daniel's way. I hope they all do. I hope they see him for what he is.

Then his eyes sweep over my face and he squints. "Where'd you get those black eyes?"

"Sparring with friends," I lie.

"You realize all incidents that happen in uniform need to be reported?"

I think of Kyle, I think of goading him into punching me. "Nothing to report," I say firmly.

Nkrumah nods. "Take three and four again, Lower Mean."

It isn't long into patrol when I realize that I walk the hallways with less torment than before. It was wrong, what happened with Landry, I know that. Never did I want to become a killer. But he isn't worthy of many tears—he never was. Besides, all I can do is pledge to do better tomorrow, and I'm ready to take that pledge.

Then I sigh. Perhaps the torment is less, but the heartache isn't.

Wren. It didn't help that I dreamed about him last night. In my dream I told him that I hadn't changed, that it wasn't the truth. Then I was the beast from aboveground, daggers ripping through his flesh before he shot me dead. I haven't been able to stop thinking about him since.

My boots echo against concrete; the sound is rhythmic. Almost melancholy. Maybe bodies swarm around me, maybe I am alone in a deserted corridor. I couldn't possibly tell and it suits me just fine.

Bodies.

Bodies.

What had Wren's father said on his deathbed? *Follow the bodies.* That was it. *That*, of all things.

In the Oracle I had brushed aside the words, but now...

Think, Eve.

The cleanse. Body after body after body. Zipped into bags. Hauled off by guards.

Think.

I close my eyes and send myself backward to that day, to that terrible moment in the atrium on the pristine Preme floor. Wren stands in front of me while disbelief gurgles in my stomach. The elevator doors are opening, the guards are pouring out, their arms are burdened with death. I blink in my mind's eye...

I blink and watch them walk by me, one by one, down the very corridor I know so well. The one I have traveled hundreds of times before, the one that leads to the Oracle's emergency exit.

I open my eyes and stare down a Mean corridor at nothing in particular. Bodies are taken aboveground, everyone knows that—just like that childhood rhyme says.

> *Flies are at the bodies,*
> *They're buzzing at the light,*
> *Follow the dead upstairs,*
> *Throw them out at night.*

Yes, the dead of Eleven are taken aboveground, to be disintegrated and destroyed by the sun. And so that is where the guards were going...

But if their destination was the Oracle—where Katz would unlock the door to the outside world—they wouldn't have used the emergency exit. They wouldn't lug bodies needlessly up a ladder. Not when there's an elevator.

The elevator isn't down the corridor the guards took. And so maybe the Oracle wasn't their destination, after all. Maybe the bodies weren't destined for the outside world.

Follow the bodies.

Now the sound my boots make is far from melancholy. It is driven, focused, full of intent. Several minutes later, I emerge onto the glittering fifth floor and walk the route I know by heart. First the library. Then the corridor where I met Ben, the one with no doors. The next corridor has a row of windows glimpsing into labs, doors into them, too. Fair enough. The corridor after that is the one where I first laid eyes on Addison as she emerged from Sitwell's Department of Security. It isn't likely that dead bodies would be taken there, to a government office, but still I pause. My fingers graze the cool metal as I think of her, and Wren, then I push on.

Three more corridors.

This one has no doors leading off it. The next one is the same.

Only one more.

At the very end stands the door leading to the Oracle's emergency exit, a familiar sight. But there is another door, too. Brushed steel, just like the others, and locked under passcode. Except this one is unaccounted for.

There's no way to know what is on the other side, not without getting through it, so I look over my shoulder, listen for the sound of approaching footsteps. Then I set to work.

Again and again my fingers fly over the keypad, seeking the correct combination—just as I have done with so many other locked doors in Eleven.

Nothing.

Think, Eve.

Guards are given access to passcodes for the compound. All I must do is wait for training to be complete, and then that information will be mine. Easy. Except I don't know if junior members are given that sort of information. And I can't wait another week to find out. I tap my fingers along my chin and keep thinking.

Next I pull the compound maps from a pocket in my artillery vest and find the one for up here. I smooth it open along the floor. I find my exact location and mark it with my finger.

Then I see something strange.

According to the map there is no door here, no room, either. Only the closet at the end of the hall with a trapdoor to the Oracle. For a moment, I'm motionless. These are guard maps. Official ones. It doesn't make sense for them to be incomplete. And more importantly it doesn't get me any closer to discovering what lies behind the mystery door…

But there *is* someone up here who might know. I swallow the lump in my throat and scan the rest of the map for the Department of Inter-Compound Relations. A minute later, I walk in its direction. I smooth my hair as best I can, then shake out my hands.

I can do this. It's important. It is bigger than me, and Wren.

But when I reach my destination I almost turn back. After all, this is the first time we'll see each other since he ended things…

This isn't how it was supposed to go. In my imagination, he spotted me through a crowd as I was laughing with friends. My hair was brushed and I looked well-rested. In my imagination the sight of me ignited longing in him... Then I roll my eyes. My imagination is embarrassing.

Still, though, as I lift my fist and knock on the door a small part of me wishes my face wasn't bruised from Kyle. And I wish I wasn't here to ask a favor of him.

A middle-aged woman with short hair opens the door. I expect her to recoil at the sight of a Lower Mean—this is the Preme floor, after all, where I'm not allowed. But then she smiles and I remember that I'm in uniform. Unrecognizable.

"Is there something the matter?" she finally asks. Genuine concern touches her voice.

"Um, no. I just...need to speak with Wren Edelman. Please."

"May I tell him who's calling?"

"Just say a guard. It doesn't matter who I am."

She disappears, and I lean against the wall, breathing hard. *Time to relax, Eve.* Time to ignore those clammy hands. Time to ignore the worries shooting through my head: *What if he turns around when he sees it's me? What if he's still so disgusted with who I've become that he can't stand to look me in the eye? What if he's with her?*

Just as I think that I need to walk away, he appears effortlessly beside me, and every cell in my body crackles with anticipation. He pauses when he sees who it is, his expression unchanged, then slowly he moves so that he stands in front of me. "Nice uniform." His voice is relaxed, distant. It makes my stomach ache worse than before—I didn't think it was possible to miss someone this badly. "Decent bruises, too."

I can't think of anything to say in return—maybe because of the erratic way my heart races, so I say nothing at all.

"Aren't you supposed to be in training?"

I peer at him, at those hazel eyes that are ever-watching,

then pull myself straighter and shrug. "I'm not allowed to fight the others after what happened with Landry. I've been sent out on patrol instead."

"Ah. Of course. They don't want to be down another member so early in the season."

My face burns at his words.

"I was kidding, Eve," he says. His voice is low, and even though I'm not looking, I can tell that he's grinning.

Why is he so relaxed?

He never loved me, that's why. If he had, this would be harder for him. Hard like it is for me.

"Right," I finally mutter. "Well—"

"Where did you get the black eyes, if you aren't allowed to fight?"

"It doesn't matter," I say quickly. "I came to ask you something," and before he can wonder what it is, before he can wonder if it has anything to do with *us*, I pull the map from my pocket. I point to the room with the Oracle's emergency exit and identify it. "See this hallway? There's a door here, leading off to the left. It isn't marked, for some reason, but I need to know what it is."

"Okay," he says slowly, taking the map and looking over it himself. It's a chance for me to stare openly at him, at his hair that matches his eyes, his straight nose and jawline, that smooth olive skin... I'm torturing myself, I know that. I just can't help it.

"It could be a new room," he says a minute later. "These maps were printed a decade ago, so that would explain why it's not on here. But off the top of my head, I have no idea what it's for. Let me ask around."

"I don't think that's a good idea."

"Why?"

I frown. "I don't know."

"What's all this about, anyway? I take it this isn't a social call."

"It isn't a social call," I agree. "But I think it's important. Or at least it could be. Right now it's nothing more than a hunch."

"A hunch you'll eventually share with me?"

At his words, my insides expand and contract. My heart beats even faster. "Yes."

"I'll look into it myself, then."

I wipe at invisible flecks of dust on my sleeve and nod. "Thanks," I mutter without looking at him.

Once again I think he is smiling. "I'll stop by later with what I find."

CHAPTER TWENTY-EIGHT

I ate dinner with the others tonight, a proper meal, my first in ages. Mostly we discussed Emerald's plan to ask Eunjung out and Maggie's pending date with Connor—a walk on the fourth floor. No detail went unaccounted for: not hair, not outfits, not conversation starters. It was easy and frivolous. Fun.

Now I lie on my bed and think over my first full week of training at the guardship. I laugh a little. Because it's hard to imagine it going any worse than it did.

At least the data card on my arm no longer stings. And hopefully by next week the other hires will no longer hate me. They seemed better at the end of today's session. When I stashed my uniform in my locker, they didn't withdraw from me, they didn't look at me with fear. I know better than to be hopeful, but I still am, sort of. Because I may not be looking to make friends, but I'm not looking for more enemies, either.

Finally there's a knock at my door and I stand, glancing in the mirror as I do. My hair is pulled to the side in a casual braid and I wear a plain shirt and jeans. Nothing fancy, though at least both items are freshly laundered. I don't know why I feel so nervous. *It's Wren*, I remind myself. Except when I pull open the door, I see that it's not.

Hunter stands there with his hands in his pockets. I must look at him funny, because he asks, "Is everything okay?"

"Huh? Oh. Yeah—I thought you were somebody else, that's all."

"I won't be long."

Most of the lightbulbs along our corridor have burned out, and the fluorescent light across from my cell casts Hunter in a sickly shade of green. "Do you want to come in?"

"That's okay," he replies. "Listen, Hugh got in touch with me today. One of the kitchen hires didn't work out and…well, they've changed their mind about my job application. I've been hired after all."

I clear my throat, surprised. "Good for you," I finally manage to say.

"Somehow I think you had something to do with it, and I just wanted to say thanks. So, here I am. Thanks, Eve."

There's no sense in denying it. But I don't want to acknowledge it, either. I don't know why I bothered to do what I did, or what the joy currently cutting through my chest means.

"Say hi to Maggie and Emerald for me, will you?" he adds.

"Oh."

"Sorry?"

"Nothing—"

"I'm expecting someone, too," he explains.

I nod, feeling embarrassed. "Who?"

"Just a girl I've been seeing. Vanessa Rae—a year down from us. Remember her?"

I do. Long blond hair, lighter than mine. Smart. Pretty, too. I don't know how I feel about *that*, either.

"Are you expecting Wren?"

Another nod.

"I heard you guys broke up."

"We did. We're...still friends."

In a voice that's perfectly calm, and even a bit disinterested, he says, "That's nice."

That's nice. Generic platitudes, forced politeness—and between two people who have known each other their entire lives. Who have always been as close as two people can be. How did we fall so far? And how do I stop myself from missing it day in and day out?

Then Wren is there, appearing from the shadows, eyeing Hunter with obvious suspicion. I guess he hasn't forgiven him for betraying me, either.

Hunter doesn't bother to acknowledge him. "Thanks again, Eve. For the kitchen," he says, then he goes to his door. "Have a nice visit with your friend," he adds, before he disappears inside.

A second later, I hold my door open for Wren, noting that his attitude has shifted since earlier. No longer is he relaxed. His features are stern. Faintly I notice that we both wear gray T-shirts—his mounds over muscle, mine hangs loosely over a neglected frame.

"Rekindling your friendship with that rat, I see?" His tone is casual, but a little too forced to be convincing.

"Not so much," I admit.

"What was he talking about there, with the kitchen?"

"It doesn't matter."

"I know it doesn't matter," he says as he eyes me. "That's not why I asked."

"He didn't get the kitchen job he wanted because of something I said to the staff. The lemon squares, remember? I felt bad about it, so I set things straight."

He peruses the books on my desk. Then he says, "He's happy to hear we're no longer a couple, I gather?" He doesn't look at me, just keeps flipping through the books.

I shrug. "He doesn't care. Besides, it sounds like he's seeing someone else."

Wren's hands go still for a moment. "Too bad."

Now that I'm no longer distracted by Hunter, the fact that my ex-boyfriend and I are alone together sinks in. It's strange—we've kissed each other and held each other and we have told each other secrets. But now that we are no longer dating, now that we have been stripped of that official title, it feels…different.

I sit tentatively on the bed. "Did you find out what's in that room?"

"Why did you want to know?"

"Did you find something?"

"Answer the question, Eve."

My back straightens. "Answer mine first, Wren."

He shakes his head and scoffs. "Defiant and stubborn as always, I see." But his voice is lighter than it was a moment earlier, and half his mouth curves into a smile. It makes me wonder why he was so agitated in the first place.

"Well?"

He tosses down the stack of books and considers me. "I looked it up. What I found was highly unusual."

"Meaning?"

"Meaning whatever's behind the door is classified. I have a high security clearance and I couldn't access that information. There's no other room in the entire compound that's classified."

I exhale. A dead end, sort of. Still I don't know what lurks behind that door, but I *do* know it's something worth hiding.

"Your turn."

I twist my braid, thinking. "Okay… But first, answer this.

When people die down here, what happens to their bodies?"

If Wren is confused by my question, he recovers quickly. "Tossed aboveground," he says. An easy answer.

I nod.

"So?"

"So, I was thinking about what you told me. About your father's last words. Then I thought of the cleanse. Of the guards carrying the dead Noms away. Do you remember?"

He frowns. "Vaguely. I remember we were fighting," he begins, and I can see by the way his gaze looks inward that he relives those minutes just as I did. Slowly he nods. "They turned at the library. In the direction of the Oracle."

"Not the Oracle," I correct him. "The Oracle's *emergency exit*. But if they were planning on taking the bodies outside, don't you think they'd use the elevator?"

"So if the guards weren't taking them aboveground, where were they taking them?"

"That's what I'm trying to figure out."

"And the classified room is the only room unaccounted for in that direction."

"As far as I can tell. It's possible they turned in a different direction at the end of the first corridor, but I don't think so." I look at Wren and shrug. "Maybe it's nothing. Maybe the classified room is a holding room, a place to prep the bodies before they dump them." I flinch at my words, and he notices, I know he does, but he says nothing about it. "Would Sitwell's office have the passcode?"

"I'm sure it would be in there somewhere," he says slowly. "But I doubt it's something Addison can access, if that's what you were thinking."

"We could break in."

He laughs. "Still as fearless as always, too," he notes.

I take care to hide my smile, then give him a fierce look.

"I'm made of steel, remember?"

"I'll never forget, Eve. But I'm not sure breaking into the Department of Security to steal the passcode is the smartest option right now."

"Why is that?"

"Because as a guard you might be able to access the code yourself once training is through. If we're caught breaking in, you'll be stripped of the opportunity. I'd be thrown from my position, too."

"Wouldn't want that," I say, as I nudge him.

He smirks. "While we're on the subject, are you interested in how the other compounds around here are faring?"

I sit straighter. Of course I am.

"Compound Eleven is one of hundreds in our region," he continues. "That's northern North America, in case you didn't know. Of that, about sixty percent of compounds have failed. All attempts to communicate with them have been unsuccessful. Their entire populations have been declared dead."

"*Sixty* percent?"

He nods. "The majority."

Sixty percent dead. It's hard to wrap my brain around. That and the fact that Compound Eleven might actually be considered a *success*.

"Do they know why?"

Wren shakes his head. "They suspect in-fighting or disease. Probably some combination of both."

"Any mention of up there?" I ask next.

"Not a thing, although some communication files have been emptied. I can see that something was sent or received, but that's it. So, it's possible…"

He doesn't bother to finish his sentence. I don't need him to. It's possible that Compound Eleven has deleted any reference to the world being habitable again. It's also possible there were never any references to begin with. Another dead end.

"So," Wren says. "The mystery room."

"The mystery room. You think I should sit tight, wait a week, and hope the passcode is handed over."

"I think that's the most rational option."

I am forced to agree.

"Think you can wait that long?" he asks.

I run a finger over my lip and find the scabs have completely healed—my lip is smooth. Then I consider Wren's question and decide that I can be patient, of course I can. Except I hear a voice say, "Not likely," and it sounds remarkably like my own.

I'm sure he suppresses a grin as he checks his watch—it's the way his lips press together. "Compound lights are officially off," he says a moment later. "I guess it wouldn't hurt to try to guess the passcode ourselves—it probably follows the same pattern as other passcodes up there."

Wordlessly I draw on my boots, fill them as I always do with knife and flashlight. Lastly I tuck the gun from the guardship into the waistband of my jeans.

When I glance at Wren, I see he is watching me carefully. "What?"

He shrugs and says nothing.

I draw in a shaky breath. "No time like the present, Preme." Then with as much conviction as possible, I walk out my cell door.

• • •

As always, the Preme floor seems darker than the rest of the compound. I used to be afraid of the dark, terrified even, but in the past few months I've been through so much that it doesn't seem to bother me anymore.

"I heard another guard was killed downstairs," Wren says, once we near our destination.

I switch on my flashlight before I reply. "Yeah? Think it was me again?"

"What I think is that you need to be careful," he says smoothly. "You're a walking target with your uniform on."

"I've been a walking target my entire life," I reply, amused. "I think I'll be fine." Then we stare at the door to the room that has monopolized our thoughts for the past several hours. "Don't forget passcodes always start with the compound number, then three zeroes, followed by the floor number," I remind him. "The rest is up to us. Oh, and by the way, I tried the first fifty combinations earlier."

"Of course you did."

"I'll take the next fifty, then we can switch."

He agrees, and I turn to the door. Nothing can distract me right now from getting through. Except as he runs a hand over its smooth metal, I can't help but stare at it. His knuckles are raw—he has been at the punching bag again, but otherwise the skin is smooth and opaque. Veins bulge.

"You should go keep watch," I blurt out. "It's safer that way."

He glances in the direction I indicate, then after eyeing me for a minute more, he moves down the corridor, where he is less of a distraction.

Focus, Eve. My mission right now is simple: to crack the passcode. And I have no training in the morning, no plans—no reason whatsoever to be in bed at a reasonable hour. So I resolve to be patient and begin. Before every handful of entries I am hopeful, after every handful I am disappointed. And after fifty attempts I stop altogether and pinch my wrist between thumb and forefinger, rubbing out a dull ache.

Wren joins me, taking the flashlight from my hand and turning to the keypad. He is slower than me, but not for long. I watch the muscles in his forearm engage as his fingers work. I stare at the profile of his face. I try not to relive each and every kiss that we've shared, but it's almost impossible.

"Eve," he says levelly without taking his eyes off the keypad.

"Huh?"

Now his fingers pause and his hazel eyes shift to mine. "Aren't you going to take watch?"

"Oh. Right." I move to the spot at the end of the hall. My eyes peer carefully through the darkness.

After a while, Wren calls my name. "Let's switch. I'm at 110005175."

"I thought you were doing only fifty."

"It's called chivalry."

He grins under the glow of the flashlight and I make a show of rolling my eyes, hiding my smile as I do.

Four tries later, the door clicks open unexpectedly under my hand.

"Success," Wren breathes, then he glances at me. He claps me on the shoulder. "Good to have you back, Eve."

I am lucky it's dark, and for extra measure, I point the flashlight at the floor. That way he can't see how deeply I blush, or how hard I must work to keep myself from grinning.

CHAPTER TWENTY-NINE

If I was expecting to see something out of the ordinary, something that would make my jaw drop, I am sorely disappointed. It's nothing more than a small and empty space. Why it's classified, I do not know.

But with the aid of the flashlight I see that it isn't completely sparse; a pile of empty body bags sits in the corner next to several brooms — an indication that the guards really did bring the victims of the cleanse here. And on the far side there's another door, one that stands ajar, one that is protected by a simple locking mechanism instead of by passcode. We step forward, glancing at each other, then I run a hand over its tarnished metal surface. At the same time I notice that the wall surrounding it is made of the same material.

Something crawls up the lining of my stomach, something worse than unease. Something that makes me feel distinctly unwell.

Wren grips the door handle and pulls it open. Thick and wide, and obviously heavy. Together we stare into the second room, this one a rectangle, smaller than the first. All four walls are metal and as we step inside I see that it isn't just the walls—it's the ceiling and floor, too.

A metal box.

No décor, no furnishings, nothing. But when I keep my flashlight steady I notice that the walls are far from bare. Scorch marks fan across them, singeing the metal and staining it black.

Wren and I turn to each other. "This is where they brought the bodies," I say, and my voice is hollow.

He draws in a breath. "They burned them in here instead of letting the sun do it." His eyes look like empty pits under the glare of the flashlight. "They knew the sun was no longer doing the job. They *know*, Eve."

"Yeah. They do." My face feels hot, but it's nothing compared to the feeling inside my chest.

Those in charge of our compound are holding each and every citizen a prisoner, just like Wren thought. They are assassinating Noms to control a population that doesn't need to be controlled. They are forcing their will and their way because they *choose* to, not because they *have* to.

How long have I been forced to endure compound life at their hands?

Wren runs his fingers through his hair and leans against one of the walls. "All these years I've wondered what my father meant. I thought he was too sick, too far gone to know what he was saying. It never occurred to me…" His eyes snap to mine. "You're brilliant, you know that?"

I let out a breath. "Hardly." I think I'm too disgusted by what we've discovered to feel flattery, but that can't be true, because something warm flickers through my chest, something apart from the raw and dangerous ball of fury that sits cradled inside.

"He died eight years ago. He told me to follow the bodies

eight years ago."

"Which means they've known for eight years," I say slowly.

Wren nods. "At least."

It takes a while for the words to sink through my skin, to *matter*. Eight years. Half my life. Half my life I have been forced to live in this hellhole for no good reason. A hellhole so abhorrent, I was prepared to die to bid it farewell.

Wren moves so that he stands directly in front of me. "We're going to make this right," he says.

"We're going to make this right," I agree.

"We're going to free everyone. There will never be another cleanse down there."

I stand straighter at his words. Thoughts of Avery, Monica, and Jules flash through my brain. "Those who have held us prisoner should be punished."

"They will be," he says with certainty.

"What if your mother is one of them?"

"Then she'll pay, just like the others. I'll see to it myself that she does." His eyes are alive; they are as blinding as they've ever been.

Partly I don't want to look away, but I don't want to stay in this room any longer than I need to, either. In this room where bodies that we knew and loved were *torched*. So I turn away and make to step out the door. That's when I see it.

That's when I go still, so still that it attracts Wren's attention.

"You've got to be kidding me," he mutters when he sees it, too. He takes the flashlight from my hands and steps forward— his fingers lift and drag across the unnatural sight.

The terrible one.

Scratches, across the inside of the metal door. Scratches from fingernails, from people trying in vain to get out.

Wren laughs, short and dark. "Those sentenced to death

are no longer sent aboveground. They're thrown in here."

I nod. Compound Eleven doesn't use this room to simply destroy the deceased. It uses it to *kill*.

Something clicks inside my mind. Something that Michael had said, that day aboveground. In the two years they have been watching, *nobody emerged from Eleven*. I shake my head. I should have suspected it earlier, just as I should've trusted Wren's gut instinct all along. Thank goodness I decided to return to Eleven. Thank goodness I have found out the truth—no matter how terrible that truth may be.

And so what about Jack? Did he ever make it out of here? Did he make it out there, where at least he had a chance to survive? He was taken from my mother's arms nine years ago, so just as it's possible that the world aboveground wasn't fatally hot then, it's possible this death chamber hadn't been constructed yet, either. Of course, it's possible that it was.

Then I'm distracted from my thoughts and my worries and my sorrow by a noise from the other side of the door we broke through ten minutes earlier. I glance at Wren, but he's still consumed with the scratch marks—he didn't hear.

So I move past him, out of the metal box, past the body bags and brooms, right to the door itself. But as I stand there listening to silence, it occurs to me that the goose bumps covering my arms have more to do with the death chamber than the noise. Same with my fluttering heart. Probably I heard nothing more than my mind reeling.

Just to be sure, I pull the gun from my jeans. One can never be too careful in Compound Eleven, and I almost laugh at the thought. Because all along I assumed my fellow civilians presented the biggest threat of a most violent death. That or the guards. It turns out it's the well-dressed Premes in charge.

There's no need to wait for Wren, or even for my flashlight. There is no need to fear opening the door. I reach a hand through the darkness and twist the knob.

Half a second later, there's a blast. Before my brain can process that it comes from a gun, white hot pain engulfs my arm. A scream escapes my lips, but it's cut off at once by the sound of another gunshot.

CHAPTER THIRTY

That is my finger that squeezes the trigger. Those are my muscles that lock my arm in place, preventing the gun from jumping. That second blast came from me.

It's a dull realization, just like the realization that the fabric of my shirt is slippery wet. Then Wren is in front of me and I can see in his face that something is wrong.

"We have to go, *now*." His voice sounds like taut wire. It sounds electrified.

Being in no position to argue, I hold my throbbing arm close to my body and force my boots forward. Through the door and under the glow of the flashlight, I see the problem.

A man.

A man lying in a crumpled heap on the floor, blood leaking from a wound administered by my weapon. By me.

By me.

Wren's voice reaches me through a haze. "We don't have time, Eve." Then he is forcing me forward and, though I try to resist, though I'm desperate to search the crumpled man for signs of life, to *help* him, Wren is far too strong.

"Wait—"

"Not now."

"But—"

"No, Eve! We need to go!" He pushes me roughly, through a maze of doorways so that we disappear into the night. Whenever I try to protest, he whispers at me to be quiet. On and on, until finally we stop in front of a door that I know well—the one to his apartment.

He turns on a light once we're inside, and under its muted glow he spots the blood staining my sleeve. He swears under his breath. I shake my head, brushing aside his concern, because all I see when I blink are the crumpled limbs I left lying on the floor, and *that's* what I want to discuss. "If someone were to help him," I begin, tripping over my words, "they could slow the bleeding and—"

"They'll have found him by now," he mutters. "Gunshots always attract guards." Then his fingers curl around the collar of my shirt and he rips it apart, pulling the fabric carefully from the wound. I stand there in an undershirt, trying to process it all.

The incinerator. The fact that I was shot. The fact that *I* shot someone. There is so much to process that I can think of nothing at all. Then I'm being led forward, and a moment later I stare at my reflection in the bathroom mirror. I frown at a face as white as paper.

Wren pulls a bottle from the cupboard and pours the contents over a washcloth. It smells strongly, and when he holds it to my wound, I wince.

"Sorry," he says, as his gaze tracks back and forth over my data card.

"It's fine," I say, even though it's not. Normally white-hot pain doesn't touch me. Right now, though, I have to clutch the countertop so I don't fall. This from me, a ruthless fighter.

One who doesn't shy away from pain. One who *enjoys* it.

It must be because I'm so distracted by the past hour. It distracts me from myself. So I breathe deeply and focus only on the present. It's nothing—just a sensation. One I can package up and set aside, just like when lemon juice stings my knuckles.

When Wren says, "All done," I've already gotten ahold of myself. I watch as he ties cloth around my arm, just above where it throbs. "You're lucky," he says in a tight voice. "The bullet only grazed you. So long as the bleeding stops, you'll live—no medical attention necessary."

I nod. "Thanks."

"When did you get the tattoo?"

"At the beginning of training."

"Standard procedure?"

"Unless you're a Preme."

"Quite a history of defiance."

"Quite a history of grief, too."

"Yes," he admits, as he gazes at me. "But that grief—that heartache—it makes you who you are today. Someone *with* heart. Someone strong. Someone determined to survive."

I'm not sure I'm any of those things, and it wasn't very long ago that Wren didn't think so, either. But…I want to be those things. I want to have heart, and be strong, and be a survivor. So maybe when I glance down at my data card from now on, it won't fill me with sorrow. Maybe it will fill me with determination.

"I'm going to get you something for the pain," he says next, as he helps me lie down on the bed. "Are you okay?"

I'm not okay, not really. Because what if tonight I killed a person? *Again.*

"Eve?"

"I'm fine."

I must not be convincing, because he says, "It was an accident." Then he pauses, and he gives me a strange look. "And besides, he shot you first."

Sometime later he slips a pill between my teeth, then gingerly unties the cloth around my arm. "The bleeding has slowed. You should try to get some sleep," he adds.

I glance around, unsure.

"Do you really feel up to going to your cell?" he continues, reading my mind. "Besides, the corridors are probably swarming with guards right now."

"Okay. I mean, yeah—thanks. What are you going to do?"

"Any guesses?"

"No."

He knocks me across the foot. "It's late, Eve. I'm going to try to get some sleep, too." Then he climbs into bed next to me, and just like it always has, his closeness steadies me. I didn't think sleep was possible a moment ago, not with my brain buzzing with so much activity, not with my arm throbbing with so much pain. But just for now I let my eyelids grow heavy. Just for now I tell myself that soon we will liberate Compound Eleven, that my arm will be healed in the morning, that the man in the heap will make a full recovery.

I wake to throbbing pain. I'm cold, unreasonably so, and there's a shaking in my bones. When I glance over my shoulder, I see that the bed is empty—Wren has gone. But I can hear his voice from the main room, and I hear, too, that he isn't alone.

With my good arm, I push myself upright and focus on the sound of his smooth voice. "I didn't hear a commotion last night," he is saying. His tone seems relaxed, but I know him well enough to know it's forced. "What happened?"

The sound of high heels echoes across the apartment. "One of my colleagues was shot, point-blank," comes an icy voice. It's his mother, and the realization makes me nervous. If she discovers me tucked inside his bedroom, my tenure as a guard will be over, even though our night was anything but romantic. We are no longer hiding our relationship, because there's nothing left to hide, and the thought makes me hurt worse than the bullet hole carved into the side of my arm.

"Who was it?" comes Wren's voice.

"Teddy, the poor man. Absolutely the last person who would deserve such a thing." She clicks her tongue loudly. "Jeffrey is devastated, as you can imagine. The two of them were like brothers."

Silence, and when Wren speaks, his voice is low. "Will he survive?"

"Already dead," says his mother crisply.

Already dead.

"Is that a fact," Wren says slowly.

"You hardly seem surprised," she snaps, "and it isn't every day that a man of his stature is murdered. Tell me you do know that, at least."

"Of course I know that." There's an edge to his voice that he can't hide now. "Where did it happen? Up here?"

"Do you really need to ask? Teddy would never venture downstairs, only a fool would do that." She says it pointedly, I can hear it, and I know she's referring to me. "His body was found only a few corridors past the Department of Security, which means the whole ordeal will be very distressing for

Addison. Check in with her often, won't you? You know how quick she is to upset."

"Near the Oracle's emergency exit?"

"Yes, there."

"That's an odd place for him to be in the middle of the night."

"Perhaps an alarm sounded, I really don't know," she says dismissively.

"An alarm," Wren repeats. "Is there anything of interest back there?"

"Both the Security Department and the emergency exit to the Oracle, as I said. Do you even pay attention?" she asks coldly.

"I meant anything *else*, Mother."

"No."

"There's another door nearby," Wren presses. He's as bold as I am. "One that's locked under passcode."

"That's nothing but a storage room for files," she explains. Then her tone changes. "And since when do you have so many questions?"

"Since when do you come bearing interesting news instead of your usual pedantic nagging?"

"Don't start with me, Wren."

"My deepest apologies," he says dryly. "Anything else?"

"As a matter of fact, yes. They say the bullet came from a guard's gun."

At these words, I sit straighter. Something other than guilt, jealousy, or excitement courses through me. This is dread. A smothering fear. Because they will discover it was me, and I will be sent to die in that death chamber, I will be burned alive.

"Really—a guard?" Wren asks, and his voice is more level than mine would be. "Seems unlikely. Maybe the gun was lifted by someone on the lower floors."

"Perhaps it was. You like to run around with that crowd, so you would know better than I."

"Don't be ridiculous," he snaps, his self-restraint wavering in the blink of an eye.

"Don't be a fool," she counters. "You had a good thing with Addison — you'd better hope you haven't jeopardized it with your dalliance with that...creature."

"I thought you came here to tell me about Ted, not lecture me on girls."

Heels echo once again through the apartment, and this time she's headed for the door. "Well, I am your mother, after all," she calls.

"That's one way of putting it."

"What is that supposed to mean?"

"Nothing. Enjoy your day, *Mother*."

The door slams shut, and there's nothing but stillness. Probably Wren is digesting the news that she brought. That the man is dead, and they know it was a guard.

I am in deep, deep trouble.

If I stay here, in Eleven, I'm risking everything. But if I go, I won't be able to help liberate a compound that desperately needs liberating. It is something that will be difficult to do from the inside; it's something that will be impossible from the outside. So which should I prioritize? My own life? Or the lives of thousands upon thousands of innocent people?

Wren walks into the room. "The bleeding has stopped," he says as he studies my arm. "That's reassuring."

I nod.

Then, as I lift a hand to dry eyes that are suddenly wet, he adds, "You're shaking." Concern touches his voice.

"It must be from the blood loss," I lie.

"You're...crying."

I force a laugh between my teeth. "Surprised? Hard to imagine someone with two confirmed kills shedding any tears."

He draws back and peers at me. "I take it you overheard the conversation with my mother."

"Yes."

"We have much bigger problems—"

"I don't care that they know it was a guard," I say quickly, even though it isn't completely true. I rest my forehead on the palm of my hand and tell him what's really on my mind: "I killed him. I shot and *killed* him—"

"It wasn't your fault."

"It was my gun, it was *me* who pulled the trigger. Of course it was my fault."

"He shot you first!"

"I don't care!"

"Ted headed the Department of Health and Population Control." He says it bluntly, like it's all I need to know to feel better.

I just squeeze shut my eyes. "I'm sure he was an important man."

"He was important, yeah. He was also in charge of controlling Compound Eleven's population."

"Yeah, I get it."

"Think about it, Eve."

But I'm shaking my head. "I don't want to think about anything—"

"Eve. He's the one who ordered the cleanse."

At these words, I pull myself up and stare right at him.

"The order came from him," he reiterates. His gaze is steady. "Now, can we focus on what matters?"

I can't, because *this* matters. He ordered the cleanse. *He ordered the cleanse.* Maybe he was just doing his job, or doing Katz's bidding, maybe. But when that job involves slaughtering thousands of innocents, it isn't a job worthy of defending.

"What's his name again?"

"Ted. Ted Bergess."

Now I am smiling through my tears. It's a name I have known my whole life. How didn't I see it sooner? He didn't *just* order the cleanse. He gave the order to have Jack removed, to leave an innocent little boy for dead. I shouldn't be crying; I should be *celebrating*.

Wren, meanwhile, rubs his forehead. "My mother knows about the incinerator," he says eventually. "I know she does. Did you hear what she said when I asked about the room?"

I nod.

"A lie. And if she knows about the incinerator, she knows about aboveground. I wonder if she realized that Dad knew, too." He shakes his head. "Just when I think I have her figured out," he mutters to himself. Then he fixes me with a stare. "They know it was a guard who killed Bergess."

"Plenty of guards out there."

"Maybe."

"And there's the possibility that the gun was lifted, just like you mentioned."

Suddenly he looks stern. He crouches in front of me and touches his hand gingerly to my cheek. It's completely unexpected, this touch, and it makes me feel awake. Very awake. "If I give the word, Eve, promise me something."

I watch, waiting. I don't think I even breathe.

"Promise me you'll listen. If I say go aboveground, I mean it. No time for goodbyes, no time to grab a change of clothes. Just go—I'll bring you food and water—"

Suddenly I realize something. He doesn't know that I've found a way to survive up there, without depending on Eleven's resources. "But—"

"Just listen," he interrupts, and his voice is filled with urgency.

"Yes?"

"If I show up unexpectedly and tell you to go, you go."

Because I am feeling brave, I tilt my head so that my face presses against his fingers. I let my eyes close, and for a moment everything feels okay. Everything feels right. Then his hand falls away and I busy myself examining my wound—a porridge bowl of congealed blood. "I promise," I say. "Do you think you'll hear things?"

He swipes his thumb across his chin. It's covered in a dusting of stubble that makes him look older. "I'll go out of my way to make sure I do. There's kind of a lot on the line."

"Just my life," I say softly.

"Mmm, no biggie, right?"

I smile. Then I say, "I have something to tell you."

"Oh?"

"It's about up there. I went up recently, and I found a city. An abandoned one, or so I thought."

Wren goes still. "Or so you thought?"

I tell him about Michael, about the burgeoning civilization aboveground, and watch as he absorbs the information.

"Wow," he says eventually. "I can't...I can't believe you're down here right now."

"What do you mean?"

"I mean I can't believe you have a way to survive up there, yet you're choosing to be *here*."

I grin. "I have unfinished business," I tell him.

He gazes at me, his mouth twisting into a smile of his own. Finally he taps my knee with his knuckles, then disappears into the bathroom. He reemerges a second later holding a thick padding of gauze. "I'm going to wrap your arm. Take the rest with you—it'll need to be changed daily."

Silently I hold out my arm and watch him work. Always so careful, so meticulous, yet quick. Everything he says and does glows with efficiency, even the way he moves. Nothing is ever labored, or doubted, or stumbled over.

"Does it hurt?" he asks, as he fastens the gauze in place.

"A bit."

"You need food."

"I'll go."

"I didn't mean it—that way. I mean, if you want to stay, or go…it doesn't matter."

I look curiously at Wren and see that his face looks different than usual. Uncomfortable. Flushed, even. Before I can study it any closer, he pushes a white long-sleeved shirt into my hands.

"You need to keep that hidden," he says, gesturing to my arm. "It will be a tell if the authorities notice it. They'll realize soon enough that Bergess fired his gun, too."

I take up the shirt in one hand, happy to have something warmer to wear than the undershirt that saw me through the night, then position it clumsily over my head. He helps me pull it on, and I inhale deeply. "It smells like you."

For a second we stare at each other. Then I stand. "I'm going to go."

His brow is pulled tight and I almost think he won't move out of my path. But then he stands aside, and he sighs, and he watches me wordlessly as I walk out the door.

CHAPTER THIRTY-ONE

My fist lifts, it strikes the door three times. I wear a white sweatshirt, my own, one that is loose enough that the bandage around my arm is hidden. It feels better today, and as I changed the gauze this morning I thought it looked better, too.

My father swings open the door. "I figured you had forgotten about us," he says curtly, and I know he's unhappy that I haven't stopped by sooner.

"I've been busy."

He stares at me and nods. "What's it like to work for the guardship?"

"Still in training."

"For how much longer?"

"A week."

He shuts the door behind me, calmly this time. My mother sits in her usual seat with her embroidery on her lap, and my insides squeeze. By now I should be used to it. Funny that I'm not.

"Surely you wouldn't need much training after your time

in the Bowl," my father is saying.

"I don't." Then I think of telling him about Landry. Maybe he would be impressed. Maybe he would be disgusted. I'm not sure which reaction would hurt more. "I came here to talk to Mom," I add. "Like you asked."

"And on your own schedule, too."

I can't stop the sigh that escapes my lips. "Yes, Dad. On my own schedule. Like I said, I've been busy."

He gives me a look, then goes back to the dog-eared book he was reading.

I turn to my mother, expecting it will take some coaxing to pry the embroidery work from her fingers, to snap her from her daze.

But instead she stares at me, her gaze cool and lucid and perfectly level. "I hear you've become a guard," she says from her seat along the wall.

"No choice." I say it quickly, and even I can hear how defensive I sound.

"There's always a choice, Eve."

"Not this time. I have enemies, dangerous ones."

Her eyebrows lift. "Ones you deserve?"

I stare at a spot on the wall above her head. A baby with round cheeks smiles at me, and I want to tell my mother no, that I don't deserve such enemies. But then I think of Landry, and Bergess, and all the people I have beaten and punched over the years. I think of breaking Zaar's knee, and knifing Daniel across the face. I think of all that and say, "Maybe I do."

"Was it you who shot one of the leaders?"

I blink away stars that suddenly dot my vision. "Pardon?"

"They say a guard shot and killed one of the compound leaders."

I take a step back. "Why would you think it was me?"

She merely shrugs. "It was just a question, Eve."

So I shake my head back and forth, more forcefully than I need to. "It wasn't me," I lie—a kneejerk reaction. Because nobody can know the truth, not when it's so damning. Or perhaps I just don't want to admit to my mother that I am flawed. That I make mistakes, sometimes deadly ones.

"Oh." She shifts in her seat and for a fleeting moment I think that maybe, just maybe, she is disappointed.

But that can't be.

Perhaps if it's disappointment I sense, it stems from a different reason entirely. Perhaps she's disappointed because she knows I am lying.

"He was the leader of Population Control," I say loudly.

She looks steadily at me. "I know."

I turn to the picture on the wall and feel a surge of contentedness. I bet she feels it, too.

"Eve."

"Huh?"

"Is there something else you wished to discuss?"

Instead of responding, I pull a gun from my jeans. "I took this off a guard a while ago," I explain. "I have my own now, and I think you should take this one. The guards are finished doing sweeps, so you can hide it in here, just in case."

"Just in case what?"

For a while I'm silent. There is no explanation—certainly not a reasonable one. So eventually I say, "There are changes underfoot," and leave it at that.

"And when change comes calling, you think a gun might be helpful?"

"I do."

Her gaze doesn't waver from mine, not even for a second. "Best give me an idea of how to shoot it," she says.

So I make her stand in position, show her how to grip the heavy weapon, explain how to fire it. I tell her what Wren told me, about holding it steady, about its tendency to kick. She listens carefully, even as my father exhales irritably from the corner, and when I'm finished she wraps the gun in a sheet covered with tiny red flowers, her own work, and places it under the bed as far back as it will go.

When she stands, she stands slowly, so slowly that I worry. But when she raises her head, I see that her eyes are piercing. She is possessed by something powerful. She *possesses* something powerful. "If you go," she whispers, "let me go with you. Promise me."

So I look her in the eye, and I promise.

CHAPTER THIRTY-TWO

"You again," Michael says, grinning. He looks me up and down. "And yet I don't see any overnight bags."

"I'm not staying long," I explain. "But I had some spare time and thought I'd get some fresh air."

"Always a good idea, that. There's nothing worse than stale compound air, if memory serves me."

"There isn't," I agree, then I spot Anne and AJ sorting through what looks like a junk heap off in the distance. We wave to one another.

"You must be parched from the hike. Can I fetch you some water?"

"Is there enough to spare?"

"Of course," he says pleasantly, as he drops what looks like dried weeds on the ground and motions me toward the half cylinder. "We don't run low on essentials around here."

"Where is everyone?" I ask, once I step inside the empty building.

"Most are working to collect food or supplies. Or that," he adds, gesturing to the glass of water he pushes in my direction.

"Others are off doing whatever they please."

I nod. "And the boy you mentioned—?"

"Away, Eve, watching a lid a couple hours west of here."

Away. The word hits me in the stomach. It makes my head ache. Speaking to the boy who lives here wasn't the sole reason for coming today—I really did want fresh air—but there's no denying my disappointment.

Michael must notice, because he adds, "Sorry—bad timing, that. How long have you been searching for this boy?"

The question catches me off guard. Because I haven't been searching for that boy—*Jack*—for very long. Hardly at all—I couldn't. I was locked underground, while he was locked above. So all I say is, "There hasn't been a day over the past nine years when I haven't thought of him."

Michael bows his head. "Sounds like true love, that."

Normally I don't open up to people I don't know very well, but there's something trustworthy about Michael. There's something kind that glimmers in his eyes. So I say, "He's my brother."

For a moment his normally astute gaze seems to falter. It even turns inward, like he's contemplating something deeply upsetting. But he lifts from it a moment later. "The bonds of blood are powerful, indeed," he says, and he bows his head.

Slowly it dawns on me that Michael, too, has been separated from his family. He was expelled, after all, just like Jack was. "I'm sorry," I tell him. "Sometimes I'm so caught up in my own life, that—"

"We all do it, Eve," he says, squeezing my hand reassuringly. "No need to apologize."

"Was it hard? Leaving your family behind?"

"Sure it was," he admits. "But at least I know they're safe enough down in Twelve. And if they do get expelled up here, there's a good chance they'll stumble upon my little camp." He grins.

"Why? Because Twelve is so close?"

"It'd be difficult to miss the towering buildings from the exit point, I'd think."

My mind once again slides toward Jack. Toward the boy from Michael's camp currently watching the so-called lids. I force myself to refocus on Michael. "Does anyone bother watching Twelve's lid?"

"Nah. The expelled seem to find their way here without any trouble. It's the compounds farther afield that need a spotter."

"Doesn't watching lids get boring?"

He laughs. "Thankfully we, as humans, are well diversified. That means that we all favor different things, and some of our members enjoy the solitude. And, of course, the odd time when a person does emerge, it's pretty exciting, don't you think?"

"I guess."

"How was the search?" Michael asks to someone over my shoulder. I turn to see Rex standing in the doorway holding an assortment of jugs. Most of the jugs have small supplies stored inside, like cups and cutlery.

"Successful," he says, as he lets the jugs fall to the ground. He wipes sweat from his hairline. "Hi, Eve," he adds, before pouring himself a glass of water.

Anne and AJ appear a moment later, leaving what looks like a large sheet of metal sitting outside the door. "More forks?" AJ asks, as he glances at Rex's assortment of supplies. "Nice."

"Looks like you finally worked that scrap free," Michael comments. He walks over to the piece of metal that I had assumed was garbage, and runs his hand appreciatively over it. "It's the perfect fix for our leaky roof, that," he says happily.

"Only took a couple hours, too," says AJ. "Should we store it near the rain barrels?"

"Great idea," agrees Michael, and AJ and Anne set to work dragging the metal out of sight.

"I'm going to go wash the new supplies in the creek," says Rex, returning to his assortment of jugs.

"I'll meet you there shortly to help," Michael assures him. Once we're alone again, he eyes me, looking curious. "If you were living here, Eve, which job do you think you'd gravitate toward?"

I wipe my mouth dry using my sleeve, remembering how sick Wren and I became after eating those berries and drinking that water. I think of how the scrap metal looked like garbage to me—not roofing material, and how I wouldn't know which way to turn or where to look to find spare forks or water jugs. "I don't know how to do any job," I admit.

Michael's ever-present grin widens. "Of course you don't. Wouldn't take long to learn, though," he says reassuringly. "I could see you being quite a scavenger, inquisitive as you are. Muscular too, and some of the items that are useful to us here at camp can be quite heavy."

"I look forward to it," I tell him, and I mean it. Because I don't want to simply live in this free civilization aboveground. I want to contribute to it, too.

"Since we're speaking of jobs, any chance you work as a cook back in your compound?"

I shake my head. "I'm a guard."

"Ah. And your friends—do any of them know how to cook?"

"Yes," I say, thinking of Hunter. Immediately I correct myself. "No." Because if for some reason I'm forced from the compound before Wren and I can figure out a way to expose the Premes and all their secrets, before we can find a way to open up the so-called "lid" and release the citizens of Eleven...I will tell my family and friends first. Hopefully they will choose to come with me—it will be safer for them if they do, I think, and it will be more enjoyable up here with them by my side. But Hunter is not my friend—not after he betrayed me—and so will I tell him the truth about the world up here?

I want to say no, but I wouldn't be honest with myself if I did. Hunter will always have a special place in my heart, even if we're no longer friends. Too many years of too much closeness. And then there's his confession, the one revealing his deeper feelings for me. I owe him this, don't I?

Michael, meanwhile, laughs. "Yes, no," he echoes. "I'll interpret that as a maybe?"

I shrug. "Are you looking for a cook?"

"Not really. We all cook communally, and I like it that way. It's the expertise I'm after. More specifically, I'd like to find a way to bake starches, like bread. I've been drying plants, then grinding them to a powder that I let ferment for a few days mixed with water— Sorry. I've been told I ramble on about the most mundane subjects."

"Not at all," I tell him. "I find it really interesting."

He grins. "Okay. Well, anyway—it's a solid start, my gut's telling me, but so far nothing coming out of the process is what I'd call edible."

"So you'll keep trying?"

"Until I perfect the process," he confirms.

I consider him silently. Hearing him discuss this sort of thing—the trials and tribulations of living up here, trying to develop *bread*—it's soothing. Soothing to think that life could be so simple. That instead of worrying about being attacked by Daniel, or shot by a guard, or burned alive by a Preme, I could focus on making something delicious to eat.

"It looks like you're favoring your arm, Eve. Are you injured?"

"Shot," I agree. Then, seeing the look on his face, add, "The bullet just skimmed me. It's no big deal."

"Sounds like a big deal to me. It's a shame our medic is out collecting herbs for her tinctures. I'm sure she'd have something to help."

"You have a medic here?"

"Injuries happen aboveground, too," he says with that ever-present grin. "And the occasional stomach upset, even."

"So you have a medic, but no cook," I say, and I'm smiling, too. "Interesting."

He laughs. "That about sums it up. But on the subject of cookery, I am learning a few things about the craft from books, if you can believe that. Check these out," he adds, then he walks to the back of the building. I follow him, watching as he opens a cupboard and pulls from it a stack of yellowed paper. "Cookbooks, from the old world," he says. "You wouldn't believe the number of them I find in apartments. Food culture must have been huge before the world got so hot."

"Food culture?" I ask, as I flip the closest book open. The pages are brittle and faded, but it doesn't detract from the mouthwatering pictures filling the inside.

"Strange, isn't it? I assume when the compound system was set up, the priority was survival, and so celebrating this sort of thing"—he fingers the cookbook—"evaporated. But now that we're back up here, with all this, it seems a shame not to rejoice in it. Do you know what I mean, Eve?"

I nod. Because when I'm in Compound Eleven, I'm focused only on my survival, too. But Eleven isn't my future, I know that now. *This* is my future, and I almost laugh with joy.

And yet I can't get excited about life up here, not yet. Not when there's still so much to do back there. No matter that this building with its collection of dusty cookbooks and fresh drinking water already feels like home. No matter that I enjoy chatting with Michael, or that I love learning about the old world up here, and the new one.

My day will come. Surely.

CHAPTER THIRTY-THREE

When I walk into the guardship training room Monday morning, I see that the others gather at the far end. They surround one of the thickest boys, one whose ankle looks to be wrapped in beige bandages. Another casualty of the fights.

I go to the lockers. Someone else's pain doesn't make me happy, yet I'm pleased that the others are distracted by something that has nothing to do with me. And then—just like that—I go still. My heart pumps so heavily, I become lightheaded.

Because I have an idea.

There's no time to think it through, to wonder if it's right or if it's very, very wrong. That sort of analysis will have to come later.

Now I must act.

So after I glance over my shoulder, and with the voices of the other hires still coming from the far side of the room, I pull out my gun. Then I step three paces to my left. Daniel's gun hangs from the lowest hook in his locker, and deftly my fingers lift it and replace the empty space with my own.

Into the waistband of my pants his gun goes. Three paces to the right. Done.

Then the door to the training room swings open and Nkrumah enters with two men trailing behind him. He looks at me, his gaze even seems to linger, and I wonder in that instant if he can see my fingers burning red at my sides. If he can see guilt slashing through my features like the scar puckering Daniel's face.

He must not, because he turns his attention to the group in the far corner, then calls them over. "What happened to you?" he asks the one with the bandaged ankle. Instead of listening to the boy's response, I stare at the two men who are new to our group.

One is a guard, his skin covered in divots, his receding hair pulled back into a bun. The other is well groomed and impeccably dressed. A Preme. They offer no clues as to why they're here, or what we will be subjected to next.

Maax nudges me in the ribs. "Think you'll be sent out on patrol again this week?"

"That depends. Are you guys still fighting?"

She glances darkly at Nkrumah and shakes her head. "I think we're done. See?" She points to an eye that is swollen and smudged in purple. "My first black eye. Normally I don't cry, but shit. I just can't believe you fight for the goddamn fun of it. You're tougher than you look, Two."

I force myself to smile. I must act normally right now, I can sense it.

Nkrumah clears his throat. "Our visitors here want to check your weapons. Any objections?"

My ears tingle at his words. My fingers feel swollen and hot. *Our visitors here want to check your weapons.* There is only one reason that I can think of for such measures and that is to find the gun that killed a most important man.

For once, it looks like my impulsivity has paid off.

"Everyone's gun in their locker?"

Around me people nod. All of them. I am the only one to shake my head.

Nkrumah's eyes narrow. "Where's yours?"

Slowly I reach to the back of my waistband and remove the gun that isn't mine. The guard moves forward and I place it in his outstretched hand.

"You get the honors of going first, Lower Mean. Guns are stored in the lockers the moment you set foot in the training room, unless I say different."

"I-I just got here," I stammer.

"Next time, don't be late. Lower Mean," he adds.

Before I can respond, the gun is handed back to me. I shove it in my locker, and ask, "What's this for?" My voice cracks, because I already know the answer. The expressions around me suggest that the others do not.

"Someone upstairs was shot a couple nights back," explains Nkrumah. "They're looking for a gun with recent fire. Lucky break for them," he continues, "because today we start firearms training."

The others look mildly excited by the prospect, though they look indifferent to the reason for the weapons check. I try to match my expression with theirs, but as the Preme and the guard set to work combing the lockers, I'm less than convincing.

Finally they reach Daniel's locker and when they do, I turn away. Because I know exactly what I've done: I have framed him for the murder of Ted Bergess, one of the leaders of Compound Eleven. Daniel is my enemy, I hate him more than any other civilian in the compound. He is cruel and evil and the world would be a better place without him.

But he didn't shoot Bergess. I did.

When they stall, when Nkrumah is motioned over, I shut my eyes. Soon Daniel is called over, too.

Finally I half turn; I watch out of the corner of my eye as the rest stare with open interest. "This gun was discharged recently," the guard is saying. His brows are drawn together in a scowl. "A bullet is missing, too. Care to explain why?"

Daniel's head moves with surprise, then it shakes side to side. Palms are extended. "I have no idea. I haven't shot it, I swear. I don't even know *how* to shoot it."

Nkrumah crosses his arms. "It's a decent point," he says to our visitors. "None of my hires here know how to fire a weapon."

"Point and pull," the Preme mumbles. "Not exactly advanced mathematics."

Then he takes the gun, the one that until a few minutes ago was my own, and the guard grabs Daniel by the shoulders. He points him in the direction of the door. "You're coming for a little stroll," he says into his ear.

Daniel's eyes ignite in panic. His very future must flash in front of him. Part of me has the urge to laugh—the savage side. But I don't, of course I don't.

Then, as he is pushed forward, his eyes snag on the sight of me, and he freezes, his pupils contracting. "*You* did this," he growls.

My face begins to contort into a smirk, but I catch it just in time. After all, I'm not out of the woods yet; Daniel will be shouting for my head to anyone who will listen. And there are some out there who will be all too happy to lend an ear. Now isn't the time for guilt, and it isn't time for celebration, either.

Nkrumah stares after them with his mouth pushed out. Then he turns to us, scowling. "One week in and we're already down two. How do you think that looks? Like I don't have control of my hires, is how it looks." He paces the room now.

"Here are two rules of life in the guardship—two rules I didn't think needed saying. One, never turn on your brother." He glances at me, then adds, "United in arms we stand, period. Rule Two: *Don't. Shoot. A. Preme.* Our job is to keep them alive, not kill them ourselves."

Heads slowly nod. I play along, for once listening to the man in authority and nodding too. Right now, my only goal is to make it through another day.

"Good. Now, as said, today you'll learn how to fire. All day we'll drill—don't expect to be able to lift your arms come dinnertime. Grab your weapons and follow me."

Daniel's gun feels no different than my own as I carry it down the hallway of the guardship to the shooting range. The range looks identical to the one on the fifth floor, and I realize with a jolt that I can't let the others know I can shoot. It would be too incriminating, especially after Daniel's assertion.

So I listen attentively as Nkrumah explains how to hold a gun, how to position the body, how to keep the weapon steady. The first dozen shots I aim wide and act frustrated. As far as anyone observing me can tell, I'm as new to this as the rest—I'm sure of it. But slowly the others get better, and so I do, too. I almost laugh at my cleverness, except that the dull ache in my arm grows more pronounced with every shot, and I wince instead.

After lunch taken in the guardship cafeteria we learn how to shoot while on the move, a new skill even for me. This time I really do try, I apply myself in the same way as when I fight. Full focus, and it's a much-needed distraction from the events of the morning. By the end of the day I am coated in a thin layer of sweat and my arms really do ache, and not simply from the bullet hole.

It's a good feeling, this exhaustion. The others feel it, too—I can tell by the way they groan, and as we push out of the guardship, I notice that they are no longer afraid of me, or disgusted by me, or whatever it was they were experiencing. Maybe it's because they know that Landry tried to kill me, or maybe it's because of Daniel's arrest this morning—a reminder that I am not the only cruel one in this world of ours. Or maybe it's simply the passage of time that has done it.

"Hungry?" Maax asks from behind me. Around us the corridors are thick with people, the workday over.

"Not really," I admit, as an elbow catches me along the collarbone.

"You should come, Two," she says. "We're meeting back in the guardship caf in ten minutes. It'd be a good chance to get to know the others."

I give her a look.

"They're not complete jackasses," she says with a laugh. "Besides, I know you're a lone wolf and everything, but you're going to want friends on the guardship, just like Nkrumah said." Then she's squeezed around the shoulders by a middle-aged woman with a laughing face and thick, shiny hair. They have the same sloping eyes.

"Caught you," the woman says.

"Eve, this is my mom. Mom, this is the girl I was telling you about. The one who can fight."

A hand is extended my way, and I stare at it. Sometimes when I see other girls with their mothers—mothers who are lucid and sane and present—it tastes bitter in my mouth. It pushes on my chest like a stack of bricks. I swallow the sensation and shove my hand into hers.

"Fiona," the woman says, by way of introduction. "Are you the one with the connection to the Edelman family?"

Wren and I may not be girlfriend and boyfriend anymore, but we do have a connection. There's no denying that. I grumble, "That's me."

"I knew his father," Fiona explains over the chatter of the crowd. Her face breaks into a smile as we allow the tide of people to push us forward. "Thom, truly a lovely man."

The words surprise me. Maybe because it's hard to believe anyone *lovely* could be connected to Wren's mother, Cynthia. Or even to her son. He is many, many things. But he isn't exactly lovely. "Wren talks about him from time to time."

"I hope so," she replies. "Such a terrible thing to lose a parent, especially at that age. He never had a chance to know the man."

"Still doesn't," I mutter, as I rub out my arms.

"Oh?"

Her interest catches me off guard. The whole conversation does, and I swallow. "It's nothing. His mother refuses to discuss him, that's all."

"She refuses to discuss her late husband?"

I shrug.

"You know, Thom and I were an item for years."

Suddenly I look at her with more interest. "Really?"

"Oh yes. And even when that ended, we remained close. If Wren's ever keen on hearing about him, I have plenty of stories to share. Certainly I knew him as well as anyone did, even...*her*." She looks at me and winks. "8578B is where I live; the door's always open."

Probably I should thank her. And I should smile as Maax chastises her for talking my ear off, or at least wave goodbye. Instead I am still, and silent, my brain buzzing with her words.

Maybe I'm still trying to wrap my mind around the term *lovely* being used in relation to an Edelman. Maybe I feel like I have betrayed Wren for discussing such private matters with a stranger. Or maybe it's the revelation that Thom also dated someone from a lower floor...

But they ended up friends, Thom and Fiona, just like Wren and I are now. It was never meant to be. Not for them, and not for us.

The next evening, I find Maggie dining with Connor, and Emerald dining with Eunjung. Silently I take a seat among their foursome and wish to myself that I was dining in the guardship instead.

It hadn't been that bad last night, not really. Mostly I spoke with Maax and Sam, but the other hires were friendly enough, and none of them seemed to care about my status as a Lower Mean. Mostly they discussed Daniel's arrest, which made me uneasy, but at least Landry was never mentioned. All in all, it could have been worse. It could have been *this*.

"Eve!" Maggie shouts as she lays her head on Connor's shoulder. "I haven't seen you in forever. I thought we agreed to spend *more* time together, not less."

"Seems like you don't have that much time to spare these days." I raise an eyebrow in Connor's direction.

"Will you be signing up for any fights in the Bowl soon?" he asks. "I really did enjoy your last match."

Emerald snorts. "Yeah, we all did. You should've seen the rocking after party we threw in Blue Circuit." She holds her hand to her mouth and mimics drinking from a large bottle.

"To answer your question," I say to Connor, between bites, "I won't be, no."

"Come on, girl," Emerald moans. "Blue Circuit needs you!"

"I'm working."

"Most of the fights are on the weekends."

"Guards don't get weekends off."

"Yeah, well they also don't work seven days a week." Then she sits up straighter. "Have you met Eunjung yet?"

I shake my head, and Emerald makes introductions. I grip Eunjung's hand in my own and note how delicate it is, all bone. I would wager a year's worth of allotments that it has never punched a person before. Then she smiles at me, and I see in her face nothing dark, nothing sinister, and I realize how different we are. I realize how deeply I envy her. If I were so good, Wren and I might still be together.

Then I'm knocked on the back of the shoulder and I stand, fist cocked. My brain explodes with possibilities — and my first thought is that it's Daniel, that the Premes let him go, that he's figured out I set him up, and now he's going to even the score.

But I see it isn't Daniel, and it isn't an enemy. In fact, it's the very last person I expect to see here, now, in the Mean cafeteria. All I can do is stare.

"Still can't get a handle on the basic workings of conversation, eh, Eve?" Wren says as he takes a seat. "That's okay. Most people start with hello."

Maggie and Emerald watch us closely, and I don't blame them. He *broke up* with me. So why is he here, in the Mean cafeteria?

Eunjung waves to Wren, then gestures to me. "Who's this?" she asks — a simple question, one intended to be friendly.

"Uh — nobody."

"Nobody?" Wren echoes. He glances at me. "Ouch."

I roll my eyes. "His name's Wren. He's a Preme, if you couldn't tell. And this is Eunjung," I add to him. "Emerald's…"

"Girlfriend," Eunjung fills in. She clasps Emerald's hand and they exchange shy smiles.

"Nice to meet you," he says, then he nudges me. "Is everything okay?"

"What are you doing here, Wren?"

"Eating."

"*Wren*."

"What's the big deal? I've eaten here plenty of times before, plus Connor's here. Who cares?"

"I do." My voice is quiet enough that the others can't hear. "*I* care."

"Why?"

I shake my head. Of course I can't tell him the truth. I can't tell him how much it hurts, having him here like old times. Not when times have changed.

But maybe he understands, on some level, because he lowers his voice even more, leans toward me, and says, "I come bearing news, if that makes any difference to you."

Slowly I nod. "It does."

"They think they've found the guard who killed Bergess."

I am motionless, waiting with bated breath.

Wren stares at me out of the corner of his eye. Then he exhales. "You already know, don't you?"

"No."

"You're a terrible liar, Eve—you always have been. Tell me how you figured it out."

For a few minutes I concentrate only on my dinner. Finally I turn to Wren, disregarding the fact that he watches me so closely. "Someone was accused of killing Bergess, you say?"

He gives me a look. "Not just *someone*. Daniel. And he hasn't been accused. He's been verified. His death is scheduled for tomorrow."

The words ring loudly in my ears.

"This is good news. You see that, don't you? Daniel's scum. And now you're in the clear." He pauses. "You're sure you didn't know?"

"Positive," I lie. Because I don't want to tell him the truth—that Daniel is scheduled to die tomorrow because of something I did. I don't want to admit that even to myself.

"What I can't figure out is why they're so certain it was him in the first place."

"Not sure." Then I force another bite of food into my mouth, and I force my jaw to move up and down. If it has flavor, I don't notice any. If it offers comfort, I don't feel any. All I feel is emptiness. Because even when I resolve to be good, I am bad.

"Maybe you can ask around the guardship. The other hires may have heard something."

"Maybe," I echo. I'm barely listening. All I can think about is the number three. Soon I will be responsible for three deaths. I can't live with that…and so I won't. I'll find a way to save Daniel, instead.

"I had a busy day," I announce to my friends. "I'm going to call it a night. It was nice seeing you," I add to Wren, without really looking at him.

Ten minutes later there comes a knocking at my door. Instead of answering it, I pull myself to my knees and untack the piece of embroidery that hangs over my bed. For a while I just stare at it, fingers dragging over each stitch. It's the closest thing I have to my mother's love, and that love is something I need right now. Maybe I have always needed it. Carefully I fold it into a square and shove it into the toe of my boot. Finally I go to the door.

"W-Wren," I say, tripping over his name.

"Can I come in?"

I stand aside to make room for him, then sit on my bed. "What are you doing here?"

He arches his brow. "I'm wondering why you ran out of the cafeteria mid-conversation."

"Was it *mid*-conversation?"

"It was."

"Well, I wouldn't say I *ran*."

"Come on," he says, smiling. He picks up the ball sitting on my desk and tosses it my way. "It's me."

"No, it's not *you*," I remind him, and I toss the ball back. Then my voice goes quiet. "You and I aren't a thing anymore, remember? You ended things. You can't even recognize me anymore. Which I get, by the way. You were right to break up with me. But…" I take a deep breath. "But maybe you shouldn't come to the cafeteria anymore, or here—maybe that just makes this…harder. I want to help free the compound with you, I really do, but the rest of it…"

He doesn't move. He just stares at me with something foreign flashing in his eyes. "I recognize you now."

My heart skips a beat. "What's that supposed to mean?" I whisper.

He shrugs, tossing the ball back and forth between his hands. "You're defiant and difficult as always, sure, but you're *alive*. You *care*. You're not obsessed with your own misery anymore."

"Except," I say, and the words come tumbling out, "now I've killed Bergess and, if I don't stop it, Daniel too!"

His eyes narrow. He even seems to gain a few inches in height. "What do you mean, *if I don't stop it*. Eve—what the hell are you thinking of doing?"

Silence.

So he says in a voice that is impossibly restrained, "There's no way you can save Daniel. It's over."

I begin drawing on my boots. "Just watch me."

"Come on—"

"You want to know what I'm going to do? I'm going to take him aboveground. Tonight. I'll take him to Michael and the others. I'm not letting him die."

"He tried to *kill* you."

"If I don't save him, I *will* have killed him!"

"*How*?" he demands. "How is this *your* fault? Just because you're the one who shot Bergess, you feel the need to save that piece of shit?"

"Not quite." My voice is hoarse, and I don't feel like joking anymore.

"So tell me what you did." He tosses me the ball, gently, like he's afraid I might break.

"I took matters into my own hands."

"Meaning?"

I roll my eyes. "Meaning it's time that you leave." I chuck the ball at him, but he catches it without blinking.

"I'm not going anywhere," he says smoothly. He has the same look in his eye as before we first stepped foot outside, way back when, in another lifetime. It gives me goosebumps.

Then I let out a deep breath. "I switched out his gun for mine. Yesterday. During training. It's not something I'm proud of, and it's not something I really thought through beforehand, but there you go."

"You switched out his gun. And?"

"And when the authorities showed up to check our weapons, his was the one with recent fire and a missing bullet."

Wren is silent. When I finally finish lacing my boots and glance at him, I see a smile tugging at his lips.

"It's not funny."

"No, it's not." He eyes me. "But it is impressive. You realize that at least, right?"

Instead of responding, I shove my knife into one boot and my flashlight into the other. I don't think it's impressive at all.

"Saving Daniel is decidedly less intelligent," he continues.

"Nobody asked you," I remind him.

"Any chance I could talk you out of it?"

"Nope."

"Then what's our plan?"

"Our?" I stare at him, then roll my eyes again. "You need to go. The lights will be out soon—I need to finish getting ready."

"Do you know where he is right now?"

"Daniel?"

He nods.

"Locked in his cell." I hope he can't hear the uncertainty in my voice. Or the fact that I don't know where Daniel's cell is in the first place.

"Not quite."

"Tell me."

"I'd be happy to share that information with you…"

"If I let you come," I finish.

He smirks.

"You're a jerk."

"I can live with that."

"Okay—you win." I give him an exasperated sigh. "Looks like I need your help after all."

His smirk shifts into a grin. "Don't sound so excited. He's locked in one of the holding cells in the guardship. Do you know where those are?"

"Of course."

CHAPTER THIRTY-FOUR

"**D**o remember," Wren says through the darkness, as we step onto the fourth floor, "that you've broken up with me before, too."

I peer at his silhouette, and something inside my stomach pushes and pulls. "Yeah," I manage to say. "So?"

He steps closer and leans down so that his mouth brushes against my ear. "So maybe we're even."

I shiver. "Maybe so," I breathe, as I lead him forward. Now my pulse is quick and dangerously unsteady.

But when we reach the guardship, I pause. I force myself to refocus. With the aid of my flashlight, I enter the passcode, and the reality of what I'm about to do begins to sink in. So does the realization that if I'm caught, my tenure as a guard will be over and I will join Daniel in a holding cell left to await my fate, whatever that fate might be.

Part of me thinks it's silly to risk my life for the likes of Daniel. Part of me knows I don't have a choice—but Wren does. I lift my hand to stop him. "If we're caught…" I whisper.

"I know, Eve," he says before I can finish.

"You don't have to do this."

He drops a hand onto my shoulder. "Yes I do."

For a while we just stare at each other. Then with a deep breath, I guide him forward. We find the guardship dark and still. The hallway to the left leads to the managerial offices, the hallway to the right leads to the cafeteria and other services for guards, ones I don't yet have full access to. Straight ahead is the shooting range, the training room for new hires like me, and, finally, the holding cells. It's strange to be here without my uniform on, or without the anticipation of seeing Nkrumah and the other hires. Strange and unsettling. It makes me feel like a student again, lurking in the teacher's lounge.

And then— "What are you doing here, Two?"

I jump at the sound of Maax's voice. "Uh—I forgot something in my locker," I stammer. More of her face appears through the shadows. "What about you?"

"Swiping this." She holds up a roll of knuckle tape for me to see, its stark white easily visible. "Sam dared me."

I smile. "Sam, huh? So does that mean Nkrumah's no longer in your sights?"

"Nah," she grins. "He's too nuts for my taste. Who's this?" she adds, shifting her gaze to Wren. But before I can open my mouth, she taps him on the chest. "You're the Preme, aren't you? The Edelman. Your dad and my mom used to be a thing, did Eve tell you? My name's Maax, by the way."

She holds out a hand and Wren shakes it. His movements are stiffer than usual. "She didn't tell me, no."

"Well, there you go. There's your gossip for the day. I would say it was pretty scandalous—an Upper Mean and a Preme, but hell, look at the pair of you."

I don't mention to her that we're broken up. Wren doesn't either. For a while we just stand together in uncomfortable silence. Then she says, "Listen, Sam's timing me, so I better jet.

Nice meeting you." With a wave she's gone, and the corridors relax into silence around us.

"Anything else you know about my father that you haven't told me?" Wren asks.

"Yes, actually. I heard from Maax's mom that he was a lovely man."

I see Wren's head snap in my direction at the term *lovely*, but all I do is calmly return his gaze. Then I lead him deeper into the guardship. A couple of minutes later, we stand in front of a series of metal doors, six of them in total. Only one has a thick padlock hanging from it. Only one person is scheduled to die in the morning.

I touch it. It isn't the type of lock with a passcode—this one requires a key. And the key could be anywhere, but most likely it's with the guard who locked him in here in the first place. Finding that guard—and the key—will be impossible.

"We'll have to shoot it open," Wren says, from over my shoulder.

I shake my head. "Too loud. The guards will come running."

"Which means we'll have to be quick." I must look doubtful, because he adds, "Not many work at night, don't forget, and the ones who do are scattered across the entire compound."

He's right, but as I reach for my gun, he grabs me by the wrist. "It has to be me," he says quietly.

"Why?"

"Because we're inside the guardship. The only guns they'll check in the morning are yours," and with that he draws his own weapon.

"We were in the shooting range yesterday. They won't be able to tell it was me."

"You want to take that chance? Fine. Don't forget I'm a better shot than you, and the more bullets needed to get that lock off, the quicker the guards will track the noise right here."

Reluctantly I step away from the door and point the flashlight there instead.

Wren moves back a few paces and aims the gun at the padlock. I squeeze shut my eyes and there is a thunderous blast. A second later I see the broken padlock lying on the floor. Wren scoops up the bullet and casing; I push open the door. Daniel stands just inside wearing a gray jumpsuit. He looks tranquil, but his eyes betray him. They're too wide. They are glassy with terror.

Even when he is scared for his life, I hate him. Even now, he radiates nothing but evil. So I almost hesitate, I almost leave him to die. Instead I grit my teeth, switch off the flashlight, and grab him around the arm.

"What the f—"

"Just shut up and do what I say." Then we're sprinting up the hallway in the direction of the exit, as fast as our boots will allow. I can hear shouting—someone heard the blast, and whoever it is, they're searching for its source. All around us the darkness seems to vibrate. At any second I expect guards to tumble through doorways, weapons drawn, guns firing.

I am not a lucky person, yet somehow we run on, through the guardship and into the corridors of the fourth floor. Almost immediately my ears draw up the sound of heavy footsteps, and I spot the unfriendly glare of a flashlight more powerful than the one wedged inside my boot.

"Hide," I hiss, and I drag Daniel to the wall. I press my back into cold concrete and force him to do the same. For a second, he resists. For a second, he would rather take his chances with the guards than put his trust in me. I glance at the scar puckering his face and can't really blame him.

Then Wren digs his gun into Daniel's stomach and the three of us are motionless.

"You're an idiot," Wren seethes, once the danger has

passed. I indicate for them to be quiet, then lead them forward as Wren swats Daniel across the back of the head. "They're sending you to your death tomorrow," he whispers angrily. "You really want to ask them for help right now?"

"How the fuck am I supposed to know what's going on?" Daniel asks in a strangled voice. "Care to enlighten me?"

"I'm saving your worthless life," I whisper, leading them into the stairwell. "But give me a reason and I'll throw you back to the guards."

He says nothing, not even when I lead him into the Lower Mean corridors that he views with such disdain.

It takes a while to reach the kitchen—longer than I predicted. It isn't that I fear running into a guard, not really. I could use violence against whoever stands between us and the outside world, I know that. I could get by them and see tonight's mission through to its end. But I don't want it to come to that. Because I don't completely hate the other hires. I kind of like Maax. And Sam. I kind of like Trevor. The guards aren't all bad, I have come to realize. And so I don't want to be in a position where I have to hurt one.

"What's the plan, *Eve*?" Daniel demands as we come to a standstill inside the storeroom. "Going to stash me on one of those nets with a bunch of lightbulbs?"

"What did I tell you, Daniel, about pissing me off?"

"At least tell me what the plan is."

Wren and I glance at each other. It's hard to believe that the first person we are sharing our secret with is him. But there's no choice and so I say in a level voice, "We're taking you outside."

For one glowing moment in time, Daniel is speechless. Then he shakes his head and spits on the floor. "To the same place I'll be sent to in the morning, then, you mother—"

Wren punches him in the stomach, a clean hit, one that

knocks him to the floor. "Watch your mouth," he says heavily.

"You were never going to be sent aboveground," I explain. "You were headed for the incinerator on the fifth floor, to burn alive. Still an option if you don't mind yourself."

"What the hell are you talking about?"

I smile wickedly. "Aboveground isn't as hot as they've been telling us. Isn't that right, Wren?"

"Perfectly pleasant," Wren adds, then he grabs Daniel under the shoulders and hauls him to his feet. He shoves him in the direction of the ladder. "Who wants to go first?"

"We should," I say. "If he goes first and falls, he could take us out with him."

"Good point."

"Wait. Wait." Daniel's entire body seems to shake. "You're serious right now? About—about up there? About this… incinerator thing?"

"Very serious."

It takes him a minute to process the news, but finally he glances at the ceiling of the storeroom. "And we have to climb this ladder?"

"Unless you can fly."

"To the very top?"

"We're going *aboveground*. What do you think?"

"Right. I just…I didn't know—"

"What's wrong with you, Daniel. Scared?"

Wren crosses his arms and grins. "You know something, Eve, I really think he is."

"Well," I say slowly, "you can either get a grip, or you can let this glorious compound of ours kill you. The choice is yours." Then I swing a boot onto the lowest rung of the ladder and begin the slow ascent, ignoring the wound on my arm that aches with every step. Wren's at my heels, and a minute later I hear Daniel grunt with effort.

Maneuvering onto the top net is no trouble now that I've done it a few times before, but it doesn't stop my stomach from flipping at the sight of the concrete floor so many feet below. "Watch," I instruct over my shoulder. Then I pull myself up and roll to the pile of metal that sits in the middle of the netting. I do it for Daniel's benefit, not for Wren, who pulls himself up with ease a few seconds after I do.

I don't notice the way his body moves, or the way his muscles arc under his shirt. I don't. I also don't care that now he lies beside me, or that the spot where our bodies touch feels heavy, like a throbbing pain that doesn't hurt.

Then Daniel screams and Wren lunges in his direction. He hauls Daniel over the edge of the net by the collar of his shirt. Quickly, as Daniel pukes onto the floor below, I lift myself over the metal tools and shove open the access hatch.

When I step outside I forget about Daniel; I relish the feeling of fresh air filling my chest, of the night sky shimmering an infinite number of miles above me. I don't think the sensation will ever get old.

"Which way?" Wren asks roughly while he pushes Daniel from the outbuilding. Maybe it's from vomiting, or maybe from the shock of discovering that the outside world has in fact cooled, but Daniel's face is ashen under the moonlight.

I point toward the solar panels, and by the time we reach them, Daniel is muttering something about the temperature under his breath, trance-like.

"Shut up," Wren finally snaps. "I'm not listening to that the whole way."

"The whole way where?"

"To the others," I answer. "Exiles, from other compounds. They have shelter and food. It's the only way you'll survive."

"You care about me surviving, Eve?"

"Nope. Couldn't care less. But if giving you a fighting

chance lets me rest a little easier from now on, then so be it."

"I, on the other hand," says Wren, as we walk single-file between the panels, "can rest easy no matter what. So one word I don't like from your mouth, one movement that I don't care for, I shoot you. Understand? This saving you bullshit was Eve's doing," he adds. "Not my own."

"Eve the Good," Daniel snorts. "Is that her charade now? I'm sure Landry would have something to say about that if he were still here."

I stop walking. Anger ignites inside my brain at his thoughtless words. Or maybe they weren't thoughtless at all. Maybe they were calculated with precision and intended to hurt. Maybe he meant for me to doubt myself and my actions this evening, because that is exactly what I do as I glare at him. Am I saving Daniel because it's the *just* thing to do? Or is it to play the hero inside my own head? To convince *Wren* of my goodness? Eve the Good. *Eve the Good.*

"I knew he wasn't worth saving," Wren says between clenched teeth.

"You're right," I say. Because I am not a mutant or a miscreation—I understand right from wrong, and Daniel will not take that away from me. Besides, he has no moral superiority over anyone. I shove him out of the way and turn back in the direction of the compound. "I think I'll leave you right here, Daniel. And don't think you'll make it through the night—the beasts around here are deadly. Keep your head up, okay?"

"You're doing this only because you set me up. You killed that Preme, didn't you?"

"You believe whatever you want to believe, how's that?" I call. "Good luck out here."

"Hey. *Hey.* I'm sorry, okay? You win—you win, again. What else is new. Take me to your people. *Please.* Please take me to your people."

I want to walk on, I want to forget about him. He is unworthy of my help. But I did set him up, I did kill that Preme, and so my boots slow. "Say one more word and that's it," I warn him. "I'm serious this time. This is your last chance."

"Okay." He lifts his hands. "Okay."

There is desperation in his voice and defeat in his eyes, and because of all that, I nod. Then I turn toward the city and lead my foe to the life that one day, I hope, will be my own.

Eventually towers rise up in front of us. Their faces are black and sinister in the moonlight. Daniel swears as he gazes up at them. Wren is silent, but I know by the way he holds himself that the sight makes an impression on him, too.

The journey here passed without incident. The three of us marched in single file and as the adrenaline that propelled us from Compound Eleven wore off, weariness settled in. We came across no beasts, nothing to torment us through the darkness aside from our own thoughts.

Part of me is excited to see Michael and the others. It's an opportunity to once again glimpse their beautifully crafted life here aboveground. It's an opportunity to meet that young boy, to see if maybe, just *maybe* it's Jack. But I am delivering scum, dropping it on their doorstep, and even though I plan to be upfront about it, the thought makes my stomach turn. And yet it's too late to second-guess myself, so I kick at the broken concrete underfoot and start in the direction of the half cylinder. I tell the others that we are close.

Eventually a voice lifts through the shadows. "Who's there?"

"We're here to see Michael," I call back. "Tell him it's Eve Hamilton. From Compound Eleven."

Then I hear, "Eve?" and I peer through inky blackness to see a boy approach our group, one who is tall and broad. Dark skin, an easy smile.

"Rex!" I shout with relief. "I need to speak to Michael. Is he here?"

"That he is," comes another voice, one instantly recognizable by its accent. When Michael reaches me, he squeezes me around the shoulder. "Good to see you again." Iridescent eyes sparkle under the moonlight. "Have you wrapped up business in your compound, then?"

I shake my head. "Not quite. But I had to break Daniel here out early, and I thought he might be able to stay with you for a while." I elbow Daniel in the arm until he grunts a hello.

"Is this a friend of yours?" Michael asks, and his gaze lingers over the scar that disfigures Daniel's face.

"Not at all," I reply swiftly. "But I had an obligation to save him and so I did."

Michael nods thoughtfully, then turns to Rex. "Mind getting him set up inside?"

"Good seeing you again," Rex says to me before he leads Daniel away.

"Is this one your boyfriend, Eve?" Michael asks as he eyes Wren. His tone is good-natured, just like always.

"This is Wren. And, um...not so much."

"Not so much," Michael repeats. "Okay. Sounds like I ought to leave it at that, then." He grins.

I'm not sure why, but the conversation makes Wren scowl.

"No sense in standing here in a pile of weeds, is there?" he asks as he guides me in the direction of the metal building. "Come on," he adds to Wren, "we've got a fire going around the other side."

"Now?" I ask. "In the middle of the night?"

Michael laughs. "It takes a while to cook the meat, particularly big game," he explains as we push through shoots of green as high as my waist. "Today's catch was late day, and besides, we tend to go to bed on our own time around here. I hope you're hungry," he adds.

I glance at him out of the corner of my eye to see if he is serious. He smiles at me, but I think he is.

"What compound are you from?" Wren asks.

"Twelve."

"You were expelled?"

"Me and my friend Muji. My fault, that. Compulsive curiosity to blame. But we managed up here all right, and it didn't take long to find a few others who'd been expelled, just like us. And the more hands we had, we discovered quickly, the better off we were."

"Why?"

"For starters, it's easier to catch dinner with a few people surrounding it."

Wren considers him. "It?"

"The animal," he says, grinning. "You can eat them, so long as you cook them right. We started with small game, since they're more plentiful. Rabbit, mostly. Do you know what that is?"

Wren and I glance at each other, then shake our heads.

"They're about this big." He gestures with his hands. "Cute, too, so it took a while for us to feel okay about, well, eating them. Of course, starvation helps, on that front."

"And you say you cook the animal over a fire?"

"First you've got to skin it," he explains. "Once it's cooked through, it's safe to eat. Awfully tasty, too."

I glance at Wren. "That would've been helpful to know."

"Maybe we should've cooked that thing that attacked us."

I laugh. "That would have kept us full for weeks."

"At least." He turns back to Michael. "How far away is Twelve?"

"Only about an hour from here. I'd say most of our members are from there, for that reason alone. It's hard not to stumble upon all this." And he stares up at the tall buildings that lie just beyond where we now walk.

"Have you ever tried getting word back to your compound about up here?" I ask. "You know, that it's safe and everything."

Wren looks at me sharply, but Michael just sighs. "We've made several attempts, as a matter of fact, all futile. We've given up on that endeavor, if I'm being honest. Basically, when someone from Twelve is sent aboveground, they take an elevator up, all by their lonesome. There's no viewing station like at your compound. One time we were able to time it perfectly so that we sent a note down with the elevator, but nothing ever came of it. Who knows if it was even seen. After that we began working on a plan where one of us jumped aboard and went underground, but it was too risky. Could be a bit of a suicide mission, that. It's hard to know exactly how someone will react to startling news. Remember yours when you first stumbled upon me?"

I laugh.

"Still gives me chills, thinking about it," he says as he knocks me in the arm. "It's been a long while since I've had a gun pointed my way. Why do you ask?"

I glance at Wren before I respond, but his gaze is focused on the metal half cylinder we approach and the pocket of orange air lifting from behind it. "We think the Compound Eleven leaders know the earth has cooled. We think they've known for a long time, actually." I stare at a million stars burning brightly overhead, then add, "We want to do something about it."

He nods. "Your unfinished business?"

"Our unfinished business."

"A suicide mission, most likely."

I flinch at his words. Wren's face is stony, completely impenetrable. "We're hoping not," I finally say.

"My two cents? Don't pull the trigger until you're safely aboveground."

"How are we supposed to pull the trigger if we aren't even there?" Wren asks.

There is an edge to his voice that I don't really understand, but if Michael notices, he disregards it completely: "Get creative, is my thinking. Shove flyers under doors on your way out. Give people the information they need and leave the rest up to them."

"It won't work," Wren says. "It might for a few, then the exit would be sealed and our options would be out. *Their* options would be out."

"Definitely a risk."

"A risk we're not willing to take."

Michael looks at Wren with piercing eyes. "I suppose you're thinking violence, then."

Wren matches his gaze. "I suppose I am."

"What do you think, Eve?"

Silently I consider the question. Michael's idea sounds promising, clean and doable as it is, but Wren's counterpoint is impossible to ignore. And if his is correct, probably violence is the only way. Eliminate those in charge, eliminate anyone who would stop the citizens of Eleven from escaping, and our mission is complete.

But those in power underground are plentiful, and armed. And, most importantly, they have the guards on their side. "Violence would mean outright war," I say as the wind shifts. It pushes all the loose hairs from my face. "Mass bloodshed, on both sides. But if the rulers aren't willing to let people out, then to do the job properly, it's the only way."

"Death for freedom," Michael comments. "Is it really worth it?"

Wren stirs. "Worried about losing your throne with an entire compound let loose?"

I turn to him, my brows knotting, but Michael just laughs. "It's okay," he says. "Me and your friend here don't seem to see eye-to-eye on things, that's all. At least on some things."

His words ease my mind, but they only seem to anger Wren more. Then we walk around the far side of the half cylinder and I can't focus on Michael, or Wren, or anything except the sight in front of us.

At first it's alarm that I feel. Never have I seen anything so powerful, and startling, and intense. Next I feel mesmerized. Because it dances, it licks the night sky with affection, it offers so much brightness, just like the sun.

Fire.

We walk closer, and I lift my palms. They grow hot, so hot I have to check to make sure they don't bleed. Once I know the skin remains intact, I edge closer and closer until the heat is almost unbearable. I know I shouldn't touch it, I know instinctively this sort of thing can hurt me, and I can sense it right now, too. But it doesn't stop me. I'm drawn to it—as, like they say, a moth is to a flame, and suddenly the expression makes perfect sense to me—I even smile at the thought.

Then Wren's hand plants itself firmly on my stomach. He gives me a strange look, then he draws me away.

"Too close?" I ask.

"Too close." He leaves his hand on my stomach a little longer than he needs to, and I feel the pressure from each of his fingers.

"Pretty remarkable, isn't it?" says Michael, from over my shoulder. His accent makes his voice sound light and touched with humor. Or maybe it really is.

"It's...incredible."

"How do you make it?" Wren asks.

"We've got a handful of methods we've developed for starting a fire—everything from using a magnifying glass over dried grass, to using steel we've rounded up from nearby buildings. Rex found some matches about a month ago, which makes the job easier, but when those run out we'll have to switch back to the methods requiring patience." He grins. "That or find more matches, I guess."

"How did you figure all that out?" I ask next. Because I don't think it would've occurred to me to try any of the things he mentioned.

"Trial and error, mostly. Don't forget when Muji and I were expelled, we didn't have the option of returning underground for a meal like you two evidently did."

"True."

"And we learned pretty quickly that most materials have many uses, if you think on it long enough. Your compound mate, Daniel—any chance he wears glasses? Sometimes that's all you need to start a fire, if the sun hits them just so."

I shake my head. "I think you'll find he's pretty useless." Then I lower my voice. "Listen, since we're on the subject, Daniel isn't just useless. He's someone I wouldn't trust, if I were you, and I'm sorry for unloading him on you, I really am, but he would've died back in Eleven." I take a moment to wipe away the sweat from my palms. I'm more nervous about telling Michael all this than I realized. "If you keep weapons here, for instance..."

"Weapons are safely locked away and I'll see to it myself that he doesn't come within a mile of one. Anything else?"

I shift around. "Just that...you know. I hope it was okay, me bringing him here. I wouldn't have, except you said all your members have been expelled from their compounds, and, well—"

"Relax, Eve. We're more than used to dealing with difficult personalities." He looks at me and winks.

"Thanks," I say. It feels like a weight lifts from my shoulders, but before I can say any more, food is being passed around, and Michael pushes Wren and me closer so that we both receive plates. A minute later, we stare at food that looks completely foreign. Even Wren, who grew up on the Preme floor with food far better than what the Mean cafeteria offers, looks puzzled. This food is colorful and juicy. There's a variety of textures. There is a strong and strangely alluring aroma coming from all of it. I pick up a piece of meat with my fingers, studying it. Then I look at Wren. "Cheers."

Its juices drip down my chin and I have to use my hand to catch them. I'm laughing, then taking another bite, and another.

Wren watches me and smirks. "That good, huh?"

I nod enthusiastically, and he begins to eat, too. I don't remember eating with such pleasure in years, not even after a week straight of sustenance packets. Maybe it's because the food tastes so different up here—so much richer, so much more flavorful. Or maybe it's because I'm eating in the fresh air, a cool breeze at the back of my neck, a warm fire snapping and crackling in front of me. Whatever it is, it leaves me feeling whole again. I am mended and healed, even though I was never really wounded.

And, more important than that, I'm not a killer three times over. I saved Daniel, just like I wanted.

One of the members collects plates and another passes around water. I lift an eyebrow at Wren as he examines his glass, then drinks it in one go. I think he's impressed. The rest of the time I stare around at the other camp members, most of whom I've never seen before. People are here from all walks of life—my age to those decades my senior. Nowhere, though, is there a child. No boy around the age of twelve. No one that could possibly be Jack.

"Hiya, Eve," comes a voice from over my shoulder. "I thought I heard your name making the rounds."

I turn and see Muji. Just like when I saw Michael and Rex, it feels like I'm greeting an old friend, and I grin.

"Whoa, that's a different reaction than last time. She held Michael and me at gunpoint for ages," she adds to Wren, before introducing herself.

I stare at him as he reciprocates. He is undeniably handsome, and I can tell by the way Muji looks at him that she can see it, too.

"You eat well up here," he comments.

"Live well, too. You guys joining rank or are you just unloading that thing on us?" She nods at Daniel, who chews at a bone and stands well apart from the crowd. He looks, for the first time in his life, unsure of himself.

"Unloading, for now," I say.

"And if you feel like cutting him loose," adds Wren, "no hard feelings."

She throws her head back in laughter, and in that moment I envy her. She doesn't just live in freedom; she *embodies* it. I want to embody it. I want to live here, I want to spend my days cooking over the fire, developing bread recipes with Michael, looking for new members, searching for *Jack*.

"Michael mentioned there's a kid who lives here, but I don't see him," I say to Muji. "Do you know who I'm talking about?"

"Tuck, sure."

"Tuck?"

"That's what we call him," she says with a shrug.

"What's his real name? Do you know?"

She shakes her head. "He doesn't speak, didn't Michael tell you? He was living pretty rough when we found him. I can't say what his background is, but I can't imagine it was golden. Nice kid, though. He spends most of his time far afield, watching lids. I don't think he's used to being around so many people," she adds, and she gestures to the crowd. "Why do you ask?"

"Curious."

"Yeah? What's the real reason?"

I grin ruefully. "I had a little brother who was exiled years ago."

"Ah, gotcha. Well, you never know, right? Too bad he's on a field mission, although I have to say, I don't think he came from anywhere around here."

"Oh?" I feel a burning along the back of my throat, like my body refuses to swallow this information.

"Well, who knows. But whenever I ask him if he's from the area, he shakes his head no."

"Eleven's a couple hours away," I point out.

"He's used to watching lids twenty hours away," she reminds me.

"What happens when one of the lids does open?" Wren asks, and I take the opportunity to collect myself. Probably not Jack, sure. But that doesn't mean all hope is lost. I can keep searching elsewhere—can't I? "This kid—Tuck," Wren continues, "is he supposed to bring the expelled person to you?"

"More or less," she agrees. "He's a friendly sort. Small, too. I think if you'd been expelled to what you thought was your death, then a cute little kid greets you with a smile, beckoning you through the woods, you'd follow along. It's kind of overwhelming out here if you don't know what you're doing."

"We noticed."

"Speaking of compound life," Muji says to me, "how's life been treating you back at yours?" She seems to study my face, and I'm reminded that it's still bruised from Kyle.

I want to laugh—life has not been kind. *I* have not been kind. But all I do is shrug.

"That bad, eh? All the more reason to just stay already." She ruffles my hair, then disappears through the crowd, chatting easily with members along the way.

I stare after her. I stare at all of them.

"Was it difficult last time too?"

I glance at Wren. "Difficult?"

"Choosing to go back."

"Of course not," I lie.

"We can't free the compound from aboveground."

I nod. I know that.

"But I'm not making you go back with me again, either."

His words catch me by surprise. "What do you mean?"

"I mean I need your help down there, and I want it, too. But I'm not having you hate me again. Besides, what he said is right." And he nods at Michael, his gaze narrowing as he does. "It's likely that freedom will come at a great cost. It will be safer for you here, with them." A moment later, he moves through the shadows, gone.

CHAPTER THIRTY-FIVE

All around me, people chat, they laugh. Michael and Muji stand on the far side of the fire speaking with Daniel. Nobody looks my way, so without bidding them farewell I turn and disappear into the night. I follow in Wren's still-warm footsteps. It's not until I'm inside the woods that I catch up to him.

"What was that?" I call, annoyed.

He stops, then eyes me under the broken moonlight that dapples the forest floor. "What was what?"

"You didn't even wait for me, that's *what*. Oh, and before I forget, thanks for being so pleasant with Michael tonight. You didn't make things uncomfortable *at all*."

He just rolls his eyes.

"What, Wren? What's so bad about him? What he's doing is pretty remarkable—surely you can see that. Don't forget we didn't even make it a few *days* up here."

"Yeah, I can see that," he admits. "It is remarkable. Happy?"

"Then why were you such a jerk?"

Wren squints at me. "Don't you know by now to be

suspicious of those who hold power? Do you really want to move from one controlling regime to another?"

"You don't know he's like that."

He shrugs. "You're right. I don't. So go join rank—I know for a fact he would enjoy it."

I stare at him.

He laughs coldly. "Let me guess. You don't notice how he looks at you. How he touches you whenever he can?"

Now it's my turn to laugh. "You can't be serious. You're *jealous*? Surely not, seeing as how you ditched me and everything."

"I didn't ditch you. I was trying to wake you up, that's all. And by the way, I didn't wait for an answer just now because I knew what your answer was going to be."

"Well, you were wrong, because here I am, ready to go back. I'm freeing Compound Eleven every bit as much as you are. Surprised?"

His brow lifts ever so slightly. "Okay," he says slowly. "Yeah, I am surprised. I mean, I knew you would go back and everything, but…"

For a second I stand there, staring at him blankly. The sound of rustling leaves fills the silence. Then I frown. "You knew I would go back. So why are you surprised?"

"I thought you would go back because you felt like you had to, for my sake. I left before you could make that choice. Plus, I don't know…" He stares at his feet and adds, "I want you to be safe."

"Wait. Wait, wait—for your sake? As opposed to the sake of the entire compound?" I give him an exasperated look. "I don't want this to come across the wrong way, but maybe you need to get over yourself, Wren."

For some reason, my words make laughter shoot across his face.

My muscles clench defensively, but a second later I'm laughing, too. It's senseless, but it feels good. It feels medicinal, like a long night's sleep.

When our laughter finally subsides, it's just the two of us staring at each other more nakedly than before. "I'm still mad at you," I say matter-of-factly.

He nods. "All I need to know is whether or not you're going to hate me back in Eleven."

I gaze at the stars, the few I can see through the treetops, then shake my head. No.

"Well, your temper I can deal with. Besides, I'm not sure I know you any other way."

I punch him lightly across the arm. "Watch it, Preme."

CHAPTER THIRTY-SIX

Tucked between my sheets the next night, I realize that it had been a good dream I was having. Maggie and Emerald had been there. Wren, too. All my favorite people. We had been standing in a meadow or some other field aboveground, one where swaying grass tickled my bare legs and birds danced overhead. One where my skin was stained pink from the sun. But now something cold and hard presses against my temple. Now terror sits inside my throat and stops me from breathing.

"Looks like I caught you with your pants down," comes a voice through the darkness. "Knew I would, eventually. Just had to bide my time before I could square things up."

I will my voice to rise to the surface. "Square things, how?"

Ben laughs. "Think I enjoy your boyfriend threatening me like that? You think I like that wise-ass attitude of yours? Girls like you think you can get away with murder," he hisses. Then his tone changes—he sounds excited. "Speaking of murder, did you hear about that department head, Bergess?"

"Shot on the Preme floor," I respond, and somehow I keep my voice level, even as I try to think of a way to save myself.

Of course it's useless. There's nothing I can do. My gun is on the desk, and the one digging into the side of my head means total obedience. My only option is words—diplomacy through words. Not exactly my strong suit. "They caught the person responsible for his death," I say next. Keeping the conversation going is something I should do, I think. "Didn't they?"

"One of the new hires at the guardship, same as you. Except for some reason he's gone missing, and he'd need inside help to pull off something like that. Funny, you're the only one of the bunch with a verification record."

I force myself to laugh. "So you think that, since I underwent verification—was found *innocent*—that I'm hiding him here in my cell? Turn on the light and have a look around."

"Nah. I know the second I take this gun off you, I'm a goner. I've been to enough of your fights to know how you work."

I start to shake my head, but he orders me to stop. So I say, "Daniel and I have hated each other for years. Ask around— I'm the last person in Eleven who'd want to help him."

"Could be you had a change of heart."

"I didn't," I tell him. Then I add, "Maybe you should check with Daniel's friends, if you're looking for him. It shouldn't take long; he doesn't have many."

"Especially since you offed one."

My lips press tightly together at his words, but I guess I asked for it. "It was an accident."

"Sure it was. So. How's your boyfriend doing, anyway?"

"We're not together anymore." Immediately I regret my candor. Because even without his physical presence, his Preme status provided me with some clout, some importance. It was an added layer of protection, even if I never wanted it to be.

I can hear Ben's smile through the darkness. He says

slowly and with great animation, "That a fact." Then he snorts. "Can't say I'm interested. You're one unladylike bitch, you know that?"

"So I've been told."

"You're also dead."

My heart skips a beat. "You're going to shoot me?"

"Nah. That wouldn't be enough fun. And it wouldn't look so good, especially now that you're part of the guardship and all. But it's only a matter of time before you get in more trouble, and your punishment will be a lot more painful than a bullet to the head."

I think of the incinerator, and every muscle in my body twists into itself. And of course that's what he references — guards march those sentenced to death there themselves. I wonder, though, if they know *why* the incinerator is used. I wonder if they've been let in on the truth or if they have been fed some bullshit lie.

Probably the latter. It's nothing but lies down here. Our entire existence is a lie.

Then the cool barrel of the gun lifts and I hear Ben's footsteps shuffle backward toward the door. I hold my breath —

"See you again real soon, Eve," he says darkly. Then he's gone.

I switch on the lamp as I let out a long breath. I lock the door and place my gun under the pillow, not that it would've helped. I was sleeping too deeply when he came in, yesterday's late night to blame. I let my defenses down, just as he insinuated.

After I have a drink of water, I stare at my reflection in the mirror and think to myself that I got lucky. Ben could have been much crueler. But luck will only take me so far; next time, I need to be ready. Then I crack my knuckles as his warning sounds in my head. He suspects it was me who broke Daniel free; maybe even Andrews does, too.

But I'm not the only one with problems. Those in power are rattled by Daniel's escape, by his inexplicable and unprecedented disappearance. All day the guards conduct searches, each floor of the compound thoroughly explored, people interrogated, and all day I have to bite my tongue to stop myself from laughing. It's only a matter of time, they maintain. There are only so many hiding places down here, and nobody can hide forever. If only they knew.

Then, as I climb back into bed, my eyes snag on the patch of empty wall above my bed. The spot where my mother's embroidery used to hang. *If you go, let me go with you.* Her words echo through my brain. But taking her with me isn't the problem—it's the rest of the compound that presents an issue. Because no matter how many times I rack my brain for an answer, I come up short.

We could make flyers, just as Michael suggested, ones outlining the beautiful world awaiting aboveground, ones that detail the lies our leaders have been feeding us and the incinerator they use to kill us. But we'd have no tangible proof. So maybe nobody would listen, maybe they'd be too scared. Or maybe anyone who did try to go would be killed, and we would be killed, too—if the authorities caught us in time.

Another option is crude violence. Find a way to kill enough guards, enough Premes, that nobody stands in our way. Thorough, yes. But far too cruel.

Perhaps the only person we need is Katz—the man at the very top. The man whose hand unlocks the Oracle. Perhaps with him under our control, we could safely end Eleven. Except nobody is more scrupulously guarded than he is. Nobody would be harder to reach.

I shut my eyes and sigh. There isn't an easy answer, but what did I expect?

There's another possibility: that there's nothing we can do. That unraveling the hierarchy of power that is Eleven is just a mission in futility, like Michael came to realize with his own compound. Or maybe a solution can't be found, because whenever I turn my mind to it, I think also of Wren, and just as he always has, he distracts me. Unfairly so.

CHAPTER THIRTY-SEVEN

I strip off my guard uniform and pull on my jeans. Another day of training, done. This one was spent at a desk learning about crowd control, about policing protests, dispersing demonstrations. Pertinent information in times like these. Maybe I'll pass along the information to Sully—the mouthpiece for Lower Mean contempt—and let him plan accordingly. I smile at the thought. Right now, though, I have plans of my own.

I need to speak to Wren. I need to tell him about Ben's visit, and his suggestion that I helped free Daniel. Because it changes things, it really does. Certainly I'm not looking for an excuse to see the Preme. Of course not.

But when I'm close to the Department of Inter-Compound Relations, my boots slow, then stop completely. Because the steel door that's my destination already has someone standing in front of it. Someone with high heels and freshly brushed hair.

Wren isn't my boyfriend, I know that. But when we were aboveground we shared some moments that made it seem like he might be. I remember laughing with him under the stars, I feel his hand pressed against my stomach, and I wonder all over again why *she's* here.

Maybe I should just go ask her all the questions that torment me late at night. Whether they hang out very often, whether they've kissed lately, whether *they* are boyfriend and girlfriend. But then Wren emerges, and she grabs him by the hand, and my thoughts vanish.

Then I'm pushing through the crowded corridor toward them before I can stop myself. She's upset about something, I can see that, and it doesn't take long to piece together that it's the murder of Ted Bergess and the escape of his suspected killer, Daniel Munro.

Ironic, given who she clutches. But he makes no reference to this, or to anything. He simply listens quietly and though he doesn't hold her, he doesn't push her away, either. Then his head snaps to the side; he looks over his shoulder as if he can feel my gaze.

When he sees me, he turns. He turns and her arms fall away. He doesn't look surprised to see me, or even angry. He looks, if anything, thoughtful.

"What do you want?" Addison asks me. She's clearly annoyed.

"Same thing as you," I retort, without shifting my gaze from Wren. "I need to talk to him."

He continues to stare at me in a contemplative way. I think maybe he is waiting to see what I'm going to do, so I do nothing. I just return his gaze.

It must make Addison agitated, because she demands, "What's going on? Why is she still hanging around you?"

I expect Wren to assure her that it's no big deal, that we are friends and nothing more. He wouldn't even have to lie about it this time. But instead he's silent and unmoving, even as Addison tugs on his arm. I screw up my eyes a little. *What is he doing?*

If he doesn't soothe her soon, my position on the guardship will be in jeopardy. And then, as the slightest smile turns his lip, I understand. Or at least I think I do.

"It's not his fault," I hear myself say. "He didn't ask me up here—he has nothing to do with it." And then because I'm feeling bold, I add, "I'm here because I miss him," and I don't shift my gaze from his for even a second.

Then he lifts an eyebrow, and heat rushes to my face, and I turn. I walk through corridors that suddenly glimmer. I use the back of my hand to wipe away my smile, except it doesn't work. Because back there, Wren didn't speak for me. He wasn't the Preme in charge. I think he gets me, and I think he cares about me, too.

And then, when I'm close to the stairs, a hand lands on my shoulder. For a moment I think maybe it's Wren, that he deserted Addison, and chased after me. The moment doesn't last long. The grip is too tight. A thumb digs too deeply into my flesh. And in my periphery, I spot billowing black robes.

I refuse to be intimidated by the Honorable Justice Andrews, I refuse to cower, so I stand straight—even as Ben's words of warning streak through my brain.

"Good day, Ms. Hamilton," he says. Displeasure drips from each syllable. "Why is it that I always seem to run into you up here, on the fifth floor, where you're not welcome? Seems a far walk from your home all the way downstairs on the second."

"I was returning a book to the library," I lie.

He laughs with measured restraint. "You wouldn't be here to see your friend Mr. Edelman, would you? Sources say the two of you are quite close—strange, considering your different positions in this well-planned citizenry of ours."

"Actually, I have a few friends up here," I say. Another lie.

"Ah. Perhaps it's your newfound position on the guardship. It conceals what you truly are."

"You mean a Lower Mean?"

His brow draws in. "Only in part. Does the name Ted Bergess ring a bell?"

I stiffen at the question, and ever so slightly his eyes narrow. He is watching me carefully. "Sure," I say, with forced calm. "He's the one who was killed a few days back. Everyone knows his name."

"That's right, Ms. Hamilton. Killed by a guard, of all things."

"I already heard that, too. It was Daniel Munro, one of the new hires. The one who disappeared." My expression is even; I don't think anything gives me away.

"The one who disappeared, indeed. It sounds as though the two of you have a vested interest in each other, doesn't it? Hired onto the guardship at the same time, and all."

I laugh. "I hope more than you do that he turns up dead. How's that for vested interest?"

"See, Ms. Hamilton, that isn't what I'm hoping for in the least."

Now I'm silent. Now I wait impatiently to see what he will say next.

"See," he continues slowly, "I don't think young Daniel killed Mr. Bergess, I don't think he killed him at all." He crosses his arms and places a finger to his lip in a show of thought. "It's interesting, Ms. Hamilton. Shortly after Daniel's remarkable escape from captivity, a bullet was found, one that was discharged from the gun of poor Mr. Bergess, one not far from where his body was found. It had blood on it. Now, young Daniel was thoroughly stripped by the guards before he was locked in the holding cell, standard procedure, you see. He was found to be without wound—I've checked the documentation myself."

"Oh?"

He takes a step closer so that his robes brush against the back of my hand. "Correct me if my logic is flawed, Ms. Hamilton," he continues, "but I tend to think that the person Mr. Bergess shot was none other than his assailant; the very same person who shot and killed him. That person was not Daniel. It couldn't have been, woundless as young Daniel was. And so the culprit remains at large, they continue to evade authorities. In fact, if I can let you in on a little secret, I think at this very moment, I am looking right at her."

My blood runs cold. *Andrews knows.* He knows it was *me* who killed Bergess, and it's everything I can do to resist the urge to run. Finally I channel the girl bred in the Combat League, and with my expression level and my face impassive, I echo, "You're looking right at her?" Boldly I make a show of looking over my shoulder.

"Very nice, Ms. Hamilton," he says with a sneer. "Do make a point to continue looking over that shoulder of yours. Your friend Mr. Edelman, too. In the meantime, you're coming with me."

I go still. My heart skips a beat. "Excuse me?"

He flashes a wicked smile my way. "I'd like to see if my suspicions are correct. So, unless you'd like to strip right here, in the midst of the Preme atrium, follow me."

But at that moment, before I can decide whether I should do as he says, or run, run, run—a new face appears.

Cynthia Edelman. Wren's mother. Her eyes narrow into slits when she spots me, they meander over my Lower Mean outfit as my stomach constricts. "I hope you aren't up here to see my son," she says coldly.

I am silent, too rattled by my conversation with Andrews to say anything at all.

She steps closer, eyes glinting. "If I ever catch sight of

you two together…" Her voice trails away, yet the warning remains crystal clear. Then she turns to her colleague. "There's an emergency verification about to begin concerning the rogue Denominator we discussed. You're needed to preside over the proceeding."

"Can't Carney do it?" Andrews asks.

"He's sick. Hurry," Cynthia adds. "This is the moment we've been waiting for to eliminate that Floor One lowlife."

He nods, but before he follows after her, he turns to me. "Don't think you've gotten lucky," he hisses. "I'll send a guard to fetch you tomorrow." Then he's gone, and I stare after him and Cynthia with my injured arm throbbing like a flashing beacon.

Fifteen minutes later, I turn and see Wren standing behind me in the Mean cafeteria. I wonder what his mother would say about *that*. Even though it isn't my most immediate concern right now, Cynthia's warning lingers in my mind. It leaves me unsettled—and not simply because the woman dislikes me. It's how easily she can disregard her own child's feelings that bothers me. How she can place the compound's societal norms above her son's happiness. I wonder if she cares about him at all, or if her position as a privileged Preme trumps all else.

Then Wren says, "Impressive, Eve."

"What is?"

"The restraint you showed upstairs." He smirks, then takes a seat next to me. "You didn't even punch anybody."

"Funny, Wren. Maybe you should give up that prissy job of yours and try out comedy."

He grips his chin like he's considering it. Then he shoves

me playfully. "Wait. Did you just call my job *prissy*?"

I shrug.

"I suppose any job that doesn't involve punching people is prissy in your book. Don't worry—I don't take it personally."

I roll my eyes. "Is Addison upset?"

"Not with me." He grins. "I know you rescinded my welcome here at the cafeteria and everything, but I take it from your presence upstairs that you had something on your mind."

More than something, I think to myself, then I clutch my arm where the flesh still twists from the bullet. Because not only does Justice Andrews think I was responsible for Bergess's death—he has a way to confirm it. A way to confirm it *tomorrow*. "We can't discuss it here," I whisper, then push back from the table.

He catches me before I can stand. "Finish your meal, Eve."

"Excuse me?"

"You're beginning to look like you need that gun to defend yourself. Eat."

"Watch it, Preme." But I sit down again, pick up my fork.

As I finish my meal, Wren chats with Maggie and Connor. He makes them laugh, Eunjung and Emerald, too. And for a moment in time, even though the chips are stacked against me, even though my list of problems grows longer by the day, everything feels right. Everything feels easy.

CHAPTER THIRTY-EIGHT

"Well, shit. If it isn't the girl with no name," says a voice, and I know without looking it's Sully. "Haven't seen you at any of the protests."

"I've been busy."

"Busy?"

"Yeah, I just started work. Maybe next time, pick recruits older than sixteen."

Sully, who stands just outside the cafeteria blocking our path, laughs—but I see his eyes narrow. Probably he's used to garnering more respect than I just showed him, at least among us Lower Means. "Looks like *he's* older," he adds, and he juts his chin over my shoulder at Wren.

Wren.

I glance at him and sigh. Why does he always have to wear such clean clothes? Why are his T-shirts so crisp? How is his posture so consistently upright? Sully will spot him for what he is, I'm sure of it—even if Wren keeps his hands in his pockets where his unblemished skin is hidden. Partly I laugh to think of the look on Sully's face at learning that a Preme dines among us. But mostly I shiver. Because Sully has a keen sense of injustice, and he has numbers, and he can mobilize those numbers very quickly against anyone he perceives as a threat.

"What's your story, lad?" he is saying to Wren. "Can't say your face is ringing any bells. Course, you don't look like you call Floor Two home sweet home, am I right?"

Before Wren can respond, I elbow him in the ribs. "He's a Mean," I blurt out. "And we'll make a point of attending the next rally, once we get settled in our jobs. Happy?"

"And what's your job, girl with no name?"

He catches me in a moment of uncertainty. After all, to tell him I'm a guard would be as dangerous as telling him that Wren is a Preme.

"We work for the paper," Wren says smoothly, and I half turn to look at him, surprised. Then I understand: Maggie had been telling him about her job as I was eating, and he had remembered. He elbows me in the same spot that I elbowed him. "Isn't that right, girl with no name? That's a great title, by the way. Mind if I call you that from now on?"

I laugh, I can't help it. And as we push each other back and forth, Sully leaves us be, muttering to himself about teenagers.

Then, as we start toward the stairwell, I hear it: raised voices. Angry ones, and suddenly I catch sight of a blue and green color-block hoodie.

Hunter and Zaar are yelling at each other—that's the first thing I notice. The second is that Zaar is no longer on crutches. Both of them stop when they see me, and Hunter scowls in my direction.

"Speak of the devil," says Zaar loudly. "I was just going to have Hunter here pass along another message." He cracks his knuckles threateningly.

"Another?" asks Wren. He eyes Hunter.

"We're not friends anymore," I tell Zaar, "so you can stop using him as your messenger. If you have a problem," I add, "come find me yourself."

Hunter knocks my arm. "Just go, Eve. I can take care of this myself."

"I didn't say you couldn't. But it seems silly having you fight on my behalf when I'm perfectly capable." I roll up my sleeves, no longer as bothered by my data card, and stare at Zaar. He may not be as inherently evil as Daniel or Landry, but he has always been a willing participant in their cruel games. He has tormented me alongside them since I was small. "So," I continue, "I'm excited to hear this message of yours. Let me guess—you're upset that all your friends are gone. Or maybe you're still angry about me taking your spot on the guardship, or, wait—is it the broken knee?"

"You're checking all the boxes," Zaar says through gritted teeth. "Thing is—"

"*Eve.* Get out of here," Hunter reiterates. "He's just talking nonsense. Don't waste—"

"She's not even friends with you," interrupts Wren. "So why are you telling her what to do?" His voice is quiet, yet stern, and I see that his attention is fixed solely on Hunter. Maybe because he knows how easily I can hurt Zaar. Or maybe because he knows how deeply Hunter hurt me.

"Thing is," Zaar repeats, ignoring both of them, "you're virtually untouchable for someone like me. You know, being the big fighter with the guard's gun and everything. But maybe if word gets round about your flashy job and your flashy boyfriend, there'll be someone who *can* touch you. A lot of someones, actually, and based on their track record, it's a hell of a lot more than a mere touch…"

Sully.

All he has to do is tell Sully, and I am dead. The thought

makes me feel exposed and unwell, though I'm careful to hide it. "He isn't my boyfriend anymore, first of all. And do you know who Lower Means want patrolling their corridors? Oh yeah—other Lower Means, *obviously*." I spit the words at him like I believe them, then shove him across the chest. "Threaten me again, Zaar, and see what happens."

"Whatever. Just don't think you're any safer down here with Daniel and Landry gone," he says lazily as he heads for the cafeteria. He thumps my shoulder as he passes.

I stare after him. Strange I never thought of it until now. My list of enemies has grown shorter with Daniel and Landry out of the picture, and Dennis, too. I guess I've been too focused on battling a different type of enemy lately—myself.

Besides, even though my old enemies might be gone, new ones have cropped up to fill their place, haven't they? Ben roams the compound, and Justice Andrews. And possibly Sully and his entourage, too. Good thing it never occurred to me to grow complacent. Good thing I'm used to being a walking target.

I glance at Wren and see that he and Hunter still glare at each other.

"She's not even your girlfriend," Hunter says to him in a snarky voice, mimicking him. "So why are you down here, following her around?"

Wren stares at him for a few seconds, then laughs. "You mean the way you followed her around for *years*?"

"Thanks, you guys," I say loudly, "for having my back just now with Zaar." I step between them and make a show of rolling my eyes. It's enough to break their anger.

"Having your back?" Wren whistles. "You've really gone soft, Eve. Last I remember you set a Combat League record for fastest match with that guy."

"You're funny, Preme, as always." Then I turn to Hunter.

"Tell me if he tries to pass along any more messages, okay?"

"Is that before or after I give him another black eye?"

"After." We grin at each other—until I remember I'm angry with him, that is. Then he disappears inside the crowded cafeteria.

I don't want Zaar to get in my head or under my skin; I don't want to give him the satisfaction, but I can't help myself. My eyes scan the cafeteria until I locate him, until I assure myself he sits far from Sully. Then, after a steadying breath, I lead Wren to the stairs.

CHAPTER THIRTY-NINE

"Is this a secret way to reach your cell, or something?" Wren asks.

I shake my head. "We're not going to my cell."

"Care to elaborate?"

"Well, we need to talk about the compound, and I feel like punching things, so I thought we could combine the two."

"You feel like punching things? Weird. Very out of character for you, Eve."

"What did I tell you about switching careers? Really, it's something you should seriously consider. In the meantime, we're going to the Bowl."

My exchange with Zaar has rattled me, it must have. And then there's Hunter. I don't hate him like before, I know it in the pit of my stomach. I want to, though, so why can't I find it in me? He *betrayed* me—the anger should be easy to recall. And yet I had smiled at him just now like none of it had ever happened.

What does my capacity for forgiveness say about my character? Am I softhearted, even weak? Do I crave peace above all else? Or does my love for Hunter run deeper than I care to admit?

"Why do you always fight for the same team?" Wren asks, as I lead him into Blue Circuit's training room. Since there are no fights scheduled this evening, the place is empty. He fingers a blue armband on the desk that Bruno used to occupy.

I stare fondly around the room before I answer—at the fraying couch, the mismatched weights, the old treadmill. "The people, I guess. Erick and Anil. Bruno, too, before he died. They're good guys. And Emerald, obviously."

"Mmm."

I hold open the door to the metal half cylinder that connects the training rooms to the Bowl. "Got a problem with that?"

"Not with Emerald," he says, grinning.

I stare at the back of his head for a second, then lead him through the web of punching bags that smell of old sweat. I stop walking only when we reach the spot where we first laid eyes on each other. I don't think Wren will remember, but then he says with a smirk, "Are you trying to tell me something, Eve, bringing me back here?"

I make an exasperated face. "You wish," I retort. Then I smack the hide of the punching bag a few times so he doesn't see me blush.

"I take it you *do* remember, then?"

"Meeting you here?" I shrug. "Sure."

"And you noticed how unbearably handsome you found me, of course."

"Oh, for sure. I also thought, *shit. This prissy Preme might actually beat me.*" I turn to him, grinning.

"Prissy again? Ouch."

"What about you?"

He taps his chin as if he's thinking. "Let me see. I thought you were annoying, working the punching bags while I was waiting for a Lower Mean brute to show up. I thought you had more attitude than anyone I'd ever met in my life. And I thought you were beautiful. Shockingly beautiful."

Immediately I grab some knuckle tape and begin wrapping my hands. What did he mean by *that*?

For a while we just hit the bags, not really looking at each other. Then he clears his throat. "You wanted to talk to me about something."

I strike the bag a few more times before I answer. "Ben paid me a visit last night."

"What do you mean?" Wren turns. "In your cell?"

"Yes, there. In the middle of the night. But that's not the important part —"

"It isn't?" He is yelling now. The humor is gone.

I walk toward him and lower my voice. "Wren. Andrews thinks *I* killed Bergess."

He stares at me blankly. "Andrews. Surely you're not talking about Dominic Andrews, the Head of Justice."

I nod. "He was at my verification. He wanted to verify me but was outvoted. Same thing after Landry…"

Wren exhales. Then he turns to the punching bag and strikes it, just once. It's loud, like the cracking of a whip, and it sends the bag flying. "Sounds like you made quite an impression on him."

"Not a good one," I admit.

"It doesn't matter what he thinks. Everyone believes it was Daniel. His disappearing basically confirmed it."

I go back to my punching bag and shake my head. "Not anymore. They found the bullet fired by Bergess. The one with my blood on it. And they know Daniel wasn't injured." I take a deep breath and hit the bag hard enough to make its chain jangle. "My arm still hasn't fully healed. Andrews said he's going to have a guard bring me to him tomorrow, so he can check me for gunshot wounds."

Slowly Wren nods. "That's a problem."

"A big one."

"Well, you can hide tomorrow, but you can't hide forever. So I guess that means we're running out of time down here."

In more ways than one, I think to myself, as I remember Zaar's warning.

"Do you know how the compound's leadership tier works?"

I glance at him between punches. "Not really," I admit. "Aside from the glorious Commander Katz, sitting on his throne at the very top."

"Second in charge is Anthony Boynton, Katz's deputy. Cras Thornton is the executive director, and below him are the deputy directors. My mother is one, and so was Bergess until his untimely demise."

"I thought your mother and Bergess were department heads."

"They hold dual roles. It gives them more authority than the other department heads, the ones who bring in the next tier of leadership. That includes people like Sitwell, who heads up security, and your good friend Andrews, who runs justice."

I shake out my fists and try to commit the compound's leadership to memory. After Katz, these are our targets, after all. "Do you think they all know about aboveground, even the department heads?"

He spars with the punching bag for a few minutes before responding. "I don't know," he finally admits. "Everyone above the heads, definitely."

"So that's Katz, Boynton, Thornton, and your mother. If only four people know—"

"More than that know," he says quickly. "The scientists who made the discovery in the first place. And some heads have to know. Sitwell, for instance. Half the time he's the one ordering the verified to the incinerator. There's no way he doesn't know why the sun isn't used anymore."

"Right."

"Then there're the guards."

I glance at him. "I don't think they know. I think they do their job, marching the verified to the incinerator and everything, and I think they know what they're doing. But I don't think they know why."

Wren studies the arched metal ceiling. Then he nods. "I agree. There're too many of them—it would be too risky."

"They'll be a problem, though, if we try to touch the leadership."

"They'll be a big problem," he agrees. Then he sighs. "If we want to exit people through the Oracle, you realize, we need Katz. Don't forget his handprint alone opens the Oracle door."

"Which will be difficult. Maybe even impossible. So that leaves us with the storeroom."

"But exiting a large number of people will be much quicker through the Oracle, rather than the storeroom, so—"

"So we should focus on Katz." Vaguely I remember standing in the atrium, that very man within striking distance. I think about how badly I wanted to attack, to drag him to the Oracle, to open its door. I think I was on to something.

"Maybe we should," agrees Wren. "At least with that approach, it would protect our way out, in case something goes wrong." He looks at me out of the corner of his eye. "We don't need Katz to be alive, you know."

"Well, alive or not, how do we get to him?"

He shrugs. "Might be easier said than done."

I'm forced to agree. Then I rip the tape off my knuckles and exhale. "Is it just me, or does ending Eleven feel kind of impossible?"

"It's definitely not going to be straightforward."

"No."

He strikes the bag, ten blows in a row. "Let's go back to the beginning, for a minute. My father told me to follow the bodies."

"And we did. We found the incinerator. We know what it means—that the earth has cooled, that we can live up there."

"Maybe he was trying to tell me more than that. Maybe he was trying to tell me that the entire compound is being held hostage."

"You were a kid," I remind him. "What exactly did he expect you to do?"

He shakes out his arms and faces me. "Maybe he expected me to do what we're trying to do now—put a stop to it."

He stands so close, I can smell that clean, masculine smell of his, and I have to work very hard to stay focused. "Or maybe all he wanted was for *you* to have freedom." My voice wavers, and I don't know if it's from the punching bag, the heaviness of our conversation, or his proximity to me.

"Too bad he isn't around to ask."

My gaze jumps up to his. "But someone is."

"Surely you aren't going to say my lovely mother."

I shake my head. "I'm talking about Fiona, Maax's mother. They were an item for years, and even after they split, they stayed friends. She said herself that nobody knew him better."

"You really think he told his ex-girlfriend about the incinerator? About aboveground?"

"Do you have a better plan?"

"No. I don't."

"Maybe he did tell her things. Maybe he had a plan of his own to go aboveground, or to free the compound—"

"Let me get this straight. A minute ago you thought my father told me to follow the bodies so I could free myself.

Now you think he was in the middle of hatching a master plan to liberate all of Eleven?" He looks dubious, and I don't really blame him.

"My honest opinion? No, I don't think he had a master plan. I don't think he had any sort of agenda when he told you to follow the bodies, other than the need to pass along important information before he no longer could."

He's silent.

"Look, Fiona probably knows nothing about the incinerator, or up there. You're right. But she does know your dad. She knew him well. And, since so much seems to rely on him, let's focus our attention there."

He stares at me, his eyes alive. "Okay. Let's go see Fiona."

O nce again, someone steps across my path. This time it isn't Sully, or Zaar. It's Jules, standing with her hands shoved into her pockets. "Thought I might find you around here." She nods at the Blue Circuit training room that Wren and I just exited.

"Hi," I say quietly.

For a while, none of us says anything. We don't even move. That's good, because I don't need to be reminded of the fact that Jules blames Wren for what happened to her people. I never forgot.

Then her worn-out boots kick forward, and a second later she throws her arms around him. He pats her awkwardly on the back. I stare at them both with my mouth hanging open.

When she finally releases him, he says, "I take it the order went through."

"For both of us," she confirms. "And Marcy, too."

"Good."

"Uh—you guys?" I sound tentative, unsure. "What's going on?"

Jules stares at me. "What, he didn't tell you?"

"No." I turn questioningly to him, but he doesn't look at me.

"We've been reassigned floors, Eve. Avery and I. And Avery's caretaker Marcy, too. Can you believe it?" She laughs a little, like she can't really believe it herself, then she holds up her hands to show me the burning red skin from where the number one has been transformed into the number two. "We're not Noms anymore!"

When Wren nods confirmation, I crush Jules into a hug, and suddenly we're both jumping up and down. I can feel her tears wet against my cheek. "But...how?" I finally manage. Because even though I've heard of people being moved down a floor as punishment, I don't think I've ever heard of this.

"Maybe he carries a magic wand after all," she says slyly. She winks, then heads off down the corridor. "I'll stop by your cell tomorrow, neighbor!" she shouts over her shoulder.

I stare after her for a minute as I digest the news, then turn to Wren. "Care to elaborate?"

"I've been pulling some strings the past few weeks," he explains quietly. He studies the graffiti on the wall. "I didn't want to say anything, in case it didn't work out, but—"

My arms wrap around his neck before I know what I'm doing. I don't care that we're no longer a couple—I hug him as tightly as I can, as tight as my muscles will allow. Because right now a thousand emotions are bursting through my chest. Joy. And relief. Relief that Jules and Avery have a brighter future than before. That even if Wren and I fail at freeing the compound, at least there will be that.

Not that it's my victory to claim, not in the slightest. Once again I glimpse Wren's true nature, one that stands in stark contrast to my own. The past few weeks, I have focused on one person—myself. I didn't try to make things easier for Jules, or Avery, or for anyone else. But Wren did.

I always knew we were too mismatched to be a couple, but I thought it was because he came from the fifth floor and I came from the second. That was never it, though, not really. He's a better person than me. I should have seen it right at the very beginning, right there that first time we met in the Bowl. He didn't want to fight me. He didn't want to hurt someone who couldn't match his skill because he knew there was nothing courageous about that.

And me? There was nothing courageous about breaking Zaar's knee just because I could. Or punching that girl submitting her job application, or even pushing the young man on the Preme floor looking down his nose at me. I stand in Wren's shadow, but right now it doesn't make me feel small, it makes me feel *awe*. And it makes me want to do better.

"You're amazing," I say into his ear. I push my fingers through his hair and tilt his head so that our foreheads touch. I look him straight in the eye and say it again in a stern voice, "You're *amazing*."

His mouth twists like maybe he is trying to suppress a smile. And, since I'm already staring at it, I decide to press my lips there, just to see what happens, to see if my suspicions are correct, to see if he kisses me back…

It happens in a blink of an eye—he kisses me. He kisses me like he's hungry. Like he's famished. He kisses me so hard that I stumble backward, and then his hand loops around my head so that I'm stuck right there, right where I want to be. Right where I've wanted to be for ages.

The funny thing is that I can't really breathe. He kisses me too hard, and I can't stop smiling, which is just making it worse. I don't know if it's from happiness or oxygen deprivation that my lungs burn like they do, but finally I push against his shoulders and laugh into the soft spot underneath his jaw. "*Wren*," I say as I gasp for air.

His chest beats up and down under my hand. "Too much?"

I think about it for a bit, then kiss him slowly along the chin, scarcely able to believe my luck. "Never."

"Good. Maybe next time I lay on the charm, don't take so long to clue in."

"You know, you could've just kissed me forever ago and saved us both some time."

"Except I've seen you punch enough people lately to know better," he says, and he kisses me again.

"Thanks for doing that for Jules," I murmur.

"It was the least I could do." Then he fixes me with a piercing stare. "I'd do anything for you, you know."

I swallow. "I'd do anything for you, too."

For a while we just stand there holding each other, and I realize that it's moments like this that make life worth living. It's moments like this that make it worth fighting for. "Weren't we in the middle of something important?" I finally ask.

"I would choose this sort of diversion any day of the week," he says into my hair. Then he kisses my forehead and turns. "But if you insist…"

I kick at the back of his boot. "How does an asshole Preme like you turn into such a saint, huh?"

"Hmm." He scratches his chin. "I guess it all started when that asshole Preme met a girl…"

CHAPTER FORTY

Finding Fiona's cell is difficult—the Upper Mean cells are laid out differently than downstairs, and by the time I knock on her door, Compound Eleven has switched out its lights. I almost think she won't answer; it's a dangerous thing to do at this time of night. But I knock again, louder this time, until finally the door inches open and under insufficient lighting, I see a brown eye pressed close.

"Fiona?" My voice is uncertain. "It's Eve. Eve Hamilton—Maax's friend from the guardship. I'm here with Wren Edelman. We were wondering if we could ask you a few things about Wren's father."

A moment later, Fiona slips into the hallway holding an electric lantern. It fills the corridor with light in a way my small flashlight can't manage. An Upper Mean luxury, it must be. "You're the spitting image of your dad," she says at once. "It's like looking at his ghost, except for the amount of muscle you carry. Thom was always on the slender side." She smiles easily, like Maax does.

But the words must catch Wren off guard. Under the glare

of the lantern, his eyes look hollow and unkind, the opposite of who I saw downstairs less than an hour ago.

Fiona's smile falters. "Hasn't anyone told you that before?" Silence.

I look at his stiff features, his slightly askew posture, and I can sense his vulnerability. So I step forward. "We were wondering if he ever mentioned anything to you about aboveground," I say.

Fiona stares at me like she's surprised by the question. Finally she shakes her head. "What about up there do you mean? Maybe it'll jog my memory."

"A preoccupation with it," Wren offers from the shadows.

"It's funny you use that word," she says after a while. She drums two fingers against her chin. "In the months leading up to his death, he always seemed preoccupied to me, whenever we saw each other. It was like his mind was elsewhere—he couldn't focus on a single thing I said. I worried at the time that the two of us were drifting apart." She sighs. "But aboveground? No, I can't say that rings any bells."

It's hard to keep the disappointment from my face, but then I notice Wren's. A shadow now clouds his features. "The two of you were friends when he died," he says. He states it like a fact. "Through the illness even?"

"We were friends until the end, of course. When Cynthia became pregnant all those years ago—well. We certainly saw each other less after that, but we still remained close. I still cared for him, and I always loved him." She pauses, and I notice that her eyes gleam. "I can't say I've admitted this before, not out loud, but I think on some level I always thought the two of us would wind up together again. Somehow, someday." She laughs, and it makes the light of the lantern bounce and sway. "It didn't make much sense. Not after he wed Cynthia, and had you. Then there was the no-small fact that he was a Preme and I wasn't. I suppose we had no business starting up with each other in the first place." Her eyes narrow ever so slightly as she refocuses on Wren. "Which illness are you talking about?"

"Kidney disease." His voice is harder now. More like the Wren I know.

Slowly she nods. "Yes, I do remember him mentioning it once or twice. Easily manageable. It didn't give him much grief."

Wren scowls. "It didn't give him much grief? It *killed* him."

Fiona's gaze flickers to mine. She pulls her face into a tight smile. "I wasn't aware of that," she says carefully.

"You weren't aware of how he died?"

She shakes her head. "I never knew what killed him. His death was completely unexpected."

Under the aura of light cast by the lantern, I see Wren go still. "Completely unexpected," he repeats in a distant voice. "So, then his kidneys weren't failing him. He wasn't dying."

Fiona shakes her head. "I don't believe so," she says hoarsely.

Silence, thick and impenetrable. The Upper Mean corridors around us are empty. There is no distant echo of violence, no chatter through the shadows, no boots on patrol.

"So then what?" Wren whispers. "If it wasn't kidney disease, what killed him?"

"I'm sorry. I don't know what happened at the end, I really don't. I thought of all people that you'd—"

"What? That I'd know how my own father died?" He laughs darkly. "My mother didn't care to share those mundane details with me. Maybe it's my face. Maybe it reminds her too much of him. She always hated him—an easy case of transference, isn't that right?" He turns his gaze to me. "I think I'll go ask her about it."

CHAPTER FORTY-ONE

After a quick thanks shouted to Fiona, I sprint into the darkness after Wren.

When I catch up to him, he doesn't seem to notice me at all. Same for when I say his name, so finally I grab him around the arm. "Wren, stop."

Reluctantly he turns. "I don't want to talk about it."

"You don't need to," I say with a shrug. "I already know what you must be thinking."

"What's that?"

"That for the past eight years you thought your father died of disease, and now that belief has been shattered into a million pieces. That you're wondering the same thing I'm wondering: if he didn't die of illness, *how did he die*?"

"That about covers it," he agrees as he starts forward again. "Except for the part where I'm pretty confident I know who's responsible for his death."

"Your mother?"

He nods.

"And you're going to confront her?" I ask, jogging to keep up.

"I'm going to get a confession."

"And then what?"

He says nothing.

So I say what's really on my mind. The reason I tore after him in the first place. "You can't hurt her, Wren."

"I never said I would."

"Are you going to turn her in to the authorities?"

He shakes his head. "She's too powerful—she'll already have Justice Andrews in her pocket. Not to mention the fact that she and Katz are friends."

A chill coils its way down my spine. *Friends.* Friends with a murderer. Friends with a monster. Then I go still. "Wren— *Katz*!"

He stops and gives me a puzzled look through the darkness. "What about him?"

"We could use your mother to get to Katz. It's the only way we'll ever catch him without a billion guards surrounding his every move."

For a moment he's still. Then excitement shines in his eyes—I can glimpse it under the dull glow lifting from the floor. "She won't do it willingly."

"But if you're looking for revenge—"

"Then using her to end Eleven would be the ultimate retribution." Without another word, he grabs my hand and we shoot up the stairs to the fifth floor. A guard shouts to us through the darkness, but Wren doesn't stop, his pace doesn't even slow. I expect the sound of heavy footsteps to drum behind us, that and more shouting, but a few corridors later I realize there is nothing but silence. Perhaps the guard can spot the stride of a Preme. Perhaps he can sense danger—because right now, Wren is determined. Determined to find out what happened to his father, and—the part that makes my chest burst with anticipation—to end Eleven.

This is going to happen. Tonight.

I don't know where we are, not exactly, but as I scramble to keep up, I realize I'm not completely lost, either. I have spent enough time up here with Wren, enough time studying maps of the compound during guardship training, so I know we're getting closer and closer to Cynthia's apartment.

Finally he stops in front of a door that is white and completely unblemished. He reminds me, "This isn't a person you need to feel sorry for."

I nod, more unsure than before.

"The only way she'll take us to Katz," he continues, "is under the threat of death."

"Are you really okay with holding a gun to your mother's head?"

"If she's responsible for my father's death, then yes. I am. Besides, it's for the compound. If we end Eleven tonight, there will never be another cleanse down there. There will be no more needless suffering."

I take a deep breath. "Then I'm okay with it, too."

A second later he lifts his fist and slams it against the door, again and again, hard enough to shake its hinges. With enough force that neighbors stir—I can hear the shuffling behind their doors; one even peers into the hall. Wren is focused on the task at hand, sure, but he is angry, too. Angrier than I even realized.

Bang, bang, bang.

When the door finally pulls open, his mother stands there, well-dressed, holding a glass of wine. He doesn't wait for an invitation—he just shoves the door all the way open, knocking her backward and out of his path. I slip into the apartment after him, closing the door and staring around at a room that is spacious and white, smooth and glowing, as pristine as the rest of the Preme floor. As cold and unfeeling as the woman who resides here. Funny that she warned me about this. About catching me, a Lower Mean, with Wren. Yet here we stand—united—in her very own home, and there's nothing she can do to stop it. Maybe there never was. Maybe no matter how hard society and its tenets and its so-called norms tries to keep people apart, love will always find a way.

"What the hell is this?" she demands, and she turns to Wren with abandon. "You wake the neighbors with your incessant pounding? You barge into my home at an ungodly hour? You bring *her* here, of all people? This is a new low, Wren, even for you."

"I'm not here to fight. I'm here to ask you something."

"Make it quick," she says as she eyes me.

"Tell me how he died."

"Do you fashion me a mind reader?" she snaps. "*Who* is it you speak of?"

He smiles darkly. "Thom. Your husband. My *father*."

Whatever she expected Wren to say, it isn't that. Surprise registers quickly across her face, then her gaze shifts back to mine.

"No, Mother," Wren says steadily. "This has nothing to do with her. And I can assure you that if you need to worry yourself over anyone right now, worry yourself over me."

Her chin lifts in defiance. "What a way to speak to your own mother."

"Answer my question. Because I know he didn't die of kidney disease. So, let me ask you one more time: *How. did. he. die?*"

Somehow Cynthia finds it in herself to sneer, and suddenly *I* want to strike her. My own mother may be absent, she may willingly lose herself in her own daze rather than pay me any attention, but never would she show me such callousness. I feel sick for Wren—I feel sick that he had to grow up with such a woman. It's no wonder he's remained so attached to his father, even eight long years since his passing.

But I need to stay calm. I can't get caught up in emotion, so I distract myself by staring at the lone decoration in the apartment—a painting hung over the sofa. Five black rectangles are stacked on top of one another against a white backdrop. At the very top sits a triangle. At first I think it's without any meaning whatsoever, but then it strikes me that it could represent the compound, and I stare at it with more interest.

"He always did coddle you," Cynthia finally says.

"How did he die, Mother?" Wren's voice teeters on the cusp of restraint. She is playing with fire, I can sense it. But can she sense it?

"The strange thing," she continues, "is that you didn't shed a tear when he went. See, I always knew you were a lost cause. A twisted and unfeeling boy, only he was too foolish to see—"

Wren knocks the wineglass out of her hand and it shatters across the floor, stunning her into silence. *"How did he die?"*

"Sickness."

"It wasn't, though. You ordered him to the incinerator. I know you did."

Stillness overcomes her. A heavy, sincere stillness.

"Yeah," he taunts. "I know aboveground is perfectly safe. So, tell me what happened. Tell me what happened to my father."

She should cower, but she's made of ice, just like her son. "I don't know what you speak of—"

His face twists. Then I blink and his hand wraps around the fabric of her robe. For an instant, my stomach clenches, but then I see that he is still; he doesn't push her and he doesn't wrench her close. He simply stands there, malevolence etched across his features, fabric balled in his fist. She is physically powerless under his hand, and I think what he is doing right now is reminding her of that fact.

Normally her eyes are astute, but right now they glimmer with fear. "He found out," she whispers.

"Found out?"

"About up there. And any citizen who comes across such information is executed."

Wren's face turns into a slab of concrete, ashen and unyielding—but I don't think he realizes something. That if Cynthia's right, if any citizen who comes across that information is executed, he is in grave danger. After all, the fact that he's her son means nothing to a woman incapable of love, incapable of putting anything or anyone before power, prestige, privilege. I guess I'm in danger, too. All the more reason, then, to get to Katz. All the more reason to finish Eleven, tonight.

"It's a hard truth of the compound," Cynthia adds.

"So you killed him. You murdered your own *husband*!"

"Of course *I* didn't, Wren," she says, and her voice is softer than before, softer than I have ever heard it. It sounds close to human. "Who do you mistake me for? His death was ordered by those above me—by our leader. There was nothing I could do to stop it."

"Bullshit!" His voice echoes around the apartment. "How did Katz know that Dad knew?"

She says nothing.

"That's right," he laughs. "Because you told him. He thought he could confide in you—his *wife*—"

"He wasn't *confiding* in me," she suddenly snarls. "He confronted me with it, he wielded it over my head. He would have destroyed the compound if he wasn't stopped—"

"Destroyed it? You mean *liberated* it. You think all the people living like shit downstairs want to stay?"

"Wren Edelman—a champion of the lower castes." She lets out a wicked laugh. "You've led a privileged life up here, boy, and all that would be for naught if we set loose our civilization on top of the earth. I did it for you—can't you see that? *All* of it has been for you!"

There is a lull and I think that maybe, just maybe, Wren is falling for it. Then he pulls out his gun and points it at her.

Terror shines brightly in her eyes. "Wren…"

I hold my breath. Because I'm not sure what Wren will do next, or where his mind's at. I'm worried he's too upset to be thinking straight.

Then he says, "Take me to Katz," and all my muscles relax in unison.

"Katz?" I can see her mind reeling. I can see her brain working through every problem, every nuance, every possible solution. Finally she breathes. "Yes. Katz. He's the one who's responsible for your father's death. Not me, Wren. Never me."

It's working. This is happening. We are going to get to Katz, and we are going to use him to *end* Eleven.

Then the door bangs open, and a familiar voice rings through the silence. "Drop the gun or your girlfriend is dead."

CHAPTER FORTY-TWO

Sitwell kicks the door closed behind him. The barrel of his gun is pointed at my head. "I should have known you wouldn't heed my advice to stay away from him," he says. Eyes crinkle into slits. "I should've let Justice Andrews haul you to your death. I shouldn't have hired such scum in the first place. You're off the guardship, in case you couldn't otherwise tell."

Something inside me withers at his words, then I almost laugh at how absurd it is—that I should care about a job that I loathe, especially in the face of tonight's circumstances. But with Sitwell here, I realize, with his gun aimed at my head, getting to Katz just became much more difficult.

So, maybe we won't fulfill tonight's mission. Maybe we won't even live to see tomorrow.

"You, young man," Sitwell says to Wren, "are never to set foot near my daughter again. I don't care if it's in the context of work, or if she comes to you, or if you are defending her from a lower-floor vagrant—if I catch you within ten feet of her, I'll personally see to it that you wind up among the verified, no matter that you're Cynthia's son. Do I make myself clear?"

Wren doesn't bother to look at him. Instead he stares at his mother and mutters something under his breath.

"I'll take that as a yes. Now, put the gun down. Because if you think I'm bluffing, if you think I care about ridding Compound Eleven of a Lower Mean such as Ms. Hamilton here, you're in for a rude awakening. Quite the company you choose to keep."

"Get out of here, Sitwell," Wren says. "This has nothing to do with you, and it has nothing to do with Eve. It has to do with me and my mother."

But Sitwell doesn't leave. Instead he moves closer. So close that the end of his gun brushes against my hair. Wren watches out of the corner of his eye.

I don't like the fact that he watches so closely. It means the threat from Sitwell is one that he takes seriously. Wren knows the man much better than I do, and so if he has reason to worry that Sitwell will actually kill me, it must be something to worry over.

Then Wren says coldly, "I assume Addison doesn't know. Your wife, either."

Sitwell is silent.

"No sense in denying it now," he continues, his voice tight with contempt. "I should've clued in when you kept Eve on the guardship after the fiasco with Landry. I don't have that much sway over you. But if you're trying to keep my mother happy, maybe I do. So, how long have the two of you been sleeping with each other? A few months...longer?"

A heavy quiet blankets the room.

"The funny thing is, Sitwell, you would've scored more points with her if you pissed me off."

"I don't know what you're talking about," Sitwell finally says. His voice is laced with outrage.

"I suppose it was the neighbors who alerted you just now," Wren adds. "Heard a commotion, didn't they? Spotted, God forbid, a Lower Mean? So they went to the man they'd seen coming and going—good thing it wasn't your wife who answered the door, you piece of—"

"*Wren*," his mother warns. Her voice is strained, yet somehow still authoritative. "Once again, you speak of things that don't concern you."

"Get out, Sitwell," he reiterates. "Get out or I'll tell Addison the second I see her. Your daughter will hate you and your marriage will be ruined. Is that what you want? All for this lying piece of filth?"

"Don't do this," Sitwell says slowly. "That is your mother you're talking about. Whatever it is you're currently fighting over, she's still your mother. You *must* unhand her."

"Must I?" He laughs darkly, and I wonder if it's as obvious to Sitwell that he has no intention of letting her go as it is to me. "She killed my father. Look the other way and you'll be next."

"Lies," she hisses as Sitwell taps his shoe against the floor.

Then he says, "Let's see how deeply you care about this Lower Mean, then."

Half a second later, the handle of his gun crashes down against my skull. I see a current of red before my vision goes black. My face feels warm, goopy. I am on my knees; pain almost turns my stomach.

For a minute, I am listless and drooping, but then I remember that I have been here before, on plenty of occasions. *This is lemon juice, Eve. Nothing more.* So even though the room tilts back and forth, I torque myself around, then punch Sitwell in the face just as he bends down to retrieve me.

A hard hit, right under the eye, one he wasn't ready for. It splits his papery skin—skin tinted blue from the veins running beneath it, and a wisp of satisfaction swells inside my stomach. Before I can lunge at him again, there comes a blast, one that's deafening in my ears. One that coerces stillness from me. A warning shot, evidently, and he presses the still-smoking gun to my temple before I can move.

I yelp from the pain of the white-hot pistol, and then I realize that's it. I missed my chance. It doesn't matter that bone throbs from where the butt of his gun struck me, it doesn't compare to the feeling in the pit of my stomach: I *lost*.

So. How are we going to get to Katz *now*?

"She ought to have stitches," Sitwell comments with apathy as he surveys the injury on the top of my head. "Of course, if you don't let go of your mother and hand over your weapon, there's really no point."

I can't get a good read on Wren—there's too much blood in my eyes and my head aches too badly. But in my peripheral vision I see him glare at Sitwell. "Let her go. *Now*."

"And will you let your mother go?"

For a moment, Wren just scowls. Then, after a minute of slowly stretched silence, he mutters, "Fine," and part of me withers. We just lost our bargaining chip. And without her, we have no way to reach Katz. We have no way of ending Eleven, and every cell in my body wants to yell, and scream, and cry. If only I had reacted sooner, if only I had somehow wrestled the gun from Sitwell's hand...

Then the barrel of the gun lifts. Wren shoves his mother unceremoniously forward, he hands over his weapon, and then I'm shoved forward, too. I take Cynthia's spot next to him and grasp at the wall to stop myself from falling. Before I can wipe the steady stream of blood from my eye, Cynthia edges toward the door, dragging Sitwell behind her. My head pounds too loudly to hear whatever they say, and so all I can do is stare after them, my brows drawn so tightly together, it's like they're stitched with needle and thread.

"Your behavior tonight, Wren," she suddenly calls, "has been beyond the pale. I do expect a full explanation and apology, but first, I must express gratitude to Jeffrey. Alone."

As soon as they're gone, Wren wraps his arms around me and my knees buckle. "I'm sorry," I say in a hoarse whisper.

"What are you sorry for?"

"Our chance to get Katz. It's over."

"It's not your fault, Eve," he says, as he kisses me. "We'll find another way."

Slowly the room levels out around me. "No, we won't."

"What do you mean?"

"I mean…that I think this is a trap."

He watches me closely. "What are you talking about?"

"We know about aboveground. Your mother said herself that anyone who finds out must die. It's a hard truth of Compound Eleven, remember?"

"I'm her son," he says, but the words haven't passed completely through his lips when he shakes his head, scowling. "I suppose that minor detail makes no difference to someone like her."

I don't bother confirming it. I just say, "Sitwell's the reason she's okay. Even without your gun, why would she want to be alone with you again right now?"

His gaze is unfocused. "So they're standing outside, waiting for us to open the door, ready to shoot…"

"They do things by the book. They won't get their hands dirty unless they have to." I take a deep breath. "My guess? One of them stands outside. Armed. The other one went to get the guards. I think if we stay here any longer, we're going to be arrested."

"Then incinerated," he adds.

We stare at each other. I can see how deeply he wants to

refute what I am saying. How badly he wants me to be wrong. A few minutes ago we were in control, but now?

"We need to get to the storeroom."

I nod. Our time in Compound Eleven has officially run out. We failed to end Eleven. We *failed* Eleven. And now, if we want to survive, we must flee.

Silently he resigns himself to this fact. I can see the shift beneath his features, can sense the resolve harden in his veins. "It's going to be difficult without a gun," he says eventually.

"Good thing I have mine." I pull it from the back of my jeans and hand it to him.

He stares at it for a moment. "Are you ready?" he asks, as we move in the direction of the door.

I dab away blood and nod. *Relax, Eve*, I try to tell myself, but my pulse is racing. Maybe just a little, I'm afraid that I am wrong—that I have misled Wren. But mostly I am terrified that I am right.

We glance at each other, then Wren edges open the door, and we hear the unmistakable sound of a gun being cocked.

CHAPTER FORTY-THREE

"You plan on killing me, Mother."

"Go back inside, Wren. We haven't concluded our business out here."

"We? I don't see your boyfriend anywhere."

Even with the orange beads along the floor offering the only light, it is plainly obvious that Sitwell has disappeared.

"The two of us are friends and colleagues, for the umpteenth time. Now go back inside."

"Or what—you'll shoot me?"

She smiles wickedly. "It isn't a nice feeling having a gun drawn on you, is it? Imagine, after all I have done for you, holding death to my throat as though I'm a crook. No son of mine would be so heartless."

"No mother of mine would kill her son's father."

"Oh, that." She chuckles. "How is it that you realized it wasn't disease that took him?"

"An old friend."

Her eyes narrow.

"A friend from a lower floor, at that."

"Fiona."

"That's the one. Lovely woman. Things sure went downhill for him when he decided to date you."

"And what about up there? Don't tell me Thom was foolish enough to confide in her all those years ago."

Wren shakes his head. "She knows nothing. Eve is the reason I know about up there, along with the tip from Dad to follow the bodies. You know, right before you took him to his death. No wonder he was so cryptic—you would've had your ten-year-old son killed otherwise."

"Go back inside, Wren. Now."

"So you can have the guards arrest us? Nah." His body is relaxed, his tone is casual. Then, as if his arm is mechanized, it lifts, it wraps around the gun she holds—*his* gun—in a fraction of a second.

That's all the time she needs. Her finger twitches, it pulls the trigger. A deafening blast rings in my ears.

When I open my eyes, Wren is bent in half, and I scream. But he straightens, and he wrenches the burning gun from her hands and delivers a punch, full force, to the middle of her face. It makes her crumple, and he uses the opportunity to take back the weapon.

That's when I notice the spot of red that stains his shirt, just above his hip bone. I stare at it—I stare so long and so hard that the pigment becomes tattooed on my brain, and my eyelids, and every time I blink, I see it.

"Strike three, Ms. Hamilton," comes a voice from the shadows, and another blast lights up the hallway. I glimpse billowing robes. I spot the gun that Andrews points at my head. I hear the bullet crack the doorframe in half, two inches from my skull.

Immediately there's another shot, and this time it comes from the gun that Wren holds.

But Andrews is quickly around the corner—I think for a second that the bullet missed him completely. Then I hear him groan, hear metal clatter to the floor, and I surge forward.

I expect to see Andrews bleed out on the floor. I expect to take his gun, another one for aboveground, I expect to bid him good riddance. Instead a fist swings at me and I lose my footing as I twist away. He uses the opportunity to grab me by the hair, he snaps my head back and tugs the open flesh along my skull.

I almost scream.

But I will not let the likes of Andrews see me panic. I will not let Wren come to my rescue for a second time—not with a crimson stain on his shirt and his assailant at his feet. This is *my* fight. So I lean into Andrews's hand to give my scalp a reprieve, then drive my leg between his.

He moans, and the grip on my hair is loosened enough that I can free myself. I drive my elbow into the underside of his chin and follow it with a hard punch to the jaw, one that turns his teeth maroon.

Half a second later, he lands a punch of his own, this one to my ear, shocking in its pain. Then his forehead smashes into me and it breaks my nose, I'm sure of it. Blood fills my mouth with the taste of metal.

A laugh gurgles between us that has the consistency of molasses, and I almost falter. Just in time I realize the laughter comes from my own belly. It's because this Preme thinks he can actually beat me after getting lucky with a couple good hits. Me, a Lower Mean. Me, whose entire life has been spent fighting, *surviving*. And him? He has never had to battle, to fight for his life, to experience real pain.

And though he may be strong, though I may be injured, he can't hold a candle to me.

Suddenly my feet are bouncing, my fists are held up in

front of me, and I am in the Bowl. People scream my name, they stomp their boots. I gather up the feeling of pain in my skull and my ear and my nose and I box it up, I set it aside. Then a pin inside my brain is pulled and with explosive power, I punch him with my right fist, then my left, then my right. Three strikes to the face delivered at full throttle.

Strike one. Strike two. Strike three. I mutter it under my breath.

I attack his neck next, the one with the white tabs fastened tightly around it—a reminder of his prestige atop the Department of Justice. *Strike one. Strike two. Strike three.* It makes him cough and sputter, having his windpipe blasted, a dirty move—almost as dirty as punching me in the ear.

Now he slumps to the floor. He is distracted by pain, by his difficulty to retrieve oxygen, and I use the opportunity to crouch in front of him. Even with blood beginning to soak his robes from where Wren's bullet must have nicked him, he'll live, I know that. Because there's shouting off in the distance, and the sound of heavy footsteps. Someone will save this prestigious Preme—it's only on the lower floors they leave us to die.

I don't have much time, so quickly I push my beaten face to his. "You had me all wrong, Andrews," I whisper. "I was never brutal, I was never a monster. At least not until you put the idea in my head. So if you don't make it through the night, remember something. Remember this was your own doing, all of it, right from the very beginning."

"Eve!" Wren has me by the shoulder. "Eve, let's go—now. They're coming!"

With blood still dripping down my face, with one last meaningful glance exchanged with my enemy, I turn away and follow Wren around the corner and through the darkness as we take off into the night.

Faster, farther. Away from danger.

The guards will have found the injured senior members of Compound Eleven by now. They will be hunting us with more intensity than before. The thought gives my legs renewed life and I push even faster, orange beads screaming through my periphery, Wren and I neck and neck—

But the guards are fast, too.

Along the next corridor, the fastest one spots us, fires his weapon. The blast pierces my injured eardrum like a hot knife, but we are around the corner before his bullet can reach us.

And then…even though my head feels full of cotton balls, I begin to notice something. Wren and I, we are no longer neck and neck. He is slower. And yet when we fled from the beast aboveground all that time ago, it was *me* who couldn't keep pace. *I* should be the slower of our two.

I peer at him as we run. Even through the darkness, I can see features that contort, that are rigid with effort. I see, too, that the red spot on his shirt has grown considerably. All at once, coldness enters my bones. No matter that I sweat from exertion, I feel colder now than I ever have in my life.

Soon we will be within the sightline of the fastest guard, we will be catchable prey once again. Already I can hear his footsteps echoing behind us, I can feel him closing in, snatching away a life of freedom that is now so close I can practically taste it—

"Wren."

A whisper through the shadows.

"Wren. In here."

Suddenly his fingers snag the back of my shirt, they force me to a halt when every fiber of my being screams to keep going. Only then do I notice a door ajar. Wren drags me through it and slips it shut before I can process what's happening. I hear the turning of a deadbolt, I hear him groan quietly as he hits the floor. The sound of footsteps bang outside.

Light floods a large apartment, and I blink at perhaps the last person I expected to see right now. Addison.

Her gaze doesn't linger on mine. Instead she drops to her knees and lifts Wren's shirt.

I cringe, but not because of her, or her freshly brushed hair, or even her proximity to him. I don't care about any of that. I cringe because there is a hole in Wren that is seeping too much blood and it strikes me that the guards might not be the biggest impediment to escaping Compound Eleven tonight.

"Help me to lower him," Addison instructs. I don't stop to think about it, I just hit the floor opposite her and do as she says. Wordlessly I push him backward. Next she rolls his shirt up as high as it will go, revealing skin so smooth, it makes the bullet hole look like even more of an anomaly. She mutters to herself, then disappears to a far corner of the apartment.

The surprise at finding myself here, of all places, wears away. Reality sinks in, and a lump forms in my throat. This can't be happening.

A minute ago he was fighting, he was running at full speed. And now?

No, Eve.

It isn't time for tears. It isn't time to give up. And certainly it isn't time for Wren to know how deeply fearful I am. So, carefully, I lean forward so that my face hangs over his and say his name.

He peers at me, but I can see in his eyes how much pain he's in. They are only half seeing. Mostly they look inward, and suddenly I'm surprised he even made it this far.

"Wren," I say again. "You're going to be fine. Do you understand me?" My mouth presses together so hard that my lips go numb. But I need him to be fine. I *need* it.

I think he understands. He holds my gaze and nods.

Then Addison is there, and I watch as she pushes a pill between his teeth. She holds water to his mouth so that he can swallow it. "You're strong," she says as she shoves an uncapped bottle and a towel into my hands. "Pour the antiseptic on it, then apply as much pressure as you can. It will slow the bleeding."

"And the pill?"

"It will help him cope with the pain. Hurry."

So I straddle him. I hold the bottle with one hand and the towel with the other, and I stare down at the hole that doesn't belong. And then I freeze.

I can't do it, I can't pour antiseptic on it, I can't press on it. Too much pain, far too much, and I can't be the one to cause it.

"*Now*, Eve."

It's the first time she has ever used my name. I lift my gaze and see that she stares at me straight on. There is no disdain. No disgust. We are not separated by three floors, we are not a Preme and a Lower Mean. We are two people trying desperately to save someone we care for.

Someone I love. And maybe she does, too.

I grit my teeth and douse him with the foul-smelling liquid; I push against the injury with all my strength. I close my eyes so I don't have to see him writhe, but I can't block out the sound of his panicked breaths or the groan that resonates from deep inside his chest. It hurts me more than the blast to my ear.

By the time my muscles begin to ache from holding myself in place, his breathing has slowed. I open my eyes and see that the blood loss has, too.

Addison stands off to the side, watching me distantly with her arms crossed. "How much trouble are you guys in?" she finally asks.

"A lot."

"Even Wren?"

"Especially Wren," I confirm. "But I think I can get him somewhere safe."

"Where?"

I shake my head. "I can't tell you."

"Why's that?"

"Because if the leaders get wind of it, they'll try to kill you, too."

She scoffs, but my face is unyielding.

"You're serious?" she finally asks. Her gaze becomes piercing, astute. It strikes me that if she wasn't raised in a world of arrogance and excess, she might not actually be half bad. I can almost see why Wren dated her in the first place.

"I wish I wasn't."

She still looks skeptical, but she doesn't argue. Instead she says, "I'm going to stitch him up and dress the wound. After that, you two should go. It won't be long before my father comes along to check on me, given the circumstances."

I nod, and when she disappears to retrieve supplies, I move alongside Wren. I kneel beside his head, and my blood-stained fingers graze his cheek. He is pale, but his eyes are more alert than earlier. "It's going to be a long walk from here," I say to him.

Half his mouth curls into a smirk. "Think you're the only one tough enough to take a bullet, Eve?"

Instead of laughing, another lump forms in my throat. I want to kiss him, but then Addison returns with a small metal tray holding an assortment of tools. I move aside as she begins stitching, and eventually I go to the door and hold my ear against it. Nothing but silence. Probably by now, the entire fifth floor has been combed, which means we should be able to move through these hallways unobstructed. I am not as hopeful about downstairs.

"Finished," Addison announces.

I examine a wound sewn neatly together, and I have to admire her skill. Next she places a thick square of gauze over the top and tapes it in place. Together we help him to his feet, but all at once he leans against the wall and pushes an arm over his face.

I glance nervously at him. At her.

"Dizziness," she assures me. "It will pass."

"How do you know all this?"

"My mother's a doctor," she explains as she tosses a wet washcloth and a hat in my direction. "Your hair stands out too much. So does the blood covering your face."

I wipe myself clean as best I can, then place the hat gingerly over my head. Wren and I nod meaningfully to each other, he pulls himself from the wall, and I take half his weight over my shoulder.

"Thank you," I say to her, before we go, as earnest as I've ever been.

"That safe place that's too dangerous to discuss? Get him there. Please."

I nod at her, and then we are gone.

CHAPTER FORTY-FOUR

Two hallways later and Wren stops. He withdraws his arm from over my shoulder and hobbles toward a door. Three knocks, then two, then one. A secret code, similar to the one I used to share with Hunter.

"What are you doing?" I whisper.

"Recruiting Long."

"Why?"

"Because you can't keep a watch out for the guards and carry me at the same time."

Long pulls open the door before I can protest. His smile vanishes when he sees Wren's pallid face. His brow draws together when he notices the large patch of red soiling his shirt. And by the stunned look he gives me, I'm guessing I didn't do a very good job at wiping the blood from my face. "Are you guys okay? What the hell happened?"

"We don't have time," Wren says in a low voice. He moves past Long, and once I'm inside, Long closes the door. "The guards are after us and I could use a hand, if you're up for an adventure."

"The guards?" I can sense his shock, and no wonder. It isn't often the guards target a Preme. "I mean, yeah, I'm always ready for an adventure, you know that. You okay, Eve? Nice hat. Not really your color, although it does complement those one thousand bloodstains nicely."

I roll my eyes. "Grab a fresh shirt for Wren, will you? And your gun."

"My gun?" He lifts an eyebrow. "Sounds like a dangerous mission you're entrusting to me."

"The guards will shoot to kill if they get a clear shot," I confirm.

"Sitwell will, too," Wren adds.

"Addison's dad? What the hell did you do? Wait, were you *shot*?"

"By my mother."

Long looks dazed. "So then why are the guards chasing *you*?"

"The entire compound will be after us, at the pace you're going," I interrupt. "We need to go—*now*."

So he turns to a pile of shirts strung over the back of his couch and tosses one to Wren. But when Wren starts to get changed, his movements are so slow and uncertain that I take his fumbling hands in my own and guide them through the sleeve holes. I pretend not to notice the way his body shakes or the slipperiness of his skin. I just smooth the clean shirt over his chest as though it's the most natural thing in the world.

"Thanks," he mutters.

I nod, then wait for Long to finish searching through the mess on the coffee table, lifting papers and brushing aside garbage. Finally he finds what he's looking for, and he tucks the gun and some spare bullets into his pocket. He spreads his arms and stares at me. "Fast enough for you?"

Instead of responding, I reach for the door.

"Hold up," he says. "What's the plan? If the guards are looking for you, don't you think—"

"We're leaving the compound," Wren explains. "You can come, too, or you can turn around once we're there. Right now, though, we just need to make it to the second floor."

"What's on the second floor?"

"The way out," I say, then I throw open the door.

Back in the corridor, my ears strain. I don't know these hallways well enough. I don't like my odds up here. Floor Two beckons me, it calls my name, even if it is swarmed with guards.

"Here, Eve." A cold gun slips into the palm of my hand.

"But—"

"It's yours. I've got my own," Wren assures me.

I nod, then lead the way forward, through the short, narrow corridors of the apartments and into the wider canals that take us toward the fifth-floor atrium. Then I stop. "The main stairwell will be watched," I say, and I don't know why I didn't realize it sooner. "We need to find another way down."

Wren shakes his head. "The other stairwells are too far. Besides, we're armed."

"I'm not shooting anyone. Not if I don't have to."

Long stares between us. "I'm with Eve," he says eventually. "Sorry, man. I know you're hurting and everything, but if you guys are in as much trouble as you say you are, they'll have guards stationed at all the major checkpoints."

Wren shuts his eyes for a moment, and I watch him closely through the shadows. I can only imagine how weak he feels. How exposed. The longer I lead him in circles, the worse his odds of survival become, and the thought makes me shiver. But he resigns himself, he must, because he opens his eyes and turns away from the atrium. A few corridors along and we hear it. Footsteps. Terse voices.

"This way," Wren whispers, then he lifts his arm from around Long and walks toward a door I've come to know well. He punches in the passcode as the footsteps grow louder. Without time to spare, we slip inside the department that until tonight was his own. Desks fan out around us, each stacked with yellow paper and computers and tidy containers holding pens. It isn't a sight I've ever seen before, not in person. These important jobs don't exist downstairs.

"Is there another door?" Long asks. He has to jog to keep pace with Wren as he leads us through the room.

"Yes."

"Slow down, will you? I'm supposed to be helping you right now, remember?"

"Long's right," I call. "You need to save your strength for when it matters."

Wren throws a dark look over his shoulder. But his stride shortens, and he allows Long to help him forward once again. The pain seems to reemerge as soon as the burst of adrenaline wears off, and I see him swallow.

I swallow, too.

Out the back door, we're tentative, even more than before. Only when we're sure the Preme floor slumbers around us do we inch forward and, after what feels like an eternity, Wren points at a door with a rectangular pane of glass. A stairwell.

Without appearing to, I watch him closely as we descend. Under the dull orange beads, I see him grimace with each step, even with Long's help. I think of the ladder waiting for us in the storeroom that he'll be forced to climb all on his own, and a shiver grips me so hard that I almost lose my footing.

Slowly we pass the fourth floor, then the third. No guards wait for us, and my head and face ache with less intensity, or maybe I'm just getting used to the constant stream of pain. Perhaps I will have the opportunity to slip inside my cell and grab a few things for the outside world. Perhaps I can knock on Maggie's door and tell her to come, too. Perhaps the path between here and there and the storeroom will be completely unobstructed, and we will make it out, we will make it to safety, and then when Wren is stronger we'll try again to end Eleven.

Then the shadows stir, and from near the door leading to the second floor comes a voice. "Gotcha."

Looking down the barrel of a gun has never suited me. That feeling of powerlessness is crushing. So is glimpsing the end when it should be just the beginning.

"Three against one," Wren reminds the guard. His gun is drawn, so is Long's.

"You shoot me," begins the guard, "and every other guard on duty will know exactly where you are. No sense in putting up a fight. It's over."

His voice sounds familiar. I squint through the darkness, but it's too murky to make out his face. Then it hits me.

"Trevor?"

He hesitates. "Eve?"

He pulls out a flashlight, eyeing Wren and Long. Then his gaze sweeps over me. It lingers on my nose, which I assume is swollen, and on the dried blood that tangles my hair.

"One male, brown hair—Preme. One female, blonde—Lower Mean. Both tall, injured, and extremely dangerous. That's what they said. So, it's you they're after?"

"It doesn't have to be," I say quietly. "There are three of us, see? And I'm wearing a hat. We don't match the description at all."

"They say you attacked the Head of Energy. And the

Justice Minister."

"Only after they tried to kill us."

He shakes his head. Then he says three words that make me squirm. "I'm under orders."

"But—"

"Move over, Eve," Wren interrupts from over my shoulder. His voice sounds strained and impatient. "It's the only way," he adds, and the sound of his gun being cocked fills the stairwell. I see Trevor look at him nervously. I see his hand grip his gun harder than before.

Quickly I move so that I stand between them. "No."

"Eve—"

"You're not shooting him."

"He's a *guard*."

"He helped me. Do you remember, Trevor? Do you remember when I was letting that Upper Mean kick me around, and you set me straight? I still think about what you said to me—I think about it all the time. No amount of guilt can change the past, do you remember?"

He nods slowly.

"If you arrest us right now, we'll be killed. All three of us will be—I know that for a fact. Save yourself the guilt, and let us go."

"I'm just doing my job."

"Please, Trevor." My voice is desperate. If I can't persuade him to lower his weapon, bullets will fly, from all directions. It's likely that all four of us will end up dead. "*Please*. You know I'm a good person. You knew it more than I did, at one time."

For a while he's silent. Then he shakes his head. "Don't go near the main corridor," he whispers. "Or your cell."

I blink at him blankly, then my chest swells. Just like when I first met him downstairs, his kindness erupts unexpectedly from the darkness. It erupts with so much force it makes me wonder why I've spent so long thinking the worst of people, why I've spent so long with so little faith in humanity. I squeeze his arm as I slip past, vowing silently to repay the favor, then I pull open the door to the second floor and lead the others into the dingy corridors that are my own.

Through the pulsating pain in my head, I spot out a chipped brown line painted along the wall, and I notice that the ceilings are particularly low. We are near to the feeding dock, then, and that means the kitchen isn't far. The finish line is within sight.

Even so, every couple of minutes I make Wren and Long stop, I make them smother their breaths so that I can listen for the echo of footsteps. There come none. The corridors are desolate, so desolate it feels like we are the only ones in all of Eleven.

I exhale. It will turn out okay—*everything* will turn out okay—even though we failed to get to Katz, to end Eleven, even though we're being forced from the compound before we're ready, even though Wren is injured. Everything will be okay. Wren will heal. We'll return and we'll get Katz and we'll open up the compound for every last citizen. Yes, everything will be fine. Except at that very moment, I remember something.

If you go, let me go with you.

The words twist through my brain, they feel like weights stacked on my shoulders, and the pounding inside my head ratchets up a notch. My mother wants out of Compound Eleven more than anybody, even me. It has been unbelievably cruel to her; it has stripped her of her very own child. She will never know happiness so long as she is down here, and I can't leave her to rot for another day—not one. That means I can't count on coming back to get her—it means I need to get her *now*.

I glance at Wren over my shoulder. Face gray, rimmed in sweat. The exertion of the walk is already too much—I can't ask him to go farther. So I'll have to go alone.

When the door to the kitchen appears through blackness, I punch in the passcode with unsteady fingers. It's empty inside, and I lead the others quickly around the butcher blocks, past the shiny knives that catch the glare of my flashlight, and finally into the towering storeroom. It should be relief that washes over me, but all I do is bite my nail.

"What the hell is this place?" asks Long as he cranes his neck and stares at the ceiling.

"The compound's storeroom," I reply. "Wren can explain everything to you while he rests. Go over there, on the other side of the nets where you'll be out of sight." I try to act nonchalant as I add, "I'll be back soon."

Immediately Wren's eyes narrow. "What do you—"

"I have to take care of something."

"Eve—"

I shake my head. "I made a promise, and I intend to keep it. I'll be back soon."

He withdraws his arm from Long and walks toward me. His first few steps are upright, but then the pain makes him double over. "You're not going out there," he says hoarsely. "It's too dangerous. We're lucky we even made it here."

"It's a promise I can't break."

"Well, I'm not letting you go." He says it flatly.

His resolve, now, makes me smile. "You and I both know you can't stop me," I say softly.

"Then I'm coming with you."

"You're not coming with me, Wren." I lift his hand and run my index finger along his palm, committing each detail to memory. "But—"

"Eve—"

"No—just listen. If something happens… If for some reason I don't come back, don't go looking. Go outside, go to Michael, just *go*."

"You know I can't do that."

"Yes you can."

"Not a chance."

"*Wren*."

He edges closer. "*Eve*."

Tears prickle suddenly behind my eyes. "Please tell me you'll go. Please do this for me."

His hand slips around my neck and I notice how clammy and cool it is—not like the Wren I know. But the way his eyes flash leave me without a doubt. "Whoever you made a promise to," he mutters, "break it."

"It was a promise I made to my mother."

Something in his eyes shifts. He knows, I think, that it isn't a promise I will break.

"I told her I had a way out of Compound Eleven. I promised her I'd take her with me. You know what she's been through—I can't turn my back on her now."

He tilts his head down so that his forehead rests against mine, mindful of my injuries, conscientious no matter how much pain he's in. "Come back, then," he whispers. "Make *me* a promise."

I laugh shakily. "Okay."

"Say it."

"I promise I'll come back," I tell him, even though it's a promise I'm not sure I'll be able to keep. The realization hits me like a brick.

Then he kisses me—gently this time—and I'm grateful that if I die, this moment will be fresh in my mind. This moment will carry me to whatever comes next.

"Rest," I urge him. I squeeze his hand one final time, and a minute later I emerge back into the corridors of Floor Two. The air is damp, it leaves me feeling cold and exposed, although maybe that's because I'm no longer nestled in Wren's arms. But right now I need to focus, because getting to my mother means traversing the main corridor, and Trevor had warned me about that.

I understand why, ten minutes later. As I peer up the second floor's main artery, I spot two guards on patrol with their weapons at the ready. Probably another pair are stationed at my cell door, and probably at Wren's apartment, too. And the rest? Not many work nightshifts, but these are desperate times. So, how many other guards have been called from their beds? How much longer until Maax and Sam and the others are roused from their sleep, given orders to suit up even though they aren't even finished with training, and hunt me down? Time is of the essence, I realize that, but as I watch the guards stroll in the direction of the Giving Tree, I think of something.

Someone out there has a knife and a distaste for authority. A penchant for violence, too. Probably it's generic, warranted unrest. But it's possible that someone besides us knows Compound Eleven's secret. After all, if we found out about aboveground, maybe someone else has, too. Someone who hasn't been murdered like Wren's father. Someone who isn't about to be forced from Compound Eleven, like us.

A second later I dart from my hiding spot, start along the main corridor trailing after the guards with my heart in my throat. If they turn right now, they will spot me. But a gulf of space separates us, I wear a hat, and I travel alone. They won't shoot me right away—I'm almost certain.

But, since I'm not completely sure, I'm light on my feet. I don't make a noise—I don't even breathe. A few more steps and I'll veer left. I will be out of their sight line, I will be in the heart of a floor I know like the back of my hand. Right now the taller one tells a joke. The other kicks a can that ricochets against the wall. *Almost there,* my brain screams. Then, as I twist around the corner, the taller one turns—

I don't wait around to see whether or not I've been spotted. Instead my legs burst forward with adrenaline, up one corridor and along the next. I leap through a supply closet, I run and keep running at all costs. I sprint so fast the orange beads lining the floor don't simply blur into one unending line, they ignite like the fire I saw aboveground, they propel me around corners, closer and closer and closer to the woman who gave me life.

Then I stop. I stop so quickly that every tendon in my body contracts as one.

Because voices come from just ahead, from around the corner, the very last corner before that familiar hall I've known my entire life. The one I used to stalk with Maggie and Hunter, the one I used to play kickball along.

Guards—they must be. As soon as they round the bend, I will attack, I will disarm them. I will hit them hard enough that it will be several minutes before they can pick themselves up again. I will not shoot.

Seconds pass, then minutes. The voices don't grow louder. Footsteps don't approach, combat gear doesn't come swinging around the corner. Then I understand. The guards don't patrol the corridor. They aren't passing from one hallway to the next. They are stationed at my parents' door.

I run my hands down my face and will myself to stay calm. Then I peer around the corner. I see that Ben stands closest. I can tell it's him by his squat shadow and his watery voice. Ben doesn't deserve my kindness, but the other? I don't know the other, and that thought makes me worry. After all, I promised

Trevor I wouldn't make him regret his decision to let me go. More importantly, I don't want to commit unspeakable violence ever again. But there's no other way to remove my mother from inside her cell.

Slowly I pull out my gun. For a while I stare at it, considering its weight, both figurative and literal. Then I lift it, I aim it through the darkness at Ben's head. My finger strokes the trigger, the muscles in my forearm feel taut as wire—

Shoot, Eve.

I visualize the blast, two of them, I see the guards slumping to their knees, then over onto their sides. I feel a surge of adrenaline as I imagine dragging my mother over their bodies and around the pools of blood they leave along the dirty floors. I hear her shoes chasing me through the night to freedom.

But I can't do it. I can't let blood coat my hands. Not now, not ever again, and so I will not keep my promise. I will not take my mother with me aboveground. Instead I must leave her to rot.

I am not courageous; I am a coward.

The disappointment is so profound that I move slowly along corridors ripe with danger, my heels drag noisily as I retrace my steps, and I'm being careless, I know that I am. So after a while, I force myself to stop and I squeeze my eyes shut.

I made a promise to Wren to return to the storeroom, didn't I? I feel his forehead pressed against mine, I feel his fingers against the back of my neck. I feel his strength when he should be weak and it makes me strong, too.

My eyes flick open. Just for now I will tell myself that I am not a coward. I am courageous, and I will not break another promise to someone I love.

CHAPTER FORTY-FIVE

That's a gun trained on my forehead.

It happened in a fraction of a second, just as I emerged from a supply closet. Just as I was retracing my steps back to the storeroom. A guard that happened to be passing by caught sight of me from the corner of his eye.

"Can I help you with something?" I ask the question in the same voice I used during my verification, the one brimming with innocence.

"You can help me with a job promotion is what I'm thinking, girly." The guard with the gun laughs.

All pretenses drop from my voice. "How's that?"

"Top points to the guard who snatches the most-wanted, for starters."

"You think I'm wanted? I'm just out for a walk. My boyfriend dumped me, and all that shit. Leave me alone."

He points his flashlight in my face so that I'm forced to squint. He chuckles. "Tall, blonde, injured. You hit all the boxes, aside from being accompanied by a dude. Oh, and the one about you being dangerous." He scoffs. "I guess a bunch of pussies put that report together."

For a moment I smirk, I can't help it. "If you want that job promotion so much, you might want to catch that much more dangerous male I'm with." I lick my teeth. "Or are you too scared?"

He steps closer and examines me. "I'm a guard, sweetheart. There isn't much that scares me. So—"

He doesn't finish his sentence, because the two of us are no longer alone. It's the scuffling of boots. The rustling of fabric. We peer through the darkness, both of us on edge, and my heart sinks when I notice the outline of the guard's uniform that our newcomer is wearing. Two against one, then. I'm done for.

But as I look closer, I see that this guard isn't as large as the other guards—a female, then. I also notice that she's struggling to fasten her face mask, and that her vest laden down with ammunition is ill-fitting. Like she's never worn these items before.

When she shifts, her nose ring catches in the dull light cast from the floor, and I almost gasp. *Maax*. Part of me swells with relief, but part of me panics, too. The Premes must be really desperate to catch Wren and me if they're sending out the new trainees on patrol.

"Who are you?" the guard grunts to her. "Fresh blood?"

I hear her low voice agree. Then her gaze shifts to me, her hand reaches for her gun. But then she goes still and I know even through the muted light, she recognizes me.

"This is the girl the Premes are looking for," says the guard to Maax. "But she travels with a guy, and I haven't found him yet. You can help me."

Maax doesn't take her eyes off me. "A guy?" I bet she knows it's Wren. After all, she has run into the two of us wandering the halls in the middle of the night before. "What's your name, anyway?" the guard continues, trying to peer at her while keeping an eye on me.

"Joss," she lies.

Relief bursts through my veins. Maax isn't just my friend — she's an ally. She believed in my goodness following my fight with Landry, and she believes in it now.

The guard turns to me. "Are you going to tell me and Joss where he is? Or do I have to smack it out of you."

I shove a thumb over my shoulder in the direction of the supply closet. "Holed up in there. Waiting for you to swing open the door so he can beat your face in."

He eyes me, then the door. "Quite a tongue on this one," he says to Maax. Then his eyes narrow as he gives me a hard look. "You kiss your mother with that mouth?"

"Not really, no."

Then he does just what I want him to do. He shifts the barrel of the gun so that it's pointed at the supply closet. "Let's see what he does to your face, how about. Open the door."

"Open it yourself."

"Open it or I shoot you, girly."

Slowly my fingers curl around the door handle. Squealing hinges reveal a black rectangle. The guard inches forward and lifts his flashlight. At that moment, I jump away from the supply closet as though the most wanted man in Compound Eleven is about to come tumbling out and the guard who calls me girly — he's even more skittish than I had hoped. His gun discharges into a room full of brooms and in his moment of distraction, I smash my fist to his nose, I grab his arm and twist it until the gun comes loose.

Maax sends him headfirst into the supply closet, I scoop up the gun, and then her gaze meets mine. There isn't time for thanks, no time for hugs. But I smile at my friend and she smiles at me, then we are running in opposite directions.

The other guards will be moving, the sound of gunfire their beacon. And so there is nobody left to patrol the main corridor, to slow me down or stand in my way. For a while I am laughing, but then I think of my mother and the laugh catches in my throat; it turns at once into a sob.

CHAPTER FORTY-SIX

"Eve?" Long whispers through the darkness.

"Is Wren okay?"

"Ask a stupid question," Wren jokes from behind him. But with the aid of my flashlight even I can see that it isn't that. He is plaster-pale.

"I told you to make him rest," I almost shout, rounding on Long. "Didn't he?"

"Nah, not really. Too busy worrying about you the whole time."

Wren walks slowly toward me. "Where is she?"

I close the space between us, then slump against him, mindful of his injury. "There were two guards stationed outside her cell."

"And?"

"And I couldn't... I just couldn't."

"You did the right thing, Eve."

I cling to him, even though it should be the other way around, and think maybe he's right. Maybe more death and destruction really wasn't the answer. And my mother has

made do for years down here, whittling away each day with
her embroidery work, and so surely she can whittle away a
few more. That's all I'll need to get things sorted aboveground,
to get Wren well again. Then we will come back and retrieve
her—my father, too. We'll figure out a way to definitively end
Compound Eleven, and with that thought blazing through my
brain, I lift my head and kiss Wren on the mouth.

"You guys will be the death of me, you know that?" Long
interrupts. He shoves a shock of black hair from his face.
"Make me wait another minute and I'll start throwing fists."

I peer at him from between Wren's arms. "Concerning," I
retort. "What are you suddenly in such a rush for, anyway?"

"Oh, not much. Just to know what it feels like to stand on
top of the planet instead of inside it."

I lift an eyebrow.

"Wren told me everything. I can't believe all the shit you
guys got up to. I mean, you think you know somebody." He
smacks Wren on the back of the head. "And now I've got to
carry his ass all the way to the Holy One, right? What's his
name again—Mitchell?"

"Michael."

"Right. Well, we should get going before the guards think
to check in here, shouldn't we?"

I nod, then turn back to Wren. My face is swollen, it's still
speckled with bits of dried blood, my hair is twisted with more.
My brain feels heavy and thick and my heart does, too. But I
gaze at him straight in the eye and feel a connection to him
that is difficult to describe.

"You okay?" His voice is low.

"Are you?" Mine is hollow.

He makes a sound at the back of his throat. "Now that
you're back? Yeah. I am."

I smile in spite of myself—in spite of the terrible series

of events that led us here. Then I turn. "Wren goes first, up the ladder."

"Fine by me," Long agrees.

But Wren is still. "You go first. If I fall…" His voice fades into nothingness.

"If you fall, I'll at least have a chance of catching you if I'm below. So, as I said, you go first."

He scowls. "This is your life we're talking about, Eve."

"This is *your* life we're talking about too, *Wren*. I'm not stepping onto that ladder until you do, and the more time we waste standing here talking about it, the more likely we are to be caught."

"You're not dying for me," says Wren in my ear.

"You're not dying, period."

He stares at me for several seconds, then shakes his head. But he starts forward, and I notice that he moves with more vigor than before. He is going to be okay. *We are going to make it out alive.*

The first ten rungs, he is strong and fast. But by the time we reach the midway point, his pace has slowed. He rests often. Half my time I spend looking over my shoulder, gazing at the door, listening for the sound of approaching footsteps. The rest of the time I stare at Wren's boots, wondering with every step if it will be his last. If he will lose focus, if he will be unable to bear the pain any longer. I wonder, too, what will happen if he falls. There is a chance, a good one, that we will all die.

"Almost there," I say. Maybe I'm imagining it, maybe it isn't as bad as I think. But when he finally mutters his agreement, I know that it is. Because that voice isn't one I recognize. It's wounded and fatigued, weak. Everything he is right now, everything he normally is not. Eventually, though, we make it to the very top of the ladder, and freedom is so close I can almost feel it across my fingertips.

Slowly Wren moves his broken body so that it drapes heavily over the ropes, then inches to the nets. This is good, this is very good. This is progress. As I start across the ropes myself I see under the glow of my flashlight that he lies on the second net from the top, the same spot I used all that time ago to rest. My arms were shaking then. They were tired and aching. And I did not have a bullet wedged into my side.

I don't shake this time; I am not fearful of the height, or of falling. I'm too distracted, too focused on Wren, too committed to the end. Then I'm lying beside him, watching as he wipes sweat from his face. Just as I did in the Bowl a few hours ago when everything was different, I think of the first time I saw him. How, even then, I thought he had a kind mouth.

How right I was.

Because, though he thinks a monster lurks within, it trembles in the shadow of his innate goodness. He is not evil, or twisted—his mother was wrong. *I* was wrong, to ever doubt him. And then the moment is shattered by the unmistakable sound of the storeroom door swinging open.

I scramble to switch off the flashlight and we are engulfed in darkness, ears our only useful sense. Too bad mine are full of rushing blood. Too bad one still hums from Andrews's fist.

Voices. Definitely there are voices. Then the lights are switched on, their stark brightness forcing my eyes shut. The sound of ticking footsteps rings through the towering room. Surely the kitchen staff don't wear heels…

Perhaps it's someone powerful. Perhaps it is someone powerful looking specifically for us. Perhaps it's Wren's mother.

No. She is too injured. Isn't she? Wren is thinking the same thing, I know he is.

Long is at the very edge of the net, the most exposed of

our three, and his eyes are electrified with fear. He doesn't even breathe. But finally, after what feels like an eternity, the voices fade and the light is switched off. I exhale loudly as I turn on my flashlight.

"Wish I brought a change of underwear," Long says as he maneuvers himself sideways. I start to grin, but then I catch sight of Wren and I see his mouth is pinched at the corners. I spot the patch of red staining the T-shirt that Long lent him.

The wound. It has reopened.

Something cold slinks over me, like a wet sheet, because the climb… It was too much for him. Long swears under his breath when he sees it.

"Is it bad?" Wren murmurs.

"No," I lie. "It isn't bleeding like before."

"Okay."

"How are you feeling?"

Carefully he presses the heels of his palms over his eyes and breathes out. In. Out. "I'm not sure," he says eventually.

Long and I exchange a look. It was a large admission, for him, and that means he's struggling. Really struggling.

He *cannot* die. It can't end like this. It *can't*.

"Come on," says Long, and together we drag him inch by inch to the edge of the net. I maneuver myself onto the top one, I lie stomach down and use every muscle in my body to lift Wren on with me. He is heavy, dead weight, and it takes several minutes before we manage it.

There. *There*. We are at the top of the storeroom. We evaded the guards, we will taste freedom. Now if only that shiver would lift from my bones…

But I hear his moan, I feel his agony against my chest as if it's my own, so quickly I push open the access hatch into the outbuilding. I crouch, so that my head lifts above Compound Eleven, and I remind myself that this will be the last time I am here, in this capacity. The last time I am a captor of this cruel and unkind civilization.

It's a shame I couldn't enjoy it more.

It's a shame we couldn't get to Katz and find a way to end Eleven tonight. It's a shame I didn't have time to tell my friends, to spread the word to my fellow Lower Means before we left. And then there is my mother. I made her a promise to take her with me. It's a promise I cannot fulfill, not yet. I prioritized the lives of others over hers, because I couldn't summon the will to pull the trigger.

I am a coward. Aren't I?

Too many thoughts, too many emotions.

At least I am free. At least I am with Wren, together again, just as we always should have been. I just have to keep him alive until we reach the others…

When he no longer pants from the exertion of making it onto the top net, I stick out a hand. He grabs it, and with Long's help I drag him to the top of the earth.

"You can go back, if you want," I tell Long, as I throw down Addison's hat.

"You can't carry him on your own." His voice is terse. He is worried for Wren, more worried than before.

I nod through the darkness. A second later I open the door.

The air is cleansing, it is invigorating. It leaves Long speechless, and I think it even gives Wren a renewed sense of life, one he desperately needs. I can see it in his eyes. It's the way they shine as they look out onto a world that is now our own.

Without asking, I wrap his arm around my shoulder, I absorb half his weight as Long absorbs the other half, as the bloodstain on his shirt grows larger. Together we start forward in the direction of the solar panels, but all the while

I consider the glass pyramid known as the Oracle. It glistens under the moonlight. It is a silent reminder of the mountain of secrets housed below.

"This isn't the end, you know," Wren says darkly from behind his curtain of pain. When I chance a look at him, I see that even though he clings to consciousness, his eyes flash with intention. "They're not getting away with this."

"No, they're not."

Suddenly that ember of injustice inside my belly sparks to life, it roars with fury, and I wish I could return to Compound Eleven's corridors to liberate the lower floors this very second.

For now, though—for now, we can only hobble forward, licking our wounds and biding our time, swallowing the bitter taste of failure and regret, bracing ourselves for whatever awaits in this brave new world we now call home.

If Wren lives.

And then I'm distracted, so distracted that my thoughts are fractured in a million different directions. Because for the first time since coming or going, I notice something new up here, and it isn't the plants, or the trees, or even a beast.

It is a set of eyes, human ones, belonging to a young boy who peers at us patiently through the darkness. A young boy who looks vaguely familiar.

END OF BOOK TWO

ACKNOWLEDGEMENTS

I owe so much to my agent, Rachel Beck, and my editor, Stacy Abrams. Thank you, Rachel, for believing in the *Eleven Trilogy* from the very beginning. Thank you, Stacy, for your patience, guidance, and vision throughout *Unraveling Eleven's* journey to publication. It's a privilege to work with both of you.

I also want to thank the entire team at Entangled Teen for their competence and kindness. It remains a true pleasure to work with all of you.

And, finally, I'd like to thank my family and friends for their continued support, which means the world. Thank you!

Unraveling Eleven is a fast-paced, exciting dystopian novel full of intrigue and romance. However, the story includes elements that might not be suitable for some readers. Violence, bodily harm, death, and allusions to a previous sexual assault are included in the novel. Readers who may be sensitive to these elements, please take note.

Fans of Veronica Rossi will love this thrilling The Count of Monte Cristo *retelling that sheds light on the dark struggles of humanity.*

STING

CINDY R. WILSON

They call me the Scorpion because they don't know who I really am. All they know is that someone is stealing from people with excess to help people with nothing survive another day.

But then a trusted friend reveals who I am—"just" Tessa, "just" a girl—and sends me straight into the arms of the law. All those people I helped…couldn't help me when I needed it.

In prison, I find an unlikely ally in Pike, who would have been my enemy on the outside. He represents everything I'm against. Luxury. Excess. The world immediately falling for his gorgeous smile. How he ended up in the dirty cell next to mine is a mystery, but he wants out as much as I do. Together, we have a real chance at escape.

With the sting of betrayal still fresh, Pike and I will seek revenge on those who wronged us. But uncovering all their secrets might turn deadly…

Confront the impossible. Discover love in the most unexpected places. And, above all, find hope in the face of the unknown.

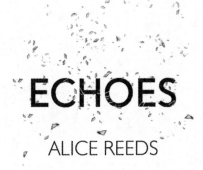

ECHOES

ALICE REEDS

They wake on a deserted island. Fiona and Miles, high school enemies now stranded together. No memory of how they got there. No plan to follow, no hope to hold on to.

Each step forward reveals the mystery behind the forces that brought them here. And soon, the most chilling discovery: something else is on the island with them.

Something that won't let them leave alive.

*An intricate paranormal romance about a
girl trying to discover how she entered the
Underworld, perfect for fans of Kiersten White.*

SMOKE

AND

KEY

KELSEY SUTTON

*A sound awakens her. There's darkness all around. And then
she's falling...*

She has no idea who or where she is. Or why she's dead. The
only clue to her identity hangs around her neck: a single rusted
key. This is how she and the others receive their names—from
whatever belongings they had when they fell out of their graves.
Under is a place of dirt and secrets, and Key is determined to
discover the truth of her past in order to escape it.

She needs help, but who can she trust? Ribbon seems content
in Under, uninterested in finding answers. Doll's silence hints at
deep sorrow, which could be why she doesn't utter a word. There's
Smoke, the boy with a fierceness that rivals even the living. And
Journal, who stays apart from everyone else. Key's instincts tell
her there is something remarkable about each of them, even if
she can't remember why.

Then the murders start. Bodies that are burned to a crisp. And
after being burned, the dead stay dead. Key is running out of time
to discover who she was—and what secret someone is willing to
kill to keep hidden—before she loses her life for good...

For fans of Keira Cass's Selection series and Lauren DeStefano's Chemical Garden series, Perfected *is a chilling look at what it means to be human.*

PERFECTED

kate jarvik birch

As soon as the government passed legislation allowing humans to be genetically engineered and sold as pets, the rich and powerful rushed to own beautiful girls like Ella. Trained from birth to be graceful, demure, and above all, perfect, these "family companions" enter their masters' homes prepared to live a life of idle luxury.

Ella is happy with her new role as playmate for a congressman's bubbly young daughter, but she doesn't expect Penn, the congressman's handsome and rebellious son. He's the only person who sees beyond the perfect exterior to the girl within. Falling for him goes against every rule she knows...and the freedom she finds with him is intoxicating.

But when Ella is kidnapped and thrust into the dark underworld lurking beneath her pampered life, she's faced with an unthinkable choice. Because the only thing more dangerous than staying with Penn's family is leaving...and if she's unsuccessful, she'll face a fate far worse than death.

Let's be friends!

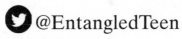 @EntangledTeen

 @EntangledTeen

@EntangledTeen

bit.ly/TeenNewsletter

entangled teen

an imprint of Entangled Publishing LLC